Blake pulled at the jet ski controls with all his strength, the heat from the jet engine now burning at his feet, the monsoon rain pelting his face. They weren't going to gain altitude at this point, but nonetheless the jagged mountain peaks rising up rapidly below them were at worst towards the middle on his hierarchy of worries.

Looming more prominently were the broader implications of maintaining speeds over 300 km/hr in a commercial blimp, whether the Hoa-Ky order would arrive at the radio array before nightfall, and exactly how much of this relied on a 3'4' wad of chewing gum.

Was he regretting some of his earlier decisions? Certainly, but there were still scenarios where they could get out of this alive. Most or all of the remaining ropes would have to hold, and they were in uncharted territory with the atmospheric resistance. But they were approaching the point where they could just glide the rest of the way, barring the wayward boxcar theory of lateral spin.

Someone had in fact written a report about this. Not exactly this, of course, in many ways nothing even related to this, to the extent that none of this had relevance to much of anything. It was more a general inquiry, into key flaws in security protocol, low probability-high impact scenarios. All of which could have been avoided with a few surprisingly inexpensive interventions.

In the blink of an eye the diner was empty. Quite literally the time it took to look up from your plate after demarcating and separating an adequately sized piece of pie. He waved at the crowd shuffling sporadically by, unsure of what in fact was lacking from the frozen dessert beneath his fork.

Now was not the time for philosophical musings, such as to the metaphysical implications of a solid 220 kilogram mass of platinum vs. just under two thirds its weight in collectable gold coins. Or how a presidential candidate internal polling had 17 points behind could win in a landslide, for that matter. No, it's just a matter of keeping the nose level, and hoping the wings don't fall off, assuming of course the wings go up in the first place.

Can I get a hurrah! Can I get a hoo-ray! Onwards, onwards, a merrily-lo, doo-wop a ding-lang-long. Now they are dancing around the fire, beating drums as they make their way to the mountain top, literary ripple pond reflections gallop-running blind through the great grand karmic *unfolding outwards*, with swashes to be buckled and speed bumps to eventually be held on over, the ritual is never lost, but *distracted from*, soon the horses ride for the forest, the leaping goats linger long under the moon, 0000100111

ALL
AS THE
DICE

DYLAN KYLE

This is a work of fiction. Names, characters, places, and incidents either are the product of the author's imagination or are used fictitiously. Any resemblance to actual persons, living or dead, events, or locales is entirely coincidental. Real cities are used for expediency, and any referencing is meant only a tip of that hat - neither are meant to represent.

Version 1

Cover design: Kier Ryan V. Arlegui
Mandala: Sadaf Urooj

ISBN: 9798553893835

"Baseball is the only field of endeavour where a man can succeed three times out of ten and be considered a good performer." --Ted Williams

1

Blake was bored. Or less boredom, perhaps the French captured it better, some point between ennui and blasé. The dilute disquiet of an unfulfilled passage of time, something almost bittersweet. Tempered with all your standard existential angsts, maybe some lop-stepping philosophical compass spinnery, all backdropped by a wobbling disorientation. It was the distinct sort of sensation you got when you were freshly arrived in a new town, with nothing to do but have another drink in the hotel bar.

Which didn't seem like such the bad place. They did have a particularly nice scotch, bitingly peaty with layers of finish, had been on the earth almost as long as he had. It had been a pleasant surprise when he saw the bottle, it was one he had in fact been meaning to try. He wondered if he could almost read that as an omen.

For he was there on the whims of the great mover of humanity, the grand transcendental magnet by which all our destinies are ordered and arranged. Business, in the form of Wildon Textiles, a particularly innovative wholesale fabric manufacturer, San Diego's - and, arguably, Southern California's - leader in the 'specialty modern fabrics' category, sales up into eight digits, maybe a dozen employees stateside, how many, close to 50, was it, down in Mexico.

They were a company with whom – if things went well – he would be investing a large amount of money, and possibly even be taking a managerial role. He had an instinct for these things, and he had a good feeling about Wildon Textiles. Everything he had seen so far suggested a solid operation, with even a blue sky for future growth.

Admittedly, he didn't know much about textiles, and there were certainly some red flags – they had debt, profits had been down, they weren't there yet with their most innovative fabrics. But that was where you found the jackpots, wasn't it? Not in the easy obvious investments everyone wanted a piece of.

Blake wondered, then, where that *ennui* was coming from. It had a certain nagging hovering quality. Was that his instinct, warning him? He had trouble telling sometimes. Maybe he was just bored.

He had read somewhere, that it was a disease of affluence, boredom. They did a study, on a tribe out in some remote wilderness, and they could just sit around a fire all night, that was entertainment. Not him. He wondered, could you just see it all, do it all – or at least enough of it – and there be nothing interesting left?

Perhaps he was being melodramatic. Certainly he had no right to complain. For he was - no need to beat about with it - *well off.* Or better rich, to the extent that filthy was likely the best word for it. He lived a life which could basically be described as one of leisure and adventure, if he did at times dedicate himself to business such as the investment at hand. In all truth he was rarely in a state of mind that could be captured by the various synonyms of the word bored.

And San Diego seemed like a good town. Any city on the beach in California, what? He cast his gaze around the bar. It was a proper British style pub, with people at a couple of tables, a couple of guys playing pool the other side of the bar.

Blake wondered if he almost should have taken Jack Wildon up on his offer to meet him at the airport and go for a drink. His plane got in pretty late though, and you never knew when people went to bed. Everyone was just always up for another drink or what have you, it was sort of your job as the investor to know when to take them up on it.

He was strangely awake now though, especially given that it was almost one AM in New York. He supposed he could get a cab downtown, explore the city a bit. Although he did have the meeting tomorrow, and they had that nice scotch here. He could have one more.

He finished his drink in one go, and held up a couple fingers to the bartender, a rather portly fellow with a bushy beard.

"Celebrating something?" asked the bartender as he poured out another neat scotch tall in the glass.

Blake shook his head, and made a noise in the negative. Couldn't you just like nice scotch? He liked to consider himself a man of taste. Blake wasn't sure if he should say something, strike up a conversation, but the bartender turned back towards the TV. On the balance Blake was feeling a little introspective anyways.

He took a sip of his scotch, and looked at his reflection through the line of bottles in the mirror behind the bar. The lighting here suited him well enough, his features sharp, his black hair slightly tussled. Middle age was on the horizon, but he felt young, and everyone told him he looked ten years younger than he was.

He allowed himself a little half grin. He wondered what they would make of him here. Blake Adersely Myntbanke, BA/MA/MBA, investor extraordinaire, adventurer, Renaissance man. Direct descendant of the famous botanist, Knight of the Empire, organizer of the Wild Summers Festival, historian with publications in no less than the Chronicus Latinae.

If nothing else, Wildon Textiles would look good on his resume. Talking to Jack he got the impression that he could still stay on a month or two even if he didn't want to invest, do a management consultancy thing with them. He could probably even maneuver his way into a nice snazzy corporate title.

Blake had a feeling he could find his stride here. He didn't know much about textiles, but business was business. It certainly wasn't that it was all the same, but in the end it was all similar enough. And he had investing in his blood. Well, not to make any sort of statement towards nature vs. nurture. He did himself tend towards the luck, social position, and hard work school of thought.

One way or another his family hadn't had to be rich, that was certain enough. Their branch of the Myntbankes had been part of an endangered, middling sort of British nobility when his father was born. Growing up Blake watched many of his peers clutch at the old ideals, trying to eke out a life of opulence from withering estates as they slowly slipped into the middle class.

His father would have none of that. Rather than try to live off his estate, he mortgaged or sold off enough of it to fund a variegated spread of investments, while his mother brought the fortune of a great French industrialist's granddaughter. Together they invested in a multitude of companies, and had doubled their pooled fortune before he was even born.

They were your model investors, only investing where it generated real value, finding mis-managed businesses and turning them around 180. A hotel near the French border, saving it from bankruptcy had been as simple as lowering prices to increase occupancy. A box manufacturer that wasn't making custom shapes and sizes, a taxi company that was making too many one way trips, they made it all look easy.

Blake entered the world in a traumatic birth, in which his mother almost died. While she made a full recovery, with the risks of another pregnancy - and the long hours they kept - he would be an only child.

You hear all these stories about terrible childhoods, but his was actually pretty idyllic. His early years were spent on a sprawling estate near London, riding horses, practicing at the archery range, learning to read on fantasy stories. He studied at a decidedly upper middle class private school, his mother making a stand against an alliance between an Aunt and Blake's grandfather. It was in many ways as normal a childhood as you could expect, given the circumstances.

His fate had not been to stay in the UK, however. When he was twelve his father had a row with the British regulatory authorities, over a huge new furniture manufacturing venture they were setting out on.

To this day Blake wasn't sure exactly what it was about, something to do with using human operators with automated cutting machines. It was sort of about safety regulations, but then not actually about safety. Either way his parent's factories were some of the safest in the country. Better to have them there than overseas where the rules were more lax. His father said it was pure crony protectionism, plain and simple.

They had a growing presence in America, and there were no regulatory barriers there. So they decided to at least temporarily re-locate their operations to New York. They bounced back and forth at first - between summer holidays and business trips, they were really half the time in London. But gradually they began to spend less and less time in the UK, and America became his new home.

Blake made friends quickly in New York, and even had some old chums who made the same leap a couple years earlier. He was a bit the rascal, got elected to student council once, with predictably disastrous results, managed to be in a couple of bands despite rather limited musical ability. He did do well enough in his studies, if he didn't always dedicate himself as he should. Part of it was just him helping his parents research their investments - studying maths could seem trivial when there were million dollar decisions being made.

In America his parents began to focus their energies entirely on the high-tech sector, with a view to mix business and philanthropy. They had visions of revolutions in solar power, cars that could survive any accident, new medical devices that could cure several diseases at once. They could have lived quite well just off the interest at that point, and investments like that were risky. But who else had the ways and means to invest in those things?

But even in pursuing these more civic-minded endeavours they again struck gold, this time in automation. There were new frontiers opening up, they bought into or founded a series of companies which took the assembly line to new levels. Complex multi-use instruments, hand-like machinery, new worlds in intelligent monitoring.

None of it was particularly revolutionary, but it was all a step up, and it all had practical use across the manufacturing sector. Within a few short years they were focused almost entirely on manufacturing tools for other manufacturers themselves.

Blake even got to play in the factories a few times. That was something, playing tied to the conveyor belt, using the pneumatic press to crush things, fencing with robotic arms. When he was a bit older he stole the keys and had a couple bush parties. He got in a lot of trouble for that though, there were liability issues.

After revolutionizing - if by degree - American manufacturing, his parents did finally take some time off. His mother started an art gallery, and they did a lot more travelling, Blake joining them when he wasn't in school. They spent a summer on the yacht in the Mediterranean, with the work phone disconnected, just sailing from port to port.

Then one afternoon Blake was called into the office at his school. His parents had been flying his father's plane back in Britain when a freak storm hit, and they never landed. It was a few days before they found the wreckage, but Blake knew the truth as soon as he was told. He was devastated, left rudderless, it seemed like something impossible. They had both been young, healthy, in their prime.

While their will did spread a lot around, and the government took its share, Blake was the primary benefactor. But his parents had always provided him with anything he needed, as long as he worked hard, at least. The money was nothing but a terrible new responsibility.

He had new 'friends' coming at him, from your standard opportunistic moochers, to gold diggers, to professional con-artists. He had to figure out what to do with his parent's businesses, a lot of them didn't just run themselves. He had always expected to play a role managing them, and even eventually take them over. But he couldn't run an empire himself, especially not at 17. Things had to be sold, CEOs had to be hired, corporate structures re-arranged, all while he was still in mourning.

To top it all off the paparazzi were suddenly after him, wanted to make a celebrity out of him. Apparently his was the type of story that sold tabloids. They showed up at the funeral, greasy guys in sunglasses giving him their card, wanting to do a series on him, asking if he had been to any good parties lately. They probably even sent a girl at him once. He swore it must have been them, trying to feed him hard drugs and get him to do crazy erratic things like steal a boat.

He finished his drink in one go. That was a dark period in his life, which he didn't like to dwell on. He could see the group at the one table was gathering up their stuff, so he pre-emptively motioned to the bartender for another drink.

The bartender made another generous pour, Blake symbolically sliding over on his stool to make space as the group arrived at the bar to pay. He half-listened as they talked to the bartender, the shepherd's pie was amazing, it sounded like they had managed to do the key tourist sights.

Blake would peg them as a group of friends or relatives who had been visiting for the holidays. Maybe half the group was from here, half was from out of town? They had a sort of last-night-of-vacations melancholy to them, light and bittersweet, the holidays were over, back to work.

There was a lull in the conversation, and Blake felt a sudden impulse to contribute. "Do you know how often the boat runs to the Coronado?" he asked, hoping he wasn't overstepping at all.

There was a momentary silence, then the bartender spoke up. "Every hour, on the hour."

One of the women smiled at him. "You have to check it out, it was really cool."

Blake smiled, and nodded. "I should be here a little while, I'll make sure to go."

And then they were leaving, the one woman smiling politely again at Blake. With the big group gone he had a decent view of the rest of the bar. At the one table were three guys, all on one side of the table staring up at the TV.

They had the look of salesmen, if he had to make a wager. Three was a big number for sales, certainly, but it wasn't unheard of, or maybe it was buyer and seller together. And it was a safe enough bet, a hotel this range, Thursday night. He supposed they could just be San Diegans here for the big TVs, there was a sports game on.

One way or another they seemed pretty focused on the screen, whoever they were. Blake looked over at the pool players, noting that it was one of the bigger British style tables. He actually invested in a company that rented out pool tables like that, it could even be one of theirs. They did a lot of business on the West Coast, and bars like this often avoided buying their own tables.

He watched as one guy lined up and took a shot, then the other. The one was a well-dressed grey haired white guy, maybe in his fifties or sixties. The other was a fairly built young guy with a shaved head, early-mid twenties maybe, long shorts and a t-shirt. Looking at the guy, Blake was struck by the fact that he couldn't even guess at his ethnic background, and his skin was a shade of brown where he couldn't even tell to what extent it was natural or sun tan.

They seemed like an odd pair. At that Blake felt a momentary twinge of guilt, it seemed like sort of a mildly racist thing to think, he wasn't sure. He wondered who they were, why they were playing pool at that bar tonight. They could be salesmen as well, he supposed, although they didn't have the look of it. Could be they worked at the hotel, he could even see the old guy being the owner. They could just be two random guests that wanted to play pool.

Although they now seemed to be having a fairly involved conversation, that suggested some degree of familiarity. They had stopped playing and were standing there, cues in hand. Something seemed odd about them, their movements, a tenseness, maybe?

Blake watched as they returned to their game. The young guy took a shot, then said something to the older guy, he looked pissed off. Then they separated to opposite sides of the table, like magnets repulsing. The way they were moving around the pool table, Blake had the impression of wolves circling each other.

Although then the old guy went up to the young guy and said something, and they were both laughing, the old guy mock-punching him in the arm. Maybe it was just his imagination then, they seemed pretty relaxed.

Feeling slightly self-conscious, he looked away from them, and took another sip of his scotch. All in all there didn't seem to be a lot going on. Which was fair enough, it didn't seem like the sort of place people would go for a night out on a Thursday.

Blake wondered how much it would cost, to open a pub like this in San Diego. He could ask the bartender if he knew what the rent was, although that was always sort of a strange thing to ask. But if he were to end up staying a while, that would be the thing to do, wouldn't it? Open up a nice little pub somewhere.

That had been one of the first things he had done with his money, in fact, found the Stonehaven's Rest. A proper pub, all stone and oak, not far from the University he had started in at in Britain. It became a legendary bar, if he did say so himself. They got away with having bands on the weekends, he was way ahead of the curve with microbrews.

It had been quite a thing to own a bar at that age, and all things considered it might have been rather a bad idea. He passed his undergraduate years in a dissolute fashion, the sum of which was a blur. It had been a strange time for him, stepping into adulthood with a limitless pot of cash.

But he survived it, at least he could say that. He even managed fairly decent grades. His major was in History, specifically of the Dark Ages. It was a subject for which he had developed quite a passion, and in which he continued for a master's degree.

Those were happy days. He settled down ever so slightly, and truly began to dedicate himself to his studies. It was during this time that he began working on his Magnum Opus - it was to be a great grand history of the middle to late Dark Ages. His focus was economic, but it went into pretty much everything, technology, culture, geopolitics, even climate.

He had in fact brought some research materials along with him. His feeling lately was that he had been neglecting it - originally he had wanted to be a professor. He had continued on in his studies, but after his masters he felt compelled to branch out into something more practical. For this he returned to America, to pursue an MBA.

While he had dabbled in investing during his studies in Britain, it was in America that he began to truly carry on the family tradition. Within a few weeks of arriving he was partner in a local music festival, was funding a new sunglass designer, and had started publishing an edgy sort of music, politics, and cars magazine. From there he did a bit of retail, a clothing store, a couple of record stores. He had a bookstore for a while, it was a nice place just to hang out. If the customers did tend to get on his nerves sometimes.

After getting on a kick eating healthy and cooking all his own food for a change, he financed and organized a grocery store co-operative. It was based entirely on a consumer-owned model - people gradually obtained shares in the company the more they shopped there. Like air miles or a coffee shop card, only transferring ownership of the company from him to the customers, who could then own up to a fraction of a percent each.

He also funded a couple art flicks, friends of his in the film department. It was really out there avant-garde stuff - pastiches of bizarre unconnected scenes hinting at semi-coherent narratives that inexorably seemed to collapse inwardly on themselves before achieving meaning. That was what the one review had said, at least.

He even got into the first stages of starting up a major motion picture company, but it didn't really get off the ground. It would have been a pretty big investment, even for him, and he preferred the smaller independent projects anyways.

What else? He bought an amusement park once. Just a little place off the highway, in upstate New York. Ten rides or so, mini golf, go carts, that sort of thing. He bought it at a discount with a lot of debt, and in the end it turned out it was going out of business for a reason. But he kept it going for a couple years, it had been a lark, they closed it down and had some good parties. If he did get a particularly steep fine. Apparently it was against the law to use an amusement park as a live music venue, and any talk of a liquor license was a non-starter.

In all his investments there was, however, one universal constant, one great unifying thread. With but the fewest of exceptions, none of his business ventures had turned a profit.

A fair number broke even, and a decent percentage came close. If there were others where he took some fairly substantial losses. But he already had money, that wasn't what he was in it for. Some things were more important in life, he felt a responsibility to invest.

After getting his MBA he started really doing a lot of live

shows, helping out a promoter friend who had good connections but lacked the funds to put on properly epic events. They started out making decent money, putting on shows around New York, booking some major acts.

But Blake always wanted bigger and better bands, larger venues, more smoke and lasers. You didn't want ticket prices too high either. It just forced out students and artists and all exactly the sort of people you wanted coming to the shows.

From live shows, it was a natural progression to funding bands, starting a recording studio. That turned out to be a bit of a sinkhole for money as well, but he got some really good music out there.

He recorded a lot of different stuff, rock, metal, electronic, jazz, a couple of early music ensembles. One band was an edgy over the top glam-punk act that went nowhere, then a few years later The New Direction Orchestra topped the charts doing basically the same act. He felt safe in saying they were ahead of their time.

Why was it that so many of the best bands just weren't that popular? Like entirely aside from anything he recorded. There were all your conventional arguments, certainly. Cultural inertia, art-snobby attitudes that people couldn't appreciate the good stuff, to business and political interests having an irrational fear of anything new, or a biological tendency to lock into the music of one's adolescence. Maybe it was just the long-tailed vagaries of taste, like there were just lots of small markets for very specific things. But it still never completely added up to him, he couldn't make sense of it.

And people did come to their shows, the albums sold - often quite well. But the costs were high, he made sure the recordings were always top notch. So many times a band would reach the end of their budget, but only really have half the album done properly. Was he supposed to stop them there? That was where one hit wonders came from.

Risky new technological ventures were another favourite of his. He invested in a lot of alternative energy projects, tried to cure malaria once, funded a couple of anti-aging pills.

He considered these investments a form of charitable spending, if they did have the potential to turn significant profits. He in fact preferred that sort of benevolent investing over simply giving money away, if he did contribute to a number of charities.

It was a bit of a complex argument, but if you did the maths, he thought it made sense. The chance of profiting on a normal safe venture was higher than on a risky ethical one, and in the end that difference was equivalent to a charitable donation. You could even quantify that into a dollar figure, graph it out economically with intersecting lines.

Of course, try explaining that to a group around a table at the bar, you never heard the end of it. Even though none of those ventures had ever really made money, which Blake took as a vindication. If he did hold what he considered to be some fairly valuable patents.

And some of his ventures certainly did alright. The Stonehaven's Rest was still doing well. If they had changed the name, and he would probably be better off with a long term savings bond, the returns Hampton was paying him. The co-operative grocery store had actually expanded into a few outlets, and was now completely customer owned. Success there was failure from a capitalist standpoint.

And with something like the bands, often he would just sort of have to let the profits go. As the investor obviously you got paid first. But if you had a band that toured for six months, and only made a few grand, you just weren't right taking that from them. It was still a win on paper, he supposed.

In the end, he could take the negative view, say he wasted all that time and money on a venture, and never made a cent. But really, if you created something in the world - started a business, put on a show, made a movie - and you broke even, it was like creating that thing for free. Or on the cheap, if you were just near the break even point. That was how he liked to see it, at least.

And if striking gold remained ever elusive, he at least managed to generally stay away from the con artists. You certainly met enough of them, when you had money and travelled in as many different circles as he did. He could smell a scam a mile away, at this point. Although it was always the ones that you couldn't just smell that were dangerous.

And sometimes you just had to take the risk. There was one project, to this day he still didn't know if it had been completely legit. It had basically been a budget hyperbaric chamber, those decompression chambers used to treat scuba divers that came up to the surface too fast.

Usually they were really expensive, a dive town would just have one for everyone to use. But in their most optimistic price scenarios any medium sized dive shop would have been able to afford one. It could have revolutionized the industry

The tank itself was really something as well, they had a fully functional prototype. The issue was never being able to build it, but mass producing them at an affordable cost. The way they designed it, you could fill it with warm water and have a float, it was quite meditative. Then you could turn the pressure up, and get nitrogen narcosis.

But in the end they couldn't get it anywhere near their price points. They would have had trouble competing with regular hyperbaric chambers, in fact. The government was really giving them trouble as well, the safety standards were almost stricter than for airplanes. Once things started to obviously go sour the project's developers made themselves scarce, and in the end Blake didn't know if they had thought they could really achieve those prices, or if they had been skimming the whole time taking him for a ride.

He had lost rather a lot of money on that one though, it was slightly embarrassing. That was how that kind of investing worked, of course. You make a lot of risky investments, and while a lot fail the ones that succeed more than make up the difference. But people just hear the numbers and get all worked up about it.

And he made most of it back on a stock tip not long after. Not that he considered that real investing. More a day at the casino. He would rather research a company, study their operations on the ground, then guide them to success. That's what investing was, not short-selling corn futures after your uncle's buddy told you there was going to be a drop-off in demand. He might as well be playing the real estate market. Although in all truth he was heavily invested in all those sorts of things, you had to park your money somewhere.

His drink was empty. He motioned to the bartender, holding up another couple fingers.

"That's the last of it," said the bartender, turning the bottle upside down over Blake's glass.

"Slow night tonight?" ventured Blake.

"Ya, it was crazy, up to the last couple days, actually, holidays and everything. Kind of nice to get a break." He gave a little shrug. "It's usually like this on Thursdays, but it really picks up on the weekends. We've got wing night on Saturdays."

Blake nodded, perhaps he would come in on Saturday. "Must be low season now?"

The bartender shrugged. "It doesn't actually make a huge

difference, summer is obviously the busiest, but it's pretty steady year-round."

"I guess you guys aren't too close to the tourist areas, you get more business travellers?"

"Ya, actually, I think the hotels near the beach are way more seasonal. Not that the weather is ever bad here. You here on business?"

Blake nodded, now feeling slightly self-conscious, he didn't know what exactly to say about it. "Textiles."

"Cool, like clothing and stuff?"

"No, just the raw fabrics. The company I'm working with sells to clothing manufacturers."

"Sounds like a good industry to be in. There must always be a market." The bartender grinned at him. "That's a nice scotch huh? We all get to try a bit whenever we open a new bottle."

Blake nodded emphatically. "Yes, it's particularly good, the peat."

"I think we're going to try a Glenwight premium for the next bottle."

"That's the blue label?" Blake asked, slightly excited. He knew that one, it was one of his favourites, in fact. He was about to recommend another one, when there was suddenly a sharp clatter and thud from across the bar behind him. The bartender craned his neck - a perplexed sort of look on his face - and the guys at the one table were turning in their seats.

Blake swivelled around. It must have been a pool ball, the older guy was running over to the other side of the bar. Blake watched as he ducked down under a table - righting a chair in the process - then appeared again with a red pool ball, which he held up to the bar.

"Nothing broke!" he said with a nervous joviality.

The bar was awkwardly still for a moment, then everyone sort of returned to what they had been doing. Blake turned back towards the bartender to return to the subject of scotches, but he was back to staring up at the TV.

Blake sipped at the scotch, the strong peatiness still not too much. He would have to make this one his last though, it had been too many already. That was a fairly natural place to stop anyways, the end of a bottle.

In all his investments there had, of course, been one industry in which he had made a particularly large amount of money. Even a stopped clock, the bluest of moons, an exception to every rule, all that.

Although he wasn't sure exactly how it counted - some success stories were skill, others luck, some position. And then some were just being able to pull it off in the first place. Or more accurately get away with it.

He had been living in LA, hanging out with a lot of people in the film business. He wasn't making movies or anything like that, having gone a little superstitious and swearing off investing for a while. Mostly he was just going to Hollywood parties, it was a pretty good time.

He also happened to have an associate at that time who was a particularly good connection for a wide variety of illicit substances. There was a lot of cocaine in those days, but everything, from weed to trendy synthetic designer drugs. He could get heroin, if he wanted it, old drugs from the 50s, hallucinogenic centipede venom, you name it.

If someone were looking for something, Blake would often just get it for them. After a while people just sort of started coming to him, often for very large quantities. As it progressed he started taking a profit instead of just doing it as a favour. Then he sort of woke up one morning and realized he sold drugs in Hollywood.

It probably wouldn't have stuck, but he found a particularly profitable niche. He was rich, people trusted him. He wasn't going to blackmail anyone. That was something particularly important among celebrities.

And Blake had the best product, no doubt of that. He soon had a virtual monopoly in a number of well-heeled circles. He became a fixture at all the right parties, and his face appeared in the background of a number of photos in glossy celebrity magazines. He was even mentioned in a couple celebrity biographies, if never by his real name.

Soon he was building up a network, expanding into Wall Street, Silicon Valley, doing deliveries for rich clientele across the country. It reached the point where he could just sit back and manage things from afar, which shielded him from most of the dirty work. If he did cross the border into Mexico with a bag of coke once, in part just to know what it was like to cross a border carrying.

It got so he was making more money than anyone he knew. It was pretty ridiculous actually, by the end of it he wasn't so far off from making up for all his previous losses combined. And there was no end to the less tangible perks. VIP invites to movie premieres, he never paid for meals at some of the classiest restaurants in three cities. Just the props from movies, people seemed to love giving him those. He had a dragon in his living room for a while, mounted some alien masks on his wall, was never lacking for a Halloween costume.

One of his clients - a major trader on Wall Street - had a yacht on the west coast which he almost never used. Apparently he had some great plan to sail it around to New York himself, but business never left him the opportunity. Blake got to move into it, in exchange for a bottomless supply pipeline to him and his top traders.

The thing had been a beast. It had two hot tubs, a little movie theatre, its crowning glory was a fireplace in the aft cabin. If it was a constant task to keep the firewood dry, and everyone always wanted to see it in action. He got some kind of mite in the firewood once, had to get the whole place fumigated. And the bearskin rug stunk if it got wet, and was like a magnet for sand. He only brought it out on special occasions.

Looking back on it all, it had sort of been a funny thing to do, selling drugs, especially with him already being rich. At the time it had made sense to him, if he didn't know if he would do it all over quite the same way. Maybe he would, maybe some of it, you could never really say, that sort of thing.

And as these things are wont to do, of course, the business did eventually begin to go sour. Certainly, he began to see the effects his products were having on his customers. He soon found himself doing too much as well - it was too many sunrises semi-conscious on the beach with vomit on his shirt or some such.

And he was starting to become the go-to guy when people really wanted to party. It wasn't always a good thing, pull an all-weekender and go to Vegas, even if it was with Jack Dash. But how did you say no to Jack Dash?

Blake eventually got the yacht taken away, after an incident where he crashed it into a dock at 2 in the morning. It really was amazing how much damage you could do at two knots with a big boat like that. And everyone made a really big thing of it, they made him replace the whole dock, even though only a little bit was damaged. The harbour people were clearly taking advantage. It probably wouldn't even have been such a big deal, but one of the girls had a photo shoot the next morning and she chipped a tooth. She threw a big fully violent hysterical fit, and it all got back to the owner.

Blake moved back into his apartment off Venice Beach, but it was never quite the same after that. He found himself getting pulled deeper and deeper into the lifestyle, and ultimately checked into rehab a couple of times.

He had also began doubting his ability to pay his way out of it, if he ever did get caught. The closest he came was an incident towards the end when the police raided his apartment. Really tore it up, actually, damaging a couple of antiques in the process.

They took him back to the station and everything, kept him there all afternoon with incessant questions. All like a cop show, in his face, a nice one and an angry one. Luckily enough it happened on pretty much the one day he didn't have any product.

He had always thought it funny it worked out that way, actually. It was a little bit too lucky, wasn't it? From nowhere the sensation of boredom returned. He finished his drink in one go, then looked over at the bartender, who was polishing a mug.

"We've got a nice 22 year bourbon," said the bartender, unbidden. Blake nodded. He saw they had a Mexican beer he liked, he could almost just go for one of those. But the bourbon did sound interesting.

"It's better on ice, brings out the flavour a bit," said the bartender.

Blake took a sip, it was quite nice. He suddenly felt a bit peckish, the dinner on the plane had been fairly light.

"I don't suppose the kitchen is still open?"

"No, it closes at 11. There's a nut machine in the corner, that's about the best we've got right now. There's a 24-hour restaurant a block down the road."

Blake shrugged, some nuts would do. He stood up, feeling dizzy for a second. Wobbling a bit he pointed himself towards the nut machine, which was hidden in the corner of the bar.

The game must have ended, there was just news silent on the TV, classic rock playing in the background. Blake noticed the salesmen had disappeared, when did they leave? Had they even paid? He supposed they must have, the bartender seemed pretty on top of that sort of thing.

Swaying a bit on the way, he made it to the nut machine. It was fairly fancy, actually, lots of flashy colours, some kind of handle-thing on the side that he stabilized himself on. It had three big rectangular buttons, but they were all the same thing, roast nuts.

He put a bill in, pressed one of the buttons. A light went on, a little cup dropped down, and filled with nuts. Then there was a rushing symphony of cling cling clings as it spat out his change.

It was sort of a smallish cup, but trying them they were good. The machine was still spitting out change though. He stared at it uncomprehending, wobbling on his feet, as it kept ka-ching ka-chinging, it wasn't stopping.

Had he put in a fifty? He reached into the change slot and grabbed a handful of coins, coins showering on his hand. He put them in his pocket, some ending up on the floor. He tried gathering up another handful, but it was surprisingly hard. They were slippery, and the slot was down at a weird angle. Maybe they did that on purpose!

Blake glanced sheepishly around the bar, suddenly feeling very self-conscious. The bartender was doing something at the cash register, while the pool players seemed pretty intent on their game. The music was loud enough, probably none of them could hear it.

He saw the older guy was just finishing racking up again at the pool table. That was getting to be a lot of pool to play, they had been at it straight the whole time he had been there. Maybe they were professional pool players, then, training for a tournament.

He wondered if he should go over there, introduce himself, see if they wanted a game. That was what you did, was it, when you were in new towns? Although it again looked like they were having an involved conversation. The young guy was saying something, really gesticulating, one finger forward like a gavel. Maybe they were in the middle of something then, didn't need him interrupting them. Blake wasn't even entirely sure he would be able to line his shots up straight, this point in the night.

Turning back towards the nut machine, it was still spitting out coins, if maybe at a slower rate now. A yellow change light had lit up. He grabbed up another couple handfuls, put some in his shirt pocket, his back pockets. He had a lot of pockets, but none of them were that big.

Blake looked over at the bartender. Telling him about the change suddenly seemed really complicated, it would be a hassle for everyone. Blake could tell him it was his tip, but then that was sort of a rude tip. And someone would probably just count it up and credit it to his bill anyways

He tried to fit in a few more coins, but realistically he just didn't have the pocket space for that volume of coinage. He would just leave them for the next lucky snacker, then. He made his way back to his stool, the bartender doing something with the receipts and looking pretty busy.

Blake sipped at the bourbon, he really would have to make this one his last. He didn't usually drink so much, really he couldn't remember the last time he had so many. Well, actually, it had been the New Year's Eve party, a week ago now. But that was a special case, it was New Year's.

That had been a nice party, up on a rooftop somewhere in Manhattan, a lot of old friends. Hard to believe the year had gone by already. It felt a little like the years were running together anyways, at this point. Whatever year it even was now, for that matter. In whatever bizarre alternate cosmic universe he found himself. Going out on a limb and assuming any of this was even real. Watching the news these days it sometimes felt like he was trapped in some bizarre upside-down simulacrum.

He hoped the meeting went well tomorrow. Thinking about it made him slightly nauseous, he hoped he wasn't making a mistake. He didn't really know anything about textiles, and these things could turn into great sinkholes for money.

They could just always be on the cusp of success, it could always just take a little bit more money, a little more after that. And then you'd invested so much that you had to keep investing, good money chasing the bad. Until finally they went belly up and you lost half your fortune.

Maybe he should just get back on a plane. He could go to Britain, work on his magnum opus. Or Italy, Paris, there were any number of places in Europe, he had friends scattered all around. He could just go back to New York as well, he had a lot of roots there. Or even do a tropical beach town somewhere, have some downtime, he hadn't done that in quite a while.

Although really, they did have beaches here in San Diego. They were pretty far south, just a couple of hours from the border. Maybe it wasn't tropical, but how much could you really ask for in life?

And Wildon Textiles seemed good. What if he passed up this opportunity, and they turned out to be a blockbuster? He was tired of hanging out at the cigar club with no better stories than music festivals that went 300% over budget. He could drop

Wildon Textiles when Boshy Boy told the story about him getting audited because he was losing too much money.

He wondered what old Reginald would say about Wildon Textiles. He always knew what to do in these situations, or if he didn't he could at least help Blake figure it out. He never should have dismissed him, but it just didn't do to have a butler in America, there were no end to the jokes. Even if he was technically a valet. Not that Blake could have kept him on through his dealing days, that would have been too much to ask an old traditionalist like Reginald.

Blake felt dizzy, he rubbed his head. Sometimes he wondered if having money just made things more complicated, if it was all really worth it. It felt like everything in his life revolved around it, all his stories started and ended with money.

He wondered what would happen, if he just got rid of it all. Convert it to cash, throw a big party in the desert, and burn it all at once. That would really be something, show them all, wouldn't it? He cackled to himself.

Of course, he would never actually do that. His smuggler friend from his LA days made a fairly convincing argument that it would just work out to be a donation to the government anyways.

Maybe he should join the Foreign Legion, go fight in a little war somewhere. His problem was that he was born in the wrong age. There was no adventure, no new continents to explore, no damsels in distress to rescue or black knights to be defeated. There was nothing to do but invest in wholesale fabric manufacturers and drink in hotel bars.

Was this what he should be doing with his life? Had he strayed off course somewhere? Where was he headed, where were they all headed, for that matter, on this giant spinning ball of dirt?

Maybe he was doing right, investing in Wildon Textiles. The world did need more high quality fabrics, didn't it? That's what business was about sometimes, incrementally moving things forward. And really, he was getting ahead of himself, he hadn't even seen the factory yet.

It would be nice to meet everyone tomorrow. From the sounds of it there would be engineers, scientists, product developers, he got along with those kinds of people. And Jack seemed like a good type. He had only met him once before in person, at the investor's conference, but they had exchanged a lot of phone calls and emails.

Maybe that was exactly what he needed right now, a good investment to keep him busy. And he would be in control, wouldn't he? If he liked them, he would go forward, if not, then he wouldn't. Simple as that.

Blake pulled out his wallet and fished out his business card. He ran his thumb over its rough texture, admiring the almost stonelike grey paper. "MYNTBANKE CAPITAL," it said at the top, in an understated font with big bold letters, followed by "Blake Myntbanke, Angel Investor." Then his phone and email, and a web address, which was pretty much just a placeholder site. Just the necessary information, elegant design, no clutter.

He had it printed at one of the best printers in New York before he left. It was kind of a big thing for him, he had never really had business cards before, he didn't like doing business that way. But it seemed appropriate to make some up now.

Looking at the card, however, something seemed amiss. Angel Investor. That wasn't a proper job title, was it? He stared at the card, the writing going in and out of focus. That's what he was - more or less - but you didn't say it, did you?

Blake suddenly felt a profound tiredness. He would have to get up pretty early tomorrow if he wanted to get new cards printed before the meeting. It seemed like an immense amount of work, running around San Diego trying to find a print shop. Then going to the meeting after that, he wouldn't be properly rested. He was probably going to be groggy tomorrow as was.

And what would he put instead? Venture capitalist? Just Investor? Maybe it was good to avoid anything investor altogether. Management Consultant then? He didn't even know if that was a proper title, either. Bloody hell, if he couldn't even get his business card right, how was he going to deal with cotton price negotiations or thread grade selection or whatever the devil else was involved in the fabric manufacturing business.

Maybe it could work, it was honest. He was an angel investor, so his card said angel investor. What did the other angel investors put on their cards?

He stared at the card, the 'Angel Investor' doubling in his vision, as if to taunt him. It really didn't work, did it? Just the imagery of it was all off. Blake Myntbanke, Angel Investor, flapping down from the sky on little wings. Who was he, Mary bloody Poppins? The people at the print shop probably had a laugh at him.

He crumbled the card into a ball in his fist, swaying on his bar stool. He just wouldn't have business cards, then.

Suddenly there was a sharp wooden cracking sound from behind him, loud enough to make him turn on his stool. The young guy was leaning into the face of the old guy, the two halves of a broken pool cue in his hands.

"You think I don't know half of what's going on? I don't like your fucking ends or your fucking means." He stepped back, throwing the broken pieces of the cue to the ground. "You want me to be a fucking goon? Well how about this?" he yelled.

And with that he grabbed the pool table, and then just sort of picked it up, leaning back and lifting it completely off the ground. He then proceeded to spin it around in a half circle before releasing it, chairs knocking over and pool balls rolling back to one side. The table arced through the air, then crashed into the brick wall at the other end of the bar, collapsing into a pile of broken slate and felt.

The room was still. The young guy stared at the wreckage, his face unbelieving. Blake looked over at the bartender, who was frozen in mid polish, his jaw hanging open. Then the door to the bar flew open, and men in riot gear were charging into the room.

The young guy looked panicked as they came at him, there must have been a good half dozen of them. They fanned out wide and moved towards him determinedly, wielding what looked like some kind of high-tech stun gun.

The guy backed towards the bar defensively, then they were on him, sizzling sounds and flashes of blue and white light breaking through the room. A couple of them tried to tackle him, but he stayed up, flinging them around. It was a chaotic mess of bodies, arms and legs flying out in every direction as they scrambled across the bar.

There was the sound of breaking wood as a table was knocked over. Then out of nowhere they were all coming towards Blake, throwing the guy towards the bar. Blake tried to get out of the way, but one of the riot suits slammed into him, he was falling off the bar stool.

There was a rain of metallic clinkings as he fell face first onto the floor. They were on top of him, black boots and leg armour, there was nowhere to go. He tried to dodge the boots around him, but he caught one in the chest, he couldn't get out.

There was a thud as another bar stool fell over, and the sound of shattering glass. Then in front of his face he saw a white sneaker among the black boots. With a quick motion he took his crumpled up business card and shoved it into the sneaker, then rolled away from the fighting mass.

2

Blake awoke to a pit of nausea the next morning, strange pains wracking his body, his mouth a sour rot. He was not well.

It took him a bit to steel himself to open his eyes, and when he did he closed them again immediately. The light from the window was coming in from the worst angle possible, someone had left the curtain open. He might have overdone it a bit last night then, had he?

Somewhere in the distance there was a rhythmic tapping sound, like a woodpecker on a tree. The noise reverberated in his skull, every rap sending jolts of pain all the way down into his stomach. Something about it was very unsettling, and he wished it would just stop, which it did.

Blake rolled over, which may have been a strategic mistake, and blinking a bit he opened his eyes again. He had a moment of startled confusion when he realized he wasn't in his apartment. It took him a second, that was right, he was in San Diego.

He glanced over at the nightstand to see what time it was, but the clock was knocked over. With great effort he flipped it up, jolts of pain flashing through his shoulder and elbow, which for some reason were incredibly sore. It was just a little past 9 in the morning.

There was again a rapping sound. "Hello, Mr. Myntbanke, can we have a word with you?" said a deep, authoritative voice from outside his room.

That's what the tapping was, then. Blake felt a pang of nervousness, he had the sudden sensation that something happened last night. He hoped he hadn't done anything stupid. He couldn't even remember how he got back to his room.

"Just a minute," he yelled, coughing a bit. The room spun as he stood up, he had to hold onto the bedframe for a moment. At least he was already dressed. After taking a couple of deep breaths, he tiptoed to the door, and peeked through the peephole. There were a couple of men in suits and dark sunglasses outside, standing stone-faced at the door.

Blake stared at the door a second, then tiptoed to the kitchenette. He needed a minute. Grabbing the tea kettle, he tried to remember what happened last night. Sitting at the bar, talking to the bartender, the nut machine.

He had a sharp flash of memory, wood and green felt smashed up against the wall. That fellow had thrown a bloody pool table across the room, hadn't he? Blake tried to reach through the fog of his memory, he could see it flying through the air, the riot police types rushing in.

He hadn't dreamt all that, had he? It would explain why his arm was sore, he had fallen off his stool. And why there were now the suits and sunglasses outside.

He jumped as there was again a knocking at the door. "Mr. Myntbanke? We just need a couple of minutes of your time."

"Coming," Blake coughed. He looked over at the tea kettle. Realistically there just wasn't going to be tea by the time he would have to open the door. He needed something to wake himself up. Glancing around the room, his eyes settled on the open bottle of bourbon on the kitchen counter.

He took a deep breath, then grabbed the bottle, and raised it to his mouth. But as he did so the bottle sort of spat in his face. It was in his nose, burning his eyes, running down his shirt, he was coughing. He slammed the bottle down and stared at it, feeling sort of betrayed. It had some sort of fancy pourer-nozzle thing on the top, that's what did it.

One way or another it didn't help. His sinuses were burning, he felt a nausea welling up, there was a metallic taste in his mouth. He leaned heavily on the sink, breathing deeply. It had been years since he had been sick, breathe in, breathe out, wouldn't do him any good at this point.

Slowly his nausea subsided, he was going to be alright. There was again a knocking at the door, this time slower, almost sarcastic, a leisurely tap, tap, tap.

"Coming," he yelled again. He stumbled towards the door, took a deep breath, and opened it. The two men were there, staring impenetrably at him through their sunglasses.

"Are you Blake Myntbanke?" asked the taller of the two. Blake nodded. "Do you mind if we come in?" Blake nodded again, motioning them in and stepping out of the way.

They closed the door behind them. "Do you mind if we ask

you a couple of questions?" the one continued. Blake could feel their gaze from behind the sunglasses, which seemed slightly the extraneous accessory. If he himself was finding it a little bright out.

"Certainly," he said, giving them a little grimace. "You'll have to excuse the mess. Sort of a rough night last night."

The taller one spoke again, while the other one briefly glanced around the apartment. "You were in the bar of this hotel, at approximately 12:15 last night?"

Blake nodded, and rubbed the back of his head. He wasn't sure exactly how to approach this. "I think so, it's a bit of a blur actually. I'm not sure what time I left."

"Did you see anything out of the ordinary last night?"

That really happened then, did it? Should he say he remembered? Something held him back. There was really no need, they might even want to take him in to the station or something. He made a quick executive decision, probably best just to play dumb, these kinds of situations. That was what they wanted from you in the end anyways, wasn't it?

"I'm afraid I won't really be able to help you. I got started on the plane in last night, and I had a few at the bar," Blake said, giving them an apologetic look and inflecting his accent just a bit thicker, which he generally found to be helpful with law enforcement types.

Again they stared at him from behind their sunglasses. Then the taller one spoke. "You are certain you didn't see anything?"

Blake shook his head, which was slightly painful. He hoped this would be over soon. "No, nothing."

The taller one continued, speaking firmly, professionally, like he was reading Blake his rights. "Last night there was a boiler explosion in a room underneath the bar. For reasons we cannot divulge, that is considered a matter of highest secrecy. As such, saying anything about it would be considered a felony offence. As would be telling anyone that we spoke to you today, or speaking to anyone about anything else related to the subject." The man paused. "Do you understand?"

Blake nodded grimly. Bloody felony. That was pretty heavy for 9 in the morning. He hadn't even had tea. And weren't they supposed to have shown him a badge or something? They could just be anyone off the street. "Of course, of course, mum's the word. You don't have to worry about me."

"When you were at the bar, you did not see anything

unusual. You had several scotches, then returned to your room after an uneventful night," said the shorter one, in a tone that sounded half a question and half an order.

Then they stared at him suspiciously a moment, and the taller one nodded. "Thank you for your time," he said, perhaps a slightly apologetic note in his voice. They gave the room one last glance over, then left, Blake returning immediately to bed.

3

Blake lay in bed sick the rest of the morning, half asleep, trying not to think about much of anything. Nonetheless the events of the night before kept returning to his mind. Did that really happen? He replayed it over and over again, the guy picked up the pool table, threw it across the room.

Maybe there had been a bomb or something, what had they said, a boiler explosion? Maybe there had been some incident with riot police and a boiler bomb under the pool table, and he got it all mixed up in his mind somehow. For all he knew they could have hypnotized him and implanted a fake memory. Then if he ever did decide to tell anyone, he'd be ranting off on some ridiculous story about someone throwing a pool table across the bar. Could they do that? He didn't know, really.

Eventually he just blocked it all from his mind. It was giving him a headache, he needed to rest. If it hadn't been a 2 o'clock meeting he might have almost called to reschedule. Jack had said there were going to be a few people there, he would be cancelling on all of them.

Blake forced himself up a little after noon, managed to eat a bit of toast from room service, and had a hurried shower. By the time he was leaving he was starting to feel halfway decent, if his head was still throbbing, and he was a bit unsure of the wisdom of eating the toast.

He tried to focus on the business at hand as he drove down the palm lined boulevards. He had written down some questions he wanted to ask, so he stopped outside a coffee shop to look for them. But checking his briefcase, loading up his laptop, he couldn't find them anywhere. Something about a cottons tariff, expanding into Europe? Thread cost to fraying ratio, he was going to impress them with something about that. He had drawn a little graph.

It also turned out that he had forgotten his phone, and his

business cards, which was the only place he had the number written down. He had gotten his lawyer to get him a San Diego number before he left - he just wasn't going to use his main New York number for a venture again. Getting a local number was perhaps a little premature, but if he got it down here he would have had to do all the paperwork and everything himself.

Probably just as well he didn't have it, anyways. He hated thinking like that, but it would sort of imply some things if he had a local number already. You didn't want to underestimate the effect that sort of thing had on negotiations, the least interested party always had the advantage.

He went into the coffee shop before he left, got a coffee to go. It had a nice atmosphere, a couple professional types sitting there typing away on their laptops. It seemed like the sort of place he could hang out.

After a couple of wrong turns he was finally there, a large nondescript boxy building with a small Wildon Textiles logo above the door. Inside was a largish waiting room, scattered with boxes and textile samples, an attractive secretary behind the desk. She introduced herself as Yuliana, but everyone just called her Y. He must be Mr. Myntbanke? She paged Jack Wildon, who appeared just as Blake was going to sit down.

Jack was a slightly stout 50-something, with grey-black hair, a nice enough business-casual suit, his friendly face wide in a smile. Following behind him were a couple of men.

"Blake! You made it!" said Jack enthusiastically, shaking Blake's hand firmly.

"Yes, sorry for the delay, had a bit of trouble finding the place," said Blake, realizing he was probably getting past the polite amount of late.

"No problem, we were just finishing something up here," said Jack, graciously.

Jack introduced the men as Bill and Steve, they worked in R&D. Bill was in the lab coat, bald with glasses, Steve emanating a down-to-earth professionalism in the understated suit. Both shook Blake's hand enthusiastically.

They quickly started in on a tour of the premises, out of the reception into the main warehouse. It was a huge space, two stories tall, filled with giant roll after giant roll of multicoloured textiles.

Jack stopped and had Blake feel a roll of black fabric. "This stuff, we manufacture for $2.10 a square meter. Our competitors sell something similar for about $2.75, and our best guess is that their manufacturing cost is somewhere between $2.00 and $2.40."

It was particularly nice, felt very lightweight, but strong, it would make a nice shirt. One of the scientists - it was Steve, was it - spoke. "We're also thinking double-weaving would make it more durable, and we're developing processes that use even less chemicals for these fabrics," he said, his tone really emphasizing the *even less*.

They continued down the warehouse hall, Blake running his hands along the material as they went, it was nice stuff. They started passing through rows of silky fabrics, pinks and whites and purples, they looked like they would make a good nightgown, maybe. There wasn't anything effeminate about working with textiles, was there?

They had reached the end of the warehouse, so they continued into the factory. Here there were wide webs of string being woven together, a conveyor belt carrying cotton into a huge container, giant revolving cylinders covered in fabric. It was all fairly impressive actually, if they did seem to be making rather a lot of noise.

"The real factory is south of the border," said Jack loudly, smiling. "This one is mostly dedicated to R&D these days, although we do manufacture a decent amount here. What we really have to do, is take you to see the factory in Mexico," Jack gave him a wink, "have some tequila."

Blake flashed him a grin, if the thought of Tequila didn't sound particularly appealing at the moment. "You've seen the pictures of the factory down there?" Jack asked.

"Yes, it seems quite impressive."

"We could expand on it, right now we're operating close to full capacity a lot of the time. Sometimes when we get a big order we have to keep it running 24 hours a day." Jack paused, his face taking an earnest expression. "We're paying double for overtime. We try and pay fair wages, we've even had trouble from some of the other factory owners for pushing up wages."

Blake nodded approvingly. Continuing along they reached a door with a 'LABORATORY' plaque on it. There was here a strange odour, something acrid and chemical.

"Just take a quick look," said Jack, now giving Blake a sort of grimace-smile. Blake stepped into a room full of bubbling mixtures, test tubes full of coloured liquids, multicoloured vats with strips of cloth in them. He was immediately hit by an overbearing chemical stench, like some combination of burning plastic and rotten egg, with strong overtones of mildew, somehow.

Blake felt the bile rise in his stomach, and stepped back out. He tried to breathe in and out, he could do this, everything was alright.

"There was a chemical explosion yesterday," said Bill embarrassedly. "Worst part is, we've got some fabric treatment experiments running that we can't interrupt, so we're going to have to spend an hour or two in there later this afternoon."

"I'm supposed to go to a BBQ tonight, but I think I'll have to cancel," said Steve.

"I'll show you the loading zone, you can get some fresh air out there," said Jack jovially, although with a distinct nervousness now entering his voice.

They made their way across the factory then out a door, stepping into a large parking lot. There was a forklift parked over to one side, some wooden crates, a big garbage bin maybe ten paces down. Blake breathed deeply - the air was fresh out there - and after a brief moment of terrible uncertainty his sickness passed.

"All in all we like this location, it has everything we need. We have another warehouse we can use in town, although it's a lot cheaper to store stuff in Mexico," said Jack.

Blake nodded, trying to think of something witty to say, although nothing came to mind. Jack looked at his watch. "It's almost time for the meeting," he said, then looked over at Bill and Steve. "You guys want to go set up?" Steve nodded, and they were off, then the two of them sat down on a bench by the door.

"Sorry about the lab," said Jack, sort of chuckling to himself. "Do you have any questions so far?"

Blake looked out over the loading zone, trying to remember the questions he had written down back in New York. It was actually quite a nice day, the sky was clear now. What had Steve been saying, he had a BBQ tonight? There weren't a lot of BBQs in New York in January.

"So you really think you could get your prices below your competitor's costs?" he finally asked. Jack had really been playing that angle up in his emails.

"We like to think we're close in a couple of markets. We don't know exactly what people's margins are, and you can only ever go so far in comparing two fabrics. It gets complicated, sometimes the market will only pay x dollars per cubic meter for a specific fabric. So it doesn't matter if the quality is better, that's what you have to sell it for. But if we can match prices, and offer a superior product, then the sky's the limit."

Jack gave a little shrug. "And in general, when we increase quality we can increase price. It's all just a matter of figuring out how much of one for the other."

"Elasticity," managed Blake, feeling like he was using the term correctly.

Jack nodded, and gave Blake a nervous glance. "We've got debt though, a lot of it." He shook his head. "We've been hit by a few things at once. We over-extended ourselves in R&D, and then we jumped the gun investing in some of the wrong technologies. One of our major clients went bankrupt a few months ago, and our costs have been going up. A lot of the finer machine parts have to be made out of really expensive metals."

Jack looked Blake in the eye. "I'm a believer in straight dealing, so I'll just give you my honest appraisal of our situation. We're definitely making enough to stay afloat. But if we lost one big customer, took another big hit, we'd be struggling. And we've had to make major cutbacks in R&D, when we should be doing the opposite."

Jack stopped talking, and was sort of looking at Blake expectantly. Blake rubbed his chin. He never knew what to say to people about their companies, it was sort of an awkward thing. Jack did seem like a straight-dealer, and everything Blake had seen so far confirmed his original appraisals of the company. He felt a little stirring, could he have found a golden opportunity, then?

"From everything I've seen so far, it seems like you have a pretty solid operation here."

Jack looked slightly relieved. "If you are staying in San Diego a bit, feel free to spend some time at the factory." He shrugged. "Maybe you would have some suggestions. We don't actually have that much business experience aboard right now, my background is more technical, nobody has an MBA."

Blake nodded, they had been talking about that management consultancy, as well. Jack continued. "We haven't approached many investors yet. One of the other owners, Straaval, has been a bit hesitant to bring people on." Jack paused a moment, perhaps choosing his words carefully. "If you *were* to buy a significant share, he would probably want you to be involved in things, and he would want to get to know you first."

Blake nodded. He had gotten that impression from their previous communications.

"Obviously you would want to study our operations more first," continued Jack, "but my cousin owns a 1.5% share in the company. She's about to put her kids through college, so she's looking to sell it. I think we could reach an agreeable price on that."

Blake again nodded. Really he could just buy that right now, he'd come all this way. But it was always better negotiations-wise to hold out a bit.

They were silent again a moment, and Jack looked at his watch. "They should be ready for us upstairs."

They made their way to a spacious enough conference room on the second floor, with a wall of windows looking out over the factory below. A group of about ten people were there, sitting around a nondescript conference table.

Jack motioned for Blake to sit down, then went around the room making introductions. To Jack's right was Straaval. He was a dour looking man in a grey suit, probably in his 60s. Blake picked up a certain coldness from him, although he smiled gruffly when they were introduced.

Blake already knew Bill and Steve, there was an eager looking youngish blond guy, was in sales, a Mexican guy from the factory down south, the accountant. Blake was introduced simply as 'Mr. Myntbanke', without any mention of his potential role with the company.

Just when Blake thought the introductions were over, a woman leaned forward from behind the accountant, somehow he hadn't seen her. Jack introduced her as Laura, she was in advertising. She must have been maybe mid-20s, long black hair, a depth in her gaze, sharp features. She gave him a little smile as they were introduced.

Jack then started the meeting off. Things were coming together, Wildon Textiles was moving into a new era, it was good to get them all around a table at the same time for once. Then he went off about some of their new clients, recent fluctuations in cotton prices, a favourable mention of Wildon Textiles in FabricWorld Magazine.

The meeting quickly moved on to Bill and Steve's R&D presentation. They got up and started showing slides, it was really professional. Their needle breakage rate was down 20% over the past two years, loose threads had been all but eliminated on the secondary cotton blends.

Blake sat back and put his pen to his mouth. He wondered how much of the presentation was for his benefit. It did feel like a real enough meeting, if perhaps tailored to the presence of an investor. He looked over at Laura, she seemed pretty intent on the presentation. There was something about her, just how she carried herself maybe, he could tell they would get along.

He wondered if she was seeing anyone. He felt a little pang at that though. He was sort of making a point of not dating women who worked for companies he was investing in anymore. It just always tended to end badly, and it was sort of a greasy thing to do. He could make an exception, but then if you kept making exceptions all the time they stopped being exceptions.

He supposed it wouldn't matter as much if he just ended up doing the management consultancy thing with them. What had Jack been saying back there? Maybe Blake could offer them some suggestions, that they didn't have anyone with an MBA. That sort of suggested they were open to that.

One way or another it would just be nice to have some people he could hang out with, have show him around town. Steve had been saying something about a BBQ tonight. If he was mentioning it to him, Blake could probably get himself invited easily enough.

Although was he really at a point in his life where he wanted to move somewhere new? He had spent most of his time in America between New York and LA. It could really be a process, making friends in a new town. Like getting to where you had a real network of however many people you could just call up out of the blue and hang out with on a Wednesday night.

The accountant had joined Bill and Steve at the whiteboard, Blake forced himself to focus on the presentation. From the looks of it, overall they had been driving costs down close to 5% annually for the past few years. That added up, especially if quality was improving as well.

Then they were done, and Jack was calling Laura up, she had a presentation about advertising. Blake hadn't thought that Wildon Textiles did a lot of advertising, she must pretty much run the department then.

She stood up and jumped into her presentation, which she delivered quickly and monotonically. He could tell she was a little nervous. Her findings were basically that what they were doing now was good, simple basic advertising was all they needed. Direct marketing to manufacturers, box ads in trade magazines, and trade shows, she really highlighted those. They had good product, so it was important to show it to people, let them feel the samples in their hands.

Then as fast as she had gone up she was sitting back down. Jack turned towards Blake. "Blake, you're new here, but do you have anything to add, based on what you've seen so far?"

Blake rubbed his chin, feeling rather on the spot. He supposed as the investor, he didn't really have to say anything. But if he did want to do a management consultancy with them, it would be good to at least offer up some little gem of wisdom.

"It seems like a pretty solid operation you're running here. I mean, I've only seen so much, but everything seems solid, on the ground."

Aside from Straaval they were all smiling at him, but Blake didn't feel like he was being particularly inspirational. He felt a little dizzy, and his headache was returning. He drew into his reserves, he was starting to understand the market, to see how things could take shape.

"If everything works out the way it's supposed to, you'll be in a situation where you can turn a profit while charging below the competition's production costs?" There was nodding around the room.

"Well, if that's the case, maybe you should look at moving up into other industries. Textiles are the base of the pyramid. If you can beat the competition in the raw fabric market, you can beat them downstream. I mean, why sell to shirt manufacturers, when you can make the shirts yourself? Every stage of the production process you take on yourself are more profits."

He paused, they were all staring at him. "I mean, a lot of these things, its just a matter of getting established - figuring out what to make, building a customer base, setting up the manufacturing. Once you've done all that, then maybe it just runs itself. And if you can get a jump on prices, you could get a foothold in a lot of markets at once."

He stopped talking, and there was a silence in the room. He hoped he wasn't saying something really obvious. Maybe there was a reason why they just produced raw fabrics.

Jack gave a little laugh. "Some of the manufacturers we sell to do mark things up quite a bit sometimes."

There was another brief silence, then Jack asked if anyone had anything else they wanted to bring up. Nobody seemed to, so Jack just finished the meeting with some quick business about dividing up machine maintenance duties, and Steve agreed to write a piece for Textiles Monthly. Then they all broke off into little groups, Bill and Steve talking to the Mexican guy, Laura and Straaval talking with the accountant, Jack making some notes in his notebook.

Blake went and got some water at the water cooler, he was suddenly very thirsty. After his second cup Jack joined him, smiling warmly. "That was really interesting, what you were saying there about making clothing. It could get tricky though, if we start competing with our customers."

"Certainly, you'd have to be careful, it would require a bit of finesse." Blake shrugged, feeling like he should cover his six a bit. "Just a suggestion, you'd have to do some market research. It could be more a matter of making partnerships."

"You'd have us be a conglomerate," Jack said, shaking his head just a little, and smiling broadly. His tone didn't suggest that it had been a terrible suggestion.

The younger guy, who was in sales, had sort of angled himself more in their direction, and was now stepping forward. "A couple of months ago I was talking to one of the manufacturers we sell to in Phoenix. I don't know if they were serious, but they said we could probably just make stuff like the pillowcases ourselves."

That sounded like a good idea actually. There probably wasn't a lot of processing involved in transforming raw fabric into pillowcases. Blake rubbed his chin and nodded.

The kid continued. "They sell wholesale, so I don't know how much they are charging for them. But I could try and figure out."

Jack grimaced. "Don't bug them too much."

"I'll be subtle," the kid said eagerly, smiling at Blake. "Do you have a card?"

"I'm not a big believer in business cards," said Blake, feeling it sounded like a bit of a snub. That was exactly the sort of thing he had gotten the San Diego number for.

"You can reach Blake through me," Jack quickly interjected.

Then the kid went off to talk with Steve, and a smiling Yuliana appeared with a clipboard to talk to Jack about scheduling a meeting with a supplier. Blake looked at the people around him, standing in circles, talking business. The company suddenly seemed like something very real. This was how these people made their livelihoods, how they paid the rent. Every week howevermany odd rolls of raw fabric passed through here to go across the country. It was here, in this room, going on around him. He felt a little dizzy.

"I'll just step out.. fresh air," he said to Jack. Blake made his way outside to the parking lot, and leaned up against the wall, breathing rather heavily.

If it was actually sort of peaceful there, out in an industrial part of town, nothing but other warehouses and factories around. The parking lot was really big, they must have those 16-wheel trucks load and unload here. They would probably let him drive the forklift, would they?

There was the sound of the door opening behind him. Laura stepped out, then shut the door behind her, smiling shyly.

"Mr. Myntbanke, is it?" she asked, slightly awkwardly.

"Blake." He was a little unsure of what to do, introductions had already been made. But he held out his hand, and she shook it.

"Laura. Smith." She glanced around the parking lot. "My ride should be here any minute, I've got another meeting today." She smiled at him. "That was a good meeting, right?"

"It was," said Blake, giving her a grin. They were both silent for a moment. He tried to think of something witty to say, but his mind was blank. What exactly had he been thinking, getting so drunk last night?

"Pretty late on a Friday to have a meeting?" he asked.

"Ya, it's probably going to be a long one too. There's a dinner event after we're all going to, so it kind of makes sense. We get a free dinner at a fancy place out of it, so I guess I can't complain." Her tone went sort of strained at the end there, she sounded nervous again.

Blake had a realization. If someone was picking her up for another meeting, it probably wasn't with Wildon Textiles. Was she a freelancer then? "How long have you been working for Wildon Textiles?" he asked.

"I don't know, a couple of weeks?" She laughed. "I don't actually work for them, I was just doing the advertising review. I work for Innosuasion Global, they're a big advertising firm."

Blake felt his spirits lift a little. "You guys did the re-branding campaign for that beach resort?"

She laughed again. "Ya, you saw the show?" She looked slightly embarrassed. "It was really cheesy right? Like everybody knew it was just an advertisement for the resort? And for us."

"These days I wonder if anything on TV is actually what it's supposed to be." She gave him an I-know-right look, and he shrugged. "I don't think I actually saw it, I read about it in an investment magazine. You guys do PR as well?"

She lit up a bit. "Ya, that story was really good, that's more what we're about." Then she looked over at him, slightly shyly. "What did you think of my presentation?"

"It was really good," said Blake enthusiastically.

She gave him kind of a look, like she didn't believe him, like he had given the wrong answer. "You think so? I don't feel like I had a lot to say."

"Well, Wildon Textiles doesn't do a lot of advertising, it's just the industry. A small number of producers selling to a small number of well-informed customers."

"Exactly, I just re-invented the box ad for them. I don't usually do that kind of stuff, I'm more about the creative stuff. But I do a bit of everything, PR, I've even been doing some interior design." She gave him a big grin. "I might be on the team to do the interior of a mall. I know it sounds kind of cheesy, but I think that would be so much fun!"

Blake nodded, slightly impressed. That did actually sound like a fun project to work on, if, yes, it was perhaps cheesy as well.

"That was really interesting, what you were saying about Wildon Textiles making clothing," she said.

"Yes, well, who knows if it would actually work. They might be better off just sticking to raw fabrics. There can be a lot of headaches, expanding into a whole other industry."

"I guess. Be pretty cool to make clothing, they could get a whole line of Wildon Textiles fashions going."

He grinned at her. "Maybe then they could bring you on. There's no shortage of advertising in that industry."

Here she gave him kind of a funny look, but then she laughed. "Ya, that's for sure, you wouldn't believe how much they spend on advertising sometimes."

That got her going about a campaign she had worked on for a clothing chain. They had wanted it outdoorsy, then they wanted it more arty. Then out of nowhere they wanted to film it all in the snow, they had to go up into the mountains in a big rush to make the deadline.

She seemed more relaxed now. There was a chemistry between them, was there? He wondered if she was there because of him. There was often a girl, in his experience, these sorts of things.

Not that Wildon Textiles seemed like the kind of company that would use that class of tactics. Nor that she seemed like a gold digger, she really didn't strike him as the type. If it could be a rather nuanced and variegated gradient, of course. Really, she could even be the type where his having money could work against him. Like she would be afraid her friends would judge her, psyche herself out, all that. It did actually work like that sometimes.

Or she could just be there for the meeting. The world didn't revolve around him and his fortune. Either way she was out there talking to him now. He tried to focus more on what she was saying, she had gotten off onto a business book that had a section about expanding into vertical markets.

Then the conversation sort of trailed off. She looked like she was going to say something, then stopped, then spoke. "So I heard a story.." She paused for a second. "Did you cross the Gulf of Mexico in a homemade submarine?"

Blake shrugged nonchalantly. "That really depends on how you define 'homemade'. My friend did make it at his house, but he was a professional naval engineer." He gave her a self-depreciating sort of grin. "Some people made a big deal about it, but I don't think it was actually that dangerous. There was a little while towards the end where we were worried we were going to have to bail out, but we made it to the other side."

Her eyes went wide, so he did a sort of wave. "The only thing was having to put on my scuba gear in the sub, it was a pretty cramped space."

"I heard you used to hang out in Hollywood, as well," she said, her tone suggesting that she also heard about what he used to do there.

Blake looked down. Then up again, they made eye contact briefly, then he looked down again. He felt like his face was probably going a little red. Did stuff like that get around so much? He supposed if she knew about the sub trip, she would probably know about his LA days as well.

"Just a tip, Straaval's a little hesitant to bring you on, but you could win him over." Her expression wasn't judgemental, perhaps it was even co-conspiratorial. "He's just a little old fashioned, but he's an old softie in the end."

Blake nodded. So he *was* getting a bad vibe from Straaval then. Hopefully it wouldn't be much of an issue. Problems like that tended to resolve themselves fairly quickly for people on his side of the equation.

"Full disclosure, he's a friend of my uncle's, they used to work together. That's kind of why I'm here doing the advertising review for them." She looked down. "I'm mostly just here because Innosuasion is thinking about opening up a satellite office in San Diego. I live in San Francisco."

"Ah, I guess then," Blake said, cringing inwardly as he heard more disappointment in his voice than he had intended. She looked at him, sort of shyly, then looked back down.

"If they do open the satellite office I might move down here, it would mean a promotion. Right now I'm doing a lot of work with the company we'd be partnering with."

She looked over across the parking lot. "Speaking of which, my ride's here." Blake looked over, a middle aged man had pulled into the parking lot across the way. Laura waved at him, then looked at Blake, slightly shyly.

"Anyways, it was nice to meet you, Blake."

"Likewise. We should go for a drink or something, if and when we're both in San Diego."

"I'd like that. Do you have a card?"

"I don't believe in business cards, they only get you in trouble," he said, grinning. "But I'll take yours." She gave him another smile, then fished a card out of her pocket, and gave it to him. Then without a word she turned and ran for the car, which took off immediately after she jumped in.

Blake stood outside in a sort of daze for a moment, then went back to the meeting room. Everyone seemed busy doing things, so he just made plans to meet with Jack for lunch tomorrow, then was quickly on his way.

4

There was a warm breeze in the air as Blake left Wildon Textiles, the sun right at that nice angle just before it set. He felt good, energized, all his worries and sickness lifting away. He just got in his car and drove, turning at random, up through shrubby desert hills, past tall palm trees and fancy looking malls, driving unimpeded the opposite direction of rush hour traffic.

It had gone well in there, had it? Maybe now was when he should listen to his instincts. And they seemed like a good group of people. Everything else aside, it suddenly felt like it would be a lot of fun, working with Wildon Textiles.

It wasn't until after the sun had set, him well in the outskirts of the city, that he remembered the events of the night before. It seemed like something from another world, the fellow just picked up a pool table and threw it across the room. Blake tried to reconcile it with the normalcy of the day's events, meeting everyone, touring the factory. It made his head spin, he had to pull over into a rest area and stop the car a moment.

He supposed it meant they had people like that, then, did it? That was rather an interesting thing. He had some friends in the media, for a moment he wondered if he should go talk to someone. Not that anyone would believe him, he didn't have any evidence.

He made his way back to the hotel in a bit of a daze. On the way to his room he peeked his head into the bar. It was fairly full now, lively, in fact. People at the bar, maybe half the tables full.

The old bartender was nowhere to be seen, a youngish guy in a suit having taken his place. There was a new pool table where the old one had been, and maybe a slight discoloration of the bricks where it hit the wall. But other than that everything seemed identical to how it had been the night before.

Blake didn't feel like joining the crowd tonight, however. He went straight to his room, where he ordered room service and went to bed. He had trouble falling asleep though, the hotel felt strangely awkward now, almost oppressive, even. What would he say if he ran into the bartender, for one? Blake had no clue what the unwritten social rules were for that kind of situation. Maybe you just ignored each other.

He just checked out of the hotel the next morning on his way to meet Jack for lunch. He would have to find an apartment, or at least switch hotels. The restaurant turned out to be a quite nice Britishy sort of place - they had particularly good fish and chips, wrapped in real newspaper and everything. Jack recommended some tourist sights, they talked about the parks in the area, apparently there was a good live music scene here.

It was nice, a relaxed conversation, Jack was easy to talk to. Blake could feel the subtext of money hovering in the background though. He wondered how desperate they were. He had seen a lot of their books, but he still didn't feel like he knew what their exact situation was. Like if they had cash on hand, for one.

Blake supposed there were ways he could try and figure that out. Play coy with the investment, feign disinterest. It all struck him as rather disagreeable though. He didn't want to start off on that foot, and it felt like a hassle anyways. If he still didn't mention his San Diego number.

The conversation did eventually turn to business. Jack got out his laptop and showed him some spreadsheets, they went over the past couple month's sales. Blake had managed to find the questions he had written down, they had a whole big conversation about fray rates. Jack said it was a tricky area, as fraying didn't generally happen until fairly long after the product had been purchased by the end consumer. You had to trust the manufacturers you were selling to cared about it, and were willing to pay extra.

Jack seemed to have a lot of questions for Blake, as well. Were low cotton prices here to stay, how much demand would there really be for space age fabrics? Blake tried to answer as best he could, and only give advice when he felt he really had something insightful to contribute. It did feel a bit like a management consultancy.

It was fascinating, actually, going over it all, the details. They had a lot of weird little customers, industrial stuff you wouldn't think even needed textiles. Their fabrics made good filters, for one.

Industrial bag material, that was almost 10% of their total sales, which came as a complete surprise to Blake. Or those washing instruction tags on clothing and mattresses. Companies would actually manufacturer their own fabrics, but still use Wildon Textile's tag material, it was just easier that way.

By the time dessert was arriving, Blake was agreeing to buy the 1.5% share. If nothing else it was a souvenir. If they were really successful anytime in the future he could say he was a part owner, at worst it would be a fish story. Although then Boshy Boy would probably crack jokes about the exception that proved the rule. That was exactly what he would say.

They did a handshake, Blake would fire off an email to his lawyer to take care of the transfers and paperwork. Then Jack was quickly off – they would see each other soon in the factory, but he had some chemical orders to take care of.

Blake felt good buying the share, if part of him was still sort of leery. But sometimes it was nice even just to have made a decision. So after lunch he got a couple newspapers, then went to a coffee shop to look at apartment listings. He made a couple phone calls, and one didn't mind showing him the place on a Saturday.

It was a nice apartment, big enough with a view, just off the beach. It came fully furnished, with a couple extra bedrooms if he ever had friends in town. He took it right away - you were supposed to check out at least two or three, but he could move in that very afternoon, and it rented by the month. So it was really just a place to land.

Once he had the apartment, he went to check out a car dealership. If he was going to stay, he might as well get something to drive. He was looking for something plain, professional, stodgy, even. But then at the side of the lot, flanked by palm trees, mist almost swirling around it, there was a magnificent beast. Dark fiery red, luxurious interior, low to the ground with sleek chrome.

The K-56, they called it. It was a luxury-sports hybrid, some size to it with four seats, but it drove like a sports car. He decided he could at least take it for a test drive. So off they went, up through the hills as the sun was setting, it was a joy to drive.

The girl said it had arrived from Italy just last week. They weren't even supposed to be selling them in America yet, but a private individual had imported and resold it, which got around the rules.

Blake had already decided he didn't want a car like that. Just in general in life with that sort of thing, it was too flash, people would think he had won the lottery. But the handling was amazing, the acceleration. It was really quiet in the cabin, silent almost, and he liked to listen to music while he drove. And they could give him a good price if he wanted to rent it on a monthly basis – it actually worked better for them with the importation regulations.

So he signed the lease. If nothing else he could just keep it for the month. The dealership was even nice enough to see his old car back to the rental place at the airport. He then spent the rest of the evening just driving around, turning heads and drawing honks as he explored the city.

5

And so the days began to pass in San Diego. Blake quickly immersed himself in Wildon Textiles, and was soon spending most of his time in the factory, hitting the ground running, as it were. He did a bit of everything, worked the machines, helped inspect fabrics up from Mexico, sat in on conference calls with customers. It was the mailroom to the boardroom experience, if condensed.

In spite of some vehement protesting on his part, they did eventually put him on payroll. He was actually doing a lot of work, it would be kind of funny doing that for free while he was considering investing. And he wouldn't be getting any paychecks - his salary was a loan to be paid later when their cash flow situation was better, or just credited towards a future investment he might make in the company.

They paid him a fixed management consultant's salary, the idea being high pay for just a few hours work. Nonetheless he started putting in long hours, even staying late after everyone left a couple of times. It felt good, it was honest work, perhaps he had needed a project. It almost even felt a little awkward, it must have been much more than they expected. He just came in out of nowhere and was working overtime. No one complained though.

As Blake started learning the ropes he joined Jack for some sales meetings. One was with a swimwear company out of LA, it had the potential to be a fairly big contract. The Vice President came to the factory, and they gave him the same tour they had given Blake, minus the overwhelming chemical smell.

They closed the deal, and - to Blake's mild embarrassment - Jack raved about how he was a sales superstar. Blake didn't contradict him, although his contribution hadn't really gone much past making small talk.

Another duty Blake took on was market research. This was also a good way for him to learn the ins and outs of the industry, while doubling as his own research into the viability of the company. He spent long hours reading textile trade publications, combed through government statistics on the industry, even went and looked at the clothing hanging on racks in stores.

It was a little bit bad, but he also did some calling around, trying to find out what exactly the competition was charging. This he did using a fake name, pretending to be manufacturing things like backpacks, band t-shirts, or rain jackets. He got some interesting information, although he was almost hesitant to report it to Jack. Blake had a feeling he would disapprove.

Some of it was a little disturbing, after an epic negotiating session he managed to talk someone down really low on t-shirt material. But overall, the more Blake learned about the industry, the more solid Wildon Textiles seemed. He could start to see how they fit into the market as a whole, he could chart different trajectories, and they tended to look good.

He would sit and watch the trucks load and unload some afternoons, it was a huge amount of fabric passing through. All of it real, all of it being sold on the free market because someone out there was willing to pay for it. He could see it, touch it. It wasn't a bunch of people who had rented an empty warehouse to pull one over on him.

Blake eventually gave a big presentation to everyone on the findings of his market research. He speculated on where the market was going, charted out the potential for further expansion into Europe, estimated at the operating costs of various competitors. Overall he thought there were a lot of untapped opportunities for future growth. If he downplayed the whole idea of expanding into clothing manufacturing for now. But for one thing, they weren't even selling their threads, they were just using them themselves.

There could be huge markets, he gave the example of manufacturers in Asia. High end specialized synthetic threads were the niche-y sort of thing they might really need, but have trouble finding in the local market. It could be a gold mine. At one point he said something about how there could even be spin-offs in the thread industry, and everyone had a good laugh. Thread spin-offs, he didn't even realize.

Straaval even came to the presentation, which was a pleasant surprise. He hadn't been around the factory much at all, Blake was getting the impression he was semi-retired. They didn't talk much, just briefly about how Blake was getting on in San Diego.

But he nodded along during the presentation in a way Blake found encouraging.

The week after his presentation there was a clothing industry trade show in San Diego. It was one of the biggest in the world, and naturally Wildon Textiles had a booth. It was quite an event, much more than just clothing - textiles, of course, to advertising firms, software companies, a little old lady with quilts, you name it.

They all took shifts staffing the booth, and Blake talked to maybe a dozen potential clients. He shot the breeze with the CEO of a suit company, gave a hat manufacturer some detailed technical details while Jack was getting lunch, ordered a selection of sample dyes. He brought his business cards along with him, although in the end he didn't give any out. A few people did ask him for his card though, and Jack made a joke that he should get a Wildon Textiles card made up.

One afternoon soon after that a smiling Jack gave them the green light to develop pillowcase prototypes. He had spoken to a manufacturer, and if they could develop a quality product they could sell pillowcases directly through them. It would be a markup of 15% over the raw fabric price.

They quickly got to work re-tooling some machines for cutting and sewing. From there Bill wrote some programs, and they started picking out materials, experimenting with different designs.

They put in orders for pillowcases from around the world, and every day a couple of new ones would arrive in the factory. Everyone would look them over and give their opinions, they developed a five category rating system and gave them scores out of ten. Every night Blake tried a different one, although really he didn't find much of a difference. They were pillowcases.

Blake's life began to fall into routine. Getting up, going to the factory, evening walks on the beach. He found a few restaurants he liked, did some cooking, ate a lot of meals in front of the TV with his research spread out on the table. He started going to the gym regularly, which he had been neglecting in New York.

Socially he mostly only went out with the Wildon Textiles people. Everyone there seemed to be friends outside the office, which made things easy. Bill and Steve were all about the BBQs, which were basically house parties. There was a good crowd of people, he met a couple girls.

Everyone was blown away by his car, to the extent that he just started telling people he borrowed it off a richer friend. Eventually he rented a second car - opting for a generic grey mid-sized hatchback - and he ended up driving it more than the K-56. Sometimes you just wanted something that let you blend into the world a bit.

He chatted online with Laura a few times, getting her messenger ID after sending her an email about the business book she had been talking about. They had some fairly long conversations, him sitting with his laptop on the balcony looking out over the ocean.

It turned out they liked the same TV shows, they compared notes about travelling around Europe, she went off at length about her work. He told her all about the trade show, they had just made a sale to a client he met there.

After a couple of chat sessions they did a video call as well. She had a big presentation coming up, so he let her do a practice run with him. It was all about mall interiors, she got put on the project!

He watched patiently as she walked him through hanging sculpture things and a bunch of fountains, they debated plaza layout. Her boss wasn't explicitly saying it, but she figured they wanted them to design the plaza so people subconsciously turned right and stayed in the mall.

She also said she was going to come to San Diego again soon. She wasn't sure exactly when, in the next few weeks though, definitely. Likewise Blake said he might be up her way sometime, now that he was on the west coast again he had people he wanted to see. She said they should coordinate it, so he wasn't up north when she was down there.

Blake did start making plans for an eventual road trip up through California. He had friends scattered throughout the state, and there were literally dozens of people for him to visit in LA. Really, he was so close now, he should have gone up there already.

He wondered what it would be like, seeing people from those days now. Part of him was a little hesitant, there might be some unfinished business. Things went a little strange back at the end there. There were probably even a couple of people not long out of jail, of all places.

And he had a feeling any road trip would quickly snowball out of control. If he made it to San Francisco, he had an old friend up in the woods of northern California he would want to see. And then if he made it that far north, he would really have to go up and see people in Portland and Seattle.

For now he was enjoying San Diego, living in his little neighbourhood off the beach. He got to know a couple of guys that did their work in the same coffee shop as him, a Belgian guy who was doing a year at a University there, a guy who worked in sneaker design.

There were some Latino guys, played football in the park down the way, Blake joined them a couple of times. His landlady was a chatty elderly lady, he would bump into her periodically. There was a pretty blond girl in his building, lived on the floor below him. They shared an elevator a couple times, but it never seemed like the right time to talk to her.

Blake went to a couple of live music shows. But the best music he heard by far was a busker who played blues guitar in a park down from his apartment. He was a big stocky old white guy, bald with a silver-black beard, always had sunglasses on.

While his music seemed based in the Blues, it had a bit of everything. He'd jump around from some transcendental fingerpicked blues riff to classical-style arpeggios, then throw in what sounded like an Indian Raga, even a bit of carnival music, before returning to the original blues riff. It was really something else, Blake would often find a place under a tree nearby and just sit and listen.

The guy's sunglasses were particularly dark and thick, and he kept a little white cane beside his guitar case. It looked like the official type blind people used, but on closer inspection wasn't. Blake wasn't sure if he was blind or not, and after he tossed him money a couple of times the guy started nodding as he went by, confirming his suspicions.

One day Blake gave him his compliments, asked if he had any CDs. With a flourish the guy pulled a bag out of nowhere with like fifty CDs. A good salesman always carries his wares, he said. They were all under different band names, but he said they were mostly all just him. He could just never find a band name he wanted to stick with.

Blake had been meaning to give him a big donation, so he just bought ten of them, told him to pick his favorites. The guy was appreciative, apparently he was a little down on his luck. He was just busking to make ends meet and save up for his next recording.

It turned out that he was also an inventor, and he had just lost a lot of money making high-end guitar strings out of rare metal alloys. It had been a complete flop, they were just too expensive, nobody wanted to pay that much for guitar strings. And if he was being totally honest, they didn't really sound that much better. Definitely a little, but not enough to get people buying them. In the end it had been nothing but a huge waste of time and money.

The guy had a theory. It was the invention ideas that looked good, but didn't really work in the end, those were the ones you had to watch out for. If an invention was junk, then you just didn't pursue it, end of story. But the ones that had a lot going for them, they were dangerous. They could really suck you in, then keep you chasing after that will'o'wisp.

Blake concurred, that was a good point. The guy felt like a bit of a kindred spirit, Blake admitted to being halfway to inventor himself. Once he had gotten back to his apartment and was listening to the CDs, Blake got sort of inspired. The recordings were good, but they were all just the guy playing guitar by himself. Most of them didn't even have a drum track. That could really hold you back, the way the market for music was these days. Blake had lots of friends in the recording industry, knew some singers that might really mesh with the guy's style. He could get a full band behind him, rent time in a high-end studio.

But he never saw the guy again. Blake went looking for him, the park, outside the liquor store, all around, but he was gone. There wasn't even any contact information on the CDs.

The events of the hotel bar his first night in San Diego returned to his mind a few times. But puzzle over it as he would, he couldn't make sense of it. Blake started to write it off as one of those strange mysteries in life where you never really find out what was going on. If it hadn't been for the guys in suits and sunglasses the morning after, he might have wondered if he had just dreamt it up.

One night at a bar with Bill and Steve he tried picking up a pool table when no one was looking. It was - as he had expected - quite heavy. Another night there was maybe sort of an incident, late at the bar after everyone else had gone home. This Middle Eastern guy befriended him, had all sorts of conspiracy theories. Shadow governments, fake terrorist attacks, even touched on some strange experiments on humans.

Blake wasn't sure if it was his imagination, but it was almost prodding, the way the guy talked. Like he wanted Blake to say something. Blake had to wonder, was that protocol, did they send someone to test you, after you saw something like that? He didn't say anything about what he saw, and it could have been nothing. But the whole conversation just felt slightly off.

All in all his main focus was Wildon Textiles, however. He thought he was working long hours as it was, but then one afternoon Jack got a phone call. It was a huge rush order for a number of their high end synthetic fabrics, for a company that manufactured outdoorsy stuff. They would be using them to make a variety of backpacks, tents, lifejackets, raincoats, and the like, and they needed it all ASAP.

The order was a bit of a victory, in fact, as Jack thought it had fallen through. But at the last minute the company seemed to have changed their minds, only Wildon Textiles fabrics would do. Jack figured they had been trying to skimp on cheaper fabrics. The unfortunate corollary to this was that they were already far behind schedule, and needed a few square kilometers of high end fabric yesterday.

So plans were cancelled, other orders put on hold, and both factories put on 24/7 operations. Everyone started putting in 16+ hour days, and Blake made sure he was no exception. Jack brought a couple of his nephews on, and even Straaval put in some long hours. There were some things that could only be done in the San Diego factory, which made it a bit of a bottleneck.

No one complained though, it was doubly good business. Not only was it some of their more expensive fabrics, but naturally as a rush job they were paying a premium. And on top of that they wanted Wildon Textiles to do some preparatory work, like sewing in reinforcing thread lines or cutting it into patterns. Which was sort of like the vertical expansion Blake had been talking about, Jack pointed out, if not actually manufacturing finished goods.

Blake spent long hours on the machines, helped out with answering the phone, went to get supplies in place of taking a break. Being a bit of a night owl, he also volunteered for the late shift. He kept the machines going until dawn, trying to get as much done as possible before they shipped off the latest batch each morning.

After a couple of nights it got to be an endurance test. It was hours sitting at a modified sewing machine putting reinforcement thread lines on lifejacket material. Blake forced himself to stay focused, he could imagine someone's lifejacket coming apart in the open ocean, just because the investor wanted to play factory worker with everyone else. Although it was actually pretty foolproof work, and obvious enough if he ever screwed it up. The lines would all be running at the wrong angles, and they would just have to use it for something else.

In the end they got enough of it done, at least close enough to the deadline. Blake wasn't sure if it was his imagination, but things felt ever so slightly different for him after that. He felt like part of the team. All endeavours had their rites of passage, didn't they?

He was starting to have more conversations with Jack about the running of the company. Jack opened up about his worries - it could be a fickle market, they seemed to be doing well, but small changes in their margins could have big effects. Jack had nightmares about someone cutting costs on one of their key fabrics by 50%. Not that he should be talking to Blake about that, he would joke.

They also discussed Jack's ethical concerns. There was one chemical supplier, they had the best prices, and they were quality chemicals. But there were reports of labour abuses in their oversea factories, their environmental record was pretty much abysmal.

Wildon Textiles was only buying a little from them right now, and only when they absolutely had to. But they could save a lot of money if they did, and it wasn't like their clients would be the wiser. Nobody asked whose chemicals they were using.

Jack also agonized over having a factory in Mexico. If he had his way, it would be 100% all American. But then was it even right to prioritize American jobs? They probably needed the work more in Mexico, things were tough down there right now. And another way of looking at all the R&D they were doing was that it was just putting people out of work.

Even just the fact that their financial goals all obviously involved selling more and more product. That was sort of contradictory to saving the environment. Jack hoped people would buy more of their most durable fabrics, but even then any decrease in sales was dangerous to their bottom line. Did Blake know about microfibers?

Eventually during one of these talks the issue of Blake

buying more of the company sort of tangentially came up. It felt funny talking about it, they spoke in vague terms, and only briefly. None of the parties seemed quite ready to make the jump.

The immediate talk was another small share, maybe 5%, at a slightly discounted price for all the work Blake was putting in. But from the sounds of it they would be willing to sell him as much as 49% of the company. Maybe even a controlling share.

What would he do, if they did offer to sell him half the company? Would he be like the dog who caught the car? Even a quarter share would be one of the biggest investments he had made in his life.

His market research suggested that even in the worst-case, belly-up scenarios, he probably wouldn't lose that much. Although any number of things could happen, he wondered to what extent they could be sued. What if they sold a bunch of flammable materials, and had to make a huge recall? He hoped synthetic fabrics couldn't make people sick.

And what if they were a good, profitable business, but it just ended up taking too much of his time? Maybe he would make a few million, but it would take years. Once he had put a lot of money in, he wouldn't want to leave them to run themselves.

Was that really worth it? He had gotten a tip from that mining guy at the cigar club, he always gave good tips. And he thought rare metals were going through the roof. Maybe he would be better off just buying a few metric tons of tungsten, and being done with it.

Before coming to San Diego, Blake had just sort of had a feeling, that after seeing their operations it would be clear whether or not he should invest. But now that he had more information, he just felt more confused. The words of the busker echoed in his head. Maybe Wildon Textiles was one of those business opportunities that looked good, but ended up being a huge waste of time and money.

Would he be letting them down, if he didn't invest now, was he just chickening out? Would he go looking for another company to invest in, then, if he didn't invest in Wildon Textiles? There were no easy answers, and the more he thought about it, the more uncertain he became.

6

The days began blending together, and Blake was soon paying a second month's rent. He still hadn't looked for a new apartment, or even made it down to the factory in Mexico. Nor was he any closer to taking a road trip, for that matter. He hadn't even talked much at all to his friends, he had meant to at least have made it back to NY for a weekend by now.

But they were making rapid strides with the new waterproof materials, and were on the verge of closing a deal with a pickling company that would use Wildon Textiles fabric as a strainer. Progress was being made on the pillowcase design - Bill and Steve had a prototype that wasn't far from being market ready.

And there was some interest in developing new products from there. Blake woke up in the middle of the night once, napkins! They talked it over the next day, and if the pillowcases worked out Jack thought it would be a logical next step. They even made some preliminary designs for socks - there was a huge market, big enough markups, and they had some perfect fabrics for it.

Nonetheless Blake did feel like he was keeping up a good enough work/life balance. He was still going to the gym regularly, which was a minor achievement for him. He was also doing more of his own cooking, trying to master a couple Indian and Thai dishes. In the evenings he even found time to chip away at his Magnum Opus, mostly just keeping up with the latest translations of Dark Age texts.

And he drove. Up through the desert hills, along the coast, out to old Spanish missions. He found it meditative, and the K-56 was certainly a joy to drive. He would go for hours on end sometimes, without destination, driving the direction that looked most interesting.

One Sunday he took Bill, Steve and Jack up to Joshua Tree Park. He let them all take a turn driving the K-56, it was a good trip. Blake even made it to the outskirts of LA once, but he turned around without going in. Something held him back, and Bill was giving a presentation the next day.

Blake was on one of these drives - a Sunday afternoon jaunt up the highway, in procrastination of reading a particularly onerous document on European thread importation tariffs - when an unknown number rang on his phone.

He stared at it a second before answering, slightly bemused. He didn't get a lot of calls on that number, and anyone who did call would be in his contact list. Had he ever even had an unknown number call it? Really the phone was more of a watch than anything else at that point. He hoped everything was alright.

"Hello?" he answered, slightly inquisitively.

"Um hi, um, is this," the voice was young, male, and deep, but with a note of nervous shrillness, "um, Blake Myntbanke?"

"Yes, it is." There was a silence. "May I ask who is calling?"

"My, um, name is Joe." The voice paused, and there was a bit of static in the connection. "You, um, don't really know me."

There was another silence. Blake hoped it wasn't some really awkward telemarketer or something. "What can I help you with then?"

"You, um, gave me your card."

"I gave you my card?" Blake felt confused for a moment. Then he had a sort of far away sensation, he was dizzy. There hadn't been a lot of people he had given those out to.

"Um, ya," said the voice, with perhaps a slightly conflicted, uncertain tone. "I'm not looking for an investor or anything," he quickly added.

"You're the fellow from that hotel bar then, are you? You were playing pool?"

At this Joe sounded surprised. "Um, ya, that's me."

There was another silence. Blake focused on driving for a second as he passed a particularly slow-moving truck. Off in the distance he could see a helicopter flying low over the city.

"Listen, um, I don't know a lot of people on the outside," said Joe, his tone now more confident, almost defiant, "and I kind of need to get out of town."

Fair enough. Blake's mind reeled as he tried to process the situation. So that with the pool table had been real, then. He wondered what exactly was going on, what did you do in these sorts of situations? He supposed it was really one of those spur of the moment decision sorts of things.

"Where are you?" asked Blake.

"I'm outside a mall, on Saguaro and the East Expressway."

Blake knew roughly where that was, actually. "Ok, I'm driving right now, I can be there in maybe ten or twenty minutes. I'm driving a red sports car, it's a K-56."

"A K-56? Really? Cool! There's a little green space at the edge of the parking lot, I'll be by the big tree. If I have to move I'll call you again," Joe said, then hung up.

Blake stared out at the highway ahead of him in a sort of daze. There was an exit up ahead, so he took it, cutting off a truck a bit, who honked. A little ways down he pulled into a restaurant parking lot, and found the way to the mall on the map.

He looked at his phone as he continued down the road, it was about 11:30. He probably wouldn't be making lunch with Jack today, then. He wondered what he was getting himself into.

After a bit he reached the big intersection from the map, and took the right turn. The city was thinner out here, it was more towards the edge of town, there were some apartments, big box stores. Going over an overpass he again saw a helicopter in the distance. Was that the same one? The one had sort of been off in the other direction, had it?

At a stop light he checked the map again, then after a bit made the turn-off, took the diagonal, and he was at the mall. It was a medium sized complex, maybe the out of the way sort of place you went to stock up on things. Some more box stores, a giant dollar store, a long grocery store off to one side.

Blake couldn't see any trees or green area as he entered the parking lot. He continued along, driving slowly over speed bumps, turning around the edge of the mall. Across the rows of parked cars he could see a little park. Approaching it he could see a guy in a non-descript grey tracksuit, sort of hidden away under a tree.

Blake pulled up and opened the passenger side door. With a furtive glance around, the guy quickly made his way to the car. It was the guy from the bar. He had a wild energy in his eyes, a lot of emotions at once, exhilaration, fear, confusion.

Then he gave Blake a sort of goofy grin, and with a 'hey', proceeded to push the seat forward and jump into the back seat. Which - to Blake's mild shame - was actually quite cluttered, a mix of pillowcases, business magazines, a briefcase, and a few empty fast food bags.

The guy held out his hand to Blake through the front seats.

"Hey, I'm, um, Joe."

"Blake," said Blake, reaching back and shaking his hand.

Joe looked at him earnestly, his eyes wide. "I gotta get out of here, ok?"

"Ok," said Blake. He pulled away from the curb, and drove for the nearest exit. "You have anywhere in particular in mind?"

There was a brief silence from the back seat. "Um, no, not really," said Joe. "I just kinda want to get out of town".

"North then?" It seemed as good a direction as any, given their options.

"Ya, that's good." They were silent as Blake turned onto a bigger road, which he figured would lead to the highway. Looking in the rear-view mirror, he saw Joe was sitting in the middle seat, and was sort of hunching down a little bit.

Joe looked like he was about to say something, then stopped, then finally spoke. "Um, so like, uh, how much do you remember, from that night.."

Blake paused a second, unsure of exactly how to proceed. They *had* told him not to talk about that, although this seemed like sort of a special case. One way or another, he picked his words carefully. "You took out a couple of bricks, did you? They had the wall repaired and a replacement pool table in by the time I was back the next evening."

Joe nodded, then swallowed. "You, um, should probably pretend you didn't see that."

"So I've been told."

"And, um, you probably shouldn't say anything about driving me today, either."

"I would assume that as well, yes."

"Right. Cool." They were silent another moment, passing through some suburbs, a doctor's office, a little strip mall.

The silence got to be slightly awkward. "Nice enough weather today for a drive, isn't it?" asked Blake. It was fairly overcast, actually, but it was pretty warm.

Joe nodded. "Ya, it's good." He grinned in the rear-view mirror. "Man, this is a sweet set of wheels. How long does it take to go 0-60?"

"About 4 seconds. That's according to its specs, at least. I just took it out to the desert a few days ago though, actually, and it was about that."

"Man, that's awesome. I got to drive a J-73 through an obstacle course once."

"Really, that's a nice car," said Blake, impressed. Then he saw Joe look up, panic on his face. Looking up ahead, there were a bunch of cars parked on the side of the road.

"Shit, roadblock!" said Joe, ducking down in the back seat.

"What do I do?!"

"Don't go through it!"

Blake looked around frantically. The roadblock was pretty close up ahead, the only option was a side road coming up on their left, angling diagonally back behind them. Blake flipped on his signal.

"This is going to look a tad bit suspicious, we're two thirds the way to a U-turn," he said as he turned sharply, sort of cutting off a minivan in the other lane.

"Throw something out the window!" yelled Joe.

Blake looked around, he had a half-empty package of mints by the drink holder. He grabbed them, pressed the button to roll down the window, and threw them out. Then he hit the gas, just a little bit, watching the roadblock disappear in the rear-view mirror.

They were on a more residential street now, houses and the odd apartment building. Blake let a couple streets go by, then turned down one.

"Is anybody following us?" asked the backseat, frantically.

Blake stared out the rear-view mirror, his heart pounding. There weren't any cars behind them. "I don't think so."

"Man, I didn't think there would be roadblocks. I was kinda hoping they wouldn't even know I was gone yet." He paused for a moment. "Do you, um, mind if I kind of hide myself?"

"Be my guest." Glancing back there was a flurry of activity from the backseat. "Try the briefcase," said Blake. He had taken to carrying around a set of fabric samples, just in case he did ever stumble across a potential client.

"Man, what is this, a bag of miniature tablecloths?" asked Joe.

"Fabric samples." Looking in the mirror Blake could see an arm moving stuff around.

"Let me know if there's anybody beside us."

"Ok," said Blake, slowing down a bit to stay away from a clump of cars up ahead.

"Man, I'm bleeding all over your stuff, I hope it isn't valuable," said Joe apologetically.

"That's alright," said Blake, hearing a note of anxiety enter his voice. He didn't really know much about this guy, other than that he could throw pool tables, and that he needed to get out of town fast. And that there were roadblocks today, that as well. The information that he had done something to make himself bleed combined with those previous facts was much more disturbing to Blake then any potential damage he might be doing to the upholstery.

"Are you hurt?"

"No, I'm ok. I just had a tracking device in my shoulder," Joe said, very matter-of-factly. "They hurt like crazy to pull out, and they bleed. They totally do that on purpose."

There was another pause, and more movement from the back. "I had one in my foot too. I bet they didn't think I knew about that one."

"It's always the second tracking device that gets people," said Blake knowingly, watching a police car pass on a cross street in his rear-view mirror, then making a turn.

"Ya, definitely. Do you mind if I make a bandage with some of this stuff?"

"Go ahead. The grey one with the squares might work well."

Blake saw a sign, they were on the road to the highway. "We've got the choice of going onto the highway or turning right. Right might lead back towards that roadblock."

"Um, the highway I guess," said Joe, sounding uncertain.

Blake continued straight, then merged onto the highway, northbound. There was lots of traffic, he matched his speed to the cars around him.

"How does it look?" asked Joe. Blake waited until they were on a straight stretch, then inspected the back seat. It was just a cluttered backseat, the fabric samples looked like clothing, with his briefcase and Joe's backpack on top, a couple of pillows, a business magazine, and the fast food bags, now puffed out as though they were full.

"Good. Really good," said Blake, taking another look back in disbelief. It didn't just look like there wasn't anyone there, it didn't even look like there was space for anyone. With the tinted back windows Joe had good as disappeared.

They were silent again. Blake stretched his hands out, they were suddenly very stiff and sore. He must have really been clenching the wheel. They were leaving the city now, the road here was mostly just scrubby hills, the occasional nondescript building in the distance.

Something up ahead jumped out at Blake. In the distance he

could see more cars parked on the side of the road. It was another roadblock. They were still a little ways off, but approaching fast. He looked around frantically, but there was nowhere to turn off. A concrete meridian separated the lanes, and there was nothing but ditch then hill to the right.

"There's another roadblock. We're going to have to go through it," said Blake fatalistically.

"You can't go around?"

"Not short of doing a U-turn in one way traffic," said Blake, hoping that wasn't an option.

He stared at the rapidly approaching roadblock. It was just on their side of the road, set up next to a rest area. It looked like they were stopping every car, and sending maybe half of them aside for inspection. Blake glanced at the tableau in the back seat. Convincing as it was, he didn't like their odds.

Blake slowed down as much as he felt he could without looking strange. A small line had formed at the roadblock. A minivan they had been driving behind was directed into the rest area, a station wagon waved through.

"Don't move, we're almost there," he said, then they slowed to a halt in the line of cars. He looked at himself in the mirror, and took a deep breath, fighting the panic that was rising up in him. The car in front of them got waved through, and Blake drove towards a cop on foot. His stomach dropped as the cop motioned them towards the rest area.

Blake accelerated and pulled in, stopping behind a white van which was in the process of being searched, the owner standing outside sourly. A youngish cop, sunglasses and blond hair, stepped up to Blake's car. Blake pushed the button to roll down the window.

"License and registration," said the cop, his tone neutral. Blake nodded, and reached into the glove compartment, fumbling a bit to get it open. He grabbed the documents and passed them to the officer. The cop looked at them for a couple of seconds, then leaned down slightly, peering at Blake, and into the car.

"This is your business card, sir," said the officer, holding up one of his business cards.

Blake looked at it, then shook his head and gave a dry little laugh. "Sorry about that," he said, inflecting his accent and giving what must have been a very natural aghast look. "I'm already late for a meeting with a major investor, my head's not on straight."

He dug around for his wallet, and passed the officer his driver's license.

The cop peered at his license, then briefly at the business card again. Blake could see an attractive looking female officer behind him, who seemed to be looking at his car. He gave her a little smile, held up his hand in a sort of half wave from the steering wheel.

The officer looked at Blake, then down at the license, then back to Blake again, saying nothing. Then he sort of cupped his hands over the window, peering in. Blake leaned forward to make space in an exaggerated motion, the seatbelt pushing up against him, although it probably didn't have any effect on the guy's view.

"I'm working with a company that produces raw fabrics," said Blake. "We're this close to bringing another major investor on," he continued, giving the cop a grin, and holding his fingers this-close close together.

The cop gave another suspicious look at the back seat, his gaze lingering a moment. It was a Sunday today, wasn't it? But then with a nod he passed Blake his documents back, and waved him on. Blake pulled forward and took off, onto the open highway.

7

Blake watched the roadblock disappear behind them, his hand shaking on the wheel. The desert around them seemed lit up, the colours vibrant. He felt more alive than he had in quite a while. The highway itself was strangely serene, it was almost devoid of other cars. For a moment he felt panicked. It was unnatural, why weren't there other cars? But that was normal, after a roadblock. They tended to act as a bottleneck.

He had a sense of profundity, at that. The movement of cars was like water behind a dam. It was all interconnected, the empty road, the roadblock, the fact that he got a call this morning, the incident with the pool table, that he came to San Diego in the first place. All the way up to humans building roads and cars and airports and roaming the world in the millions.

They were both silent for a bit, the Californian brush countryside now flat around them, little trees far in the distance. There was a sign for a turn off up ahead. "Should we stay on the highway? There's an exit coming up if we want to take the side roads," said Blake, breaking the silence.

"This highway should be the safest place for now. They aren't going to have two roadblocks in a row. How fast are we going?"

Blake looked at the speedometer. "Just under the limit."

"You could go a little faster. They probably aren't going to be pulling people over for speeding right now."

"Ok," said Blake, speeding up a bit, if it did make him slightly nervous. But he had just said he was in a hurry, hadn't he?

"Where are we now?" asked the voice from the back seat.

"Just passing Escondido."

"Is it safe for me to come up?"

Blake looked around. The road was still fairly empty. "Sure, I think so."

Blake watched in the rear-view mirror as Joe sat up, then
swivelled around to look out at the traffic around them. He had
a goofy, almost happy-go-lucky grin on his face, which Blake
found strangely disproportionate to the events of the past hour.

"Man, I didn't expect half that, two roadblocks. That was
fucked up," said Joe. A pained, apologetic look now came over his
face. "Man, you really saved my ass back there. You didn't have
to do that, you don't know what's going on, you don't even know
me." He now looked guilty. "I shouldn't have called you like that,
I'm sorry. You can just drop me off wherever. I can find my way
from here."

"Nonsense," said Blake. "You don't want to be out there on
foot. There's helicopters about."

Joe had an intense look on his face. "The people that are
after me, they play for keeps. You could get yourself in a lot of
trouble."

"I would assume there's an element of risk on my part."
Blake gave a shrug. "I've got a good lawyer."

Joe didn't look convinced. "They aren't going to care about
your lawyer."

Blake waved his arm in negation. "I'll take my chances." He
looked out the window at the desert hills around them. "You want
to be out there in that? There's nowhere to hide. And we must be
past the worst of it by now?"

"Maybe." Joe looked like he was about to insist again, staring
out the window, but then he nodded. "Ok, but, um, if we were to
get pulled over or something, you should say that I forced you to
drive me. I'd be in the same amount of trouble either way."

Blake nodded. That did actually seem like a good
suggestion, he wasn't going to argue with that. "Let's just not get
caught in the first place."

"You should say you don't know anything about me, the less
they think you know the better." Joe rubbed his head. "But we
should stick to the truth as much as possible. So you could tell
them you put your card in my shoe and all that. And that I called
you out of the blue and you picked me up. But then I'll say that
after the roadblocks I pulled a gun on you. You can say you
wanted to stop, you even offered me your car, but I told you to
drive."

Blake thought that sounded a bit lame on his part. "How
about we just keep it simple. You told me to drive, and I did?"

Joe nodded. "Ya, I think that works." He looked lost in

thought. "If they do pull us over, give me your phone though. I would have made you give it to me."

"Sounds like a plan. If anyone asks, this is against my will."

Joe looked up. "Hey, can you check your call history for me?"

They were on a straight stretch, so Blake grabbed the phone from the dash, flipped it open and went to the call history. To his bemusement there was no record of an incoming call that morning. The last thing was a call he made to a pizzeria a few days ago.

"All clear, nothing there," he said, slightly amazed. He didn't even know that was possible.

"Cool, I was hoping that would work." Joe paused for a moment. "You should probably take out the battery on that phone. They still might be able to detect the call, and as long as it's on it's going to be a beacon that leaves a trail."

"Right." Feeling a nervous twinge, Blake quickly opened up the back of his phone and popped out the battery, putting them both on the seat beside him.

They were both silent again, Joe looking out the window. Blake was starting to get the distinct impression that the stakes might actually be fairly high here. Whoever this 'they' were, they had certainly mobilized a lot of resources in trying to find him. For one there must have been a lot of roadblocks. Like just statistically, if they drove on a small fraction of the roads, and stumbled across two of them.

"Man, I've never been in this bioclimatic zone before. Those are cool trees," said Joe.

Blake looked out at the road beside them. He supposed there were a few more trees up here, if it was still mostly desert shrub. It struck him as a little odd, all things considered they still weren't really that far from San Diego.

"You're new to San Diego as well then?" asked Blake chipperly.

"Well, I've been coming and going a while now. But I don't really get out too much," said Joe, his tone heavy in understatement. "And when I do it's mostly stupid stuff like playing pool in empty hotel bars." He shrugged. "I've logged almost 300 hours of real world experience in America though."

Here he grinned self-depreciatingly. "Actually, I'm probably over 300 hours now. I left pretty early this morning." A slightly embarrassed expression now passed over his face. "And, like, sorry if I was out of line calling you." He looked uncertain, like he was having trouble articulating what he wanted to say. "Like, it wasn't weird? I mean, we've never met."

"Well, I didn't have any real plans for today." What exactly *were* the unwritten social rules for this sort of thing? Really Blake supposed there might not be any, it was sort of a unique situation. "I did put my card in your shoe."

Joe nodded a bit. "I wasn't going to call anybody. I was going to go on foot, or hide myself in a truck or something, maybe even steal a car." He swallowed. "I guess stealing a car wouldn't have worked with all those roadblocks. And, um, I kinda read your file. I probably wouldn't have called you if I hadn't."

A flash of worry then passed across his face. "I, um, can read people's files sometimes," he said quickly. Then he grinned. "Man, you've got a really thick file." Blake felt a flash of pride. So they did have a file on him, then, and it was thick.

"You used to sell drugs in Hollywood?" Joe asked, his tone excited, impressed.

"I may have dabbled in the business." Blake never knew exactly what to say when people were enthused about that particular episode of his past. It was sort of an awkward thing to talk about, he wasn't entirely sure how he felt about it himself.

"Man, drug dealers are always the coolest characters in the movies. Is that where you made your money?"

Blake felt his face burn slightly. "No, actually, I inherited it," he said, studying Joe's face for a reaction, but there didn't seem to be one.

"Man, have you seen West and 37th? That scene where they do the raid on the club?"

"Classic. I was hanging out on the set when they filmed the sequel. I was actually an extra in the club scene when they meet the dealer in Miami."

"ARE YOU SERIOUS? WEST AND 37TH TWO? DAMN!" Joe's eyes went wide. "Man, that must have been awesome. Did you ever meet the actress who played the speed boat captain?"

"Ya, I did, we went to a couple parties together, actually." Joe's face was awestruck in the rear-view mirror. "Did you guys, ever, like.." he asked, trailing off.

"You don't always want to go for the stars, they tend to be prima donna types." Blake shook his head. "She had a bit of a Princess complex. Maybe there was something there for a bit, I don't know. I sort of hooked up with a girl in her entourage, and that nixed any chance there might have been there."

"Ya, I guess," said a dazed looking Joe. "Your file said you had Hollywood connections, but I didn't expect anything like that."

"It's a pretty small world actually, once you know people." Blake paused a moment. "Did you see Ork Horde IV?"

"Ya, that was a good movie."

Blake made a little negative uncertain sound. It hadn't done that well in the box office, he had lost a decent amount of money on it. "I was one of the backers for that one. It didn't turn out quite the way I would have liked, but I thought it was alright."

"Naw, it was awesome. That was the one with all the flying tigers, right?" asked Joe, sounding genuine. "The whole magic sword plotline was really understated, but it was supposed to be like that. Like nothing ever happened with the magic sword, but that was just showing that things would have been better if they had never gone to war in the first place."

"Yes, there was that." That was a fairly insightful comment, not a lot of people picked up on that.

They were silent a moment, then Joe spoke again, slightly hesitantly. "Were you dealing down in San Diego?"

"No, no, I've been out of the business for years. I was working with an innovative fabric manufacturer, actually." Blake paused, not sure exactly how to frame his time with Wildon Textiles. "They do a lot of material for clothing, but everything. A lot of high-tech fabrics, stuff for life jackets, backpack material, umbrellas, industrial filters, even."

"Sounds like a good business."

Then they were silent, the Californian countryside rolling by. It was a bit lusher now, lots of trees. After a bit Joe swivelled around and watched the traffic behind them.

"I think there might be an undercover cop behind us," said Joe, staring out the back window. "The red truck, in the left lane." Blake looked in the rear-view mirror, there was a red truck a ways behind them. "I'm gonna hide myself again. It's going a little bit faster than us, so just slow down a little, and let it pass. It's probably better we don't even talk. Don't even look at it, just act normal."

"Ok," said Blake. He slowed down ever so slightly, then looked at the back seat, which was disguised again already.

After a couple of minutes the truck started coming up behind him, then passed him. It was a little nerve wracking, watching it go by. Blake had to really force himself not to look at it, maintaining an even speed suddenly seemed incredibly difficult. And then it was in front of him, just slowly gaining distance. Where else did he look?

He wondered what exactly it was about that particular truck that Joe hadn't liked. It seemed pretty normal to him. Above and beyond that, he still didn't feel like he was 100% clear on *why* there were roadblocks and undercover ghost trucks in the first place. That seemed like an important detail, this stage in the game.

Finally the truck disappeared on the road ahead of them. "It's probably safe to come up again," said Blake. There was motion from the backseat, and Joe's head popped up.

"Now, I suppose I shouldn't ask what's in *your* file?" asked Blake, feeling slightly awkward.

Joe looked nervous in the back seat. "Ya, it's kind of all top secret. The less you know about me, the better, for everybody's sake. There's some shit you just don't even want to have in your head, you know?"

Blake gave a shrug. "However much you want to tell me, that's fine. I can keep a secret, if that's what you're worried about."

Joe gave him an intense look through the rear-view mirror. "They can figure out what you know. They can do stuff like talk about me and measure your blood pressure, eye movements, put electrodes on your head. Just finding out if somebody knows something is really easy, way easier than using a lie detector."

Blake swallowed. Could they really do that? Nonetheless he felt himself overwhelmed with curiosity. "Well, they already know I saw the pool table incident. And I do know they've put up roadblocks to get you, you can read people's files, and you had not one but two tracking device implants under your skin. To me it seems like I already know the most salient details already."

"Right," said Joe, rubbing his head, and looking conflicted. "I guess technically that makes you class 4A security already."

Joe looked forward at him in the rear-view mirror, a nervous expression on his face. "If I tell you anything, you can't tell anyone, alright?"

Blake spoke firmly and clearly. "Of course. I give you my word of honour. I have never broken my word, and I never intend to. I do not give my word unless I know I can and will keep it, and I hereby give you my word of honour now, in its entirety and without exception."

There was another silence, little houses going by off in the distance. Joe looked conflicted, hovered there uncertainly for a moment, then after a deep breath he broke the silence.

"I'm sort of bio-enhanced. Like, modified." He paused, looking lost for words. "I'm kind of a project, um, like, experimental."

"Bio-enhanced?"

"Ya, some muscle re-fibering, bone fortification, a bit of synapse doubling, a lot of second-gen steroids. It's all top secret stuff."

Blake wasn't sure what all that meant. "So you've been engineered to have super human strength?"

"Basically." Joe grinned. "Want to see something cool?"

Blake said ok, and Joe disappeared down in the seat, appearing a moment later with Blake's tire iron. "Mind if I?" he asked, then wrapped both hands around the iron, took a deep breath, and gritted his teeth. He slowly twisted it into a U-shape, then around again in sort of a half circle, with the ends twisted around and over each other a bit. Then Joe tossed it onto the front seat, and Blake picked it up, inspected it. He tried to unbend it while he drove, but he couldn't budge it in the slightest. It was a tire iron.

"Pretty cool huh?" asked Joe. Blake looked at the tire iron again, then back at Joe in the rear-view mirror, still trying to process it all.

"Obviously I can run really fast too. I've got pretty much triple endurance, and my vision is like 20/5. I could even be stronger, and faster, but all my modifications are specially designed to be undetectable. They don't want anybody reverse-engineering me if I were ever captured."

Joe paused for a moment. "I'm not completely normal, and my DNA's kind of weird, but most of my mods are really hard to detect. And I'm designed so it's even harder after I die. So unless a specialist dissects me alive I basically look like a normal guy," he said, laughing, although there was also a note of nervousness in his voice.

Another grin came across his face. "And they did another experiment on me, I'm one of the first people it really worked on. I can self-regulate my hormonal system to speed up the parts of my brain that process my perceptions, so it seems like time slows down around me."

Blake was a little confused. "You can slow down your perception of time?"

"Ya, it's sort of like when you're in a car crash, and everything slows down. Or more like in the movies, when they do slow motion, it's actually pretty similar to that."

Joe's voice took on a more sombre tone. "And I'm really good at it. I used to do it a lot. The agent before me got like five types of cancer by the time he was 24." Joe swallowed. "That's how old I am now. He died like a year later, and it was really bad. They told me they knew what went wrong, it wouldn't happen to me. But man, to watch that.." His voice cracked a bit. "So for a while I wanted to slow time down as much as possible, get as much as I could, you know?"

He paused a second. "It started giving me really bad headaches, so I had to stop for a while." Then he brightened up. "And I haven't had any bad signs or anything yet."

Blake didn't know what to say about it all. He looked over at the bent tire iron again. Was all this for real? He supposed it must be.

Joe's face twisted in the mirror. "Man, I don't know why I'm telling you this stuff. This stuff is all top secret."

"Well, like I said, your secrets are safe with me," said Blake, now starting to slightly regret having asked for more information. What had Joe said, they could tell what you knew just by looking at your eye movements?

"Ya, but still, I shouldn't have told you any of this." Joe paused a second. "It feels kinda good though, actually. Like, just to know that someone who isn't one of *them* knows this shit."

"Well, it's an honour. I imagine I'm better off not knowing who *they* are, then, as well?" Blake asked, unsure of what exact kind of response he hoped to get from that particular question.

Joe nodded solemnly. "I was sort of created by this lab.." He paused. "They work for a lot of different people, there's a few governments I'm authorized to work with in some situations, and they do jobs for a lot of private individuals, some kinds of sub-military people in some places. You're really better off not knowing anything more than that."

But nonetheless he continued. "But man, there was some fucked up shit happening. I didn't even know who was calling the shots anymore." He paused again. "That was why I threw the pool table. They had to put an 'unstable' flag on my file, it disqualified me for a mission. And hopefully some people found out about some shit."

Joe's tone went more philosophical. "And I've been reading

a lot of stuff lately. I think I'm kind of a pacifist. Like, people have to fight sometimes, you gotta defend yourself, the world is a complicated place. But a lot of the stuff that's going on... Like, I mean, I just don't want to be involved in it."

He looked at Blake. "It's kinda fucked up that they made me, right? And that they are keeping me secret?" Blake gave a little nod. "And, like, all those roadblocks? Who knows what they're telling the police."

Joe paused, and gave a little swallow. "Although, um, I kind of took some documents as well. Some stuff about how I was created, a bunch of stuff." He looked kind of freaked out. "Thinking about it, that might be why there were roadblocks. They probably wouldn't have put those up if it was just me running."

Neither of them seemed to have anything else to say about that, and they were both silent for a moment. Then Joe spoke again. "You really can't tell anyone about any of this, alright?"

"Not a peep," said Blake, fairly emphatically.

"My last name is Soldao, by the way. Joe Soldao. Soldao, like Soldado, that's soldier in Spanish, or Portuguese, for that matter. If it sounds like an alias, that's because it sort of is. But it's my real name as well. My real name is kind of an alias."

Then they were again silent, Joe looking slightly distraught. It was probably a big thing for him to have told Blake all that. They were coming up towards a city, and Blake saw a sign for a gas station. Looking down at the meter, they were getting pretty low. "We need gas, there's a station up ahead."

"Ok, I'll hide myself again," said Joe, and immediately ducked back into the pile of junk in the backseat.

The gas station quickly appeared on their right. It was a big one, eight pumps and a decent sized convenience store, cars coming and going. It looked like an anonymous enough place to fill the tank. Blake pulled up next to a pump, took a deep breath, then got out of the car.

Feeling slightly dizzy, he went into the gas station. He grabbed a few snacks at random, not even really seeing what they were, then paid for more than enough gas to fill the tank.

As he was making his way back to the car he saw a flash of blue and white. A cop car was pulling in, right across from the K-56. Blake tried to look relaxed as he walked around it and up to the pump. Was it his imagination, or did they pull in too quickly, too sharply? Two cops got out, a white guy and a black guy. He felt a relief when one started pumping gas.

Blake started filling the tank, focusing on the meter as panic welled up in him. He wanted to take the nozzle out, to run, get out of there, but he stopped himself. People who drove luxury-sport hybrids generally didn't just put $1.50 in.

He cast a nonchalant glance across the gas station. Not looking at anything in particular, just surveying the area. The cops were looking at him. He gave a brief sort of half grin, then returned his gaze to the slowly increasing price.

It seemed to have an immensely huge tank for a relatively small car. It never took this long before, did it? He could hear the police talking, he tried to listen, but he couldn't hear what they were saying over the noise of the gas station. Finally there was a click from the pump, the tank was full. As Blake took the nozzle out he saw something moving in his peripheral vision. One of the cops was walking towards him.

Blake breathed in, breathed out. Just a normal day, he was running a little late, off to a meeting with a potential investor. A Sunday meeting, more a social event actually, although business would certainly be discussed.

The cop stopped a few feet away from him. Blake turned to face him, but the cop was staring at the car. Then he looked over at Blake, awe on his face.

"Man, is that the K-56?" he asked, amazement in his voice.

Blake felt dizzy. "The one and only," he said, forcing a smile. The cop looked it up and down, walked a little half circle around it.

"Oh, man," said the cop. "I didn't even know they had these in America."

"Special import," gasped Blake.

The cop gave a little nod, then returned his gaze to the car. He knelt down near the front hood, examining the curves in awe. Then he slowly, tentatively, reached forward.

"May I?" he asked, looking back at Blake. Blake shrugged. The cop slowly ran his hand along the front of the hood, then stood back up. "How fast you gotten it up to?" he asked, a mischievous grin on his face.

"Not fast enough to make my meetings in time," said Blake, his heart jumping in panic as he heard a slightly condescending note in his voice. He flashed the cop a big grin. "I don't think I got a chance to look down at the speedometer when I hit top speed, actually."

The cop sort of laughed, then went back to staring at the car.

"Whenever you're ready," said his partner, who was leaning on the police car with his arms crossed. The other cop nodded, looking slightly self-conscious now. He mumbled something about it being a nice set of wheels, then turned, returned to his car, and they were getting in, pulling out of the station.

8

They drove in silence after the gas station, Joe remaining hidden in the back seat. Blake had a sudden fear the police would appear behind them - maybe they had just been feeling him out before making their move. But no police appeared, they just continued through the flat grassy plain, a sea of little house roofs off in the distance on either side of the highway.

Finally Joe asked if it was clear, then popped his head up. "Where are we now?" he asked, peering out at the desert around them.

"We're a little ways south of San Bernardino, we've just started passing around Los Angeles."

"Man, LA, we're making good time."

Blake was inclined to agree. Although he was struck by the fact that this was good time *away*, though, not good time *towards*. Where were they even going to go? He imagined Joe would need to keep a pretty low profile.

"So, did you have any destinations in mind, when you left this morning?" asked Blake.

He was answered by another pause. "Honestly, I didn't even think about it very much. But I had a couple of ideas." Joe started, his voice sounding a bit unsure. "I thought maybe I could go to an inner city somewhere, and maybe like hook up with a gang or something. Find someplace to hide out, get a fake ID made up. But that's what they would expect me to do."

Blake nodded. "It's best to avoid those kinds of criminal types as much as possible anyways. Just associating with them, it's easy to get pulled into who knows what sorts of unsavory business."

"Ya, there's that," said Joe, slightly indignantly. "Although I have done a couple of units on gang infiltration. I was thinking about going down to Mexico as well. Although if they had that many roadblocks the border must be on lockdown."

He shrugged. "When I left this morning, all I knew was that I wanted out. If nothing else I could have just disappeared into the forest, I'm pretty hard to find in the woods."

At that Blake had a sudden thought. Good old Lee was up in the north of the state, wasn't he? Lee had even been telling Blake to come visit him, they did a phone call before Blake left New York.

"Now, I know someone, has a cabin in the woods upstate. He probably wouldn't mind putting us up, and we go way back."

Joe looked skeptical. "Is he someone we can trust? I mean, they're really going to be looking for me."

"Definitely," said Blake. "He's an associate from my Hollywood days, we were in the business together. He's semi-retired now, but he was my supplier. I think he worked as a smuggler for quite a number of years."

Blake paused. Lee had all sorts of underworldy connections which could prove quite valuable at a time like this. "If you were looking for a fake ID, I remember him having a hook up for that kind of stuff, as well."

Joe looked nervous. "I dunno, the less people involved the better."

"I would trust Lee with my life." Really, there weren't many people Blake trusted like Lee. That particular business provided the tests to a friendship that you just didn't see in normal life. "He could have disappeared with a huge amount of money or product any number of times while we were in business together, but he never did. He could have blackmailed me pretty easily, as well. There were a few people arrested, at the end there, but he never talked."

Joe still looked uncertain, but he began to nod a bit. "It would be good to have a place to lie low for a while."

"I've got his number in my phone, I could give him a call. Could well be he's not around, it's been a couple months now since I talked to him."

Joe looked a little concerned at that. "Ok, but do you mind if I take your phone apart? You probably shouldn't even turn it on without disabling anything that detects location. We should get a new phone to call him with."

"Fair enough," said Blake, passing his phone back to Joe, who pried off the casing then started fiddling around with the electronics.

Just up ahead there was a big mall on the side of the

highway, so Blake pulled in there. He found an out of the way parking spot wedged in between a truck and a van, checked to make sure Joe was hidden, then hurried into the mall.

Then suddenly there he was, walking through the wide indoor avenue, past women's clothing stores, a specialty tea shop, a big sporting goods store. It had a strange surreal sort of normalcy after the day's events. People milling about, talking on their phones, sitting by the fountain with their bags of purchases.

Off to the side he found an electronics place. To his relief they had the brand of phone Joe needed, so he grabbed one, plus some batteries, a flashlight, a stack of blank CDs for whatever reason. Then he quickly hurried out of the mall, getting a little lost on the way.

Joe immediately got to work on the phone, taking it completely apart, pulling some electronics out of his backpack. Blake wondered if he needed a sim card or anything, but Joe said no. He would just hack directly into the network.

They continued northwest now, Joe deciding it was better they take the roads west of the mountains north. Blake felt a tentative relief as they sped through the hilly desert road. It would be a stroke of luck if Lee was there, Blake couldn't think of anyone better suited for the matter at hand.

After about half an hour Joe had the phone ready, so Blake pulled into a rest area. He got Lee's number from what remained of his old phone, then dialed it on the new one. It rang a few times, kept ringing, Lee must not have had an answering machine.

Then there was a click and a rattling from the receiver. "Hello? Who is this?" asked a slightly weathered voice.

"Lee!" said Blake. "You're there!"

"Well, I'll be, Blake Myntbanke, I didn't expect you," said Lee, his voice friendly. "How have you been? Up to your neck in some great business adventure, I imagine?"

"I've been good. I have been investing, although I don't know if you could really call it an adventure. I've been working with that wholesale fabric manufacturer I was telling you about. It's actually something quite practical, for a change."

Lee laughed. "You can tell me that, but I still imagine you're up to no good." He paused. "You said you were headed back to California, are you going to come visit me one of these days?"

Blake had a sense of relief, he was up there in the cabin then, was he? "Well, actually, yes, that's why I'm calling."

"Because you're coming to visit me, or because you're up to no good?" cackled Lee, who clearly knew Blake too well. Blake wished he wouldn't joke around like that though. Joe had told him to act under the assumption the call was being recorded, even if it was unlikely.

"Coming for a visit," said Blake, slightly stiffly. "I'm starting out on a new business venture you might be interested in, and I'm going to be in the area." The term 'venture' was code they used from back in the day. Things could be projects, investments, enterprises, there were a bunch of things, venture implying a certain level of risk and questionable legality. "Are you going to be at your cabin tonight?"

"Yes, I'm here. If you're coming for dinner I'll get something out of the freezer."

"I might be late. Is there anyone else there right now?"

"No, I'm here by myself, I don't have anyone coming by for a few weeks," said Lee, slightly gruffly, a note of uncertainty now entering his voice. "Your connection is terrible, I can hardly hear you."

It was bad on Blake's end as well, so he just scribbled down some fairly complex directions to the place, which was apparently a couple hours north of Sacramento. Then he hung up, they had a place to stay.

They both seemed to relax a bit after that. They put on one of Blake's classic rock playlists, even rolled down the windows. The weather was getting pretty nice now, especially for February, the clouds had disappeared, and the sun was shining bright.

The clear skies above them turned out to be a disadvantage from the standpoint of surveillance, however. Joe said there would be satellites over California now. It wasn't a huge deal, but if they were putting up roadblocks then it was at least possible someone would be sifting through satellite images as well. It would be needle in haystack territory, but there were ways they could narrow it down.

Further down the road they passed a truck weighing station, there were a couple of big trucks pulled over having stuff taken out. Soon they were into the central valley, on a smaller side highway that cut around the cities.

Blake remembered Joe having said something about his file, so he asked him about that. Blake was in fact quite curious to know what information they had about his assets. Joe said there had been a big section, but he had only skimmed through it. He didn't remember seeing anything about Caribbean properties or Swiss bank accounts though, that was good.

There had also been a lot about him dealing, some stuff about his businesses. It sounded like he put on some cool shows. Joe had even dug up some of the bands Blake recorded, apparently his file had a complete discography.

That band that copied the punk band on his label? That was actually a psy-op. There was hardly any information about it, and most of it was in code. But the band had been groomed to be offensive, there was some mention of a 'mechanical citrus' operation. A note said a key demographic would be turned off Blake's band if they thought they were gay. Joe didn't even know who was behind it, or why. But they had obviously been saying something that somebody didn't like.

It was sort of odd, Joe knowing all that stuff about him already. Joe said there had been newspaper clippings about Blake's parent's plane crash, Blake remembered the articles. Blake told him about the paparazzi at the funeral, his withdrawal into debauchery, finding his way again in his studies.

Joe had seen that, he had a lot of letters after his name for someone who got an F in Math 11. Blake digressed a bit about his magnum opus, the work he had been doing to calculate GDP for three different points in the middle to late Dark Ages. It was actually surprising how much data you could get, given it was the Dark Ages.

What was giving him the most trouble was actually calculating inflation, comparative GDP values meant a lot less if you didn't have the inflation rate. But the concept of a 'basket of goods' really didn't carry over, there were price spikes in staple goods. Not to mention the kings were always minting new coins and watering them down with less gold or silver each time.

He had actually been trying to get permission to do a composition analysis on some coins in the Royal Museum, but no one seemed game. And even then it was debatable as to what extent the precious metal content of a coin was a measure of its real value, and to what extent they just acted as a fiat currency, like symbolic worthless paper money.

Joe opened up about his background as well. It sounded like his life had been dedicated to training up to now. And a few missions, although he couldn't talk about those. He had grown up in various types of military compounds, mostly on an island in the pacific that wasn't on any maps.

Apparently he spoke seven-plus languages, all to varying levels of proficiency. His best second language was Arabic, he could do eight different dialects and even more accents. Joe said some long phrase ending in insha'Allah five times, Blake couldn't tell the difference between any of them.

It was sort of a weird question to ask, but Blake wondered if he was intellectually modified as well, then. Joe said there were a couple of things, but not really. They just really wanted him to know a lot of languages, and he had a lot of free time. His Arabic teacher had been like a mother to him.

Joe had never actually met his real parents. Or if he had, he didn't know it. They told him he was an orphan, that they died in a car accident soon after he was born. But some of the modifications they did to him, they had to start while he was in the womb.

His best guess was that his family was from the Caribbean. But he really couldn't say, not by looking at his genes, at least. He was probably the most diverse guy Blake was ever going to meet. They chose people with diverse backgrounds on purpose, having genes from all over the world was the best way of hiding DNA editing. And having stuff spliced in made him more diverse in and of itself. It was pretty cool, to be related to everybody, right?

Although that was just one way of looking at it, maybe he was just a weird mutant freak mashup of DNA. He had a bit of animal DNA, and a lot of plant DNA, actually. Turned out some of the stuff in reeds was actually really good at keeping muscles from tearing. That wasn't weird, was it?

And apparently they were actually related, him and Blake. Like only a few generations back, which was pretty close. Plus Blake had some of the genes they spliced into his chromosome, although Joe didn't know exactly what they did, something to do with how their hypothalamuses process risk and stuff like that.

Blake wondered how he even knew that. Turned out it was in Blake's file, they had his DNA. They had a lot of people's DNA, actually, it was kind of fucked up. Like, why did they really need to know that?

From there the conversation roved around. High performance cars, the last election, Joe dug Blake's playlist. He didn't know many of the songs, but when Blake told him who the band was, he knew their big hits. He was just kind of discovering rock and roll now, like real rock and roll, what it was really about.

Up to a few years ago he was really brainwashed, apparently.

He thought the hippies were a bunch of dirty drug addicts, and half of them were terrorists. It wasn't until he was twenty one that they let him watch whatever he wanted, twenty one! And then only because it would give him 'cultural understanding' that would be necessary for some missions.

The conversation did seem to have a way of returning to Blake's time in Hollywood, so Blake indulged in some stories. Driving around at one in the morning on a Tuesday night trying to find props for what ended up being a terrible sci-fi movie. Boarding Jack Dash's yacht all pirate-style in the middle of the night and stealing a bottle of 30 year old scotch.

It even started getting to the point where it was feeling strange. Blake couldn't remember ever having a conversation about movies even half that long. He got the impression Joe didn't really get out very much, TV and movies probably filled a gap in his life.

And perhaps gave him a warped perception of reality. The subject of plastic surgery naturally came up, that much time talking about Hollywood. And Joe seemed to think he could just go to a plastic surgeon and get a new face, elude the authorities like in a couple movies he mentioned.

Blake didn't think it worked that way, it was pretty hard to look completely different. Maybe it was hypothetically possible, but it would be a huge amount of surgery. Joe was talking about it like it was a nose job or something. In the movies it was usually only a couple scene changes and presto. But in real life you were liable just to end up looking like a freaky and recognizable version of your old self.

Joe also seemed to think everyone in America lived in mansions, even if they just worked in coffee shops. Fights came up, while Blake was talking about the state of live music in New York City. Joe wondered if he got in a lot of fights, living in New York.

Blake told him no, you didn't really get in a lot of fights, not in New York, anywhere. Maybe New York was rougher a few years ago, and maybe if you went out looking for it, but no, not really. Blake personally, pretty much never. Joe seemed a little embarrassed, some of the guys might have been pulling his leg.

Likewise Joe seemed to be a true believer in a wide array of fairly out-there conspiracy theories, of which he also spoke about at length. Some of them were of the well-maybe sort, which - given his history - did make Blake a little nervous.

But a lot of it was full-on tinfoil hat. Orbital mind control lasers, brains in jars secretly running the show, satanic cults organizing clandestine human sacrifices. Half the big storms you saw were the product of weather machines.

Could that be the impetus for him making his escape? He had been saying 'they' had been doing some bad things. Blake hoped all this wasn't happening just because of some online Illuminati videos.

As the sun began to set Joe suggested they go east until it was dark. Maybe it was too much attention to detail, but that would help confuse things if anyone did ever trace Blake's movements via satellite. They wouldn't be able to track them at night.

Blake remembered there being a bunch of ski resorts nearby, which Joe thought was perfect. They drove east maybe twenty minutes, before coming across a sort of tourist outpost town at the base of the mountains.

Blake did a lap around the main drag, which was maybe only 10-15 shops, a bunch of college student looking types cheering at him as he drove by. He parked at a pizzeria, went in, and made an order for pick up, then walked a lap around the main drag as the sun set. There was something surreal, being out there, knowing Joe was hidden away in the back of the K-56. Blake had a giddy energy, he didn't know what to make of any of it.

Once it was good and dark he picked up the pizza, then they headed out, stopping to fill up the tank again. They didn't talk as much as they continued north, it had already been a long day. Blake passed the MP3 player back, and Joe put on some jazz, reggae, punk, even checked out some of the early music.

They stayed on the side highways, close alongside the mountains, passing through empty agricultural areas. After a couple hours they passed the Bay Area, then they were up around Sacramento. They stopped for gas one more time, then got onto the side roads, cutting through thick pine forests.

As they got further north there were less and less cars. Blake was beginning to find the empty dark forest roads distinctly unnerving. But Joe was happy, perhaps even more relaxed than he had been before.

If someone *had* been trailing them, waiting to make an attack, they would have done it already. This far out in the woods, there wouldn't be any witnesses. Joe had been a little worried they were just waiting for them to get off the main roads. Blake didn't know if that made him feel any better, but he kept driving, his legs aching, staring forward into the blackness, trees and concrete twisting constantly ahead of them.

9

It was well past midnight when they passed the turnoff Lee had mentioned in his directions, then rolled up the long narrow gravel driveway. It ended in what looked to be a fairly large cabin, tall trees all around it, a big stoop at the front with a dim light.

A figure stood up on the stoop as Blake pulled in. It was Lee, his trademark fedora on his head. Blake got out of the car, his legs stiff, the cold air crisp and clean. Lee came down the steps to meet him, a wide grin on his face, his hat now in his hands. His thinning hair was a lighter shade of grey now, but other than that he hadn't seemed to have aged much. His features were still slightly gaunt, as ever an intensity in his eyes.

"Lee, you old sonofabitch!" said Blake, glad to see him.

Lee looked over at the K-56 and whistled. "I see your taste in cars hasn't changed," he said, a slightly amused look on his face.

Blake looked up at the cabin. It was a fairly big place actually, halfway to being a lodge. "Nice place," he said.

Lee grinned. "It does the trick. I just got back here, actually, I've been in Mexico the last couple of winters."

There was a sound from behind them as the door of the K-56 opened up, and Joe slowly got out, carrying his backpack. "You've brought a friend?" asked Lee.

"Yes, he's looking for a place to get away from it all for a while," said Blake, giving Lee a brief look, his tone hopefully suggesting there might be more involved than just a vacation.

Joe stepped forward, nervously joining them. "Lee, Joe," said Blake.

"Um, cool cabin," said Joe.

Lee looked over at Joe, then sort of looked at him again. They all stood there in the driveway in silence for a second.

"You said you were down in the south of the state?" Lee

asked, staring impenetrably at them.

"San Diego," said Blake. "The fabric manufacturer has their head office down there." He looked over at the cabin again. "If you're looking for a place to invest, actually, I might suggest them. They seem pretty solid."

"You drove here from San Diego today?"

Blake nodded. "Heck of a drive."

Lee stood there a second, then motioned them towards the cabin, his face emotionless. They went up the wooden stairs and into a long and spacious kitchen-living room. To the left there were chairs and a couch by a TV and a large fireplace, the kitchen to the right.

"Sit down," said Lee, motioning them towards two chairs by the fireplace, then sitting down across from them. "So what exactly is the story?"

Blake looked over at Joe, who was silent. "Joe needs a place to lie low. We can't really go into detail." He felt slightly awkward, saying that. But Lee would understand, they had been in business long enough together.

"Where did you meet?" asked Lee, his tone sharp.

"Well, in a hotel bar," said Blake.

"You met in a bar?"

"Yes, in San Diego," Blake said, with an air of finality for the topic.

"What did you say your name was again?" asked Lee, looking at Joe.

"Um, Joe," he replied, slightly awkwardly.

They were all silent again. "And there isn't anything I need to know?" Lee asked, looking between both of them.

Blake would rather just straight-up tell Lee what was going on, but that was for Joe to do, not him. Nonetheless he needed to give him some more detail. They didn't want him inviting the neighbours over for dinner.

"There may be a certain element of risk, of pursuit," Blake said, looking over at Joe, who gave a little nod. "But we're confident we've evaded it. And Joe hasn't done anything wrong, it's sort of a funny situation."

They were all silent for a moment. Then Lee picked up the remote and turned on the TV. He jumped around between a few news channels, then Joe's face appeared, staring back at them in the form of a black and white mugshot.

"..was last seen outside a mall in San Diego, and is believed to be armed and dangerous," said an announcer's voice over some grainy security camera footage, a guy with a gun and a balaclava in a parking garage, some flashes of light. "The suspect fled on foot, after a failed robbery attempt on an armoured van." A picture of a maybe Hispanic security guard appeared on the screen. "The driver of the vehicle is currently in critical condition after the shootout."

"I didn't shoot anybody," Joe said quickly, swallowing and looking frantically between them. "I swear, I didn't hurt anybody, you gotta believe me, none of that is real."

"I saw the story on the nine o'clock news, it sounded like it had just broke. I had the TV on for a couple of hours tonight, and it's been on heavy rotation," said Lee matter-of-factly. Looking over at him, Blake noticed he had a gun in his hand, held loosely on his lap. Where did he get that from?

"What happened to your shoulder?" asked Lee, motioning with his chin. Blake looked at Joe's shoulder, there was a little red stain.

"I had to tear out my tracking device, I swear." Joe looked at them earnestly. "I had one in my foot too," he said, reaching forward towards his foot and looking up at Lee. Lee shook his head at him, raising the gun up a bit, and Joe sat back up.

Blake stared at Joe, a certain sick sense of panic welling up in him. How much did he really know about him? Joe seemed honest, and his story made sense. Especially in the context of him throwing a pool table across the room. But being able to throw pool tables didn't necessarily preclude him from robbing armoured vans, did it? It would just make the present situation that much worse.

"Now tell me, Bob, do the police have any leads on where the suspect is?" asked one of the announcers in a frightened sort of voice. All three of them turned their eyes to the screen.

"Earlier this evening the police made a statement that it is likely he is still in the San Diego area. But police across California and the United States have been put on alert, as well as the Mexican authorities and Interpol. Police are advising the public that he is believed to be heavily armed, and has a history of mental instability. Anyone with any information about his whereabouts should contact the San Diego police. Crime Watch is also offering a reward of up to $200,000 for information which leads to his arrest."

Lee looked at Joe suspiciously, like he was sizing him up

again, then looked over at Blake. "How long have you two known each other?"

Blake gave a little swallow. "Well, just since this morning, really."

Now Lee looked at Blake suspiciously. "I thought you said you met in a bar? That was in the morning?"

"Well, the bar was about a month ago, but it was just briefly." Blake paused a moment. "I put my card in his shoe."

"You put your card in his shoe?"

"Yes, it was a funny sort of thing."

Lee shook his head, and looked over at Joe. "You're saying this is all some kind of set up? It seems like a lot of effort to go to." He looked at him shrewdly. "Why should I believe you?"

Joe looked at them earnestly. "You don't know how easy it is for them to do stuff like that. They probably know whoever owns that mall, they've got friends in the police. They can just wall off a crime scene and nobody else gets in. I swear on everything holy, I've never done anything like that," he paused a second, nervously, "not in America."

A certain degree of puzzlement appeared on Lee's face. "And I suppose you can't tell me who *they* are?"

Joe shook his head. "I, um, can't say anything about what's going on."

Lee looked over at Blake, fixing him in his gaze with a quizzical expression. "Well Blake? What do you make of your new friend?" he asked, his tone almost more curious than anything else.

Blake looked at Joe. It was a logical scenario, maybe he needed money, decided to rob an armoured van. Escaping was generally the sort of thing that was hard to do on the cheap. Joe didn't have any big bags of cash with him, though, just the one backpack. Although they said it was a failed robbery, didn't they?

Blake tried to think back, to when he first picked him up. Joe had been in quite a hurry, but he didn't seem like he had just shot someone. Blake imagined it was a pretty emotional thing. Although he supposed you couldn't necessarily tell, someone with Joe's background. Why hadn't he asked to put on the radio, to listen to the news? That would have been valuable information, and he had been pretty interested in playing DJ with the MP3 player.

But it seemed like Joe had been honest with him. Blake had only really known him for a day, but he felt like he had gotten a read on him. And what did he really think was going on, with all the roadblocks?

They were all silent, Blake at a loss as to what to do next. He needed more information. There was a computer sitting on a desk at one side of the room.

"Do you mind if I use your computer?" he asked. Lee nodded, and motioned Blake towards it, keeping the gun focused on Joe.

"Be careful what you search for. They might look through search data," said Joe, slightly desperately.

"It's a secure connection, it doesn't trace back here," said Lee.

"Ok, but still, be careful."

Blake turned on the computer, then pulled up a directory site as the TV started in on the weather. He clicked through to the news section, opened the pages for a few different Californian newspapers. He didn't go directly to the stories about the armoured van robbery, he just opened a bunch of different news stories all at once. Something about a missing hiker, gas prices going up, apparently there were two different political sex scandals going on.

There were a lot of stories about the robbery. Blake opened up a few of them, it looked like they mostly all had the same information. Pictures of the gun fight, again the warnings not to interact with him, Joe's mug always prominent. One story had some stuff about the family of the driver who was shot, which Blake scrolled over quickly.

There was one article that seemed longer and more in-depth. Blake skimmed through it, found a map with where the robbery took place. It was somewhat close to where Blake had picked Joe up, just a few miles away. Blake supposed that wasn't that far for someone like Joe.

Something caught Blake's eye. The story referred to the robbery as happening 'this afternoon'. Blake scrolled down a bit further, then found what he was looking for.

"Wait, right there. It says the robbery took place about 12:10. I must have picked him up before noon, there's no way he could have done it."

"Are you sure?" asked Lee, a strange expression now on his face. Blake thought about it a moment, he had looked at his phone, after Joe first called him. It had been about 11:30. It was specifically 11:33, he remembered that, did he? Could he have read it wrong, a 3 for a 5?

He was supposed to have met Jack downtown at 12.00 for lunch, if it had been later he would have been heading back to town. And he had been driving for about half an hour, he must have been. He remembered leaving his apartment about 11, the idea was to get a good solid drive in, do lunch, then dedicate the afternoon to tariff documents.

Blake went over the route he took after Joe called him. Pulling off the highway, stopping to look at the map, the one big street then the other. 11:33 to 12:10, that was 40 minutes. There was no way it was 40 minutes between the pickup and the phone call, there was no way it was even half an hour. Not to mention the time it would have taken Joe to get to the mall, even if he could run at super speeds. At the very minimum it was impossible by at least ten or twenty minutes.

"I'm sure," said Blake, perhaps more relief in his voice than he had intended.

Joe didn't look offended. "I told you, that's what they do!"

Lee's eyes were bugging out a bit now. He looked at Joe, then back to Blake. "So this really is a frame up?"

A nervousness returned to Joe's face. "Ya, so, um, you aren't going to tell anyone, right? That has to stay secret, all of this does."

Lee nodded, still in awe. "Ok, mum's the word."

Blake looked over at Joe. "Perhaps we'd better give Lee some more details? If he promises to keep things to himself?" Joe looked nervous, conflicted, but he nodded.

"You'll keep anything we tell you secret, in the utmost confidentiality?" asked Blake, looking at Lee.

"Well, yes, of course. You can trust me." Joe still looked hesitant. Blake gave Lee a little look.

"I swear on all things holy that I won't tell anyone anything you tell me," said Lee.

"You can trust him," said Blake. Joe nodded again. There was a crowbar leaning against the wall by the fireplace. Blake walked over and picked it up, looking at Joe, who again nodded. Blake made a brief to-do of inspecting it, it was a normal crowbar. Then he passed it to Joe, Lee's eyes going wide for a moment.

"May I present to you, the amazing, the outstanding, the unprecedented, straight from an island in the Pacific that's not on the maps, stronger than any ox, faster than any Olympic sprinter, speaker of what, seven odd languages, the one, the only, Joe Soldaaaaaooooo," said Blake dramatically, giving a bow and flourish.

Joe grinned goofily, gritted his teeth, and slowly bent the crowbar around in a U shape, like it was some kind of malleable plastic toy. Then with a sharp noise and an almost visible burst of energy it snapped in his hands. Joe looked at them, almost sheepishly.

"Crowbars aren't made to be bent," he said, holding up the two halves. Lee gave a little whistle. "I'm sort of bio-enhanced. Like, experimental."

Lee's eyes now lit up. "I've heard rumors about those programs," he said, a look of awe coming across his face, "but I never thought they were true."

Knowing Lee, Blake highly doubted this last point. He always seemed ready with an endless stream of fairly outlandish conspiracy theories, which were generally about how the powers-that-be were doing things exactly like that. If anything, for Lee the fact the news was saying Joe robbed an armoured van was probably evidence in and of itself that he was telling the truth.

Lee gave another laugh, and then shook his head, looked like he was about to say something, then stopped. Then he looked down at the gun in his hand, almost surprised to see it. He stood up, and put it in a drawer by the kitchen.

Then he grinned at them. "Well, you can stay here as long as you want." His face went serious. "What do you think the odds are of anyone tracing you here?"

"Low," said Joe. "We covered our tracks pretty good, and we're pretty far north." He paused a moment, thinking, then looked at Blake. "But they might be able to connect me to you. Maybe not right away, but once they start running out of leads they're going to start looking into people like you."

Here he got up, paced around a couple of times. "That's going to have some implications for some things. If you leave, you probably shouldn't have anything to do with me, you could just lead them to me. But if you stay, it's going to seem pretty weird that we disappeared at the same time."

"Well, they might not figure that out, I was pretty off the grid in San Diego," said Blake.

Joe shook his head. "If you were living there, there are gonna be a lot of trails. The people you were working with, credit card transactions, your internet connection. Even just walking down the street, with all the security cameras they have." He gave a grimace. "They're going to be able to trace your phone leaving San Diego right when I escaped. Then being turned off. That's gonna look pretty suspicious."

"I had my lawyer get me my San Diego phone, while I was still in New York. I can't say for certain, but they generally don't do stuff like that in my name. Could be they wouldn't even be able to figure out I was in San Diego. I don't generally use my credit cards too much, I don't think I ever got around to finishing the paperwork for my apartment."

Joe nodded, looking slightly perplexed. Blake shrugged. "I generally keep a pretty low profile. Ex-girlfriends, telemarketers, bunk start-ups looking for investments, all that." Not to mention you never knew when you might stumble across something like this.

Joe still didn't look convinced. "I dunno, if they want to find out where you were, they're going to find out."

"Well, maybe they won't dig that much. I just saw you throw a pool table," said Blake. At this Lee looked up, sort of a smirk on his face. Blake was really surprised at how well they were both taking all this, it was like a day at the beach. "I was pretty drunk that night, the bartender would attest to that. There's no reason for them to think you had any way of contacting me, or even knew who I was."

Joe shook his head. "You'd be surprised, they can be pretty resourceful. It might be better if you just go back to San Diego and act like nothing happened. They might question you, but if you just played dumb they'd probably leave you alone."

Joe looked over at Lee, then back at Blake. "Both you guys could get in a lot of trouble. You've helped me out big time, but I should just get out of here. I'm sorry I even told you all this stuff."

They were all silent for a moment. Blake was about to brush him off. But he had been making an effort lately - sort of doing a thing - where he didn't just rush into whatever crazy venture presented itself in life. Maybe this was one of those times where he should just take a pass. Just because he stumbled across Joe didn't mean they had to work together.

Perhaps his role in all this had just been making the connection between Joe and Lee. They were pretty close to San Francisco, he could go visit Laura maybe, then head back to San Diego for a round trip. He had sort of made a commitment to Wildon Textiles, he doubted he'd be able to work with them any time soon if he stayed up here.

But an opportunity like this? You just didn't pass up something like that. It would be like denying some fundamental force of the universe. "I'll take my chances," said Blake.

Lee nodded as well. "Even if they identify Blake as a suspect, that shouldn't lead them here. Me and Blake are known associates, but the cabin is registered under a secondary alias I use. I haven't been on the grid in a long time."

At this Lee grinned. "And we'll be able to see them coming here." He went over to the computer, and flipped a switch on the side of the monitor. A set of little squares came up, some of them black, a couple with weird green and white tree-looking things, one with the front porch. Those were cameras, were they?

Joe's eyes went wide. "Are those infrared?"

"Just a couple of them," said Lee, pressing a button which lit up a light on one of the screens, it was the driveway before the house. "I've got some motion sensors as well, but they aren't set up right now."

"Can I?" asked Joe with a big grin, and Lee nodded. "Man, can civilians even buy this shit?"

Lee shrugged. "I've got a guy."

Joe went to the keyboard, moved the cameras around, switched a light on and off. It looked like he knew his way around the system. As he did this, a slightly perplexed look came across Lee's face. "Now, what I don't understand is why they are doing all this, if you didn't rob an armoured van?"

Joe looked down. "I'm not really supposed to leave without permission. Or an escort, as well, actually."

Lee scoffed incredulously. "All this is just because you left? So you were a prisoner?"

"I wasn't a prisoner!" said Joe defensively. "I'm class A2-C security, and that means in America I can only leave with permission."

"I'd say that's pretty much the definition of a prisoner," said Lee. "You're a free man, you should be able to come and go as you please." Blake nodded along a bit, it did all strike him as a little restrictive.

"Well, I'm top secret, so the rules are different." Joe paused a moment, looking unsure. "And I took some documents, as well, when I escaped."

Lee's face was taking a red hue. "That's modern day slavery, that's what it is!"

"I signed an agreement," said Joe defensively.

"You signed an agreement? Well then!" said Lee, his tone an exaggerated generous sarcasm. "No one should be able to sign away their basic human liberties. You signed this agreement under your own free will?"

"Well, I was 12, and they told me I couldn't study under the ninja master unless I signed," said Joe defensively. "But military secrets are really important. Especially weapons tech, and I'm weapons tech. They need to monitor people like me."

His tone lightened. "And, like, when I was in the Middle East, or in Africa, I would go out by myself all the time. It's just because I'm here in America. Nobody who is class A2-C security goes off base without an escort in America," he said, grinning at them like they were crazy.

"Well, class A2-C security, that explains it all," Lee said with the mock generosity again, his face reddening further still. "You should go public, that's what you should do!"

Joe now looked a little freaked out. "I really can't do that, I'm top secret. This shit has to stay between us, alright?"

"Of course you're top secret, they've drafted you a slave. It would be a PR nightmare if that ever got out."

"Enemy militaries could copy me, or terrorists could use the technologies to create super viruses. I don't even know what all the implications would be. It's bad enough that I'm here, ok?"

Lee fixed him in his eyes. "You could get away with it, you know. If you went public. There would be nothing they could do, you would be protected by the public eye."

Joe was shaking his head, but Lee continued. "We could release videos, telling your story. Find feats of strength that couldn't be faked." His eyes were lighting up. "Maybe do some surprise public performances, a bit of street theater, and then disappear. Can you pick up a car?"

Joe looked a little freaked out. "It's not an option, ok?"

Blake nodded, flashing Lee a look. "Joe knows the true nature of the situation much better than either of us, and we have agreed to honor his request for secrecy. If he says we can't go public, then we can't go public."

Lee's eyes blazed. "They've created a new weapon in you. I'd be more worried about the implications of that then anything else. How many others are there like you?"

Joe looked down at that, and Lee continued. "What if they started using people like you as secret police? Have they ever had you do anything against political targets here in America?" he asked, fairly accusingly.

"My specialty is the Middle East and Africa, there's more going on there right now," said Joe. "But I was trained in everything."

He grinned at them, perking up a bit. "Once in my training I did a scenario where the President's daughter was kidnapped by Marxist terrorists, and I had to infiltrate them. It was really cool, I pretended to be a sympathetic first year student from Ohio. My story was that I was in a study room a couple of floors below them when the kidnapping happened. I had to hide and let them find me, then develop Stockholm syndrome and everything."

Joe looked around, then grabbed a pair of what must have been Lee's reading glasses from the table. "When the black man complains of racial discrimination, his anger is misdirected unless he realizes that all racism is only veiled class oppression." He sort of put on a face while saying this, and did a voice. He suddenly looked very African American, it was a little bit eerie.

Lee cackled. "Have you read Kirpitnik?"

Joe's eyes widened. "Just a little bit. I was supposed to tell them that I was writing an essay on him for a comparative politics class, but not really understand his theories."

Lee went to his book shelf, quickly retrieving a book. "This is his best work, if you ask me," he said, passing it to Joe, who gingerly took it, a look of awe on his face.

"Are you a," he swallowed, "Communist?"

Lee shook his head. "I've done well enough by the free market." He shrugged. "There's good and bad in Kirpitnik. Any movement for a more equal society that requires a centralization of power is at the least always at risk of being derailed and taken over."

Joe flipped through the book, it was almost disbelief on his face. "I'd say that's the best translation, some of the others don't really do him justice," said Lee. "Some of it just doesn't translate well. Like the super-structure isn't a powerful force, but the broad all-inclusive basis of economic relations."

"Man, I never got to have conversations like this back on base. Not even when I was doing the training exercise," said Joe, enthusiastically. His smile faded though. "But I just can't go public. It's bad enough that I'm here now, ok?"

"Alright, alright, it was just a suggestion," said Lee. "I don't know what you're going to want to do then. There's not a lot of point in escaping just to hide out in a cabin."

Joe looked down. "Well, there was one thing I was kind of thinking about, before I escaped," he paused, looking sort of hesitant. "I could move to a big city, and kind of like fight crime and stuff. If I used a disguise then it wouldn't matter about the armoured van stuff on the news."

Joe looked slightly embarrassed after saying that. "I mean, that's probably a stupid idea, isn't it?"

Blake gave him a little look. What, were they going to get him a neon spandex jumpsuit and a cape? "That's what the police are for. As long as they're doing their job properly, at least," he said, looking over at the TV.

Lee gave a little laugh. "That's maybe the one thing you could do, if you don't want to go public. You won't be able to show your face for the next ten years without someone recognizing you."

Joe looked at them, a strange uncertainty now in his eyes. "Well, I dunno what I should do. But I *could* get plastic surgery."

Blake was about to say something, but Joe had a funny look on his face. With a swallow, Joe reached for his backpack, and pulled out a briefcase. Slowly and purposefully, he fiddled with the combination lock, staring at them a moment before opening it. He pulled out a folder, went through it, pulling out a few papers. Then he quickly shut the briefcase again, and passed them the papers.

"My face has been specially modified so I can change it with plastic surgery. Some fat injections, bone carving, a bunch of stuff like that."

Blake stared at the sheets of paper. There were diagram after diagram of faces, with little dotted lines, arrows, instructions in fine print. Some of them had titles on top, like "brutish", "everyman", "Casanova", "nobody." Flipping through the pages there were some ethnicities, "Pakistani", "North African", "Sri Lankan." Blake had never seen anything like it.

While they were on the topic of Joe's face, it again appeared on the TV. They all turned towards it, falling silent. It seemed mostly to be the same clip as before, but Blake had been a little distracted the last time it was on.

Apparently it had been an ambush. The fellow – they said Eugene Cudneck was his name - had known the van would pass through at that time with a full load of cash. The guards resisted, and there was a shootout, in which the driver of the van was shot in the shoulder. They wouldn't have actually shot the guy, would they?

They mentioned the time of the attack, and this time they said 12:14. That was a relief, he had been worried they might suddenly revise it to half an hour earlier. If they had it that precise then they probably had the time right. Something like a shoot-out in a parking garage, people would have heard it.

Blake had a little realization, though. They must have gone through that first roadblock just a little before 12:14. 12:20, at the absolute latest, and it took a little while, to set up a roadblock, didn't it? Seemed a little sloppy on the part of whoever was doing this.

He supposed it wasn't easy to throw together a fake armoured van robbery. And the roadblocks could have been there for something else, he supposed, although that would seem a little contrived. That was the sort of thing conspiracy theories were made of.

The story ended, the news replaced by an ad for a fabric softener. Lee got up to get some first aid stuff for Joe, who then went to wash out his wounds and put on proper bandages. Lee also poured Blake a much needed scotch, and offered them something to eat, which Joe took him up on.

Blake took his shoes off, then sat back and tried to relax a bit, it was all still a little much to take in. What were they going to do with him, then? Maybe that was the question now. There had to be something you could do with a supersoldier. Like Lee said, there wasn't a lot of purpose in Joe escaping just to hide out in a cabin.

He looked over at the plastic surgery diagrams. It would open up a lot of options, if Joe could get a new face. But what? If you thought about it, strength was only so important these days, outside of things like being a supersoldier.

Joe would certainly be good at manual labour, but that seemed like a waste of his talents. What, were they going to get him a job with a carnival? Maybe if they couldn't think of anything better. There had to be some kind of golden opportunity.

Lee and Joe rejoined him, Joe with his foot bandaged up, wolfing down a huge sandwich. Lee went to his computer, and started looking up stories about the armoured van robbery. He thought his connection shouldn't trace any farther than a hotel in Minnesota.

The news had moved on to sports. There was a story about some player renegotiating their $5 million dollar contract, the announcer thought they were going to get more this year. He was playing a lot better than someone else, who was getting $8 million. Blake stared at the screen.

"Are you guys watching this?" he asked.

They didn't answer, and the TV continued. "And rumor is Garcia is asking for $16 million. Do you think he's going to get it?" asked one of the announcers. "I don't know Jim, that's a lot of money, and his stats just aren't there yet after his injury."

"Those are some big numbers," said Blake. He looked over at Joe and Lee, who both looked back blankly.

Then Lee gave a cynical snort, and shook his head. "It's ridiculous, the amount of money they're making these days. You could have ten or twenty teachers for every midrange player. Although I suppose it's better than the team owners making it all." He paused, shaking his head. "There was a record-breaking contract just the other day, some baseball slugger."

"Really, how much?" asked Blake.

"$30 million, I think, or something like that," said Lee, cocking an eye at Blake. "It's probably in one of the newspapers there by the fireplace."

Joe looked on confusedly as Blake went over and dug through the newspapers. Going through a few of them he found the story, it was on the front page of the sports section. "$30 million, a five year contract! What's that, $6 million a year, just to hit a ball around a field?"

Lee smirked at him. "It's probably $30 million a year."

Blake skimmed through the article, and there it was. The total value of the contract was $150 million. He knew there was a lot of money in sports, but he never realized it was that much. "Well, then, $30 million a year."

Comprehension was dawning on Joe's face. "You don't think I should.." he looked at him incredulously, "I mean, seriously.."

Lee had a smuggish grin on his face. "There's fairly stringent drug testing in professional sports these days. I'm sure they could figure out something funny was going on pretty fast with someone like Joe."

Right, there was that. Blake felt a little crestfallen, he would be disqualified pretty fast. But no, what had he said? "Your modifications were made to be totally undetectable, even to

Russian bio-enhancement specialists and the like?"

Joe's eyes bugged out a little. "Maybe if I messed with my hormones I could pass the tests. I dunno if that would be the problem, they're probably looking for other things." He looked over at Blake like he was crazy. "But do you seriously think I could play pro ball?"

Blake looked him straight on. "Well, I think I'm safe in assuming none of the other players could even hold a candle to you. Did you ever play any sports back on base?"

"Ya, a little bit. It wasn't really fair for the people who weren't modified though." A smile played across his face. "Once, when I was playing baseball as a kid, I hit the ball so far, it went into a lower security area. Everyone there was wondering where it came from, but they couldn't explain it, this baseball just fell out of the sky."

His faced straightened. "But you aren't serious though, are you?" He laughed. "I mean, I couldn't do that."

"Why not? Stranger things have happened, haven't they?" Blake locked him in his gaze. "Do you know what you could do with that kind of money? You could have sports cars, sail boats, you could buy your *own* private island, with a mansion, retire after just a couple of years."

Lee's expression was a little sour. "You'd rather he play ball than go public?"

Blake looked at Lee, then Joe. "Well, like you said, going public is out, isn't it?"

Joe nodded at that, and Blake continued. "In the movies, having money never matters in the end. The hero always turns down the money for more important things, or people are only truly happy once they've lost it all. But that's just the message the media sends out. They have to, everyone can't be rich, so it's really just best they convince everyone it's better to be poor."

Joe was silent, so Blake continued. "But in the real world, with money, you can have it all. Cars, luxury mansions, the girls. And the money wouldn't even matter with the girls, because you'd be a sports star. You could do whatever you want in life. You want to just up and go to a tropical paradise for the weekend, stay in luxury hotels? You get a bunch of friends together, and take the private jet."

A bit of a grin started to form on Joe's face. "Man, I always thought it would be cool to have my own jet."

"You could afford a few at those wages, you could build an

airstrip in your back yard." Blake paused a moment. "You could do a lot of good with your money as well. Give to charities, donate to political campaigns, any number of things. Even if you just gave away a sliver of your earnings, that would still be a huge contribution."

Joe's expression was puzzled, but there was still sort of a smile on his face. Blake saw a paper napkin on the table, so he grabbed it, and got out a pen. "Say you got half of that contract. That would still be $75 million. And that was just a five year contract. How long of a career do you think someone could have in baseball?"

"On average they are pretty short," said Joe, "but the guys who are really good play for twenty years sometimes."

"Well, you would be better than all of them!" Blake started scribbling down some numbers. "It would probably take a bit to get going. But once you were established, you could keep making good money pretty easily. And there would be sponsorship deals, merchandise sales, who knows what else. You could probably even get into movies."

"Man, I studied a lot of acting, like for when I'm on missions. I bet I would be an awesome actor," said Joe, grinning widely.

Blake added up his scribblings. "Over the course of a full career, it could be as high as $500 million to a billion, maybe even more. Do you know what you could do with *that* kind of money? You could build a media empire, cure a disease, or change the course of an election, without even spending a fraction of it."

Lee looked fairly amused by all this. "You could probably take over a small third world country."

Joe shook his head. "Man, I don't know, that would be like cheating. And they would be really pissed off at me. There's no way I could get away with that." He looked around, and suddenly laughed, goofily. "That's crazy, I couldn't do that."

The spell seemed broken. Lee looked at his watch. "Its past 3 am, you've both had a long day. You guys go to bed, I'll take the first watch."

"I'll take the second, I can get by with a nap for now. I don't always need that much sleep," said Joe.

Blake nodded, now feeling a little sheepish. "Wake me if you need me," he said, suddenly feeling very tired. He had been driving all day. He groggily followed Lee as he showed him to his room, then fell asleep as soon as his head touched the pillow.

10

Blake awoke the next morning in a new bed, the air crisp and moist from the half open window. The light outside had a vibrant glow, it was almost otherworldly, playing off the tall trees. It confused him for a second, why was the light like that, until he realized it must not have been much past dawn.

He just lay there a bit, revelling in the warmth under the sheets, the events of the past day slowly returning to him like a vague, half-remembered dream. He wasn't sure what to make of it all, if it was all even real. But that seemed like a subject for another time.

Early though it was, he didn't feel tired. So after a little bit more time under the blanket he got up, braving the cold to get dressed. He heard voices talking as he made his way down the hallway, wobbling a bit on his stiff legs. He supposed any number of things could be waiting there for him. The police, men in suits and sunglasses, a TV crew. Maybe this was where they did the big reveal.

But it was just Lee and Joe, putting motion sensors into pine cone arrangements. They poured him coffee, said the night had passed without any new developments. If the Mexican news sites had started running a lot of stories in the past couple hours, which Lee thought was pretty early.

The plan for the morning was to put up the motion sensors around the cabin, then hike to a hill nearby - Joe wanted to get the lay of the land. It looked like it would be a cloudy day, so they wouldn't have to worry about satellites.

Lee packed them up a lunch and they headed out, Blake noticing that Lee had already thrown a tarp over the K-56. They looped around the cabin a couple times - it was a nice spot, nestled away in the pine forests at the base of the hills, a little garden plot a ways down around back.

Joe then started setting up the motion sensors, as well as a couple of extra cameras Lee had in storage. He had them walk by, wave their arms, throw rocks, Blake had to crawl on his belly through one section of bushes. You had to get the sensitivity just right - they didn't want an alarm going off every time a rabbit went by, but they needed to know if they had visitors.

Once Joe thought they had the area covered, they started up a little deer trail that cut through the woods. Joe analyzed the terrain as they went, he might run this way if someone came to the cabin. He was basically uncapturable in a forest like this, especially if he had a head start. There were walls of brush, he could jump from tree to tree, the visibility was really limited. Lee said there was a creek a little ways down, that was good to know.

The trail meandered up through rocky meadows, past giant trees stretching high into the sky, the air fresh with pine resin. Blake and Lee told stories about their Hollywood dealing days, which Joe couldn't seem to get enough of. Pool parties on the beach, crashing movie premieres, smuggling product under Jack Dash's limo.

Then Lee told a story, from back when he had been an assistant manager of an international cargo shipping company. They had been moving semi-hot electronics from factories in China to be sold on the black market in Indonesia. It had been a pretty low-key operation, half of it was just avoiding customs taxes.

But then one haul the captain came to him in a fit. He admitted they were carrying guns that time – part of some grand trans-Eurasian operation - and the authorities had been tipped off. They had to unload big crates full of AK-47s onto a little inflatable dinghy in the middle of the night, there was a chase, but they lost them in the reefs. Which worked out well enough, but could have ended badly.

It also turned out that both Joe and Lee had spent some time in Mogadishu - Lee supervising a waypoint in the hashish trade, Joe on a sort of half-training exercise he couldn't really talk about. They swapped some stories, they both knew the one expat bar, they commiserated about the heat.

They started climbing a bit, going up through a thickly wooded area along the side of the hill. Joe thought it could be a particularly good place to shake a trail. Did they mind if he scouted it out?

He sped off into the woods, jumping and swinging on a tree over some bushes. About five minutes later he came back, here would be perfect. He could run along the ledge to the west, then push a boulder to block the trail.

Joe just needed the boulder. Did they mind spotting him? They walked a little ways through the trees and brush to where there was a huge boulder, it must have weighed a couple of pool tables. Joe sort of got below it, had them stabilize it, rocked it around a bit. And then with a grunt he was lifting it up, it was a truly giant rock, Blake couldn't believe it.

He carried it a good ten minutes – along some fairly precarious sloping hillside - Blake and Lee both helping him hold it in place. He wasn't going to drop it, but if he did they should get out of the way as fast as they could.

Finally after crossing a particularly sheer slope they came to a narrow gully. Joe dropped the boulder at the top of it, did a few stretches, then got to work pushing a couple of trees over. That was pretty impressive as well, roots coming up out of the ground, wood breaking, Joe jumping to the other side to lower them down.

All he would have to do now was push the boulder down the gully, and it would block the path. It would buy him a lot of time, even if it was another supersoldier chasing him.

Continuing along, the going got a little rough, they were climbing up through the bush. Blake in particular was getting pretty muddy at that point, Lee figured he had some clothes that would fit them.

Then finally they scrambled up one last rocky slope, and they were there, the top of a forested ridge. They walked over to a break in the trees, and looked out over the valley below. It was an impressive view, a sea of trees, misty hills in the distance. Blake couldn't see any trace of civilization, you couldn't even see the cabin from here. Maybe a little grey line between the trees, that must have been the road.

There was something intense about it. That was the world out there, stretching out around them in every direction. Blake felt a sense of accomplishment, they had made it past roadblocks, highway patrols, helicopters, satellites. A circle centered on San Diego with Lee's cabin on the edge would cover a lot of ground.

They had lunch sitting on some rocks overlooking the valley. Lee wanted to know about the company Blake was investing in, so he dutifully told them about Wildon Textiles. All the fabrics they made and the manufacturers they sold to, the epic shifts keeping the factory going 24/7 with the rush order from the outdoors company.

Blake went into some detail about the report he had been working on before he left, all about European import tariffs. It got kind of complicated, each country had their own rules, if they were moving towards parity. And it wasn't necessarily fixed what industry categories their products fell into. Like, the material they used for the life jacket casing, that was 'ferretaria misceláneo' in Spain. It was a special category, and there were almost no tariffs for it there.

And they were sending each shipment individually. They were sending enough to Europe to justify combining shipments, which was significantly cheaper. It would be a little more complicated, and it might mean some of their customers had to wait a little longer. But Blake's impression was people didn't need things in a rush, if anything it was more the opposite. There were actually a lot of small obvious business 101 mistakes like that, which were probably costing them a lot of money.

It felt good to deliver his report to someone, even if they had nothing to do with Wildon Textiles. He was supposed to have presented his findings this week. Lee did say they sounded like a solid company, maybe he would go in with Blake on an investment somewhere down the road.

After finishing lunch they headed back towards the cabin, taking another little half trail along the other side of the ridge. Lee made an innocuous comment about the defensibility of a ravine they were crossing, and they started analyzing the strategic value of the terrain as they went.

A hill with some boulders and big trees, it would be a solid position, nobody from the meadow could get to you there. A spot with some thick thorny bushes, you could shoot through those, then run to the gully and throw grenades. The rocky bit of trail ahead of them, with thick bushy trees on both sides? That would be a perfect place for an ambush. They all went quiet, passing through there.

The conversation started getting a bit post-apocalyptical as they got closer to the cabin, Lee going off about how modern society was inevitably hurtling towards a cliff. It was your standard scenarios, climate change causing simultaneous disasters, a stock market collapse, massive civil unrest, a downward spiral of crisis-domino chaos feeding into more chaos. The end result being a world of small armed groups roving around fighting for gasoline, guns, and toilet paper.

It was all very pessimistic, if he did actually make rather a good case for it. Blake wondered if he shouldn't put more of his holdings into gold, he had been thinking about that a bit lately. Gold would go up, at least on the way to that, would it? He supposed it would reach a point where you were better off just buying barrels of oil and burying them somewhere.

Once they got back to the cabin they started planning for its defences in said scenario. The two of them figured they could sleep at least 20 soldiers in the cabin. In an attack maybe 12 would stay in the cabin, four would be down past the garden - they could do a surprise counter-attack - another four along the driveway ready to fall back.

They were soon circling the cabin, figuring out where exactly people would go, what kind of traps they would put where. Pit traps and snares, those would be the big ones. Apparently there was good access to the roof, they could build a system of rope bridges, or at least zip lines, and then have crow's nests with machine guns up in the trees.

Joe really seemed to be enjoying himself, but Blake found it all a little disturbing. Maybe in different times he could see the fun in it, but under the present circumstances it was just morbid.

Then Lee got sort of a funny look in his eye, and took them around to a room at the side of the cabin. It was a spacious storage room, stacked floor to ceiling with a variety of supplies. Canned food, bags of rice, medicines, even a couple big barrels of gasoline. Lee would have no trouble come his apocalypse, then.

They weren't there for the supplies, however. Lee had Joe move some shelving, pry up the floorboards, then lift a heavy looking slab of rock. Beneath was revealed a porthole hatch, with a ladder going down. They descended one by one into a surprisingly largish room, it must have been a few meters square, crates up against the walls.

Lee opened one of the crates, revealing a stack of AK-47s. Another beside it contained handguns and grenades. Joe was pretty impressed, he put a cartridge into one of them then took it out, tossed one of the grenades up in the air.

Apparently Lee had an associate, did some arms smuggling. Different guy from the guy in Asia. Had a deal go bad, had to unload them fast. Lee actually got them below the list price, it had really been a matter of literally taking them off his hands.

Nonetheless Lee said it was a terrible industry to be involved in, he generally tried to avoid it like the plague. Just the risk:benefit side of things, and the kind of people you had to deal with. The people who had illegal weapons to sell, the people who wanted to buy weapons, the people you had to move them with, the whole chain of it. Drug people could be a little erratic at times, but they were nothing like weapons people.

Lee admitted to not really knowing what to do with it all. It was hard enough to find a buyer, and he didn't want to sell them to just anyone. All things considered, he would probably just keep them there. It was good to have an emergency stockpile hidden away somewhere. What was the argument? You never knew when someone *was* going to try and take over the world, there was actually enough of that in the history books.

They were all a little worn out after the hike, so they settled in on the stoop of the cabin, and the conversation moved back to lighter issues. Joe went off about how nice it was to be off the compound, not having to do whatever pointless training exercise, report on all his movements, all that BS. They talked about Hollywood a bit more, a bit of everything. Eastern religions, the geology of Northern California, was there a bubble in tech stocks.

Girls, Joe hadn't met too many girls on base. Dating was hard sometimes, when you were a top secret supersoldier. They had to get security clearance first, which could kind of put a damper on things. One time he rescued a girl, on a mission, but there was no way she could ever get clearance. It was really messed up.

He had sort of made some progress with a couple of civilian agents. Spy chicks were really hot sometimes. Although apparently his lab wasn't making any female supersoldiers yet. It was too much work to do another gender. The hormones were all different, so they just focused on men. Kind of sexist though right?

And with the changes at his lab, they were even stricter now about that, about everything. They had kind of implied that if he wanted a steady girlfriend he should just get married. They could set him up with someone with the right background and psychological profile.

Which was kind of fucked up, right? Like, he wasn't necessarily opposed to it, he didn't want to be some pick up artist or anything. But it would be cool to go out on dates, play the field a little bit.

The conversation did eventually venture into sports, and the idea of Joe playing was again raised. Like go out there, in the real world, play pro-ball, was that what Blake was talking about? Blake was slightly hesitant, but that was the idea, yes.

Neither Joe nor Lee seemed particularly opposed to it, more just skeptical. They didn't really seem to take it seriously. After a brief discussion Blake was forced to admit that it probably wasn't feasible. Lee seemed amused just that he had brought it up again in the first place.

So the conversation moved on to, well, suppose, just hypothetically, alternate universe, he was actually to do it, what sport would he play? Joe said it was tough, he always had to be careful about not hurting people. He got these weird muscle spasm things sometimes. It hardly ever happened anymore, but it was always a risk. He really messed up his karate teacher once when he was 14.

So anything involving a lot of physical contact was definitely out. He would even be a little nervous about something like basketball. And even if he were able to risk, say, hockey, he'd have to learn how to skate, shoot, pass, all that. The other players might not be bio-enhanced, but they would have a lot of hours of practice on him. He kind of sucked at golf.

Joe supposed the one to do would be baseball. It was straightforward enough motions, hit a ball, throw a ball, catch a ball, run down the field. Maybe he could hit the ball too hard, but the pitchers were generally pretty awake.

Joe turned out to be quite a baseball fan, in fact. Before Blake knew it the conversation was off about last year's season, both Lee and Joe had followed it. The star players, all the epic home runs, some ill-advised trades.

Joe had gotten into San Diego for the first time towards the end of the season last year. But they wouldn't let him go to a game, they just kept dangling it in front of him like they always do. Then San Diego made it all the way to the playoffs. And then he definitely couldn't go, the playoffs! It was a big media event, the eyes of the world were on it. So fucking nice of them to buy a new big screen TV especially for him though.

Which again got him off about how nice it was to be off the compound, he thanked them again for giving him a place to stay. It was sort of funny, as intense as all this was for Blake, it was probably actually the opposite for Joe. He was stretching out, kicking back like it was his first day off in years.

And fair enough, maybe in some ways it was. Joe's good mood even seemed slightly infectious. Blake felt himself relaxing a little, and they all just sat back, watching the sun set behind the trees.

11

The theme of baseball and their lighthearted optimism of the day faded from their minds with the setting sun, however. The armoured van robbery was again on the evening news, Joe's mugshot again staring out at them.

Nervously they watched as the announcers said the police were now confident that Eugene Cudneck had left San Diego. Joe figured they must have scoured the city pretty thoroughly, and would be expanding their search to a wider area.

It all made Blake decidedly uneasy. He wasn't going to sleep any time soon, so he offered to take the first watch - Lee and Joe both looked pretty exhausted. He then passed the night with his eyes glued to the security screen, just staring out at the trees of green light swaying in the wind. It was a little gruelling, he had a constant hovering sensation that twenty of those riot gear types were going to appear.

If something about it was meditative, as well. Like chanting a mantra or focusing on your breathing. Staying so intensely focused on what would otherwise be a meaningless image, the trees, the row of bushes, the black corridor that was the driveway. It was always the same, but his state of mind was constantly changing.

Joe got up to take over at maybe three in the morning, looking slightly embarrassed at having overslept. Blake managed to eventually get some sleep after that, and didn't wake up until close to noon.

They planned out shifts over his breakfast. Joe seemed convinced that - at least for now - they needed someone watching the cameras 24/7. So they split the day up into three eight hour shifts, and three eight hour sleeps. The idea being that there would always be someone on the cameras, and only one of them would be asleep at any given time.

Blake would take the first night shift, from a little after

sunset until 3 or 4 in the morning. Joe would be awake during his shift – night was obviously the most dangerous time. Joe would then watch the cameras from the end of Blake's shift until mid-morning. Blake thought that was kind of an awkward time for him to go to bed, but Joe thought it was perfect, he could get all his sleep in the safest part of the day. Lee in turn would take over with the day shift, as to be awake all day if anyone came to the door.

This naturally raised the question of what they were to do if someone did come to the cabin. It was actually quite well fitted in terms of escape routes, with exits on all sides. One was in fact designed with quick and discreet decampment in mind, a trapdoor in one of the bedrooms that lead to an area covered in bush.

They needed to prepare for all eventualities, so they spent the afternoon doing drills. Out the window, low through the bushes, up through the woods. Did Blake realize how much noise he was making?

A day passed, then another. Coverage of the armoured van robbery was dropping off, if they had raised the reward to half a million dollars now. There was no evidence of any search parties, in fact only a couple of cars had gone by Lee's road. Apparently there was nothing but empty lots up the road, then a logging road further along.

They spent some time making the cabin look uninhabited, and continued with the escape drills. But other than that there wasn't a lot to do. Fortunately Lee did have a fairly extensive library of books and movies, and even an old video game system buried away. For someone who thought TV was the Illuminati's primary brainwashing tool he also had a fairly comprehensive cable package, so there was at least always something to watch.

Aside from the ever-present lingering fear of some kind of squad descending on them, it was fairly relaxed. Sort of like a normal weekend at the cabin, except with the outdoorsy hiking and kayaking sort of stuff cut back, and the hanging out in the evening watching movies stuff expanded. In some ways it was nice, Blake had been meaning to get caught up on movies.

Lee did most of the cooking, which turned out to be a bit of a task - Joe seemed to have some fairly specific dietary requirements. He was generally fasting 16 hours a day, but when he did eat he would take in huge amounts of protein, or want meals entirely without carbohydrates. Did they realize they were running themselves entirely on glucose?

Lee soon suggested that he go on a supply run. While he did have his cellar stocked for the apocalypse, they didn't want to live off canned food, not to mention they needed clothes. Joe and Lee also both seemed convinced they needed more cameras, extensive as their existing system was.

Lee also suggested they leave some sort of trail under Blake's name, using his credit card, maybe. Doing this could help reduce the risk of someone figuring out that he disappeared at the same time as Joe. Lee would also check in with Blake's lawyers and make sure the San Diego number didn't lead back to him.

They also decided he should send an email to Jack, from Blake's account. They didn't want Jack filing a missing persons report or anything. They just composed a quick message, something had come up, Blake wasn't sure when he would be back. The way it was worded, it sounded like he was leaving now, not a few days ago.

Lee headed out bright and early the next morning, returning in the evening with a trunk full of groceries, clothing, video games, and movies. He had also hit up a spy store, Joe was impressed by the selection of signal jammers, flashbangs, miniature cameras and the like he had picked up. All of them got special cell phones that communicated over an encrypted local radio network.

For Blake he had a bass guitar - he had found an out of the way music shop near LA, and paid with Blake's card when they were particularly busy. It seemed like the sort of thing Blake would pop out of nowhere and buy.

Blake's lawyer had said no one had been asking about him, and the phone number had no connection to him. For now it would have a new life as the backup phone for a travelling insurance salesman, then they would cancel it in a couple months.

It was nice to have the new video games and movies, and Blake played around on the bass a bit. He had actually been meaning to pick it up for a few years now. But all in all he did find the pace a little slow. Valentine's day came and went, and he didn't even realize until a couple of days after, he had passed the day playing video games.

Blake almost wished someone would come to the cabin sometimes, get it over with, have a little excitement. Even having lived in Hollywood investing in film, he had never watched so many movies in his life.

They did some marathons, Lee had bought the entire series of a classic underground sci-fi TV show. Blake couldn't help but identify with the characters, trapped in their spaceship hurtling through space. With the night black out the windows the cabin began to feel like a spaceship.

It even got kind of eerie, in one episode the characters were staring out the portholes navigating through an asteroid belt. Towards the later parts of his shifts it started feeling like a giant space rock could crash into the windows at any given moment.

The theme of sports didn't come up again until one rainy afternoon, when they were watching a particularly epic hockey game. Joe got going about how they used to play baseball back on the island he used to live on. It was all high security people, so he hadn't had to worry about hiding his abilities.

The way it worked out, he was just always an automatic walk - after his first couple plate appearances they wouldn't throw him anything but intentional walks. Once he was on base, he could usually get all the way home on pretty much any hit, at least as long as nobody else was on base. He tried running past people a couple times, but they said that was against the rules, which was total BS.

Stealing bases was a breeze, aside from home, which could actually be kind of hard. So it wasn't like he was a guaranteed run every time. There were even times where people would intentionally strike out if they went up before him. Like, bases loaded, no outs, he was up next. That could be an intentional strikeout, people just wouldn't swing. You didn't want to risk the double play.

Talking about it, he thought they should go outside, do some kind of sport, anything. He was going nuts in there. They all agreed - Blake was feeling pretty cooped up himself. They figured they were safe enough out in the woods, it was a cloudy day. They could spend a couple of hours away from the cameras.

Lee realized he might even have some baseball equipment stashed away. He went and dug up a battered old bat and ball, then they hiked through the woods to a flatish meadow a couple of kilometers from the cabin.

With little ado, Blake passed the bat to Joe, and took the position of pitcher. "Seventh inning, bottom of the ninth, last game of the playoffs. A cheer goes up as the great Joe Soldao steps up to the plate, and the pitcher winds up.." said Blake dramatically, swinging backwards then throwing the ball towards Joe in a decent enough underhand.

He watched it fly towards him, then there was an almost invisible swish of movement, a loud thwack, and Joe was standing sideways to where he was before. Off in the distance the ball was soaring up, up, into the sky, in the clouds, it was a little hard to see. Blake stared at it, trying to see where it was going to land, but it didn't even begin to descend, it just sort of disappeared into the horizon.

"We'll have to be careful where you hit them, there's some cattle graze a few miles south of here," said a grinning Lee.

Joe held up the hilt of the bat, which was broken in two. "You got another bat?" he asked, and Lee shook his head.

Blake looked back up at the sky again, then looked at Joe. "You could do it, you know that?" he said fiercely. Joe looked at him, an incredulity again returning to his face, but Blake continued. "You could beat out any of them, be the greatest player there ever was, there ever will be."

"Yeah, but.." Joe stammered.

Blake fixed him in his gaze. "You don't know the opportunity you have. People work their whole lives, pull 80 hour weeks, sacrifice everything, for the kind of money you could make in an afternoon."

Joe looked dumbfounded. "I dunno," he said, looking down at the broken bat in his hand, a sense of bewilderment and wonder now crossing his face. "I mean, do you think it would even be possible?"

"Would it be easy? Probably not. It would probably be incredibly difficult. Maybe it's impossible, maybe it's crazy even to think it. But all the best new business ideas sound crazy when someone first comes up with them." Blake gave a little shrug. "In all honesty, it would probably be a breeze, compared to any of the other ways you could make that kind of money."

Lee had an amused grin on his face. "There are certainly worse ways to make a fortune, and we don't have a lot else going on. If you just trained during overcast days, it probably wouldn't be *that* much of a risk," he said, his tone perhaps suggesting in fact an element of unnecessary risk.

A goofy sort of grin came over Joe's face. "Well, maybe we could play a little ball, just for fun."

12

And with that began Joe's training. If it soon became evident it would more be training in reverse - for most skills the issue seemed to be overperforming, not underperforming.

With the ball gone and the bat broken, they just started with base running practice. Lee measured out a track of 100 meters and told Joe to run it like it was a game. On his first pass, Lee figured he probably beat the Olympic speed record by more than a second. Then on his second he was too slow, Lee said he was out at first base. Then he broke the record again on his third.

They spent the rest of the afternoon doing sprints. And from the looks of it, there was actually a surprisingly narrow window between running faster than humanly possible and getting tagged out. After a few dozen it seemed like Joe was starting to be able to keep it in range, although occasionally he would just go way too fast. Suppose he *was* ever to play in a professional game, there would be cameras recording his every move. Even if he could stay at the right speed 99% of the time, breaking that barrier even once would be too much.

They were due for another supply run, so early the next morning Lee went to Sacramento. Blake gave him a brick of cash, and told him to spare no expense. Lee came back with a full load of equipment, including a variety of baseball books and videos, a professional grade pitching machine, and even some proper bases.

It was another cloudy afternoon, so they got right back out there, Lee happily staying in to watch the cameras. They measured out a rough baseball diamond in the meadow, as well as marking off where the field would end.

After a bit of fiddling they got the pitching machine working, and Joe started practicing hitting various distances. Groundballs to the field, sure-out pop flies, top of the fence 50/50s. Being a ballplayer wasn't all strikeouts and home-runs.

Joe generally managed to keep it within the realm of human potential, if he did hit a few zingers that went far up and over the trees. Blake spent most of the time just gathering up the balls and delivering them back to the machine.

It felt good, to be doing something, to be out of the cabin. It was a nice enough day, if the clouds were thick in the sky, and there was a decent amount of rain. In the end they stayed out until after the sun had set, returning to the cabin muddy and exhausted.

That night they found some spring training games on TV - it turned out they had just started a couple of days ago. Joe seemed to know all the players, and gave them a running commentary as the game went on. It was almost like having another announcer in the room.

Then they were out there the next day, and the day after that - there was a series of rainy overcast days, with never a touch of blue in the sky. They practiced a bit of everything, more hitting and running, throwing, catching, slides. Bunting was a big area, Joe didn't really have much of an advantage with that. It was just a matter of holding the bat in the way of the ball.

With his ability to speed up his perception he was pretty good at catching, although he still did miss a few. They rigged up the pitching machine to shoot hits for him to catch, and the biggest issue seemed to be that sometimes he would get excited and run just a little bit too fast. So they tried to specifically practice catches that were on the border of human ability, Blake watching from the distance to tell him when an epic catch looked just a little bit too epic.

There didn't seem to be a lot of issues with his throwing - just the mechanics of throwing, it was easier to keep it within the bounds of human ability. They practiced a bit of pitching, although they assumed he would probably just be a hitter. Joe had a pretty mean fastball – those were more brute strength - but he couldn't really get any of the various sliders, knuckleballs, or curveballs to properly go off.

Tired though he would be, Blake would continue late into the night after the training sessions. He watched spring training games, or read through the books Lee had bought. Baseball history, player biographies, classic works of fiction, statistical analysis, he devoured them all.

It did strike him that it was really a lot of time they were dedicating to baseball. All just out of nowhere, he marveled at it a bit. Maybe they had needed a project, there wasn't a lot else to do in the cabin. It certainly felt more productive than watching the same movie from Lee's collection for the third time.

Even Lee seemed to be bitten by the bug, he joined them for some of the less rainy training sessions. He knew a fair bit about the sport, discussing the finer points of the game's strategy and regaling them with stories of seasons past.

Lee did seem to have a sort of amused demeanor about it all though. Blake even felt slightly patronized. He had a feeling the only reason Lee was going along with the baseball idea at all was because he didn't think it would work. Maybe he was just waiting for them to get it out of their system. Like Blake's thing would fail, then Joe could be convinced to go public, was that his game?

Blake supposed they could well be up against some long odds. He would wake up in the mornings, nerve-wracked after strange dreams he couldn't remember, and it would all seem impossible, a fool's errand that would get them incarcerated or worse. But by late afternoon - watching Joe blast balls into the trees - it almost seemed like it could be too easy.

Blake tried to approach it logically, to break it down into its individual challenges. Any business venture was just a series of tasks, of obstacles to be overcome. And once you broke something down into its component tasks, things that seemed impossible could actually start looking very feasible.

Talent clearly wasn't a problem. The problem there would be keeping the true extent of Joe's abilities secret, and he was progressing well enough with that. They would need to get him a pretty good fake ID as well, and the plastic surgery would have to work. Probably be a process just getting him on a team. But none of those seemed like insurmountable obstacles.

The biggest issue seemed to be getting past whoever exactly it was that had created him. Really anything involving them was a bit of a wildcard. Especially as Joe didn't seem to want to divulge any information on who exactly they were. But one way or another they were people, they could be made to see the financial benefits of letting Joe play.

And the potential pie to distribute was so huge that it probably wouldn't even matter. Blake almost wondered why they hadn't gotten Joe into pro ball themselves. He didn't want to get ahead of himself, but he did research endorsement deals a couple of times. And some of the numbers were really amazing – mind blowing, even.

He had always known it was a lot, same as the salaries. But it was even crazier than those. A player like Joe could get into ten figures just through endorsements alone. Then on top of that the super star salary. What else, merchandise, he could write books, make his own dip brand, make another few million there.

Blake wondered if he should almost bring up the subject of how any profits from baseball were to be divided. It seemed rather uncouth though, and certainly premature. If you *were* generally supposed to do that at the beginning of a venture, he imagined he would be bankrolling things. But it really didn't do to mention it, given the fundamentals he felt the three of them could work something out if and when profits were turned.

Joe also seemed to be developing more of a comprehension of the financial stakes. Blake got the impression he hadn't had a lot of experience handling money in his life to date - everything had been paid for back on base, he was given room and board, supplies for whatever mission. Joe said it just kind of worked out that he never really bought anything.

Joe read an article online about mechanic jobs, and he thought it couldn't be right, he couldn't believe how little they made. A good pair of night vision goggles was like three month's wages. To this Blake added that after food, rent and all that, a mechanic would only be able to put a certain amount of money aside. It would probably take a year of savings just to buy those goggles.

Along with the baseball training, Joe was also eager to continue his military and personal training. This was a sight to see, he did strength training with boulders, or giant crates of canned goods from the storage room. After a while he started to find those limiting, so he made up weights of his own out of concrete and scrap metal, they were huge.

Lee got them some paintball guns, and Joe had them shoot at him while he dodged around. They would do it out in the open, Joe with little or no cover, but try as they might it was rare for them to hit him. It was quite a fascinating thing, and a little frustrating. Joe would jump, duck, dodge around, even do some dance moves, moonwalk, and the paintballs would just fly by him, splattering on the trees.

No point in having super strength if you can't dodge bullets, he said. Although he admitted it was as much a matter of looking where people were aiming and faking them out. He got kind of freaked out when they did hit him though, and would just stare at the paint on his leg.

As they continued with his training, Joe also began to open up a bit about his past. His previous training sounded pretty intense, they would do things like drop him off in the jungle with nothing, he would have to find his way back with people chasing him. Or taking on a helicopter with nothing but a knife and a grappling hook, having to swim under a ship to defuse a bomb on one breath.

He had been tortured - just a little bit – while on truth serum. He never gave up his secrets though. Which made it that much more fucked up that they were having that conversation.

It was all pretty hard on the body, as well. He had some advice for them, never fuck with your hormones. Of all the things you could do to yourself, it was the worst. Nothing ever worked the way it was supposed to, and everything had side effects. Half the shit they did to him was fixing side effects, then fixing the side effects of the stuff to fix side effects.

He was full-on horseshoe bald by the time he was 14, he'd been shaving it since then. It really freaked people out, seeing a kid like that. He grew it out for Halloween once, it was an instant costume.

He couldn't always think straight, he got brain fog, or got confused making decisions, it was weird. And they dulled some of his emotions, as well. He didn't feel fear like normal people, he should probably have PTSD by now. Well, sometimes he got freaked out, it all came back. It was kind of messed up.

Same with pain, he only felt like half as much pain as he should. Which was also kind of messed up, you feel pain for a reason. There was another guy, they overdid it with him, he only ever felt pain if he was seriously injured. That guy ended up in psych ward.

And it was cool to be super strong and everything. He couldn't complain about that. Although he *always* had to do *everything* back on base. They had to carry some giant part across a field or up into a mountain somewhere? No need for a truck, Joe could do that! Every single time there was a shipment to unload, it was good exercise, wasn't he bored of the gym?

After that pool table incident, they made him unload like 500 tons of supplies. Did they know how much that is? And they had all these excuses. They were doing an overhaul of the loading equipment and a huge shipment of 'top secret' parts just arrived, only he could do it. It was nothing but car parts, it was complete

BS.

Conversations about his background did tend to lead to questions from Lee towards the 'who' element of his creation. On this subject, however, Joe was mum. It really was better they didn't have that stuff in their heads. Blake wasn't sure if Joe knew exactly who he had been working for himself. Likewise he wouldn't say how many others there were like him, or if he was one of the more advanced soldiers.

Lee was also quite curious about what kind of missions inside America would require someone with Joe's particular skill set. On this front he finally broke down and gave them some details.

To start with, he wasn't allowed to do a lot of stuff. Supersoldiers were actually really regulated in America, even if they didn't officially exist. He was really only here because of what he knew – he could do missions involving classified information, because it didn't matter what he saw.

After a bit more prodding he told them about his mission, the one he got himself disqualified for by throwing the pool table. There was a medical research lab, and they had figured some stuff out. Nothing that big, but it was stuff that lead to other stuff that they really didn't want getting out.

The lab got shut down, but the lead scientist took a hard drive and a bunch of petri dishes and went into hiding. They knew where he was, and he didn't have a lot of protection – the mission report said a dog and a handgun, and he probably wasn't going to use the handgun. They just needed someone who wasn't going to learn anything new to go in there, destroy the research, and tell him to cease and desist.

But it was a government funded project - which was fucked up in and of itself, those were tax dollars - and the shit they were studying wasn't that bad. It could have a lot of good uses in medicine. It was kind of fucked up that they hadn't made that research public already. And what if the guy refused to stop the research, or tried to make the results public? Whose job would it have been to convince him?

Another recurrent element of their stay in the cabin was the continuing coverage of the armoured van robbery. While it was now rare for anything about it to be on the news, it did seem to periodically pop up in a few places.

One night a sort of second-rate fugitive TV show did a whole big bit on him. They had a criminal psychologist on, said he was a pathological liar, suffered from bizarre delusions of grandeur. They really played up how dangerous he was, said people should avoid engaging with him at all costs. Lee thought they were nervous he might spill the beans.

Lee would also print out the latest news for them when he was out on supply runs. It was kind of heavy to read. Fortunately the armoured van driver who was shot seemed to be making a full recovery, Blake was glad of that.

Going through it all, Blake couldn't help but get little bouts of paranoia. Joe couldn't really have done that, could he have? Obviously they had a better explanation. But seeing it on the news really made it feel real. What if he had set his watch an hour off when he came in from NY? Had he been showing up an hour early to all the meetings with Wildon Textiles?

Could the police report have been wrong, was that possible? It was just a small window, maybe twenty minutes, and it would at least be physically possible that Joe did it. Maybe there was some bizarre reason why it was absolutely vital the public think it happened later than it did. That first roadblock *was* set up before the time when they were saying Cudneck committed the robbery. When was daylight savings time?

But Blake trusted Joe, and by this point it felt like Joe would have just admitted to doing it anyways. Whatever fears Blake had were eased somewhat when a news story broke about an armed robbery of a convenience store in Chicago, which was apparently committed by Cudneck. He was believed to have gang connections there, who were believed to be hiding him. The way they covered it, Joe thought that they really thought he was in Chicago. Which meant they were less likely to be combing the woods of Northern California.

More unsettling, then, was the fact that they were harbouring a fugitive who someone would go to those lengths to pursue. Lee seemed to think that sort of thing happened regularly, like half the people you saw on the fugitive shows were really activists or supersoldiers or whistleblowers or what have you. That was the joke, actually, whenever they saw a fugitive on TV, was he a friend of yours.

To Blake, on the other hand, it seemed like a disturbingly rare event. Everything else aside it was just a lot of moving parts. Any number of people would see things, journalists, mall workers, the doctors treating the security guard.

All in all it was a lot to have hovering over you. It put a bit of a damper on the training, for one. They were out there doing timed base runs after the report that Cudneck might be in Chicago, and Blake couldn't get it out of his head. Every time Joe ran by he saw his mugshot. Blake even got a little jumpy, he could swear he saw people at the edge of the woods a couple of times. But Joe ran to check it out, and there was nobody there. If there was a deer once.

Joe's training did seem to be coming along quite well - it was now rare for him to do anything outside realistic human performance. Too rare to properly estimate a rate, although Blake figured it was maybe 1 time in 500.

But they didn't want him doing anything impossible even once. How many times would a player hit, run, catch? 1 time in 10,000 was still too many. Joe could just never cross that line. If he were to play in the big leagues today, he would have to run slow, probably too slow, just to avoid running too fast.

They kept at it, but Blake was almost feeling relieved on the days when the skies cleared up and they couldn't go outside. It didn't feel fun anymore, like it had at first. Lee was also getting mad at them, Joe was running trails into the ground. Satellites could see that kind of change. Not to mention they had been going out on some only semi-overcast days. Blake got the distinct impression he thought they would have lost interest in baseball already.

A streak of sunny days soon in fact put their training on hold, so Blake dedicated himself to studying the road ahead in more detail. And every time he thought he'd solved one problem, another two would come up. It turned out that when you really looked into it, getting a supersoldier into pro-ball could be a logistical nightmare.

First off they would need a pretty high level fake ID, which according to Lee wasn't easy. And getting the ID itself would be decidedly problematic until Joe had a new face. Even if he could miraculously change his face as he claimed, there was still the question of how exactly to get a plastic surgeon to operate on Eugene Cudneck. Apparently Lee knew a guy, but he was in hiding in South America somewhere, so that wouldn't do.

The process of getting Joe on a team was actually looking more difficult than Blake had originally thought, as well. From his research, there was a fairly standard process players had to go through to get into the big leagues, and it sounded pretty involved - they would probably have to find ways to skip over a lot of it.

Normally a player would start in high school, maybe go on to college ball, before getting drafted to play in the minor leagues. Then finally years later they would get onto a major league team. It also seemed like there was fairly stringent drug testing these days.

Compounding all this was the fact that the major league season started in a little under a month, on the first day of April. At first that had seemed like an advantage, they could get going fast. But given everything they would have to do, it was really the worst time possible. Blake researched the rules, and technically September 1st was the absolute last day teams were allowed to add new players, although the main deadline was the end of July.

Would they have to wait a year before playing? Joe seemed into the idea of baseball right now, but that was a long time to wait. They didn't want to hang out in the cabin for a year. The importance of momentum could never be underestimated in these sorts of ventures.

It was only now that Blake felt like he was truly beginning to appreciate the enormity of the task they were setting out on. As great an opportunity they had here with Joe, part of him couldn't help but pine for the simpler days when he was working with Wildon Textiles.

13

They were soon passing through March, the days a little sunnier, rain falling a little less often. Eugene Cudneck was still on the lamb, no one had yet come by the cabin, and they were all developing varying degrees of facial hair.

They did a little celebration one afternoon, champagne and everything - it was Joe's 1000th hour of real world experience in America. He acknowledged that hanging out in a cabin watching movies was pretty low-key real world experience. But technically he was in a different security class now.

They were now making their way through some war documentaries, a couple Japanese anime series, reading old comic books by the box - Lee had bought out a couple of second hand stores. On a very fundamental level, however, there was only so much time you could spend watching movies, playing video games, listening to books on tape. Blake found himself becoming increasingly restless. He didn't know if he had ever gone quite this long without contact with the outside world. The people at Wildon Textiles must be wondering about him, for one.

Whatever exactly it was they were going to do, they weren't making any progress hanging out in the cabin. If anything they were stagnating. Blake would sit on the stoop, staring out down the driveway. What lay ahead of them, down that road? The real world was out there, pulling at him with a strange ominous magnetism. It was alluringly enigmatic, exotic, even.

They were enjoying a particularly nice pasta Lee had whipped up for dinner one evening, with a spring training game on in the background, when Blake saw with clarity what had to happen next.

"I need to get out there, into the world," he said, looking over at them, and muting the TV. "I need to test the waters, to see what happens."

A concerned look appeared on Joe's face. "They might be looking for you. If they are, it's gonna be really dangerous for you to go out in public. I can get a new face, and they have no reason to connect me and Lee. But you're at least going to be a person of interest."

He gave Blake an earnest, almost apologetic look. "I dunno, it might be better for you to stay in hiding for now. We really don't know what's going to happen if you go out there."

Blake shook his head. "But that's the point, we don't know, and we need to. And the longer I stay off the grid, the weirder its going to look. Whatever we are going to do, it's going to be a lot more difficult if I can't show my face. We're going to need money, for one. I can get a lot anonymously, but in the end only so much."

Blake felt a pang of nervousness. He hadn't been thinking about his investments too much, he might have even been putting off thinking about the subject. But there were probably things he should be doing, should have done already, financially speaking. He tried to give them an easy grin, but it felt weak, a chill descending all the way down his spine. "I don't know if my portfolio is maximized for avoiding an asset freeze, for one."

Joe nodded. "Right," he said, a perplexed look coming across his face. "The biggest issue is that you disappeared at the same time as me, on the morning of the 7th. Other than that nobody really has any reason to suspect you. You said you were really off the grid in San Diego?"

Blake nodded. "Ya, in San Diego, just in general." He paused a moment, thinking. "Like I said, my phone wasn't in my name, I never got around to submitting the paperwork for my apartment. Not a lot of people knew I was living there, I generally use cash."

Lee grinned. "The more well-off in society can be notoriously difficult to track down. That would work strongly in your favor."

Joe stood up, and started pacing the room. "Maybe you aren't on their radar, they don't have a lot of reasons to connect us. Do you know who exactly has your San Diego phone number? I know they can get some cell phone movement data in California state, and that's exactly the kind of thing they would investigate."

Blake thought about it a moment. "Just a few people, I think, Jack Wildon, most of the Wildon Textiles people. My landlady,

I'm pretty sure I gave it to her."

Joe rubbed his head, and did another lap around the room. "Wildon Textiles wasn't in your file, I would have remembered that. So it could be they haven't connected you with them. But if they really look into you, they would probably find them, right?"

Blake swallowed. "Yes, I did send Jack a lot of emails. And I called him with my New York phone a few times before heading to San Diego. It's probably not registered in my name either, but a lot of people have it." He paused a moment, what else? "There's probably some publicly available information about me purchasing a small share of the company mid-January."

Joe nodded, and then was silent, circling around the room again a couple of times. Blake chastised himself at not having taken more precautions. Wildon Textiles had to be the one investment he did completely on the level?

"I think Wildon Textiles is the key information point, maybe your landlady too," Joe said finally. "If my people have talked to them already, we should assume you're a prime suspect. If not, maybe you're good. So maybe you could talk to them, see if anyone was asking about you."

A pained look came across Joe's face. "Although the longer I stay down, the more likely it is they are going to start looking into leads like you. Even if they haven't talked to Wildon Textiles yet, they still could at any point in the future." He paused a moment, then gave Blake a funny sort of look. "Um, how well do you know this Jack Wildon guy? Like, do you think you could get him to lie for you?"

Blake sat back in his chair, and rubbed his head. How well did he really know Jack? He had only worked with Wildon Textiles for about a month, but he felt they had gotten to know each other fairly well in that time. In many ways he felt like an old friend. You could be good friends with someone, see them for drinks every few weeks, but hour for hour that was nothing compared to working with someone every day.

Could he get good old Jack to tell a little white lie on his behalf? It would be a rather glaring violation of investor ethics. But that sort of thing happened, didn't it, out there in the world, at least periodically enough?

"Perhaps," said Blake, trying to think. "Although really there's a half dozen people who would at least know roughly when I disappeared. It doesn't seem prudent to ask all of them to lie."

Joe tilted his head "That might be alright. If they haven't investigated you yet, they probably aren't going to dig that deep, if and when they do. My people aren't necessarily going to want to leave a big trail themselves. If Jack is the boss and the guy you had the most dealings with, they would probably focus on him. And maybe there's some ways he could mention something to everyone else."

Lee chimed in. "I'm sure Jack Wildon is a respected figure in the community. An alibi from someone like him could stop an investigation in its tracks."

Joe paused to think again, although now he was nodding, looking more confident. "Even if they just thought you left San Diego a few days later, that would probably be enough to clear you. It would be a little risky, but them catching you in a lie isn't going to make a huge difference if they figure out we disappeared at the same time."

Joe looked Blake straight on. "Jack wouldn't turn you in just for asking him to lie, would he?"

Blake shook his head. "I really don't think he would."

Joe did another couple of laps, then slowly started nodding. "Ok, maybe we can do this."

And with that Joe and Lee embarked on a detailed analysis of Blake's situation. They grilled him about his time in San Diego, making him go over everything he did in minute detail. Who he saw, where he shopped, they wanted to know every single time he was out in public. It felt like a bit of an interrogation, it got a little personal. Yes, he did actually eat quite a bit of fast food, if you sat down and figured it out.

They spent a lot of time on his San Diego phone. Joe had Blake try to remember every single person who could have his number. It was pretty much just the Wildon Textiles people, and his landlady. The car rental places, maybe, ya, both of them as well. Blake didn't think he actually gave it out to anyone at any of the sales meetings. Maybe one or two of the girls at the BBQs, he had gotten their numbers, at least.

They turned on Blake's phone and went through his call history, call by call. There were actually very few calls. Blake usually just showed up at the factory and made social plans there, it was generally everyone heading off somewhere after work.

There was a bit of back and forth with Jack, Steve had called him once when they switched restaurants at the last minute. There were a couple of delivery places, a pizzeria and a Chinese place, hopefully he was alright there. The first call he made with the phone was two days after the pool table incident, to his landlady from a café. That could be worse.

Later in January there were a bunch of outgoing calls. It took Blake a minute, but right, those were the market research calls. He had been trying to get competitor pricing information. He had actually been using a fake name, if that helped. Joe didn't think it would hurt, maybe they could even get lucky, wow.

Moving on to Blake's laptop, Joe thought its security software was pretty good. If, certainly, somewhere there would be something connecting to his apartment's IP address. Blake wasn't online all the time, so it would only look like he stopped accessing things like his email or chat programs around the same general time as Joe disappeared.

The bigger worry with emails was if any of the Wildon Textiles people sent emails discussing his disappearance. Fortunately it looked like Wildon Textiles used an internet service provider that was good about protecting privacy. Blake's impression was that everyone generally used their @Wildontextiles addresses for work emails.

Lee eventually went to bed, while Joe continued with the questioning, alternating between pacing the room and writing out page after page of notes. Where was the K-56 parked, what exactly had he told his New York friends about Wildon Textiles, how often he went to the gym, how exactly he would characterize his relationship with Straaval. Joe zeroed in on the guy at the bar with the conspiracy theories, wanted to know exactly what the busker had said, even made him go over where he went for walks on a map of his neighbourhood.

Around three in the morning they started going through the week before Blake left San Diego day by day. It had been a slow week, they had just finished off some big projects, there hadn't been as many people around. Blake had spent a lot of time in his apartment just plowing through European tariff documents.

Once they were done that, they dug up Blake's agenda and had him imagine how the week after he left would have been. There were meetings on Wednesday and Thursday - how would they have gone, who would have been there? Was anybody else going to be at the factory, any big deliveries? Blake thought it would have been a slow week as well, although he had been slated to make that presentation.

There were some unknowns, try as he might Blake couldn't

remember which credit cards he used for which purchases. The larger share of Blake's credit cards were in the names of what he thought were reasonably anonymous holding companies - he didn't like having his name on credit cards, people looked him up, and then things magically appeared on his bill, he started meeting people in the hotel lobby who were looking for investors.

He had been using one that was under his name a bit lately, however. He only used credit cards for big purchases, but there had been a few key purchases in San Diego that were worrying Joe. Specifically the hotel, the car rentals, and the apartment.

They had a panicked realization. That could be a link, a credit card in Blake's name, to the car dealership, to his San Diego phone number. They made a frantic rush out to the K-56 and found the paperwork, it was under the Big M Ventures card, that was a relief. Big M Ventures?

The sun had risen, Lee up and making them coffee, when Joe was finally ready to deliver his verdict. As far as he could tell, Blake *was* pretty off the grid. But there was still a lot of stuff that could connect him to incriminating evidence. And as per their initial worries, his San Diego phone number seemed to be the most important issue.

There were a few different places Joe's people could get that number. And in any scenario where they went to enough effort to find the number, they would probably also look at its movement history.

Anything beyond a superficial investigation would lead them to Wildon Textiles. And Jack would be expected to give them Blake's number, and answer questions honestly. As would Blake's landlady, or the people at the car rental places. They wouldn't necessarily come at them in suits and sunglasses, they could pretend to be an old friend looking for Blake, someone trying to make a delivery, any number of things.

If, however, they hadn't investigated him yet - or hadn't investigated him that deeply - then it was possible that with just a little bit of subterfuge Blake could hide his trail reasonably well. He would never be able to withstand a thorough investigation, there were any number of things that could give it away. A lot of people must have seen the K-56 drive north, for one. They could triangulate call records, or look at all the numbers that hung out around Wildon Textiles. Even just the various water/electricity/internet meters in his apartment.

But the point was just to be able to withstand a small to medium sized investigation. If Blake could do that, they probably wouldn't investigate him again. So Jack Wildon - and to a lesser extent Blake's landlady - would be both key information points and vital strategic objectives.

The first step of the operation would thus be to call them, and try to see if anyone had talked to either of them. If someone had – or if they just seemed weird - then Blake was to abort immediately and come back to the cabin.

If everything was normal, then he would go and see Jack in person, and establish an alternate day of departure. Blake could just ask Jack to lie over the phone - with the technology he would be using, someone would have to bug Jack's physical phone itself to listen to the call. And if they were bugging Jack's phone he was probably made anyways. But there would always be that risk, and some things were just better done in person.

There was, however, a complicating factor here - Blake remembered that Jack was going to be travelling for much of March and April. Blake had it in his agenda, but it didn't specify dates, there was just a line through the second half of March with 'Jack away' written on top. From what Blake could remember, Jack had a couple of meetings in the Midwest, then a big trade show in New York at the end of the month. Blake had been planning on joining him.

That was just as well, as Joe thought it best Blake make the calls from a couple of time zones to the east anyways. Best someplace far from the cabin, and apparently the networks on the west coast were relatively harder to hack. It was easy enough to do anonymous, untraceable phone calls. But they specifically needed an anonymous phone call that didn't look like an anonymous phone call.

If and when he talked to Jack, if everything was clear, Blake would enter into the second phase of the operation. This would involve taking a flight to another city - Joe was thinking maybe LA - and marking up the grid by checking into a hotel, going out in public, and just generally hanging out and being normal.

At that point Blake would have to be ready for anything. They could bring him in for questioning, or they could just watch him from afar, there were a few different scenarios.

If everything seemed clear, then Blake was to subtly disappear, then come back to the cabin. If he *was* interrogated - or if for whatever reason he thought he was made - then it was probably best he go to another location and wait for Lee to contact him. Blake could go work with Wildon Textiles again, or better just go back to his normal life in New York.

None of them could see any gaping holes in the plan, and it really seemed like their best option. There was perhaps a case for them all just to flee the country, Lee did have connections with some people smugglers. Maybe they could fall back on that if someone had talked to Jack.

So without further ado, they began preparations for Blake's trip, which they had now dubbed 'Operation Groundhog', based on a suggestion by Lee. They wasted no time getting ready - Blake had already been off the grid for too long. That was sort of a mistake on their part.

Joe was immediately to work hacking a phone for him. They also figured out some places to meet, should they be unable to communicate. If nothing else outside a specific diner in Minneapolis, the afternoon of April 15th or May 15th.

They did a few practice interrogations, which were pretty grueling. Joe and Lee demanded precise details, there were a lot of what-exactlies and but-didn't-you-says. They were good at it, they caught him in a couple of contradictions, his covering got a little hokey.

Joe also seemed to have an endless set of rules for him to follow. Everything from procedures for checking into hotels to how to react if he met someone named Joe. It got to be a bit much, Blake was having trouble keeping track of it all. He hoped they weren't overestimating him. Eventually he just took the rest of the night off, tried to rest, prepare himself.

He hadn't realized going out into the world would be such a massive undertaking, he wasn't even sure if it was a good idea anymore. Maybe they *should* just flee the country. But he needed to protect his assets, they were just sitting there, a lot of them not even in offshore holding companies.

14

Joe was ready to leave when Blake woke up the next afternoon, suited up with giant backpacks of supplies front and back, as well as a couple of duffle bags. They had decided it was best he just camp out in the woods while Blake was gone. There would always be the risk of Blake leading someone back to the cabin when he returned, and it would allow Blake at least the option of telling all in an interrogation without giving away Joe's location. Joe's people could be pretty persuasive.

Still it felt a little unnecessary to Blake. It would be cold and wet, wouldn't it? But Joe didn't seem to mind at all. He liked living in the woods, it would be a nice change of pace, Lee had given him some books on meditation. He sort of even seemed surprised that Blake was making a big deal out of it.

Then they all wished each other luck, and without further ado Joe was off, shambling with his eight odd bags into the woods. Lee then set to work sterilizing everything Blake would take with him - they didn't want a single strand of Joe's DNA on him. Lee even had a whole new set of plastic wrapped clothes for him to change into.

They left the cabin in the late afternoon sun. Lee would drop him off a couple hours south, outside a town where Lee happened to have a car stashed away. Blake would then be able to drive through the night, being in a nocturnal sleep schedule from doing watches. Lee in turn would go run some errands, like getting the car rental places to delete Blake's phone number.

Lee gave him a map with a route marked off to study as they drove, as well as a folder with fairly detailed profiles of a couple men. One was an industrial welder, the other a backwoods tour organizer. They could provide Blake an alibi if needed - he had been staying on a ranch outside Austin, Texas, if he had to commit to a specific place. Likewise Austin would probably be the best place for him to first appear.

They arrived at the sprawling apartment complex where the car was parked a little after sunset. With a wish-me-luck Blake got out of the car and into the new one, a non-descript grey sedan. He put on a hat and some glasses Lee had given him, then looked at his reflection in the rear-view mirror. Between that and the beard he really didn't look anything like himself.

Adjusting the mirrors he pulled out of the parking lot, turned left after the diner Lee had mentioned, and took the second right. Then he was on country road. Two lanes stretching south through what must have been fields, little lights of farmhouses in the distance.

There was agriculture all along California's central valley, laid out in a vast checkerboard of perpendicular roads. Blake was to stay on these most of the way to LA - they didn't get a lot of traffic, and weren't really monitored. On the highways there would always be the risk of his car being photographed. Which wasn't terrible, but was better avoided, especially to start.

He sped up on the empty road, feeling a little adrenaline rush. He was out there, in the world, the game was on already. He had to be ready for anything, he could just stumble across a roadblock or witness an accident or something, and get taken in because he was on a watch list.

They had gone over how he should talk to the police, and had a basic plan of action worked out. He would need to stay in character, in any sorts of interrogations that might happen in the coming days. Blake Myntbanke, rogue investor and all that. He should try to be as relaxed as possible, talkative enough, maybe even a little flippant. Being chatty wasn't always the best strategy in legal situations, but this wasn't about the law, it was about convincing anyone who might be listening that he knew nothing about Joe.

Lee had suggested a strategy of delaying cooperatively at first. Give them a few vague details that didn't commit him to any particular story, get confused over the exact dates, if they wanted exact dates. Blake could spend a lot of time digging around for a phone number or something. Then if they kept questioning him, he could get offended, like they were wasting his time. Draw them out on stuff that didn't matter, then clam up when it did. If they said something that could be misread as more offensive than it was, misread it, that sort of thing.

The police probably wouldn't know anything about Joe, so they might interrogate him about something else. Joe's people could get access to some police files. Or he might get passed around, Joe didn't know what exactly to expect.

If Blake thought he was talking with someone who did know about Joe, he could also sort of have a realization, wonder if it was about the guy in the hotel that night in San Diego. That was a risky strategy, and was probably best avoided. But it could be effective, even get them to scare. Blake was a rich guy with friends in the media.

Lee had also sprinkled a very small amount of cocaine in the trunk, having had some left over from a deal he did a few years ago. It was only a trace amount, but if they did a proper detailing of the car it would be enough to show up on the tests. If they caught Blake in a lie, or he felt like he seemed suspicious, he could also fall back on a story of him having done some kind of a delivery.

Any story like that would be risky, of course, and would probably be better left implied than admitted to. But it would give him a pretty solid excuse not to talk, while explaining any number of inconsistencies with his story. It was a realistic enough scenario, maybe a bunch of retired old dealers had some product land in their lap, nobody wanted to do it, Blake finally stepped up.

Blake didn't think he would get pulled over though. They had a pretty solid route picked out for him, and how often did you get stopped, just driving down country roads? One way or another it would be a long drive. He didn't mind in the slightest though, not at the moment at least. It felt good to be behind the wheel, out in the world, making progress. He hooked up his MP3 player and put on one of his favorite playlists, mostly classic rock, but a bit of folk, some early music as well.

It immediately started with a classic 60s-70s driving song. It was on random, that was sort of good luck, was it? If he had actually put a lot of songs about driving and the road on the playlist as a lark, it had been his main driving playlist back in San Diego.

His long drives in the K-56 felt a world away now. He went just a little over the speed limit, south for a while, then east for a bit, back south again. There were hardly any cars, and as it got later the traffic got even lighter. When there was someone he almost made a little game of it, staying ahead of them, or staying behind them. He lost if anyone ever got close enough to see his license plate.

He hoped it was all worth it, whatever exactly it was they were trying to achieve with all this. Were they going to keep on with baseball, then? They had been spending a lot of time training. Lee wasn't out and saying it anymore, but Blake had the impression he would still rather Joe go public with his story.

Blake supposed they shouldn't rule that out, either. He had never really paid the idea much thought, Joe had always been so staunchly against it. But he could sort of see Joe eventually getting behind something like that.

Blake felt a rush of nervous exhilaration. That would really be something, to be the guys who blew the whistle on a supersoldier program? It would be front page news, to say the least. They'd make some enemies, doing something like that, but also some friends.

There would be money in that, as well, if nothing on the scale of baseball. And they would probably have a pretty high security bill, for one. Sometimes you made a lot, but you spent a lot too. But there would be bestselling tell-all biographies to write, they'd be able to do the talk show circuit, endorse political candidates, there would probably be a few things, actually.

If he was probably seeing the money angle too much with all this. Just in general, in life. He was always thinking about money, investing it, who had it, even just how much things cost. He had actually been meaning to not do that as much, it was sort of a thing for him.

Although maybe he had it backwards, given the facts of his present circumstances. He felt another pang of anxiety, this time resonating deep in his bones, and he sped up a bit on the road. The sooner he talked to his financial people, the better. He needed to get moving with his assets.

Would they really hit his assets? He had never known anyone to get their assets frozen. Well, a couple of people in the drug business, they had gotten their assets seized, actually. But that was all proceeds of crime stuff. There was a big legal distinction between that and stuff that was legally acquired.

But it did happen, didn't it? He swallowed. Like not very often, just in those rarest of cases. All the other rich people tended to get pretty huffy. But this could well be one of those cases. Those men who came and visited him back in the hotel in San Diego had seemed like rather serious types, and they had been talking felony.

Although that had been for revealing what he saw, and he'd

kept silent. Technically they had no complaint there. That was actually a strength, legally speaking, was it? They had specified all the things he was and was not to do in regard to the fellow with the pool table, and getting him into pro ball wasn't on the list.

Although Joe was a fugitive, on the news and everything. Blake supposed that sort of negated that. Maybe he could say they were on some sort of retreat in the cabin, getting away from civilization all together, they hadn't turned the TV on once. Lee had banned it as a tool of capitalist brainwashing or some such. They couldn't tell if you had been watching TV, could they? Certainly, that was a hokey story, but all his legal team would need would be something that was at least hypothetically true.

Although really, he didn't know how well legal teams did, in general, situations like this. Maybe they could just threaten to go public. By some measures the criminals were the ones faking armoured van robberies. Assuming they didn't just get disappeared, of course.

Blake felt a panic welling up again, he was having a little trouble breathing. Between having his assets on the line and the risk of getting shot the stakes were pretty high with all this.

Really, there were lines they had yet to cross, maybe they weren't that far gone yet. Blake could have a proper conversation with whoever was running whatever supersoldier organization, tell them he had been on their side all along. Maybe he just thought Joe needed to get something out of his system. He wasn't going to betray him by turning him in, it was something Joe needed to figure out on his own. Blake was just handling a sensitive and complicated situation the way he thought best.

That they had been training for baseball actually worked pretty well, in that context. Like, what, did they think that *he* thought Joe was actually going to play baseball? Blake felt a twinge of bewildered disappointment at that, it worked a little too well.

It was all a little heavy, he could mull it over later. He was getting to the end of the country side roads, he was going to need to get gas. There was soon a sign for the highway ahead, he merged onto the southbound highway that cut through the mountains towards LA. Looking at his watch it was just a little past midnight, he supposed he was making good time.

There was a bit of traffic, some big trucks, but generally the road was pretty empty. It took a little while to pass through the mountains, his gas gauge moving ominously towards the 'E' mark. He was almost even getting worried about it, but then the one specific gas station chain Lee had told him to use appeared on the right.

He took a full service pump, told the guy to fill up the tank. Blake couldn't see any cameras, and it didn't seem like the guy would have gotten a good look at his face, not that he even looked like himself. He paid in cash, telling the guy to keep the change, then took off again onto the road, easy as that.

Blake wondered then, as he cut through the dark desert night, what was the *right* thing to do, with all this? That was another important question to ask, with any new venture. In many ways they had an enormous responsibility thrust into their hands. Lee seemed to think they had a moral obligation to go public, although you could probably argue just as well they had an obligation to keep it all secret.

Certainly, Blake would rather the general public know about projects like Joe. There were a lot of implications, they could be debating it on the pundit shows. But he wouldn't want the technology falling into the wrong hands either. There were any number of groups out there he wouldn't want making an army of Joes.

Maybe the question was less who had them, as long as it wasn't one band of people with supersoldiers running things. Could a decentralization of power like that create chaos? He supposed in the end he just didn't have the answers, he didn't even really know what was going on.

Maybe only the people with all the security briefings could ever really decide if information like that should be made public. The heads of spy agencies, presidents and prime ministers, all them. But then, did you just have to trust those people? What if they were in the wrong, or working towards less-than-honest ends? That happened often enough, if you read a little history.

And that was assuming those people were themselves equipped to make those decisions. He didn't even know what *they* knew. Maybe no one had all the answers, could have all the answers, maybe it was fundamentally unknowable. That was the nature of reality, some problems just didn't have good solutions.

But where did that leave him then? Maybe it worked out to a moral coin toss. Given the information they had, it was equally likely that their actions would cause good as they would cause harm. He supposed Joe knew the most out of the three of them, so maybe the decisions were best left to him. But whatever happened, it was on all three of them, there was no denying that.

It all made him slightly sick to his stomach. Morality had been easier, in other times, hadn't it? When doing right had been about making sacrifices when the time came, being brave in the face of danger, telling the truth when it wasn't in your interests, not going about raping and pillaging.

This day and age, it felt like a logical puzzle sometimes. You wanted to do right, you had to ponder every angle, meticulously take apart every detail, consider all the unintended consequences.

Or maybe it was all simple, maybe he had been reading too much industry PR propaganda. Maybe you just sort of knew, based on the sum of your life's experience. You could figure out quite a bit over a few days of intense soul searching. Although he didn't know what to do, here and now, so it had to be reasonably complex, didn't it?

Maybe he was a brain in a vat, come to life in a simulation three months ago, with infinite financial resources and access to Joe. Part of some bizarre trial at the end of the universe. Maybe he had been a steroids scientist responsible for a vital leak that turned out to be the root cause of World War Three.

Or maybe he was the guy who could have adverted the supersoldier take over, for that matter. It didn't really seem like something he could second-guess. Maybe it was a driving simulation of twenty random people's nights, that was entertainment 300 years in the future. Would a simulation even let him have these thoughts? None of this felt real, that much was certain.

He hoped he had done right so far, right enough, at least. Maybe morality under uncertain conditions was just having your heart in the right place. If you were operating under the right principles, you would just make the right decisions when the time came to make them.

The potential for financial gain was at least colouring his decision making with all this, he couldn't deny that. Although if he thought Joe was a more solid investment than Wildon Textiles, his sin was probably foolishness over greed.

At this he felt a little twinge of disappointment. He hadn't really been thinking about Wildon Textiles that much, but really there was no way he was going to be investing in them now. Straaval had been worried about his reputation as was, he didn't want to draw them into any unsavory business. Well, at least not any more than he had to.

Doing a defensive re-arrangement of his portfolio, it wouldn't make sense to invest in Wildon Textiles anyways. As a legitimate America-based business they wouldn't be secure, and he wasn't going to talk to Jack about setting things up in an offshore trust. They needed to keep things with Wildon Textiles squeaky clean.

Just the process of moving his money around in general was dangerous, it made noise. He really didn't want to get audited right now, and whatever they were doing with Joe was probably going to take some spending. Not that he would even want to risk two big ventures at the same time. What if they both went sour?

As it stood, he was down at least 10-20% over the past decade, maybe even more. It was hard to even calculate, with inflation, estimating true valuation, just counting everything up. But he had originally planned to have at least doubled his fortune by this point in his life.

And actually, he would be down a lot farther, but he had all that stock in that clothing company. They had been paying dividends like crazy while their stock prices went through the roof. But the last couple years there had been more and more stories in the news, more of the same accusations of unfair labour practices and environmental damages. There had been that fellow who sort of looked like him at the big sit-in protest.

At some point you just had to stop believing the VP of PR's stories about misguided social justice warriors that were probably being paid by the competition. And Blake was their single biggest shareholder now, with that pension fund having dropped them. If you did the maths, environmental laxity and 3rd world union-busting did lead to lower prices. And their low prices were clearly enough the reason why the company was doing so well.

That had been one of the reasons why he had gotten involved with Wildon Textiles. They seemed to be doing well enough without pumping chemicals into endangered wetlands. He supposed he could just sell his shares in the clothing company, as part of this defensive rearrangement of his portfolio he was embarking on. Although they were in a pretty solid holding company, and they weren't legally based in America anymore. Not to mention their stock was probably a little undervalued right now.

Blake felt a brief frustration, at that. It was one of those great ironies in life, the more money you had, the poorer you felt, sometimes. Even if his fortune was just a little bit bigger, it would give him the confidence to make those cuts. Or to take on the big risky projects he dreamed of.

There was an idea he had kept coming back to over the past decade. One of his greatest successes was the grocery store co-operative. It was still going, had just opened another couple locations, actually, and was still 100% customer owned. What if he could do that with a big proper company?

He was thinking automotive manufacturing, but any number of industries would do. He would start out owning everything - like your standard enterprise - then gradually sell off the shares to the cooperative's members, the customers who were buying the cars. He could even set it up so he made a profit, that wouldn't be so bad for his efforts.

Originally he had been thinking of transforming it into a worker owned co-operative. But that would still have all the various counter-productive incentives of the profit motive, like planned obsolescence and all that. What he was thinking now was a consumer owned co-operative, like the grocery store. Just basically a non-profit company that for all intents and purposes owned itself.

He thought he could make it work with a sort of subscription model. People would pay an annual fee - which would basically make them an equal owner in the corporation, with a vote for the board of directors - and for that they would receive an extendable lease on a car.

One way or another the fundamentals were all there. If a company was taking in enough money from its customers to be profitable, then those customers intrinsically had the capital to own the company. It was just that the money was spread out between tens of thousands of customers, and it would need a lot of capital to get it going in the first place. Really, a non-profit consumer owned co-operative should be more competitive, as it wouldn't have to pay out profits to the owners.

But it would be a huge up-front investment to start. Then there were product failures, cost overruns, unseen delays. Who knew if someone would attack it just on principle. And he would be on the hook for it - if it succeeded it would benefit society as a whole, but if it failed the losses would all be his.

That was a noble enough use of a fortune, though, wasn't it?

And really, whatever they were doing, here, now, with Joe, it wouldn't be about the money. At root it would have to be some great cosmic prank, some profound piece of socio-political theatre. Whatever they ended up doing, he should consider himself lucky to break even.

If it did always make for a better story if you made off with a big haul. Then you were the romantic rogues. Otherwise you were liable just to look like misguided fools meddling in places they didn't belong. He was risking everything from an asset freeze to getting shot. He could be justified in expecting at least the potential for some sort of financial returns, couldn't he?

Something on the road caught his eye, down across from the overpass he was going over. It was a mall complex, with a couple of glowing neon signs, the empty parking lot dimly lit by sporadic street lamps.

Was that the mall they stopped at, him and Joe, to buy the phone to call Lee? It looked familiar, the big doors at the entrance, those trees along the one side. He must be passing over the road they had taken north.

There was something profound in that, it felt auspicious. Full circle. Or perhaps a home run, even. If he didn't exactly feel like he was safe at home. Was it too superstitious to read it as some kind of small gesture from the universe? He supposed he was inevitably going to cross his trail somewhere, he might have even already. But to pass that mall like that?

It was a nice idea, at least, he could allow himself that little superstition. He turned his attention to the road, the turn off for the side highway he was to take east through the desert would be coming up soon.

His playlist was now belting out a slightly abrasive live version of some old 70s-80s rock anthem, which felt like a bit much, their new vocalist was a little screechy for this time of night. It had played once already anyways, he had been behind the wheel long enough to make it through the whole playlist, then.

Turning the stereo off, the night around him was still, peaceful. There wasn't another car on the road. He was soon reaching the turn off to the desert highway, which was hardly a highway at all. There wasn't even a stop sign at the turn off, and the paving was pretty rough. Some of the side roads he had been on were bigger.

Blake didn't even know what the speed limit was, there was

no sign, but he sped up a bit. It seemed like the last place a cop would pull him over at four in the morning. Although then he slowed down again, it was a pretty isolated place. What if he did get a speeding ticket, and his name was flagged? He'd rather there be some traffic around, actually.

He continued on, the desert empty and black around him, little shrubs lit up by his headlights. As it began getting closer to dawn he started looking for a place to stop. Joe had wanted him parked somewhere before first light, as a minor precaution against satellite tracking - they wouldn't know which way he had been going.

A little further down the road there was a sign for a rest area, so he pulled in. He walked a few laps around the shrubby desert - stretching his legs was bordering on ecstatic - then sat down on the top of the picnic table to wait for the sunrise.

His mind was going a mile a minute, but he tried to slow it down, empty his head. Usually he had trouble with that, but he managed really well for a little while. Watching the sun slowly come up over the desert, he felt connected, awake, all oranges and reds and purples behind the clouds, revealing the scrub desert terrain around him.

A few short hours from now he could be in a little room, an agreeable and a not-so-agreeable cop grilling him on every detail of his past month. That was something pretty intense, actually, but he felt no fear. He almost wished they could interrogate him now, he didn't know how he would feel later.

More than anything, at that exact moment he just wanted to know what was waiting for him out there. For a moment he tried to analyze everything they had been over with Joe, like he could somehow logic it out here and now.

But reality, the future, it was unknowable. Joe's people had whatever evidence they had, they either suspected him or they didn't. From where he stood it was probabilistic, random, a roll of the dice. He had to act under the assumption that all scenarios that could be true were true, and take actions that worked under all of them.

This was the real world, without stunt doubles, where the good guys didn't automatically win, strangers you met on the street weren't plot devices to help move the scene along, and everything didn't just wrap up nicely at the end of 90 minutes, 120 with commercials. No, it was a random clusterfuck that came at you 24/7 from every direction, and you just had to keep hanging on for dear life and hope you didn't get sideswiped by anything.

He was in control of his own destiny, that was something you could forget sometimes. His actions would mean the difference between success and failure. And have who-knows-what implications for the whole rest of the world.

Hopefully everything would become clearer as time went on. Maybe they were on the right path with all this, maybe they weren't. They didn't have to play baseball, or go public with Joe's story. Or not do those things, either, for that matter.

If he was so worried about that clothing company, then he should just sell the shares. He got these weird psychological hang-ups sometimes, like he had some kind of bizarre subconscious aversion to doing that. He didn't know why, it was the easiest thing in the world to do. What difference would it really make? Moving his money somewhere else meant at worst maybe 5-10% lower returns on a small part of his holdings. A percentage of a percentage.

He felt a relief, at that. If also a strange sort of nagging doubt, he couldn't identify exactly where it was coming from. But why even bother listening to their excuses. He had enough going on, he would just unload the shares and be done with them. Staring out at the stark desert stretching around him, he suddenly had a very strong sensation that if he found the right path he could find his way with all of this.

15

The sun was well above the horizon when Blake took off from the rest area. He continued east along the desert highway, now feeling a little tired, a strange inexplicable déjà vu lingering in the back of his mind. It was around when he would have gone to bed back in the cabin, but the sunrise seemed to have given him energy.

Around noon he stopped at a gas station outside Phoenix. From there he was passing desert mountains, little towns that stretched alongside the highway, a palm lined oasis. Lee had given him an address where there would be a motorbike for his return to the cabin, so he went over that a few more times, made sure it was burned into his memory. He also spent some time going over all his various investments in his head, trying to catalog them by their level of susceptibility. He would have to start slowly with the re-arrangement of his portfolio, it might even be better to avoid selling the most obvious stuff first.

Mid-afternoon he napped for a few hours, hidden away in a rest area in New Mexico. It was dark when he left - he had been out for longer than he intended - so he drove fast. Joe said he needed to make the calls at night - something to do with the load on the networks - and he didn't want to call Jack too late. The idea was to have a long conversation, really get a read on him, which probably wouldn't happen if he woke him up at 1 in the morning.

Later into the evening he stopped at another gas station and filled up. As he approached the Texan border he turned on the phone Joe had given him. A no internet symbol appeared on the top, which meant that he still wasn't in range to make the calls.

He crossed the border a little before midnight Texas time, which was two hours ahead of San Diego. Nothing was happening with the internet symbol on his phone, so he sped up even faster. After another half hour or so of driving the network symbol started flickering back and forth. Finally, a little before one in the morning, the internet symbol came on, and stayed on.

Blake kept going a little bit further, then pulled into an empty rest area. Walking out into the desert, he found a rock to sit on. He felt an urge to procrastinate - there was at least the possibility that their phones would be bugged, and anything he said now could come up later if they were ever questioned. But he just put the phone on to record, took a deep breath, then dialed his landlady's number.

She answered after a couple of rings, and he introduced himself, Blake in apartment 801, sorry for calling so late. Could she hear him? The reception was a little bad, but it worked, and her voice didn't sound like she had been sleeping.

It took her a moment to remember who he was, but then she sounded happy to hear from him. He hadn't been around, had he? Blake said no, he left, well, about a month ago, the middle of February, actually. There was no need to give an exact date, the 7th was just never mid-month.

He confirmed that he had paid for February, but said he owed her for March, apologized for getting behind. It had been crazy, she wouldn't believe. She said that was alright, she had called him. Blake made a mental note of that, it was a link to his San Diego number in the call records.

He said he would get the money to her right away, and she asked if he wanted to keep the place. That was one of the reasons why he was calling, actually, he didn't think he would. Could he send some people in to pick up his stuff? He wasn't sure if he would have time himself. She thought that would be alright, she gave him another number to call.

He tried to keep the conversation going. It felt a little awkward making conversation that late in the night, but she seemed happy enough to talk. Apparently he had been missing out on some record-breakingly sunny days. She said the reception was bad – which it was – but he said it was perfect on his end.

Then just when they were saying goodbye, Blake remembered something, oh, hey, had anyone been in to see him? He had an associate that was going to drop off a package. She paused, thought for a moment, she wasn't sure. She said she could check, and put him on hold. He stared at his watch as he waited, it was 11:15 in San Diego already.

She came back on the line, there wasn't anything for him.

Although thinking about it now, a couple of men had been in to see him. Blake's stomach dropped. He asked who it was, trying to sound normal, nonchalant, the bare minimum of curiosity in his voice.

She didn't know, it had been a couple of weeks ago, and she hadn't been there. She thought they had a package with them, but they didn't leave anything. She could call her nephew tomorrow, he had been there when they stopped by, they might have left a number.

Blake's mind raced, what did he say? It could have been Jack. Should he ask for the number? Anything like that made noise, Joe had been saying it was best not to draw attention to himself. Could be strange to get the number and then not call it, as well.

The pause in the conversation had stretched on too long, it was almost an uncomfortable silence. He said no, that was alright, he knew who it was. Then Blake remembered one last thing, he had a new phone number. Could she change it in her phone now? The old one was lost, gone, he wouldn't be using it anymore, she should delete it. Ok, that was good, she yawned, she would change it now.

He gave her a New York number Lee had gotten for him. Hopefully she would just immediately put it into her phone, replacing and thus erasing the San Diego number. Then he said he'd let her go, he or his people would be there in the next couple of days to clean his stuff out of the apartment.

Blake had a sick feeling when he hung up the phone. Someone had been by the apartment. Could it have been Jack? They had sort of figured out that nobody at Wildon Textiles had his address. Although he doubted the Men in Black types would have come bearing gifts. Either way the next step was to talk to Jack, he could just ask him directly.

Blake paced a couple laps around the desert plain, taking another couple deep breaths. Then he dialed Jack's number. The phone rang a few times, then there was a click, and an alert enough Jack answering with a bemused 'Hello?'

"Jack, is that you? It's Blake!"

"Blake? Well, I'll be." Jack's tone was warm. "You're still alive then?"

"Yes, more or less. Sorry about," Blake paused for a second, unsure of what exact wording he wanted to use, "about not getting in touch sooner. I imagine you must have been wondering about me."

Jack laughed. "A little, you really disappeared back there.

Blake gave a little blowing-offish laugh. "Ha, yes, I suppose I did, a little." He laughed again, and inserted a humorous note in his tone. "I hope you didn't file a missing persons report or anything."

Jack laughed as well. "No, no," he said, although with a nervousness that suggested it might have crossed his mind.

"Where.." started Jack, although Blake interrupted him.

"Are you in San Diego right now?"

"Well, yes, right now. I've got a flight to Japan first thing tomorrow morning though."

"Japan, really, wow!" said Blake, a little confused, he hadn't remembered anything about a trip to Japan. "I thought you had meetings in the Midwest in March."

"That was originally the plan, but we've got a potential customer in Tokyo, they really like our reinforced cotton blends. It could actually be a pretty big sale. I'm also going to visit a couple textile mills in China, I might even make it to Thailand for a day."

"I was thinking of coming to San Diego in the next few days, are you going to be there long?"

"Well, I've got a lot of meetings in Europe right after the ones in Asia. I was going to go to a trade show in Chicago, but I don't think I'll make it." Jack's tone was turning negative, apologetic. "I might just go straight to Europe, there's a couple more meetings there now. I might not be back until mid-April."

Then Jack gave a little laugh. "Who knows, maybe I'll even get some sightseeing in. Where are you these days?"

"Well, out in the middle of nowhere right now. But I'm on my way to LA, eventually." Blake's mind raced. "It would be nice to see you, if you do come back to the states. The trade show in Chicago sounds interesting."

"Steve is going to the trade show by himself, I'm sure he could use a wingman. He's driving me to the airport tomorrow morning, I can ask him about it if you want." Jack paused a moment, then continued before Blake had a chance to speak. "Hey, a factory in Thailand is looking at buying some threads. I think that was your idea."

"Really?" asked Blake, slightly impressed with himself. "Which threads are they looking at?"

Jack started off about the Thai company, they made duffle bags, they needed something to reinforce where the handle connected to the bag. As he talked Blake tried to figure out what his next move was. He needed to get out there now, but he needed to talk to Jack first. Joe had been saying the very act of him appearing on the grid could trigger an investigation in and of itself.

Jack had said he had a flight tomorrow morning, Blake didn't want to ask what time it was. That was a good way to end the conversation, it could be five in the morning. Either way too early for him to make it there in time. Mid-April was too long, but seeing him in a few days wasn't so bad. It sounded like there was at least the possibility he might come back earlier.

Jack was now asking him how he had been. Blake forced himself to focus on the conversation. He said he had been good, it had been crazy, he had been a little off the grid, lost his phone actually, was out in the country the last while. Blake tried to affect a bit of a foppish air, like he didn't even realize there was anything strange in him disappearing like that. Like maybe he had been off on a beach with a girl or something, and just forgot to get in touch.

Then Jack gave a yawn. "Well, I think I'm going to have to let you go in a minute. I've got a long day tomorrow, with the time change I get in just in time for an afternoon meeting. I've still got a bit of packing left to do, although my suitcase is full of fabric samples. I'm going to have to buy clothes there."

"Sounds like an adventure. Well, if you *were* going to be in town after Asia, when would it be? It would be great to see you. I'll probably just be hanging out in LA, so it would be really easy for me to pop down."

"Well, I've got the meetings.." Jack paused distractedly, he must have been going through his agenda. "Not this week, maybe early next week?"

"That would actually be really good timing," said Blake, sounding slightly surprised at how well that worked with his busy schedule. Although his stomach dropped, that was another week away. He should have been out in the world a couple of weeks ago.

Jack paused again, then his tone went hesitantly positive. "I have been meaning to go to LA. There is a customer there you could help me out with, a hotel chain, if you wanted to come to a meeting." His tone fell again. "But it's going to be really hectic as is. Realistically I probably won't be back for a few weeks."

There was nothing to it, Blake would have to talk to him

now. What was his move then? Joe had said that he could talk to him over the phone if he had to, and Jack didn't sound like he had been questioned by men in suits and sunglasses.

Blake needed to keep him on the line though, Jack was saying something about finishing packing. Blake remembered a story Jack had told a couple of times, something to do with having to lie to a customer for their own good, he couldn't remember exactly. But that seemed like a good place to start, it was sort of a half message in and of itself. So Blake asked him about the story, he had mentioned it to a friend, but couldn't get it right.

Jack seemed slightly puzzled at the request, but dutifully obliged. It was about a client that had their heart set on one fabric for lining their shoes. Jack had known it was the wrong material, had to sort of trick them into buying what they needed.

What were Blake's objectives, then? Changing the day he left, and erasing his San Diego phone number from Wildon Textiles. There was other housekeeping, as well. "Mmm, hey, did you guys stop by my apartment in San Diego?" Blake asked, interjecting into Jack's story.

"No, I don't think anyone here did."

Blake felt his anxieties rise a notch, he tried not to let it affect his voice. "Hmm, someone stopped by, I'm not sure who it was." He paused a second. "Do you guys even have my address there?"

"I don't think we do, actually. I have your New York address."

"And nobody was in to see me? There was a package, I gave them your address as a back up."

"No, nobody."

Blake scrutinized his tone, it was normal, was it? "Well, that was probably who stopped by the apartment then. Not sure why they didn't just drop it off." Blake paused. "Anyways, I'd give you that address, but I'm moving out of that place. I've also got a new number, if you want to put it into your phone."

"It's this number that's calling?"

"No, it's another one." Blake read off the number that Lee had given him, then gave a little laugh. "Anyways, forget that old number ever existed. I'm never going to use it again," he said in a sort of humorous, exaggerated tone, which he hoped suggested an inside joke, some great ironic tale about why he could never use that number again, perhaps to be told at a later date.

"And tell Steve, when you see him tomorrow, to delete my

old number and put the new one in. He can tell everybody else at Wildon Textiles to do the same," said Blake, speaking slowly and deliberately, now.

"Ok, I'll tell him," said Jack tiredly, an air of finality in his voice.

"Oh, right, and there was one more thing. There was a meeting I missed, in the morning, the day before I left San Diego. I can't remember the name of the company." Blake tried to think, how would he approach this. "It was with the furniture people, they use that nylon blend on the inside of their couches. I remember the last time I talked to them, the one guy had a bunch of recommendations for hiking trails."

"Ya, that's Jones Upholstery. They're all big hikers." Jack sounded slightly puzzled. "I don't think you were there that day though."

"No, I was there. I just didn't get to the factory until five minutes after they left, then I didn't stay very long," Blake said, again speaking slowly and deliberately. "You said I must have passed them on the road. That meeting was the 9th, right? It was really rainy, that day."

Jack paused a moment, he must have been looking at his agenda again. "Ya, it says that was the 9th." He sounded pretty confused. "I can give you their number."

"No, that's alright, I just needed to know who they were, I can look it up. And sorry again about cancelling that lunch, a few days before that." That was everything, was it? "Anyways, I should let you go, you've got an early flight tomorrow. Give Steve my number, he can get everyone to change it!"

"Ok, will do," said Jack, sounding slightly relieved. "I'll get in touch when I know exactly when I'll be back in America."

"Sounds good. Just leave a message on that voicemail I gave you." There was one more thing. "Oh, right, and if you email me, use the one with the 555, I check that one the most these days." Then Blake wished him luck at his meetings, and quickly hung up.

16

Blake just stared at his phone after making the call. It had all gone well enough, had it? He had sort of been improvising. He imagined Jack would be pretty confused by the conversation. But hopefully he would be able to piece things together pretty quickly if men in suits and sunglasses came asking about Blake's whereabouts last February.

Blake felt a chill though. They hadn't been to the apartment. There weren't really a lot of other people it could have been. That was about the level of investigation Joe had said to expect. Maybe he was just a low-level person of interest, they stopped by, he wasn't around, and they decided to check back later. Maybe they *were* waiting for him to appear on the grid. He felt a wave of anxiety. Joe had thought it was really better if they didn't know about the apartment.

A car drove by the rest stop, Blake jumping at the sound. He had been there making calls for quite a while, it was time to move. Was it mission accomplished, then? The next step after talking to Jack was to make his first appearance, in Austin. It felt a little sketchy, not knowing who stopped by, and relying on Jack being able to read between the lines. But he should have been out there already, he wanted to get it over with. He needed to protect his assets.

With another glance at the road he began composing a text message to Lee, trying to remember their code. Any communications between them carried a degree of risk, but Joe thought it was greatly reduced if he kept it under a minimum number of characters.

'Deal solid on phone. Land thing a maybe, but good. Now Tex for AM.' This communicated that he had successfully talked to Jack on the phone, that there was evidence the apartment may have been investigated, but Lee could go ahead and get someone to clear his stuff out, and that Blake was now headed for Austin.

Pulling out of the rest area, Blake started going over his backstory. He had been on a retreat, a ranch off in the middle of nowhere. The sort of place city people went to get away from it all and play cowboy for a couple of weeks. Rustling cows and riding horses and eating steak by a fire and whatever else cowboys did.

The logic behind Austin was that it was a place where they wouldn't have been looking for him - if they were looking for him - while still being the sort of place he would be expected to just randomly pop up. And just basic psychology, if someone like him was nervous, playing innocent, they would go to a city they were more familiar with. Not the capital of Texas.

Although that was complicated slightly in that if he *was* working with Joe, he could be expected to do the opposite of whatever it was he would be expected to do. But even then Joe had thought it worked pretty well. And best it was something similar to the cabin - sometimes if you had been hanging out in a cabin for a month, you would just *seem* like you had been hanging out in a cabin for a month.

Blake put on the recordings of the calls. Jack sounded pretty normal, if Blake thought he himself sounded a little weird in a couple of places. If nothing else, Jack would have at least found some subtle way of tipping him off, if he had been talked to, wouldn't he have?

Listening to the conversation with his landlady, he rewound the part about the men who were in to see him several times. He couldn't really get much new information out of it. Although he wondered if she could have got him mixed up with someone else who had a package delivered.

He had asked *her* if anyone had delivered a package for him. That had been a mistake, he introduced the package, he might have put the idea in her head. She hadn't been sure, had she? It was a realistic scenario, her nephew had said someone was by with a package for someone else, but she associated it with him because he was calling and asking about packages.

Blake wondered if maybe he shouldn't have gotten her to get the phone number of whoever stopped by. He almost wanted to call her back, but that was the sort of thing paranoid people who were harbouring fugitive supersoldiers did. At least her nephew probably hadn't had his phone number.

Once he felt he had gotten everything he could out of listening to the calls he deleted them, as per Joe's instructions.

Then he put music on again and sped up, the empty roads were flat and straight.

It was another few hours of driving through the empty night and he was approaching Austin. He took an exit from the highway and was soon driving through what must have been the far edge of town, some bars, live music, hip looking shops. They had been getting nice weather here, fairly warm, a few light rains.

After making a wrong turn and circling back, he arrived at his hotel chain's spacious covered parking lot, the first rays of light just breaking on the horizon. He briefly wiped down the car for fingerprints, and put a parking pass Lee had given him on the dashboard. Then he grabbed his backpack, and made a dash for a little park beside the hotel.

Blake felt better with every step he took away from the car. It was really best he wasn't associated with it, there could be traffic camera photos of it driving anywhere along the way. Aside from the keys in his pocket there wasn't anything connecting him to it now. Any point from now on he could get the make, model, and plates wrong. It was a borrowed car. And if he ended up going with the drug muling story, the deal could already be done.

He just walked a while, down semi-residential streets, stuffing his hat and glasses in a garbage can along the way. It seemed better he not call a cab, so he just took turns at random, the sky now changing colour behind the trees. He felt a bit like an itinerant worker, newly arrived in town ready to look for a construction job or some such.

Turning onto a bigger street, he saw a bus stop further down the road. A bus would work. There was a black guy with a skateboard and a studious looking Asian girl waiting at the stop.

"Do I get the bus downtown here?" he asked.

"Ya, you want the 20 to Congress," said the black guy. Blake thanked them, then took a space by the bus stop and waited. A 20 soon appeared, and he hopped on.

Blake had a dazed sort of energy riding the bus. It was strange, surreal, being in public again. There were people from all walks of life, talking, listening to music on headphones, reading books. All going about their lives, off to whatever they had to do today, not knowing a thing about Joe or supersoldier programs.

He tried to relax, get in character. He was back in civilization after an extended stay at a ranch. It had been a good time, he had learned a lot about himself, picked up some new skills, made lasting friendships. Or maybe not so much lasting friendships, Lee's people were only to be used in case of emergency. He wondered if he would ever see any of his fellow ranch hands again.

After about half an hour the bus stopped in what looked like downtown. Maybe half the bus was getting off, so he joined them, with an enthusiastic 'thank you' to the driver.

Still in a daze he walked down the street. The city was just waking up, shops opening their doors, joggers going by, a white guy with dreads in a suit talking on a cell phone. Blake got off the main street, went down a side street.

There was a thrift shop across the way. He did need to buy extra clothes, actually, and he could ask for directions to a café. The store was empty, must just have opened, the cashier girl smiling at him when he went in. He wandered down the aisles, grabbed a nice enough shirt that looked like it would fit.

On the way to the cashier he passed a section with cowboy boots. There was this one pair, brown leather with etchings of some hills with cattle grazing pastorally in the background. Bands of bright multicoloured Mexican-style weavings stretched up and around them, it must have been rhinestones along the sides.

They seemed like the sort of thing he would have acquired during a stay at a ranch, so he grabbed them, they were only a couple of bucks. The cashier complimented him on his choice as he paid, and he asked her if there was a big coffee shop nearby. Apparently there was, just around the corner, in fact.

Blake hid his purchases away in his backpack, then went to the café. It was a sprawling bohemian sort of place, strange happy energetic music blaring out, pop culture murals and bizarre abstract art covering the walls. There were plenty of bearded men at the other tables, Blake felt like he blended in nicely. He grabbed a newspaper from a table, then found a booth hidden away at the back, asking for the Wi-Fi password and getting a tea for now.

Turning on his laptop, he set up the webcam, put on headphones, then dialed his lawyer's number. Now was the time to call him - he needed to make the call from a public place, and once he was properly on the grid he would have to act under the assumption his every word was recorded.

At the prompt he keyed in his lawyer's extension, and after

one ring his lawyer answered with a 'Mr. Myntbanke?' Blake sent him a link to the webcam, and they made small talk as he set it up. They were remodelling the office, apparently his daughter was going to spend the summer in Copenhagen. There was something very relieving in hearing his voice.

Then the webcam turned on, revealing his lawyer, tufts of grey in his hair, smiling at him in a suit and tie. Blake held up the newspaper, then picked up the webcam and passed it over the bustling café a couple of times, before again aiming it at himself. He held two fingers to his left eyebrow, put both his thumbs flat under his chin, and tugged three times on his right ear.

His lawyer now sounded more relaxed. Blake's old associate had been in touch? Yes, he was to do what he said, Blake had sent him. No one suspicious had been asking about him, although the textile company had called, and the people with the pub in the UK wanted him to sign some papers when it was convenient.

Blake said he was just calling because he had been reading a lot about real estate in Europe lately, was thinking he didn't have enough of it in his portfolio. European real estate being code for a defensive re-arrangement of his portfolio.

His lawyer thought that was a good idea. He had just read an article about how the rural economy was hollowing out in a lot of places, little villages were being abandoned. In many ways it was a tragedy, but there could be some good deals.

Blake was thinking he could sell his magazine holdings to start. Maybe the properties in the East Village. They could gradually start getting rid of anything publicly traded here in America as well, actually. He just didn't know about the stock market right now.

Then Blake bid him good day, feeling fairly relieved that they were getting that started. Next he loaded up the email program, set it to automatically download all the messages from his three different accounts. Joe had set it up with firewalls and VPNs and other security software, so they were confident it wouldn't lead to his location here in the café. But it would leave a digital trail showing that he had accessed his account, so technically it was his first appearance on the grid.

He opened the Myntbanke Capital address first. There wasn't too much there, it was a new email address, although Jack had emailed him a few times. Blake read the messages from Jack carefully. They hadn't heard from him for a while, he hoped everything was ok, let him know when you get this, that sort of thing.

There was nothing that explicitly gave away the date Blake left, but some of it did make him a little nervous. Jack referenced missing the lunch in one place, then a presentation Bill was going to give in another message. If someone really took all the emails apart they could maybe piece some stuff together.

Blake deleted all the messages, both sent and received - no need to leave unnecessary trails to Wildon Textiles. Next he started going through his other two main email addresses. There was a lot more there, but skimming through it he didn't see anything that was overtly from law enforcement or a supersoldier lab.

There were a lot of messages from people inquiring as to his whereabouts. He had missed a big party in New York, a few people had messaged him about it. It seemed like there was a movement to get a bunch of people together to rent a cabin this summer. And Adrianna was still emailing him then, after everything that happened?

There were a few emails from people looking for investors. Blake read them suspiciously, was that how someone would approach him? The one guy had been at that investor's conference, had he? The girl representing a business software company looked like his type. He read over that email carefully, it was pretty generic, looked like boilerplate that would be sent to everyone on their investor list. Certainly the opportunity seemed too good to be true, but then they all sort of did.

Here was something. There was an email from a Dark Ages scholar, postdoc at a university in Boston. He was writing a paper about the evolution of minting practices in the 13th and 14th centuries, said a colleague had given him Blake's information.

The guy had a bit of a write up about what he was working on, thought Blake might know about or have access to some relevant source documents. It would aid him greatly if they could talk, he left a phone number, also mentioned he was working on a project in New York right now.

Blake re-read the email a couple of times, staring at the screen. Something about it felt off, the hairs on the back of his neck stood up. No one bit in particular, just the overall whole of it. It didn't feel like something a Dark Ages scholar would have necessarily written.

Hadn't he read the staggered acceleration theory about the velocity of medieval coinage? He should have mentioned that in the third paragraph, the bit about the devaluation of silver in France. And he just happened to be in New York? Who was it that recommended him, it was a little odd just to say 'a colleague.'

If Blake was being completely honest with himself, requests like that were few and far between for him these days. He was long out of university, he hadn't been actively carrying out research for quite a while now. Really, it was something he had been neglecting, in life.

Could it be someone playing to his ego? That would probably be the way to do it. Although would they really send a fake Dark Ages scholar after him, could they recruit one? It didn't sound particularly plausible.

Either way he saw no pressing need to reply to the guy. Or anyone for that matter. He was notoriously bad at getting back to people.

Next up was his chat program. There were a few messages from his friends, asking if he was in New York, a few sending him links to stuff. He saw Laura had sent him a couple messages, 'hey are you there?', then a few days later, 'Jack is looking for you'.

Looking at the messages, though, he had a sudden recollection. She had been talking about coming down to San Diego, and he had given her one of his numbers. Would that have been his New York number?

Frantically he scrolled back through the message history. There it was, his San Diego number, all ten digits staring back at him. That was bad, really bad, wasn't it? He didn't know exactly what information Joe's people could get, but it seemed more likely someone just stumble across his number there than by something like questioning Jack.

He didn't know what to do, if he should just pack up and head back to the cabin. That was something Joe should probably know about. He read the message over and over again. Well, if you are in town, here's my number. What had he been thinking?

Hovering over the message with his mouse, a little box popped up. There was an 'x' icon. Did that mean he could delete the message? He stared at it in disbelief. Would that work? He hovered over one of Laura's messages, there was no x, that's what it must be. That was handy.

He read over the messages a couple of times. If he deleted the message with the number, and his message after that, it would sort of work. It made the text slightly awkward, made her say a non-sequitur. But one way or another it was better than having his number there.

Blake clicked on the xs, and his messages disappeared. He took a deep breath, feeling slightly short of breath. This was hard work. Bullet dodged, he moved on to the last order of business, his credit cards. He got out the anonymous events holding company card, and logged into his account.

Going through the records, there were a decent number of recurring charges. A few charities, a music service, there was a subscription to that cable TV channel he really liked, he had kept that going just out of principle when he left New York. There was the K-56, but they already knew it was on that card. And both the San Diego apartment and the second car rental, that was a relief.

Moving on, he logged into the card in his name, jumping back to the start of the year. There was the charge for that hotel he stayed in the first couple of nights, and his flight to San Diego. He scrolled back a bit, through the charges for the previous year. There were again lots of little recurring charges, but other than those he didn't really use his credit cards very much. Flights, the new computer he bought, a couple of hotels going back to his trip to Europe, he had mostly been staying with friends. It wasn't like there was a sharp drop off after he fled San Diego.

Going back to January though, something caught his eye. A twenty dollar charge at 'NY Slice' late January. What was that, it didn't sound like a magazine subscription or anything. Recollection flooded back. The bloody pizzeria. He only had large bills, the guy hadn't had change, he put it on his card.

Blake felt his throat constricting, the floor was falling away. He would have called the pizzeria with his San Diego phone, to have a pizza delivered to his apartment, paying with a card in his name. That linked everything up.

That was exactly the sort of thing detectives looked up, wasn't it? Pizzerias must keep that kind of data. Market research, sending out flyers to lapsed customers, just to simplify things when people made another order. They had to have a way of calling you if they couldn't find your place.

He tried to think of a way he could call them, get them to delete his records. Maybe he was getting too many fliers or something. But anything like that would be too obvious, it would be even more suspicious. And an enterprising detective could probably just get a list of every phone number that called that night, go through them one by one.

Blake stared at the charge, one fateful little line in his

statement. Who the devil doesn't carry change? It wasn't that big of a note. What, was he going to give it all as a tip? Would the pizza have been free if he didn't have the card, was the guy going to go down the street to get change?

He tried to breathe. Maybe it wasn't obvious, it was hidden away in the other charges. They would have to do some digging to get his phone number. But it was a thread, someone could follow it, and he would be made.

What did he do? It was all borderline. The next step was to check into a hotel, officially cross over onto the grid. Or go back to the hotel parking lot then drive back to the cabin. He didn't want to make that decision.

Maybe he was made already, maybe they were waiting for him to show his face, then they would pounce. Maybe all he was doing with all this was establishing that he was lying about the day he left. Who had been at his apartment? It suddenly seemed like a vital detail. If they had figured out where he had been living, they probably would have figured out a lot of other stuff as well. He considered calling his landlady again, but it didn't seem like a good idea.

The dye people. At that big trade show. He had really liked their dyes, they were going to send him a big sample package. Had he given them his home address, not the factory? There hadn't been anything for him at Wildon Textiles. He must have talked to them for a good twenty minutes, they would have seen him as a serious customer.

He had been thinking about setting up a station in the guest bathroom and testing the dyes on a variety of Wildon Textiles fabrics, hadn't he? That suggested he would have given them his home address. He probably should have checked with his landlady about that, actually.

You would think they would have found some way to contact him. Although they could have thought they had the wrong number if they called, his phone was in someone else's name now. Either way it made more sense than agents, if they came with a package. He tried to remember the name of the company, but he couldn't.

Blake's head was hurting, he felt dizzy. He needed to crash somewhere. He didn't know if he would be able to sleep, but he needed to be away from it all. Every day he spent off the grid made him look more suspicious, and it wasn't going to change the facts on the ground.

He motioned to the waitress for the bill, and asked her if there were any hotels nearby. She said there were a few, just to the left and up around the corner.

Before he left he put the car keys in an envelope, wrote a note with the address where the car was parked, addressing it as directed by Lee, to a PO Box in Ohio. Out on the street he found a postal box along the way. He stood beside it a minute, once the car keys were gone it would be a lot harder to turn back. But then he just unceremoniously dropped the envelope in the box.

Blake found a hotel quickly, a mid-range sort of place, it looked like it would do. It was fairly empty when he went in, he took a deep breath then went up to the receptionist. In a southern drawl she told him they had rooms, he would take a deluxe single.

He passed her a credit card, using one in his name, but not the one he had used for the pizza place. It felt momentous, he tried not to stare as she swiped his card. This exact moment was his first real appearance on the grid. She typed a bit on the computer, then passed him his card back, with a room key. At least his card had worked.

He thanked her, then headed up the stairs, found his room. He locked the door shut, put the chain, then collapsed fully clothed on the bed.

17

Blake awoke groggily mid-afternoon, slightly surprised he had even managed to sleep in the first place. It felt like a minor victory that no one had come knocking on his door.

Half-asleep he went to take a shower, then stopped himself as he was going to run the water. His bag was in the other room, and he was never to leave his stuff unattended. Even taking a shower was too much, Joe had in fact specifically mentioned showers as an example. He had been pretty emphatic about it - anything left unattended for more than 30 seconds was to be considered 'unclean', and potentially full of bugs and tracking devices and the like. If you were always overly careful, that meant you were always careful enough.

So Blake went back and turned on his laptop, switching on the camera and placing it in a corner of the room from which it could see all the potential entrances. Joe had set it up with some sort of tamper-proof camera system that would send pictures to an encrypted folder on his phone if it detected any movement. Apparently it would still work even if the internet and mobile networks were down. Likewise his phone was never to leave his sight.

Then he had a nice long shower, and clipped his beard down to a long stubble, another minor precaution in case photos were taken of him driving. From there he ordered up room service, and put on the TV, jumping through the channels and managing to not really think about much of anything.

As the afternoon began to turn into evening, he decided he should probably go out, see if the night had anything in store for him. The payment for the hotel would definitely have processed by now - if Joe's people had access to his credit card records, they would know where he was staying.

Blake did know a few people in Austin, but it didn't seem like a good idea to call anyone up out of the blue. So he just killed a bit of time reading the live music listings over more room service, then set out on foot for a part of town where he remembered there being a lot of good bars.

Leaving the hotel he cast a quick glance around the lobby, a little unsure of what exactly he would be looking for. He didn't see any mustachioed types watching him over newspapers.

After a nice walk through the warm night he found a studenty sort of bar. There was a maybe Indy Jazz band playing, with a bit of a gypsy jazz sound, a wizard on the clarinet, so he settled in to watch.

The band played a couple of sets, and the night seemed to pass uneventfully. Blake talked to a couple of people, a girl who was studying film, a research biologist guy, he made small talk with the bartender. In-between sets he complimented the clarinet player, struck up a brief conversation. The melodica *was* an underappreciated instrument.

No one seemed overly friendly, or asked probing questions about anything like where he had been. Blake left a little before midnight, and stopped for a slice of pizza on the main drag. Then he took the long way back to his hotel, detouring along the river a bit.

Once he got back to his room he checked online and found an early flight to Los Angeles. He felt a sense of foreboding as he filled in his information, and once he was done he just stared at the airline's booking page without clicking 'buy'. One thing Joe had been sure of was that his people had access to airline databases. If someone had gotten Blake on a watch list, then the moment he was on a flight manifest they would know about it.

Finally with a deep breath he clicked the buy button, then lay back on the bed, feeling inundated with a heaviness and low-level dread. Was a light flashing somewhere, someone getting an automated alert, Person of Interest Blake Myntbanke had just booked a flight from Austin to Los Angeles?

He tried to force himself to fall asleep, but it was no use, he was wide awake, so he put on a movie channel. After a couple of movies – both cheesy, lighthearted comedies - it was getting on time to go. So he ordered up a coffee and had a shower, tried to get himself as presentable as possible.

He checked out of the hotel, then flagged down a cab on the still dark street. The driver was a bit chatty, wanted to know where Blake was from. He must have been there for the music festival? Blake hadn't, would have liked to, had been out on a ranch, actually. He felt his head throb a bit at that, he hoped he hadn't missed an event. That was suspicious, he liked music festivals, put them on himself.

After a bit he just shut his eyes and slouched back in the seat. He didn't even want to risk talking to the guy at that point in the morning. It was around his bedtime in the cabin, and he suddenly felt very tired. Part of him wanted to just cancel his flight, get another one later. He would need to be on the ball for an airport. But it was kind of a suspicious thing, cancelling flights.

With a now pounding headache and medium to severe nausea, he made his way to the counter and got his boarding pass, not checking any bags. The stewardess asked about the music festival as well, but this time he just sort of made a non-committal noise.

Making his way towards his gate he tried to look as normal as possible. Joe had been saying everything in airports was filmed. He could get away with being tired, maybe he had a mild hangover. But he didn't want to look strung out, or nervous. He got another coffee, and tried to look tired but chipper. Off to LA, what fun!

The line for security was fairly long, it was an ordeal just standing there. Filling up the scanner bin he dropped his wallet on the floor. Then after his bag went through the x-ray one of the security guards called him over, was asking him about electronics, wanted him to open his bag.

In a bit of a daze Blake complied, and the guy put on gloves and dug through his cables. Blake felt like he should make some kind of witty remark, something that was relaxed and in character, but nothing came to mind.

Then the guy asked him to turn on his laptop. Blake gave a little nod then opened it, pressed the on button. Panic surged through his system, but he tried to remain calm on the surface. That went beyond the normal sort of thing they asked for.

His laptop lit up with the welcome screen, and the guy sort of said ok. Blake wasn't sure if that meant he could go, but it seemed like it did. So he closed the laptop and repacked his bag, then hurried towards his gate.

He was soon in the air. He tried to watch a movie, but he couldn't focus on it, it was making his headache worse. That was the first time in his life, he had ever had to turn on a laptop. And he flew a lot. Maybe he had heard about someone having to turn on their laptop, he vaguely knew it was a thing that happened.

Nothing had come of it, certainly. They hadn't asked to make a copy of his hard drive or anything. But it still struck him as decidedly strange. What were the odds of something like that happening now?

He felt self-conscious, he couldn't get comfortable. He was squirming around too much in his seat. Were the stewardesses watching him? It sort of felt like one of them might have been.

He was getting nausea in waves. It was claustrophobic, there was nowhere to run on a plane. Or once they landed, for that matter. What exactly was he going to say, if he got pulled aside in security? They could ask a lot of questions sometimes.

Was a ranch a farm? It sort of was, and that was one of the questions they asked you, on those little forms, had you been on a farm. If he said yes, they might want to know all about it. What plants and animals there were, what the address was, what were the exact dates. Could he just sort of forget to check the box? He told the taxi driver he had been on a ranch.

Blake forced himself to breathe. They only asked you that stuff when you were arriving in on an international flight. Nobody cared if you were on a farm in America. The Texas Boll Weevils or what have you could make it to California easily enough without him carrying them by air. He needed to get it together.

The flight dragged on, although in the end part of him wanted to stay in the air. He was safe up there. Finally they landed, a little before 10 in the morning LA time, and he was out of the gate and into the main thoroughfare without incident. With the same credit card as before he rented a car - a nondescript grey midsize sedan - then left for a hotel he knew in Santa Monica.

Checking in, it seemed like the kind of place where Joe had been telling him he should stay. It was located on a main street right off the beach, and it was really busy. There would be people from all around the world to witness it, if anyone *were* to make a move on him. There was something reassuring in that.

Once he got to the room he collapsed on the bed. He still couldn't sleep, but it was nice to just lie there, he felt his headache subside a bit. He was just drifting off to sleep when a realization struck him. If he fell asleep now, he could well be out for a good eight hours. If he *had* just been on a ranch for the past few weeks, he should be getting up at dawn. Not staying up all night and sleeping through the day. There would only be so much to do after sundown on the ranch.

Blake ordered up a double espresso, and had a cold shower, again after setting up his computer to watch the room. Then he went to his car, and just drove. He toured through some of his old stomping grounds, up into Beverly Hills, around through downtown, Hollywood, back into Santa Monica, down along the beach. Memories flooded back, he had some good times here. A lot had changed, but a lot had stayed the same, that late night waffle place was still there.

All the time he kept an eye on the traffic behind him. He didn't see anything particularly suspicious, not that he could really tell. Had that silver car been following him for a while? He was starting to feel like he was being followed. Could you tell, did he have a sixth sense? According to Joe's rules he now had to act under the assumption the car was bugged and had tracking devices. It had been sitting unattended in the hotel parking garage.

Looking in the rear-view mirror, there was a cop car, just a couple of cars behind him. Breathing evenly and regularly, he continued along, through a couple of intersections, past a little mall. It stayed behind him, just one car between them now.

He felt like he was looking in the rear-view mirror a lot, he forced himself to stop. Could they tell when you were looking in the rear-view mirror too much? Joe had seemed to think that level of attention to detail was necessary.

Feeling his pulse quicken, he took a left turn onto a smaller side street. The cop car followed him, it was directly behind him now. He tried to breathe in, breathe out, look at all the nice little shops going by. It was a normal day, back from the ranch, out for a drive in LA after all these years in New York. Blake felt distinctly unready for questioning, he tried to go over all the details in his head, but he couldn't remember half of it.

The cop stayed behind him for a while, then after a couple of minutes turned down onto another main road. Blake felt an immense sensation of relief. Although really, was it going to be a cop, following behind him, pulling him over in the middle of the day?

That was rather a disquieting thought, which suddenly seemed fairly obvious. Blake still didn't feel like he was 100% sure about how exactly the relationship between the legal authorities and Joe's lab worked. But going with the police would probably just add unnecessary complications for them, things would have to be done by the book. More likely it would be someone with a similar skill set and physical makeup as Joe, but less agreeable as a dinner-guest.

The gas meter was getting low, maybe a third of a tank. What if he got in a car chase? There was a big gas station at the next intersection, so he turned into it, pulled up to a pump and went in.

It was busy inside, people coming and going, having coffees and muffins at some tables off to the side. It was all strangely reassuring. At that exact point, that singular moment in space-time, he was safe. Part of him wanted to grab the people around him, call for the media and tell everyone there everything he knew. He would be protected by the crowd.

Blake took a deep breath, he had absolutely no evidence anyone was watching him. He grabbed a chocolate bar and a coffee, paid for gas, then filled the tank. Pulling out he saw a big mall across the way, that could kill a chunk of the day. Shopping seemed like the sort of thing you did after an extended stay out in the country.

The mall was a sprawling complex, he wandered through it sort of lost. It was almost too much, the noise, there were people everywhere. He found a coffee shop and skimmed through a newspaper. After a bit it started giving him a headache though, it was nothing but puff pieces and obvious politicking, so he got up and wandered around again.

There was a big open plaza with plants and sculptures, it was quite well done. Blake wished he had a camera, he could show it to Laura sometime. He noticed, though, across the other side of the plaza, there was a guy, in a suit and sunglasses. He was looking right in Blake's direction, was he looking at him? Blake looked away, and didn't look back. Maybe *he* had been looking at *him*.

Blake tried to look normal, he felt an urge to swallow, but he supressed it. It really felt like the guy had been watching him. And it was a little weird, people didn't usually wear sunglasses in the mall. The place had a reasonably dark lighting scheme, he'd be liable to bump into things.

Although all things considered Blake himself had probably worn sunglasses in a mall once or twice. And if they were sending someone to watch him, they would probably blend in a little better, wouldn't they? Blake felt somewhat relieved, but he didn't want to show that, either. He just continued through the mall thoroughfare into a clothing store, not even looking the direction where the guy had been. Browsing through he bought a change of pants, a couple of shirts, and a nice outdoorsy all-weather mountain climbing jacket.

From there he checked out a novelty knick-knack store, they had a really neat automatic card shuffler, he bought it on impulse. He would have to get some cards. Passing a lottery kiosk, it turned out there was a big draw, so he bought a few tickets, you never knew.

There was a really big bookstore, so he took his time in there, ended up with half a dozen books. All mostly business books, and a historical novel set in the Dark Ages he had been meaning to read.

Then on the way out he hit up a big electronics store, browsed through the various nifty new devices on offer. They had a home DJ beat box sort of thing, he played around with it for a while in the store, it was really something. He ended up buying it, as well as a fancy new MP3 player - that was enough that he would be expected to put it on his credit card, which was another mark on the grid.

Blake felt strangely calm leaving the mall, like it was a normal day. The sun was bright overhead now, worries of supersoldier pursuit only in the back of his mind. If he was slightly encumbered with his bags.

At this he felt another little throbbing in his head. He would eventually have to find an excuse to ditch all his stuff. Joe had specified he was to get rid of everything before his final return to the cabin. All his new toys were really nothing more than expensive receptacles for tracking devices.

It was now getting into late afternoon. Blake felt like he had put in enough time out and about in the world, he really didn't feel like being in public anymore. He headed back to his hotel, whipped through the lobby, then collapsed on the bed.

Feeling like he should eat, he ordered up room service, picked away at a sandwich. As he was doing so, however, a strange sort of dizziness came over him, he felt just slightly odd. Could it be possible someone might drug his food?

That would be a way to get him. Knock him out, have someone pick the lock on his room, then smuggle him to a location more convenient for questioning. There would be logistical difficulties in that, infiltrating the kitchen staff for one. But it probably wouldn't be so hard for someone like Joe to carry him out in an oversized duffle bag.

Feeling his heart rate ramp up, Blake stood up, and stumbled towards the door. If he was going to pass out, he'd rather be in a public place with lots of witnesses. Feeling dangerously lightheaded he hurried down the hall, not towards the elevator, there were stairs, the stairs were better.

He hurried down the stairs, not knowing what he would do if there was someone there. Fortunately they were empty. There was a shirt, hanging from the handrail, that was kind of weird.

Making it down to the lobby, Blake sort of felt alright. He probably hadn't been drugged. Nonetheless he didn't want to go back to his room yet. So he checked out the pool, went down to the gift shop and bought a business magazine. He was still feeling normal. But he might just avoid room service for now. It wasn't such a big hassle to go order food from randomly selected restaurants.

Blake went back to the room and jumped through the channels a bit, then settled on another movie. Eventually he must have fallen asleep, because he looked up at the clock and it was almost eleven.

He tried to fall back asleep, but it was no use. He was still exhausted, but wide awake. Nonetheless he turned the TV off, he needed to act like he was asleep. Time passed excruciatingly slowly, he just tossed and turned. Part of him was worried about looking tired tomorrow, part of him was afraid of falling asleep.

Then sometime in the night, maybe around 3 in the morning, there was a sound right at his door. Someone was rattling the handle, trying to open the door. Blake stared out in the dark, letting his eyes adjust, adrenaline pumping through his veins.

The room was silent, minutes passed and the door stayed closed. He had an intense urge to get up, look out the peephole. But that would be suspicious. Maybe that's what they wanted him to do, could it be a test?

He spent the rest of the night wide awake, jumping internally at any noise outside his room. He finally felt like he could get some sleep as the dawn began creeping in through his shaded window, but he forced himself to get up. Really, if he had been on a ranch, he shouldn't just not be nocturnal, he should be getting up with the sun.

He put the 'do not disturb' sign on his door, and went down to the lobby. The hotel turned out to have a big buffet breakfast, which was open already. This gave him pause - it would look a little suspicious to go eat somewhere else. Not only was it free for guests, but it looked like a pretty nice buffet. But it was basically sitting there unattended. It would be a lot easier for someone to drug that than the room service, if he was worried about being drugged.

In the end he grabbed a plate and went for it. There was enough different food that he could pick and choose. Maybe they'd put truth serum in the coffee, and everyone would be brutally honest at their family get-togethers or sales meetings or what have you. But that didn't seem likely, he was probably overthinking things a bit.

Blake managed to eat a croissant with some eggs, had a couple of coffees, he felt alright. There was an older guy there, said hello, commented he was up early. Blake mumbled something about having been out on a ranch. Apparently LA was going to have good weather the next few days.

After breakfast Blake was at a bit of a loss as to what to do, so he went for a walk along the beach. It was nice out, the early morning sun gave him energy. He just forced himself to relax, to be in the present. He sat down on a bench, watched the people go by. Venice Beach was just waking up, lots of joggers at this hour, roller skaters, people out walking their dogs.

There was a little newsstand, so he bought a couple of newspapers and the latest issue of his favorite British newsmagazine, then went to a coffee shop by the beach. Maybe the last days on the ranch had been crazy, he needed some downtime.

Blake passed a good part of the morning there, ordering a few coffees by the end of it, and pretty much skimming the newsmagazine cover to cover. If he was having trouble focusing on it. Why had they asked him to turn on his laptop, there was no reason for it, it wasn't even an international flight. He had never even *seen* anyone have to turn on their laptop at airport security.

He wondered how much progress his lawyer had made so far. He had rather an intense urge to call him, there were a couple more things he was thinking he should sell. But now that he was on the grid, the last thing he wanted to do was call attention to his assets.

Eventually he felt like he had to move on from the coffee shop, so he went walking along the beach again. He really didn't know what to do with himself, he walked to downtown Santa

Monica, browsed the windows of some boutique shops. Then he went to a supermarket, got some junk food, and finally just went back to the hotel and put on the TV.

Jumping through the channels, there was an exposé on steroids in sports, it sort of pulled him in. It was kind of heavy to watch though - more and more teenagers were using them, some of the health effects were actually pretty heavy. Like, he already knew that, but still, just hearing about it. Personality changes, chronic fatigue, infertility. There was a golden boy quarterback who was terminally ill, all his heroes had been using steroids.

It sort of felt like research watching it, but he really wasn't in the mood. He put on the news for a while, but then there was a story about some fugitive on the lam, had also been an activist, apparently. It made him sick to his stomach, he almost changed the channel, but stopped himself. Even something like that was best avoided, the walls could have ears. So he waited for a few more news stories to pass, then put on a movie channel that looked to be nothing but cheesy comedies and lighthearted action flicks.

Sitting there watching a particularly bad slapstick romantic comedy, Blake began to get a very distinct sensation that he was doing too little in LA. He used to rule this town, there were literally dozens of people he should be seeing. It was a Thursday, that was close enough to the weekend in LA.

He had some numbers on his computer, he went to look through them. Who should he call? Old Jake, he was generally out to the clubs half the week. Blake had talked to him a while ago, it sounded like he was still in LA doing the same old, was working in set design. Better a friend from the film business.

After a brief contemplation of the security issues, Blake dialed the number, and after a couple of rings Jake answered. Blake Myntbanke! He would be, it had been ages, hadn't it? It had been a little while, Blake had been living in New York, although lately he had been bouncing around quite a bit. He was here in LA now though. Well, they were all going clubbing tonight, Blake should come along.

Blake got the address of the club where they were all meeting up. Apparently there were dinner plans beforehand, but he said he would just meet them there. Then he just sort of lay in bed, somewhere between sleep and wake, half watching another couple of cheesy comedies until it was time to leave.

He got dinner from a fast food place a few streets up, then

took a cab to the club. He stood outside a moment, staring up the stairs before going in. Inside it was really busy, flashing lights, they had a DJ who was playing pounding electronica. He really wasn't in the mood for it, and the DJ sounded kind of cheesy, just lots of fast noise. Well, he wasn't there for a good time, just to make an appearance.

He went to the bar, ordered a drink, then after doing a lap found his friend. Jake was looking well, had a goatee now. They had a yelled conversation, Jake had some story involving scaffolding Blake only got about a third of. Then Blake was introduced to his friends, another guy from the movie business, there were a couple of girls.

They all hung around, bounced up and down on the dance floor. After a bit it started getting a little crowded, so Blake went and got another drink, yelled a bit more with Jake. Apparently there was talk of an Ork Horde VIII, all very early stages, of course. Blake just mostly sort of made noise when Jake asked him what he had been doing lately, to which Jake nodded along intently.

One of the girls joined them, a blond in a slightly revealing blue one-piece dress. Apparently she was new to LA, was working a couple different jobs, had done a bit of modelling, was trying to get into acting. She seemed a little nervous, and the conversation got onto Blake's ranch, stayed there even with his subtle attempts to sway its course.

He didn't really say much other than it was a ranch, a ways out of Austin. They had done a lot of hiking, actually. But for a moment he couldn't help but wonder if she could be working for someone. Really, he didn't know how well she knew Jake. She could very well have just latched onto him that night before Blake arrived. Maybe they seemed like they knew each other well enough, but really Blake couldn't tell. He wasn't going to ask.

Another DJ came on, and they all went back to the dance floor to bounce up and down again. The new DJ was getting on abrasive though. Maybe it wasn't that bad, if he had been in a better mood he might have called it innovative. But for now it was just making his head throb, he was feeling exhaustion creeping in. He had put in his time, made an appearance, had he?

Blake said goodbye to Jake, he really wasn't feeling it tonight. They would have to catch up again later. Jake concurred, Blake was looking pretty tired, apparently. Blake saw the girl on his way out, so they talked again briefly and exchanged numbers, him giving her his new New York number.

There was an empty taxi waiting outside, but he didn't feel like taking it. That other taxi had been asking about the music festival. So he went for a little walk down the strip, got some pizza. After letting a few cabs go by he flagged one down, and went back to his hotel, exhausted, the city alive around him on the drive back.

18

Blake slept fitfully that night, every noise in the hall jolting him awake. Once the sun started rising he sort of felt like he might be able to get some proper sleep, but he again forced himself to get up. He skipped the buffet breakfast, and went for a longish walk, finally stopping at a diner a ways down the beach.

Sitting there over their breakfast special, he began getting the feeling LA just wasn't the place for him right now. What exactly was the protocol if he ran into someone he knew? People would want to know what he had been doing, would want to go for a drink and have big long conversations. He could get tied into backstory, get caught in a lie, lying worked like that.

And if he was going to hang out in LA, he should really be going out with his friends, renting an event space and throwing a big party, even. That was another thing they should have realized, making plans. LA was the last place he should be hanging out right now. Not to mention he would need to get his room cleaned soon, and the logistics of that were actually kind of complicated if he wanted to maintain airtight security.

He knew a beach town, a couple hours to the north, he had gone up there for the weekend a couple of times when he lived in LA. Maybe he wasn't feeling LA right now, what he needed was some low-key R&R. He wouldn't know what to say to some of the people from his LA days anyways, even if all this wasn't going on.

Going back to the hotel, Blake quickly checked out, then headed west along the coastal highway. It was a nice day for a drive, he was on the scenic route, the sun was shining.

Out there with the window down, the blue of the ocean cutting through the trees along the highway, Blake slowly felt himself begin to relax. It had been more than 48 hours since he had bought the plane ticket, and about 72 hours since he first used his credit card. Aside from maybe a couple of strange things, nothing had really happened.

If they did suspect him, wouldn't it make more sense just to come and have a chat? It seemed like a lot of work to have agents trailing him, secretly watching his every move. Agents had to have pretty high hourly wages. There must be fifty other equally suspicious people they would have to spend the same amount of time on, if they were investigating him.

Although that was sort of assuming they didn't have much reason to suspect him in the first place. A wave of nervousness again passed over him. If they did think he was involved, just following him around in silence could really be their best strategy. If they approached him now, his orders were to deny everything and go back to New York to live his normal life. But otherwise he *would* eventually go back to the cabin, and meet up with Joe there. He supposed he shouldn't rule out their best strategy, should he?

Blake felt like he was looking in the rear-view mirror too much again. He tried to push it all out of his head, he turned up the music, and just drove. A little further on he stopped for lunch at a restaurant off the highway, sitting at a table from which he could see his car. All his stuff was still 'clean', it had always either been within his sight or under the watch of his computer security system.

Continuing north he made slow time, he stopped at a couple rest areas, took in the views from a cliff over the ocean. He made it to the beach town in the late afternoon, the sun bright and the sky clear. Driving a lap through town, it was basically as he remembered it. Maybe some new developments on the outskirts, the same fountain was still in the plaza, he remembered the one restaurant being good.

Blake drove past a couple hotels, before stopping at a bustling mid-sized boutique-y place right off the beach. It seemed like an upscale sort of place that would have good security. The receptionist said they had a room, it was slightly overpriced, but he took it, again paying with the one credit card in his name.

He was feeling pretty burnt out by that point, so he just set up his security system, then went up the road to a fish and chips truck for dinner. He got it to go, then ate in front of the TV, they had the same cheesy movie channel he had been watching in LA. He considered going out briefly - he remembered the town having decent nightlife - but he just closed his eyes for a moment, and he was instantly asleep.

When Blake awoke it was dark, the hotel silent. Looking at his watch, he was surprised to see it was after midnight. That was actually a bit of a relief, he had needed to get caught up on his sleep. It also made him slightly nervous though, that would look a little strange, it was a weird time to get your sleep. Maybe it was within the bounds of an early night ranch time, Austin was a couple of hours ahead.

The hotel was eerily quiet, all he could hear was the rhythmic crashing of the waves on the beach. Feeling a restlessness, he got up and went outside for some fresh air. The reception was empty as he passed through, the halls silent. He did a little loop around the neighbourhood, but the streets felt abandoned. It made him a little nervous just being out there.

Getting back to the hotel, he noticed the parking lot was empty, there was just one car other than his. That gave him pause. There had been cars that afternoon when he had checked in, hadn't there?

He couldn't remember exactly, but no, there were lots of cars. He had to drive to the far end of the lot to find a spot. That's why his car was off away on the other side of the empty lot. He had wondered if they were going to have a room.

Everything in town was within walking distance, and would be closed by now anyways. And it was a Friday night. Maybe it wasn't high season, but it couldn't be low season either, it was the shoulder. Had everyone been there for the mid-week rush, then left Friday afternoon to go home for the weekend? He couldn't make any sense of it.

Feeling a growing anxiety, he went back into the hotel. The reception was still empty. Going up to the desk he saw there was a phone with a little note, dial 5 outside of normal hours to talk to the receptionist. It was a big enough hotel, they should have someone there all night.

Blake went back to his room, and turned on the TV. Then he turned it down a bit. Between that and the waves, he wouldn't be able to hear anything in the halls. He went over his arrival at the hotel again in his mind, the parking lot had been full. He hadn't seen any other guests, but he hadn't been hanging out in the lobby.

His mind reeled. It was decidedly strange that the hotel was empty. Could someone have emptied it out? Maybe a busted pipe, some kind of biohazard. Could they have filled the hotel up with their own people, then subliminally implanted the place in his mind somehow?

That didn't seem realistic, for one they wouldn't even have known where he was going. But from all external appearances he was now in an empty hotel. Joe had told him to watch out for magician-level stuff, things that would seem impossible. Maybe there was an easy way to do it, something he couldn't even think of right now.

He couldn't make any sense of it. How the devil were there no cars outside? Maybe the receptionist and the cleaning staff went home, but that was 2-3 cars, not 10, more than 10.

He felt a sick sensation. He still hadn't heard any other noises from the hotel. No snoring, no opening and closing of doors, no running water. It could very well be that he was alone in the building. Maybe it was paranoid, but he needed to act under the assumption that there was an operation against him going on this very moment.

What did he do, if someone came? He looked out the window, it was dark beach, waves breaking a little ways in the distance. Glancing around the room there wasn't a lot that would work as a weapon. The lamp maybe, that was about it.

Maybe he should wander around the hotel, see where all the exits were. What were his victory conditions? It wouldn't be a matter of taking a supersoldier down in hand-to-hand combat, just getting away to someplace where people would see what was going on. Joe seemed to think his people wouldn't want to get caught doing anything. Blake wondered how far his shouts would carry, he liked to think he had a decent set of pipes.

He tried to focus on the movie, it was all lighthearted slapstick, dick jokes and the like. Something in it was strangely reassuring. Two in the morning came and went, and he lay down like he was finally going to sleep, the TV still on in the background. He didn't know if they would be able to see what he was doing, but it was suspicious to stay up all night, wasn't it?

He managed to keep his eyes closed briefly. Then he opened them, expecting to see an evil Joe standing beside his bed. How was he supposed to sleep without anyone on watch? That suddenly seemed like something that was missing from modern society. Just in general he was getting complacent. His apartment in San Diego hadn't even had a doorman. That had worked out well enough, but what if someone had tried to kidnap him?

For now he didn't even want to feign sleep. It seemed like they might be less likely to make a move on him if they knew he was awake. It was late, the town would be asleep, now was when it would happen.

Blake got up, went to his computer. People just had trouble sleeping sometimes, evening naps could screw up your sleep schedule. He found a video about changing your circadian rhythms, sat and watched it. There was his excuse, if anyone was listening.

The movie finished, and another started up. The hotel around him was still silent, there hadn't been a peep from any of the other rooms. Around three in the morning there was some sort of sharp sound from the street outside the hotel, a yelp, or a holler, he didn't know what it was.

A little bit later there was the sound of a car idling outside, it must have been pretty close to the hotel. They had talked about him bringing a gun along, Joe had sort of been surprised Blake would even consider going out like this without one. But Blake didn't usually carry a gun, it would have been suspicious, especially with the flight.

Now he just felt naked, it wouldn't even have to be loaded. He wouldn't want to go up against a Joe with a lamp. He wouldn't even want to go up against him with a gun.

4 AM passed by, then 5. Blake began to relax, people would be getting up, the sun would be up soon. There was some ambient noise from outside the hotel, a few cars going by. Finally the sky outside his window started changing colour, he had made it through the night.

19

Blake watched the sunrise from a bench on the beach that morning. There was something almost glorious in it, it felt like a victory. Although had he really somehow thwarted their plans just by staying up all night? One way or another it didn't add up. He had no clue what, if anything, had just happened.

After a bit he wandered into town looking for a restaurant, but there wasn't a lot open. So he decided he would find another hotel - his survival until dawn aside, he didn't want to stay another night in that place. He walked by a few hotels, then went into a big one in the middle of town that was already busy.

He asked to see a room, and they certainly weren't as nice, but they were surprisingly cheap. They even had one with a kitchenette, which sealed the deal for him - it gave him an excuse to change hotels, while allowing him to cook his own food. He only had to go to the wrong restaurant once.

Blake paid for the room with the same credit card in his name that he had been using. Then he went back to his other room to get his stuff, castigating himself as he did - he was breaking with Joe's procedure for keeping things airtight. His new room was sitting there without his security system set up. Technically someone could be entering it at this very moment and setting up hidden cameras and listening devices and the like.

His original hotel was still empty, there wasn't even anyone at the desk yet. It was sort of eerie, he just got out of there as quickly as he could, then drove back to his new hotel.

He was getting hungry, so he went ahead and got breakfast from room service. If someone *was* going to infiltrate the cooking staff, it would at least take them a couple of hours. As he was eating, he checked his email, and there was one from Jack, from yesterday.

The trip was going really well, the food was amazing, everyone really friendly, he was close to closing a couple of big deals already. And apparently there had been some rescheduling, he was going to be back in California, actually. If Blake was still going to be around, maybe he could come to a meeting in LA on Monday with a big hotel chain. Either way Blake was to let him know, the sooner the better.

Blake stared at the email. He had sort of forgotten about Jack, it hadn't sounded like he was going to come back. Had the call in Texas gone well enough? Blake felt like he had basically gotten the necessary information across. There could be advantages to talking to Jack again, although being on the grid he wouldn't really be able to say anything now.

Maybe there was some risk of leading them to Wildon Textiles. But if they *were* surveilling him now, he had a feeling they would probably know about Wildon Textiles already. Jack was coming all the way to LA for the meeting, and Blake had made rather a big deal of wanting to see him. Going to the meeting was what he would normally do. What was his excuse if he didn't go, he was too busy hanging around doing nothing in beach towns?

Blake clicked reply and typed a quick message, he was almost sure he could make it, what were the details? Sending it he felt a little nervous, it was a significant enough departure from the plan. But being 'on the grid' was more than just leaving a trail of credit card payments, it was seeing people, doing real things.

Blake tried to have a nap, then watched another movie. He was feeling pretty groggy, he would like nothing more than just to stay in the room watching TV all day. But he was at the beach, it looked to be nice out. His mission was just to go out and be boring in a resort town for a couple of days, until he went on to whatever big off-the-grid thing he was about to do next. In all the world's history of missions it was a pretty easy one.

He slapped some water on his face, tried to wake himself up. Then with a deep breath he went out, down the hotel hallway and into the town centre. It was nice and sunny out now, quite pleasantly warm. He went into a couple little stores, gift shops, beach clothing. He bought some swimming trunks - he wasn't sure about the logistics of swimming, as he was supposed to keep his phone on him at all times. But even if he wasn't actually going to go swimming, he should at least look like he was planning to go swimming.

Then he went down to the beach, which was reasonably busy now. Sunbathers, kids making sandcastles, a couple people in the water. There was a promenade along the beach, so he walked along that.

He noticed a youngish guy, sort of disheveled hair, coming towards him along the promenade. It seemed like the guy was sort of looking at him. As they passed each other the guy said one word, 'we', then kept walking.

Blake continued along, feeling his stomach do a somersault. After a bit there was a park bench, so he sat down and stared out at the ocean, trying to look unaffected. Why the devil had the guy just said 'we' to him?

Blake felt an uncertain nervousness well up. Had something just happened there? He got out his phone, played with it a bit, resisting the urge to look over at the guy.

"We." What did that mean? Like them? A group of people? It was enigmatic, it didn't make sense. We're watching, we know, it's we, what? Maybe that was the strategy, they did something weird like say 'we' to you, and watched to see if you freaked out. Was that their weird fucked up way of introducing themselves?

Did he need to look bemused? Maybe it was some new thing the kids in California were saying these days. Trying to look nonchalant, he looked down the beach the other way, then towards where the guy had gone. He was standing a ways down, talking to a couple of hippyish looking girls.

Maybe he had said 'weed', had he? That made more sense. Blake relaxed on the bench a little bit. The guy certainly didn't look like an agent, more a professional surfer.

A thought did occurr to him. He could just go and buy some weed off the guy. That wasn't something you did when you thought the Illuminati was watching you. Joe had been saying he should try and do stuff like that sometimes.

Was that a crazy idea? It could be a good way of testing the waters, it could even be an excuse for someone to question him. There was something strangely appealing in that. More than anything he just wanted to know if someone was on him.

He had slept close to eight hours last night. Might as well have them come at him when he was feeling on his game. And really, the laws in California, it would be strange if he got anything more than a fine. Which would then be a good grid-mark to have in the scenario of someone investigating him a month down the road.

Blake sauntered in the direction of the three of them, steeling himself as he did. As per Joe's instructions he had to act under the assumption that they were agents, or at least that the conversation could be recorded. Dapper wit felt like the angle. That was just objectively hard to do when you were freaking out about super agents. Your timing had to be right, you couldn't be nervous, or it would just all be off.

"Now, you three look like you could be from around here," said Blake as he came up next to them, inflecting his accent a bit more strongly, almost comically.

The guy smiled. "Ya, the last couple summers," he said, in a proper California surfer accent.

"Ah perfect! I would assume, then, that you have an extensive knowledge of the local cuisine?"

One of the girls, a brunette, smiled at him. "Ya, there's lots of good restaurants. The ceviche shack on the main road is really good, my friend works there."

"Yes, it's been really good, what I've had so far," said Blake, pausing for a moment, slightly puzzled. "I've noticed, however – as is the case for many restaurants, along this particular stretch of the American Coast - that everything is *gluten free*." They were all silent at this, so he continued. "I was wondering if you knew, if there was anywhere that had more," he again paused, unsure of his words, "gluten-rich food?"

The brunette was now looking at him like he was kind of weird. "Ya, I dunno dude," said the surfer guy, squinting at Blake a bit, and looking slightly nervous. "Like, maybe anywhere that doesn't say gluten free?"

"Well, yes, there must be," Blake looked over at them, almost apologetic. "You see, I have this unfortunate dietary condition," he paused a moment, obviously trying to think of something. "A gluten.. deficiency! That's it." He scratched the back of his head. "So what I'm really just looking for is some wheat. Do you guys know a good place to buy wheat?"

A grin appeared on the surfer guy's face. "You're looking to score some wheat?"

"Ya, that would be great," said Blake.

So the guy just glanced around the beach, then got out a little bag and showed it to him. Blake got the feeling it was actually pretty low-key buying weed here then, all his conversational machinations about wheat had been unnecessary. It looked good, so Blake bought a couple of overpriced grams of what the guy said was truly killer bud, them exchanging bag for cash right there in plain view of anyone who might be watching.

Then they just talked a bit. Blake got another couple of restaurant recommendations, there was one bar that was worth going to this time of year. Apparently it was still the off season, but maybe even as soon as next week it would really get going.

They liked his wheat bit. He said his alternative was an understocked kitchenette in his hotel, he needed pots, or actually just one. They dug it, that was almost better than wheat. Blake said people didn't get that one sometimes, just thought you were trying to borrow cooking ware.

Then the blond asked him what he was doing there, if he was hanging out for a while. Blake just said he had been travelling a lot lately. He had been in LA for a couple of days, but he wasn't feeling it. She agreed, it was way better up here.

It felt like an opportunity for any of them to ask more about where he had been, but none of them did. He bid them adieu, they said they might see him around, then he walked back into town. One of the souvenir stores had pipes, so he bought one. There he was, buying weed, buying pipes, if anyone cared. Was he going to smoke some then?

Blake wandered a ways down the beach, away from the crowd. Down past where the sandy beach ended he found a decent sized park, it seemed reasonably out of the way. He sat down at a picnic table in the corner of the park, waited while a jogger with a dog ran past, then packed the bowl.

At this juncture he hesitated, however. If he had been afraid the room service was going to be drugged, he probably shouldn't smoke weed. A surfer dude drug dealer could appear and disappear, carrying an illegal, unregulated substance. That was ten times riskier.

Although now that he was out there, sitting in a park with a full bowl, it would be sort of strange not to. That was exactly the sort of thing Joe had been talking about. He could fake smoke some, but that sounded like the worse idea still. For one he would pass a drug test. He had sort of painted himself into a corner, had he?

The park was a public place, it was the middle of the day. They would have to carry him pretty far if they wanted to capture him. The real issue here was not looking paranoid. Without further ado he lit up, and took a nice big puff.

It had been a while since he last smoked, it made him cough, it seemed like it was good weed. As soon as he finished, however, he had a very heavy sensation. Had he just smoked weed specifically to get caught for it? It suddenly seemed like a very bad idea. He no longer wanted to talk to the police.

Blake lay down on the bench, anxiety flooding his system. He had an intense sensation of being watched, of a hostile other, floating just beyond his view. There were potentially people out there, out to get him, watching him now. It was a pretty heavy trip, this was probably just a bad time to smoke weed in general.

He had a sensation like he was moving really fast, spinning, like he was lying at some weird impossible diagonal angle. His arms felt heavy, he felt them drop down to either side of the bench. He probably couldn't stand up if he wanted to. It didn't feel like a normal weed high, it was too heavy, overwhelming, in fact. His vision was disappearing at the edges.

He felt sick to his stomach. Had he just been drugged, then, had he skipped merrily into their trap? He felt himself slipping away, a circle of black now ringing his vision, stars and sparks floating before him. He tried to focus his consciousness. He needed to stay awake, by force of will alone if nothing else.

Should he yell for help? He didn't know, that would be pretty suspicious, he didn't feel like he should be making decisions like that right now. But was he about to get captured? He gave a little cough, his voice wasn't there.

The surfer guy and his friends had seemed so normal. Maybe they were unwitting agents. They could have just slipped the guy a few hundred dollars and a special bag of pot, told him it was reality TV or something.

Blake tried to turn his head to the side, to see if they were coming for him. He couldn't see anyone, but the physical act of moving made his stomach do a flip. He tried to pull himself up, almost falling off the bench in the process, then jumped to his feet. There was a wall of green bushy hedgy trees ahead of him, he aimed himself for it, an acrid stream filling his mouth as he fell forward.

He retched a few times, clinging onto a branch above him, his head in the foliage. It actually felt good, it was cleansing, liberating. This was a special case, there were extenuating circumstances, it didn't really count. If nothing else he hadn't been sleeping properly, that really made his stomach sensitive sometimes.

Once he was done he pulled himself out of the bushes, and looked around, his cheeks burning. He couldn't see any witnesses. Stumbling a bit, he walked in the direction of his hotel.

He was pretty dizzy, but he didn't feel like he was going to black out.

He must have taken a wrong turn on the way back, however, as he was suddenly in the centre of town again. There were people everywhere now, it was too noisy, he didn't know which way his hotel was. It wasn't a huge town, but things just weren't where they were supposed to be.

He needed to get off the main drag, he felt like people were looking at him. He went to go down a side street, but as he was going to cross the road there was something cold on his arm. Someone had bumped into him, it was ice cream. He apologized and stumbled across the road, wiping the white residue off his arm.

Could they drug you through your skin? Then he wouldn't know if it was the ice cream or the weed. The residue was all over his hands, on his arm. Blake wanted to scrub it off, but that would be suspicious. There were no napkins nearby, he was outside, on the street. He didn't want to go to the hotel. He had already figured that out, that was how they got you, when you went to your room when you were drugged.

He just walked, down a residential side street, trying to gauge his psychological state. *Had* he been drugged? He was still conscious, so there was that. But there were drugs that did things other than just knock you out. How did you know if you were on truth serum? Was it like everything was normal, but you told the truth? Or were you so blotter that you just didn't know what you were saying?

He kept walking, back along the beach promenade, then sat down on a bench where it was less crowded. He stayed there for a while, just staring out at the water, gathering his senses. It was probably just good weed. He needed to get it together, his behaviour over the past hour would probably seem pretty erratic, if anyone was watching him.

The afternoon sun was descending towards the water when he finally felt ready to risk standing up again. As he was making his way back to the hotel someone stopped him in the street, a middle aged guy in a ball cap. Did he know which way it was to the supermarket?

Blake thought for a second, hand on the back of his head, he wasn't from around here. The sun was just right behind the guy, in his eyes, Blake couldn't really see the guy's face. Maybe it was two or three streets down, then to the left?

The guy thanked him, and was on his way. Then as Blake was turning down the street towards his hotel it seemed like someone was coming at him. He jumped a bit, but there was no one there.

Blake managed to find his hotel this time, then hurried past the reception, and sprawled out on his bed. He was feeling pretty good now, actually. That happened with him sometimes, smoking weed. It was really heavy at first, then it mellowed out. He stretched out, staring up at the ceiling, the fan revolving leisurely above him.

What was he doing with his life? Lately it felt like he had been going from misadventure to misadventure. More than lately, all his life, maybe. He wondered, sometimes, if he should just settle down, get a cottage somewhere.

He had been having a nagging sensation, that he had his priorities all wrong. Like he was sort of missing the plot, in life. Did he have too many options? It felt like that sometimes. He hated making choices, but everything was a big huge smorgasbord of opportunity in every direction.

Maybe that was the problem with modern life in general. It was just an endless stream of big life-changing decisions, with only so much to ever really tell you if you were making the right ones. You just had to periodically look at where you were and try and guess at how you were doing.

Blake sat up in bed. Were they really going to try to get Joe into professional baseball? Now that he was out there in the real world, the idea suddenly seemed strange, alien, even a little ridiculous. He couldn't focus on it, his mind just spun around. Maybe he had been thinking about it too much.

There was a knock on his door, interrupting his reverie. Blake felt a deep sensation of dread. Part of him just wanted to ignore it, hope it went away. But he forced himself to get up and go to the peephole. There was a middle aged Latina woman in a uniform outside, so he opened the door.

In a thick undeterminable accent she said she was there to clean his room. Confusedly he told her no, he just checked in that morning, it had been really early, he didn't need cleaning. He would let them know when he wanted the room cleaned. They could leave it a few days, actually, did she know how much chemicals and water and soap get used washing hotel sheets every day? It was a travesty.

But she got kind of insistent, if he wanted his room cleaned today, it had to be now. And he had a twig in his hair. It all felt slightly bizarre, given that he didn't want the room cleaned at all.

Her spoken English was pretty good, but he got the impression she didn't really understand him. Some people were like that with languages, and he wasn't sure how coherent he was. For the life of him he couldn't even tell what her accent was. She looked Latin, but it wasn't a Spanish accent. It sounded Eastern European, it was messing with his head.

He finally showed her the room, look, it was clean, he checked in today. That seemed to be enough for her. She left, and he collapsed down on the bed.

Had something been going on *there*? Certainly, he had checked in early. But hotels were usually pretty good at organizing their cleaning schedules. And she had been really insistent, almost weirdly so.

Could she have been an agent? That didn't seem particularly plausible, were they going to pay off the cleaning staff? He supposed she could have been a fake cleaning lady. He wouldn't know any better, if he tried to check her credentials that would be a giveaway in and of itself. Now might be the time they would want to talk to him, while he was high, he would be more likely to give something away.

There might be easy ways for someone to send her, aside from co-opting the cleaning staff or placing agents or what have you. They could have just put in a request to have his room cleaned. Or even have distracted her, and made an alteration to whatever document they used to organize the cleaning schedule.

But what purpose would that really serve? All he would be expected to do would be tell her his room didn't need cleaning. Was that really what he thought was going on there? It seemed crazy to even think all that, could he hear himself?

Blake had an immense sensation of relief. He lay back on the bed, feeling himself relax, his worries releasing. Coincidences happened, and that wasn't a particularly big one. His aberrant behaviour could even be triggering aberrant behaviour in others. Maybe the hotel people thought he was setting up a meth lab in his room or some such.

Although aside from that there were a lot of little things. He felt his anxieties return, like the swing of a pendulum, his mind was spinning around and around.

Having to turn on his laptop at the airport was pretty weird. And how often did people rattle at your door handle? It happened, but that very first night after flying? It was all stuff that was explicable purely by chance, but he couldn't say there weren't a lot of weird coincidences, that much was true.

He rolled around, uncomfortable in the bed. In many ways it was almost weird that they hadn't contacted him. You'd think he would at least merit an email or something, if they went to all that effort with the roadblocks.

It was pretty strange that those people from the dye company hadn't contacted him either, for that matter, if it had been them at his apartment. He must have at least given them his email. Maybe it could have landed in the spam folder, but no, he checked it in Austin. Realistically it was pretty unlikely that it had been them. Which would mean it was either agents, or that his landlady got confused.

There was a lot of information they could get on him, if they knew where he lived. Even just his water, electricity, internet usage, Joe had mentioned those. All three of them would have dropped off to nothing the same day that Joe fled.

How precise would the metering be? Blake remembered his power bill in New York, it had a graph of day-to-day usage over the month. He could visualize it, little bars in a rectangular box, he had thought it rather neat at the time.

Going to his apartment was a different MO than whatever they were doing now, if someone was doing something now. But maybe they had gone to his apartment as part of a routine investigation, and figured out his phone number. And now they were being more subtle. Maybe they didn't know if he was involved, but they suspected him. Agents *were* expensive, maybe they needed to figure out how much time they wanted to spend trailing him.

Blake felt a chill. Everything weird that had happened fit with an MO of poking at him to see if he reacted. The ice cream hadn't been drugged, he had been fine. But it was the kind of thing that people who were worried about being drugged might freak out about. How had he not even seen who's ice cream it was?

They hadn't searched his laptop, but it scared him half to death having to turn it on. Had the door handle rattled too loudly? That guy in the mall, with the sunglasses on. The guy had really been looking right at him, and had sort of appeared in his field of vision. Those agents had been wearing sunglasses indoors, that was something he would be expected to react to.

One way or another he had spent his first night in the beach town in a seemingly empty hotel. He shivered. There had been a police car following directly behind him, right when he first arrived in LA.

What had the surfer guy said? He said 'we', didn't he? Who said 'we' for 'weed'? Blake tried to remember the exact moment, replay it in his mind. It had been a pretty distinctive 'we', there had been no 'd' sound. You didn't say, hey let's smoke some we, my nephew's growing like a we, I'm going to go we the garden.

And 'we' was exactly the sort of word that would freak out paranoid people. If the guy had said 'Ganj' or something, that was neutral. But *we* was *them*. That was two things at once, one in a thousand meets one in a thousand.

Blake turned again in his bed. He always gave his email to people, that was the first thing he gave out, before his phone number, address, anything. In any scenario where the dye people had gone to all the effort of going to his apartment, and couldn't connect with him on the phone, they probably would have emailed him. Which pen had he been using that day? The ink tended to run on that fancy black one, and he sort of had messy writing...

20

Eventually Blake must have gotten a bit of sleep that night, although he was wide awake well before dawn. It was again a relief to see the sky changing colour. If nothing else it was an excuse to get out of bed, there was something morbidly disheartening about lying there feigning sleep.

After a brief consideration of the security issues, he decided to go ahead and go for a swim. He just left his phone in a bag on the beach, it was pretty empty at that point in the morning. Then he didn't even worry about it as he bodysurfed in the waves.

Out there in the cold water, with the dawn breaking over the beach, Blake could see everything with clarity. The final truth of the matter was that he just didn't know what was going on. But if they *were* poking at him, trying to get him to respond, then that in and of itself implied that they didn't know if he was involved.

If they already knew, then poking at him would be the last thing they would do. It would just make him suspicious, and thus less likely to lead them to Joe. So the most important thing he could do now was stop worrying and act normal until he disappeared.

Blake got stuff for breakfast at the grocery store, then checked his email. The meeting was on for tomorrow, Jack was getting into town this afternoon. That was that, then. Blake had been a little unsure about going, but now it definitely felt like the right move.

He had a leisurely breakfast, watching a particularly cheesy comedy on the movie channel. It was the third one he had seen with the same actor. As it got later into the morning he went for another walk through town. He browsed the tourists stores again, bought a highlighter pen from a little stationary store.

On the way back he passed by his original hotel. The parking lot was again full of cars, he couldn't make sense of it. Although, looking at it, the hotel was right on the beach. There wasn't really a lot of parking that close to the beach, the nearest other spot was up at the little shopping centre. Maybe they just let people park there this time of year. Blake felt a little rush of relief, there were logical explanations for these things.

He then spent the rest of the morning stretched out in a hammock in his hotel's common area, going through the business books he had bought, periodically highlighting things he found interesting. With the highlighter pen he was no longer killing time, he was *doing something*. Maybe he was doing a management consultancy with someone, and these were the books their current strategy was based on.

He had a few short conversations with the people coming and going in the hotel, the hammock was in a high traffic area. A couple of girls from LA, had just been up for the weekend. They really liked the ceviche place as well, Blake would have to try it. A middle aged guy waiting for his family to get ready, apparently he sold insurance, they talked about the industry briefly. A young Swedish couple headed eventually for San Diego, he gave them a reasonably detailed summary of the key sights in Southern California.

Blake tried to be outgoing, to never shy away from conversation. No one asked him any weird or prying questions. The one guy came and went without Blake ever seeing the family, but there were other exits they could have taken leaving the hotel.

Finally about three in the afternoon he went back to his room to call Jack. Blake briefly considered making the call from somewhere outside - technically his room could have bugs. But that felt kind of weird as well, to make it worthwhile he would have to go find somewhere without anyone around. Sometimes there was no perfect way of doing things.

Jack answered after the first ring, and sounded relieved to hear from him. He was in LA, had just finished checking into his hotel, the trip had gone well, it was a heck of a flight.

They had a meeting loosely scheduled for two tomorrow. Blake said that was perfect, then Jack jumped into a rundown of what the meeting was about. It was all very preliminary, but the hotel was looking for someone to supply the material for all their linens in California, and possibly duvet covers as well.

It would be a huge deal if they could close it. The hotel had been asking about some of their more expensive fabrics, which they had a higher markup on. And hotels went through linens pretty quickly, apparently. Jack thought he knew who they were using now, and it was a cheaper manufacturer.

Then Jack said he had to run. He gave Blake the address to the hotel, which apparently also doubled as the California corporate office. And oh, Laura would be coming down for the meeting. Did he remember her? She was there at that first meeting in San Diego. Then Jack said he looked forward to seeing him tomorrow, and hung up.

Laura was coming. Blake ran this development over in his mind. He could try and make sure she didn't have his San Diego number in her phone, he had sent it to her in that chat. But that might be hard to bring up, he would have to act under the assumption that the walls had ears.

His instincts were telling him it was probably best she not even be there. From the sounds of it she was just tagging along, he supposed it was even at least hypothetically possible that she was just coming to see him. It didn't feel right to involve her, if there could be someone trailing him. Bad enough he was involving Jack. Blake felt a little pang at that though. When exactly in the future would it be a good time for that sort of thing?

He dialed her number, and let it ring, hoping she would pick up. She seemed like the type that might ignore an unknown number. Finally she answered, and sounded happy to hear from him, once she realized it was him. How had he been!? He really disappeared back there. Blake said he was good, had been out on a ranch, actually, and now a little beach town the last few days. It was pretty low-key.

She asked if he was coming to the meeting, he must have talked to Jack? Blake said he was, but he thought it might be a fairly boring meeting. Was she really coming all the way down to LA for it? He wasn't going to be in LA very long at all actually, he himself. Although he might be making it up to San Francisco in a few days.

At this she sounded a little annoyed, her tone developed a noticeable chill. It was a big meeting, Jack had a lot on the line. She sort of admitted to in fact playing a very small role in setting it up, Innosuasion had been doing some advertising for the hotel chain.

She was just going to be in LA briefly as well, actually. She was going to a resort in Palm Springs early the next morning, they were going to take pictures for a brochure she was working on. Then she was off to New York in the afternoon for a conference, which meant she wouldn't be able to stay at the resort. She felt ripped off, they had offered her a free night. Also, it was a separate hotel chain, apparently she had been working on nothing but hotel advertising for the last while, it was crazy!

Blake's mind raced as she went off about the intricacies of hotel pool photograph angling. She was coming to the meeting then, was she? It didn't sound like he would be able to dissuade her. He tried to run over all the logistics again in his mind, it felt like there were lots of little things that could go wrong.

Her tone changed, she wasn't talking about hotel brochures anymore. Maybe she shouldn't be telling him this, but Jack had been planning on offering him a title with Wildon Textiles, right before he disappeared. She didn't know what, it was just something symbolic. Maybe Vice-President of Innovation or something, he probably could have made something up himself, ha ha.

Blake laughed, but something caught his attention. What exactly had she said, 'right before he disappeared'? Not around when he disappeared, or a more general 'if he hadn't disappeared'. 'Right before' suggested a high degree of precision, the knowledge of an exact day. Perhaps that of his scheduled lunch with Jack.

She was saying she had actually ended up being in San Diego that week. Just for like a day and a half, but she had stopped in at Wildon Textiles for a couple hours. Blake felt an urge to ask if she called him, which he suppressed. But that was getting to be too much.

Could he ask her to lie about the day he left? He hardly knew her. Although one way or another he might sort of have to, if she knew the exact date. He would need to find an opportunity to have a talk with her tomorrow, he couldn't do it now over the phone. But when? A dinner after the meeting maybe? It sounded like she had a pretty busy schedule, she might just go to the meeting then disappear.

A thought had just occurred to him, he said. There was something he needed to pick up, in San Francisco. He had been planning on picking it up later, but he was already most of the way there. Really he might as well get it now. Then he could pick her up tomorrow morning, and they could drive down, make a road trip out of it.

She sounded slightly taken aback. Blake hoped she hadn't

bought her plane ticket yet, or perhaps better that it was refundable. But ya, she thought a road trip would be fun, actually, maybe that could work, her tone still a little uncertain. It was better for the climate. Blake pointed out that it was probably only an hour or two longer by car, once you took into account getting to and from the airport and waiting for the flight.

She made some mulling-over noises, then agreed, sure, they could do that. Good thing he called now, she had been about to book her flight. They agreed to meet up at 8 am sharp, and she gave him her address. Then she said she had to run, she had some emails to send and she hadn't even started packing yet.

Blake fell back onto the bed after hanging up. This was getting to be more and more of a departure from Joe's procedure. He couldn't see any fatal angles though, he was doing what he needed to do.

It was all exhausting, thinking about it. Blake tried to sleep for a while, but his mind just wouldn't shut off. Nonetheless it felt helpful, just lying down with your eyes closed was restful, wasn't it? Around eight in the evening he got up, and it didn't feel like he had been lying there awake for four hours. So he must have gotten at least some sleep.

He made tea, and after a short deliberation decided to drive up to San Francisco that evening. He could get another hotel up there. Exhausted though he still was, he wasn't going to fall back asleep any time in the immediate future. Might as well get the driving done now.

Blake packed up quickly, carrying his stuff to the car all in one go, and checking out on the way. Leaving town he stopped at a gas station to fill up, and bought a case of energy drinks. He had one right away, and cracked another as he headed out onto the highway.

He went over everything again as he drove north. Joe had a lot of rules for him to follow, he didn't want to forget anything. There was the phone he had on him now, as long as it was turned on they might be able to trace his movements, either now or in a later investigation. He didn't necessarily want to lead them to Laura's place, maybe he would turn it off later. He could say the battery died.

There was another thing. He had told Laura he was driving to San Francisco to pick something up. He would need said item. Maybe something for a market research project, that would work. An investor friend wanted his opinion on some product,

Blake was to use a bunch of different brands then report back on his experiences.

Although nothing he had in the car seemed like it justified the trip. Maybe something with the DJ box, but why not just have that sent in the post. He felt a little wave of panic, it was almost 10 at night on a Sunday. Where was he going to find something? Maybe he could buy a gas station out of some knick-knack. But everything they had at gas stations was just generic stuff you could buy anywhere.

There was also the issue that if he had an agent on him now, they would see him buy the stuff, which was sort of weird. There were again different scenarios, agents magically watching his every move, agents putting a tracking device under his car. Or just investigating him a month from now.

The surface story could be that he was actually picking something up. Then if he got interrogated later, he could quickly fall back on admitting it was just an excuse to pick Laura up. That sort of worked. It was pretty creepy, certainly. But if the worst that came out of all of this was that they thought he was a creep, that wasn't so bad.

Maybe this was his Big Mission. The people on the ranch were the ones investing in the business, and it was his job to pick up a whole bunch of sample product. That was a little less creepy. He was still using it as an excuse to pick her up, but it was something he was going to buy anyways. He felt like he could pull that story off in an interrogation room. That just left him needing whatever product it was he was going to research.

There was a sign for a town coming up, Blake had been there before. He remembered it being a fairly small place, but it was getting late. He might not get a lot of other chances. He took the exit, drove a little ways. Then on the other side of the road he saw one of those big everything stores. There were a few cars parked outside, the lights were still on, it looked open!

He parked outside, taking a spot right in front of the main doors, and grabbing his backpack with the computer with him. The odds of someone breaking into the car seemed small, but if he followed Joe's protocol strictly - which was what he was supposed to be doing - he would now have to assume there were bugs in the DJ beat box or the card shuffler, even the business books.

Stepping through the sliding doors it was a blast of fluorescent light and muzak. Blake grabbed a cart and hurried down an empty aisle, it was men's clothing. There was a lot of selection, but it was all pretty cheap. It felt like clothing could complicate things anyways. He didn't know how exactly, but Wildon Textiles was in the clothing industry.

Likewise he skipped over the sporting goods section. There was an announcement through the store's loudspeaker, they were closing in ten minutes, please bring your purchases to the cashier. He went down a general appliance aisle, there were a bunch of big fancy coffee machines. They seemed like too much though, they were all really expensive.

Blake had a realization. If he was on a mission to buy some specific product, he would already know what it was. He needed to be looking for something in particular. Skipping over kitchenwares, he hurried down a general computer and electronics aisle. There were video games, but they didn't seem right, little portable speakers, maybe if he couldn't find anything else.

Then he saw it. Mice! He wasn't sure exactly why, but for some reason a ludicrous amount of mice seemed especially fitting for the circumstances. That was what it all came down to, finding the one perfect product in the endless labyrinth of a box store.

They had a few different types, he threw a couple of each of them in his basket. What was the angle, why were they investing in them? Looking at them, they were all mostly the new style, just one brand was the older style. Well, maybe he liked the older style, but he wanted to incorporate the innovations of the newer models - some of them were pretty flash, and wireless was obviously better.

Like vinyl records, everyone thought they were going the way of those 8-tracks you used to see, but now they were hipper than any CD or MP3 could ever be. It was a metaphor, that's what it was. Or something like that. That difference between the old and the new, that was the essence of the thing, what it *represented*.

He made his way to the cashier as another closing announcement buzzed through the store. "You've sure got a lot of mice," said the tired looking cashier, looking slightly in awe as he rung him through. Blake made an acknowledging noise, and paid in cash. He hoped he wasn't twitching, he felt like he might be twitching a bit.

Blake threw his purchases in the back seat, then quickly set off north again. He didn't feel good though. It felt like everything he was doing was wrong, like he was making stupid mistakes. His behaviour back at the beach town had been pretty erratic. And now this? It all felt like too much. Just the fact that he was driving at night, he should have spent the night at his hotel then gotten up early to go pick Laura up.

He felt really greasy as well. What kind of guy does something like that, just to have an excuse to drive a girl across the state? Was it a wacky romantic thing? He didn't think so, it was probably more serial killer. Blake rolled down the window and threw out the receipt, he didn't even want to have it on him. What if it fell out of his pocket, or he got arrested and she saw it?

Really though, if he sat down and did the maths, it was a lot worse that he was involving her in the first place. Assuming he would even get the chance to talk to her, it suddenly seemed like an exercise in futility. He had to assume the car was bugged, how much time would they really spend outside of it on the drive down?

Blake glanced back at the backseat. It looked very empty, like he just didn't have enough mice. He was driving all that way just to pick up something he could have bought at any generic superstore? He needed a proper collection, what he had back there would just look weird.

Although now that he had them, he was sort of stuck with his story. But he had to pick up Laura at 8. Where was he going to find a store that early? Maybe he could be late, find a place that opened at 8. But it was going to be touch and go getting to the meeting as was, it was a long drive. By the time he bought the stuff and drove to Laura's place it could be pretty late, 8:30-9:00 was probably optimistic with rush hour traffic. Then the only way they would make the meeting on time would be if he sped, if he really sped. And he wouldn't want to risk a ticket, not now, especially not with Laura in the car.

It was all of Joe's bloody rules, he was getting tangled up in them, there were too many moving parts. One of the key reasons for going to the meeting was to look normal. But a drive like that, there would be a lot of opportunities for her to say something that gave things away. It would be a great strategy if he was actually innocent, but he wasn't.

Maybe he should just abort. He was pretty close to the town where Lee parked the motorbike for him. He could just cut east and park the car at a hotel, then disappear into the night. That would be flakey, and erratic, especially now that he was en route to pick Laura up. But he could just say he was sick, fall back on the old schoolboy standard.

Every course of action seemed flawed. Maybe he just needed to get it together. He still didn't have any real evidence anyone was on him, he just had to act under the assumption all scenarios were true. He glanced at the back seat again. Maybe he just needed more mice.

Continuing north Blake made good time, the highway was empty. A little after one he began approaching the vast urban conglomeration that was the Bay Area. He pulled into a truck stop on the highway, he could probably just sleep a couple of hours there in his car. Checking into a hotel suddenly seemed incredibly complicated.

There was a diner style restaurant, so he pulled in right up front then took a seat overlooking his car. He had a piece of cake, then another one. People came and went from the restaurant, truckers, a family, some teenagers. He tried to feed on their normalness, none of them had been harbouring fugitive supersoldiers.

Finally he paid, leaving a big tip, and asked if they minded if he just sleep in his car for a couple of hours. The waitress said it was alright, so he just went and stretched out with the seat back. He was enough of a rough, adventurous sort, he didn't need a feather bed.

Time passed slowly, Blake didn't really sleep. Finally his alarm went off at five thirty in the morning. He turned off his phone, then got out and stretched, did a couple of laps around the parking lot. Then - taking his backpack with him - he went and quickly freshened up in the bathroom. Looking at his haggard face in the mirror though, he felt distinctly unprepared. Now more than ever would he need to be on the ball.

Going back to the car, he dug around in the back seat a bit, just in case that receipt he threw out the window had flown back there. It felt like his headspace was all wrong, he was strung out, over-analytical, paranoid. When he should be the opposite, relaxed, maybe a little bored. He had just spent a week doing nothing after his adventures on the ranch.

Blake tried to look back fondly on the ranch, to visualize it. Riding horses, sitting around a fire. It all felt fake though, like a movie. Why had they picked a ranch, it seemed really complicated, what did he know about ranches? There were any number of details he could get wrong.

Then he remembered something. He had those boots, the ones he bought in the thrift store in Austin. He went around to the trunk, and dug them out of his bag, their bright colours glowing vivid under the LED lighting of the truck stop. Sliding them on, they fit well enough, he felt a transformation. They were a gift, from an old cattle handler to a new one. They marked a rite of passage. Or maybe they were more a gag gift.

He could see them all, sitting around the campfire the last night. A grizzled old rancher giving him the boots, everyone laughing heartily, he had earned his stripes. It was almost like it was all coming back to him. Getting saddle sores the first week, trying a cactus stir-fry, relaxing watching TV on the big screen after a long day of hiking through the hills.

Re-energized - and with another energy drink - he continued on his way. The sky began changing colour as he headed north, it was getting towards 7 as he approached San Francisco. There was starting to be a lot of traffic, which was making him nervous. He pulled into a gas station to fill up, and asked the guy at the till whether there were any big stores nearby that might be open this early. The guy wasn't really from the area, but he figured there must be something.

Speeding down the road, it felt like the entire operation was hanging by the mice, it was the singular detail on which everything else depended. Going over an overpass, Blake saw a grocery store, it had a 24-hour sign. Maybe it was a long shot, but it looked fairly big, and he might not really get a lot of other chances. He took the turn off, pulled into the parking lot, and hurried inside.

Blake headed down an aisle that looked promising, magazines and stationary and stuff. They had mice - they were twice as expensive as the other place, and of obviously lower quality. But they had them. Price aside he still grabbed a bunch. There was only the one brand, but if he arranged them strategically no one would notice. He hurried to the till to pay, the cashier again making a comment towards the large amount of mice Blake had.

Blake got a couple of recommendations from the guy for big stores in the area, they were sort of in the direction of Laura's place. Then rushed back to the car and arranged his purchases in the back seat. It still didn't feel like enough, but it helped. It took a lot of mice to pull off an operation like this.

Hurrying on, he was soon passing by a number of big box

stores. Art supplies, home & bath, clothing, they were all closed. Then he saw another big everything kind of place, with some cars parked outside.

Blake pulled up to the entrance, went to the doors. It wasn't open yet, but it opened at 7:30, that was five minutes away. Feeling an immense relief, he did a little walk around, waited by the door. Stores like that opened right when they said they did, did they?

7:30 rolled around and the doors opened like clockwork. Blake hurried in, and asked a very pregnant cashier which way it was to electronics. They too had a ton of mice, he filled his basket, and grabbed a big duffle bag on impulse. The cashier sang a little song as he paid, about all the mice the guy had, ok. He asked her if there were any electronics stores around that would be open, and she said there was one just around the other side of the store. That was handy.

Blake went back to his car, then drove maybe 100 meters, there was a giant electronics store, someone leaving through the front doors with a big bag of purchases as he pulled up. He hurried in, raced around aimlessly until he found his section. They had more mice than the other stores combined. They were all 10% off, although the prices looked slightly higher than the everything stores, and reading the small print it said there were no returns on sale items.

He grabbed a couple of each of them, then grabbed a few more. He felt like he could get away with some duplicates with market research. He also grabbed some weird giant ones that were half video game controller tablet things. If you had giant mice like that they were sort of a different beast, but he figured they still counted.

Blake paid with his credit card – he was just hiding what he was doing from Laura, not from any super-spies that might be tracking his financial trail. The acne-ridden cashier actually seemed slightly freaked out about the amount of mice Blake had. There was something weird with disabling all the anti-theft devices, but in the end he figured it out without having call his manager

Feeling immensely relieved Blake hurried back to the car then headed the direction of Laura's place, driving opposite to the main flow of traffic. That had been a lot easier than he had expected, actually. This was America, he supposed.

As Blake continued down the road, he saw a big hardware

store on his right. There were a decent number of cars in the
parking lot, it looked like it was open. There was a point, where
you just had more mice than would do you any good, was there?
Maybe so, but he pulled in anyways. If he was quick he wouldn't
even be late.

There were a couple of bored looking cashiers sitting at the
tills, one slightly androgynous with green hair. Blake asked if
they had mice, and the one made a non-committal noise, while
looking vaguely offended, then sort of made what could be read
as a head movement towards the interior of the store.

Blake raced down the aisles, almost ready to turn back. It
didn't really look like the kind of place that would have anything.
But he found an office supply aisle, and they had a section with
some surprisingly huge mice. Blake grabbed a few different
colours and hurried back to the cashiers, who boredly rang him
through, completely nonplussed by his gigantic mice.

Hurrying back to the car, Blake noticed there was a big self-
storage place across the way. The sign said it was open 24 hours,
that could actually work pretty well in the context of a later
investigation.

Looking at the back seat, his purchases were pretty much up
to the top of the seats. He had found his mice, then. Having
achieved his goal, it now suddenly seemed really unnecessary.
He wasn't exactly sure what he had been thinking. He could have
just said the DJ beat box thing had special top secret copyrighted
beats saved on it or something.

But nonetheless he felt a strange tranquility. Never mind the
mice, in some strange way it felt good just having bought more
stuff. He gazed back at the boxes, the light reflecting off the
various multicolored plastics. He had paid his dues to the deities
of commerce, like the old sailors who would throw a gold coin
into the ocean before a voyage. If nothing else it was good for the
economy, he had gone all that time in the cabin without buying
much of anything, he had been feeling a little guilty.

Blake pulled out of the parking lot, drove down the main
road, onto another road, then past the park Laura had
mentioned. It was about five to eight when he saw the sign for
her street. He turned down it and watched the numbers until he
came to her house.

21

Laura's place was a biggish row house on a hill, up a bit from a park, and not so far from downtown. It seemed like a nice enough place, he remembered her saying something about roommates. He would even peg it as part way to a party house.

Laura appeared at the front door as he was parking, hurrying towards the car with a backpack slung over one shoulder. He got out of the car, and she gave him a quick chaste hug.

"The mysterious Blake Myntbanke returns!" she said, slightly awkwardly.

"Yes, I'm back in California for now," he said, unsure of what exactly to say about that. He opened the trunk so she could throw her almost burstingly full backpack in, then she hurriedly opened the passenger door.

"Did you get Jack's email? He wants us there early now, we need to do some prep for the meeting," she said as they got in. Blake nodded and started the car, pulling out the way he came.

Laura swivelled around and inspected the back seat. "You literally have a ton of mice!" she said, laughing. "I guess that's what you were picking up?"

"Ya, it's product research for an investment I'm working on." Blake glanced towards the back seat. "I'd offer you one..." he started, but she cut him off.

"Well, I kind of overpacked a little," she said with a little laugh. "Those mice wouldn't even fit in my purse."

Blake felt an ironic sort of relief. It did actually feel much less creepy that he had come all that way to pick her up. Thinking about it, if he *was* paranoid, worrying about agents tracking his every move, would he have really bought all that?

There was a pause in the conversation, Blake felt a little unsure what to say. Then Laura broke the silence. "You really disappeared back there. Off gallivanting somewhere, I suppose?"

"Well, yes, I felt a bit bad about that, leaving without giving people a bit more of a heads up," Blake said, affecting a tone of just slight exasperation, with a touch of confusion. Like why was everyone making a big deal about it, when he hardly disappeared at all.

"I headed up north, for LA, then ended up on a ranch in Texas. I lost my phone out in the middle of nowhere, I didn't have anybody's numbers, you wouldn't believe the hassle..."

"You were really on a ranch?" she asked, and he detected a slight note of incredulity in her tone. "Is that where you got the boots?"

"Yes, they were a gift, my last night there." A thought occurred to him, they were rather a large fashion statement for a meeting. "I've got shoes I can change into, in the trunk."

She laughed. "Whatever, I think these guys are cool. People who work in the hotel industry see a lot of stuff. How was the ranch?"

"It was quite an experience, camping, riding horses, cooking on a campfire, even a bit of herding." Blake hoped he wasn't committing too many details about the ranch, he didn't actually remember anything herdable in Lee's folder. "It wasn't like all out on the range either, they had a really nice entertainment system, you wouldn't believe the TV."

He quickly continued, feeling the need to change the subject. "Last little while I was just hanging out on the beach. Reading a lot of business books, actually, part of another project I've been getting behind on. Have you read The Profit Prerogative?"

"Ya, I have!" she said, which was a pleasant surprise. Blake thought it was an interesting book, was glad to have someone to talk to about it. She thought it was good, but she thought it was actually a little biased *against* small business. They both thought the hostile takeover case study was crazy.

Business books seemed to in fact be a shared passion of theirs. Blake gave her a summary of one he had read in the cabin, they compared notes on some classics, she gave him a couple good recommendations.

From business books, the conversation moved on to the meeting today. From the sounds of it, Laura had actually played a fairly big role in setting it up, although she was being really demure about it for some reason. They had been doing some PR work for the hotel, and she gave someone Jack's number after a fluke conversation about their recurrent linen problems.

From there the conversation got on to travel. They had both traveled fairly extensively in Europe, both really liked the same beach in Spain, they both wanted to spend more time in India. Turned out she had studied anthropology, she was supposed to be living in a remote village in Asia by now.

Blake dropped a couple stories about the time he had a bar in Goa, talked about his days with the Stonehaven's Rest. They were good times. The way he was talking about it, it did feel a bit like he was throwing his money around. But given the circumstances he might need the leverage.

She just got kind of cold though, and changed the subject. Which in and of itself was sort of refreshing, he had that sensation again, like she had absolutely no interest in digging gold. It wasn't even that, it was like he was just a normal person to her, like his money wasn't even on the radar. Sometimes people got really awkward, or weirdly critical, there seemed to be a lot of baggage with the subject.

They hooked up his new MP3 player, and took turns putting on songs as they passed through the low desert hills. After a bit he put on one of his early music playlists, she said it was good travelling music. Well, a lot of it was old pilgrim songs, that's what pilgrims did.

Not everyone liked his music, but she seemed genuinely into it. Which was nice, he had been a little worried putting it on. You couldn't think all knights and dragons and elves, you just had to appreciate it as music. They were songs that were close to a thousand years old, and there were still bands playing them today. She could dig it.

Blake wasn't always as coherent as he would have liked, he had some trouble putting his ideas together sometimes, but it was good conversation. He was basically running on fumes. He had another couple of energy drinks, her giving him a look after he cracked the third one. Apparently you weren't supposed to drink more than two in any 12 hour period, it said on the can.

The conversation did seem to keep returning to her work. Eventually she wanted to end up in the non-profit sector. Or maybe PR, if she could find a company that worked on good causes. She only took the advertising job because it was a good position with a big company. She was learning a lot, making connections.

But it was still advertising. Apparently Innosuasion had just been hired to design the packaging for a new 'healthy' chip. They wanted it to look all rustic and natural and wholesome, and they were like, oh, get Laura to do it, she loves health food. But it wasn't any different than other chips, if anything it was a little worse. You wouldn't believe how much sugar something could have without tasting sweet.

Blake didn't think that was all that bad. She had no control over what clients her company took. She had to pay the rent, from what he knew about Innosuasion they sounded pretty ethical. Definitely no worse than your average marketing company. Turning down a contract was halfway to a boycott.

But she really wasn't having it. Did he realize how many hours of human labour go into convincing people to eat more junk food? She kept going off about it, he didn't know if she was sort of venting, or what. But it was making him feel dirty. He was going to ask her to lie for him? It suddenly felt like an incredibly difficult thing to do, now that she was here, in the flesh sitting beside him, with a guilt complex about working in advertising.

How was he even going to bring it up? Oh, ya, hey baby, can you pretend I skipped town on the 11th? Ya, can't say why. Give a big wink and point a finger at her. Don't worry about it sweet cheeks.

It all felt horribly wrong. What would she think of him, it felt like everything was going so well. Not to mention the sheer amount of mice involved in his excuse to come pick her up. He wondered if that was the sort of thing they might tell her about, in an interrogation, to get her to flip.

Whatever he was going to do, he needed to do it fast. There were the ethical concerns, but also logistical ones. He might not get a lot of chances to talk to her. Assuming she didn't have a bug in her purse, a restaurant could be a safe place to talk.

Looking at his watch, it was a little after 11. Did she want to get something to eat? She was getting hungry, but suggested they get fast food. They were running late as it was. Something a little fancier would probably work better for Blake's purposes, but they really hadn't been making good time, there had been a lot of traffic.

There was a fried chicken place just right up ahead, so Blake turned in and parked next to a big glass window. It looked busy, hopefully it would be fairly loud. They went in and ordered, Laura confessing a guilty pleasure in fast food, which Blake concurred with himself. If she did order the salad in the end.

As they went to sit down he sort of took the lead. Glancing around, there weren't a lot of secluded tables, he took one which had his back to a glass wall. At least from there he could see everyone around him, and basically the car.

Blake let her talk about the interior design of the place as he tried to figure out his next move. A family with kids had just vacated the table closest to them. There probably wasn't anyone within earshot.

But again he didn't know what to say. He couldn't think of any way of asking her in code, through the lines, like he had with Jack. Did he even trust her enough for something like that? He sort of almost felt like he did, but this was only the second time they were seeing each other in person. Maybe he was reading too much into their online chats.

A young couple came and sat down where the family had been. That could be earshot. For all he knew there were lip readers with cameras recording his every mouth-movement. Here wasn't the place to talk to her.

He got a moment of relief from that, he could just enjoy his chicken strips. While Laura was in the bathroom he chugged another couple energy drinks he had hidden away, throwing the cans in the garbage before she got back. Then they were quickly back on the road.

Laura started off about Wildon Textiles again, but he couldn't follow it, she was saying something about them making a deal with another t-shirt company. Jack had sent her an article, about the t-shirt industry, it was really interesting, there was a lot of growth in the market, it was a staple product. Her words were a strange drone, t-shirts this, t-shirts that.

When he spoke, his voice sounded strange to him. It was alien, like when you were listening to a recording of your own voice. It was rather disturbing to think, there might be a bug in the car. There was either someone recording the conversation or there wasn't, it was one of those two things, and he didn't know which.

Laura was asking him something, something about a fabric. He didn't really get the question, and just said he didn't remember. That seemed like an acceptable answer, just the way she had asked it. He hoped it hadn't been a non sequitur.

His tone had sounded weird again. What if someone was listening to that, replaying everything he said over and over, looking for non sequiturs, analyzing his every tonal nuance? He could see little spots of black, forming at the edge of his vision, he had to swerve a bit to avoid a car that was passing around him on the left.

Maybe everything he said would be in a report. Blake could see an agent, faceless, suit and tie. They all wore the same uniform. He was sitting in an airplane, in first class, reading the report.

Blake tried to peer at the report, looking over the agent's shoulder he could almost read it. It was page after page of text, everything Blake had said, word for word. Although no, it wasn't word for word, not all of it. He could see big summaries of his conversations.

Blake felt a fear, but also a strange camaraderie. Here on the perimeter the distinction between hunter and hunted became immaterial. Friends, enemies, co-workers, brother-in-laws, taxi drivers, it was all illusory. It was just a pattern, experiencing itself subjectively, a blooming of hungering beings, chasing their drives, ever changing their forms so very slightly with every generation, a strange stillness in the chaos as it reached the crux of the process.

He had an immense sensation, a connectedness, it was profound, oceanic. He could feel the beating pulse of the universe all around him. The agent wasn't an agent anymore, and the report wasn't a report, it had never been a report. It was something else, all lines of text speeding fluidly by, like they had been spun on some strange wheel, Blake couldn't read any of it. He could see very far from here, and he was suddenly very sure he was near the Root of All Things.

There was someone else there, as well, not the agent, not Laura, not god, nor the devil. Some silent, neutral observer, perceiving, interpreting, he could sense them, but only for a moment. They wanted him to focus on the road. Then they were gone, or just beyond his reach, he didn't know. It was all fading like one of those dreams you forget without even remembering what it was about in the first place.

Blake felt his fear return, he could see the agent again. The agent was still on the plane, now he was reading the report and listening to the recording at the same time. The recording was at the exact point where Laura was talking about granola bar packaging, and the words in the report were being written as she spoke.

The base would be earth tones, but they wanted some bright

colours, so it was about balancing them out, not contrasting them, although you did want contrast as well. She thought they should use more metallics.

Blake heard himself agreeing, and she was saying they should at least have one mountain or mountain-like shape. The agent was underlining something in the report. Was it what he just said, or something he had yet to say, could he change it? Blake tried to read the report, but it was too far away, it fell away as he tried to look at it.

He was no longer sitting flat on the road, but staring straight down a tunnel. It felt like the car was speeding up. His vision was dissolving into static at the edges, like an old TV on a channel you didn't get. But the static was hieroglyphics, in some strange language he had never seen. It made up the true substrate of the universe, and it was dissolving the reality around him.

Had the agent sent him down this pit? The alien letters sped by, now thousands per second. The agent was turning towards him. As it did so its face transformed, it was reptilian, strangely cartoonish, yet horrifying, it was beaming him a message telepathically. It could smell the echo of his footfalls, and would be along for the big parade. Then with a puff of smoke it was all gone, the report, everything, and there was just road in front of him.

Laura was now talking about a multi-day hiking trip she had done last summer. That was nice of her, just to talk, he had probably stopped uh-huhing a little while ago. His vision around the edges was just black now, and was starting to return.

He breathed in and out, and tried to focus on what she was saying. It sounded like she really enjoyed her trip, picnics in alpine meadows, swimming in the river, it was really cold. If you thought about it, that's where we used to live, out in the woods, it was our natural environment. But 99% of the time it was just city city city, no wonder we were all so out of touch with everything.

Blake knew exactly what she meant. That was one of the reasons why he was spending so much time at the ranch. He tried to focus, pull all his energy into having a normal conversation. He thought long hiking trips were great. Or just big parks where they had proper facilities. You could get the best of both worlds, hike all day then get dinner at a nice restaurant and sit in a hot tub.

She laughed, that was true. They both agreed that there was something to be said for roughing it as well. Blake didn't think it was some myth. She could take a turn driving, if he was getting tired. It was a long drive. But they were almost there, maybe half an hour away, he said he could pull it off.

Then they were silent a bit. Which was alright, they had been talking a lot. He would rather just sort of focus on staying within the white and yellow lines at that exact moment anyways.

Blake looked at the clock on his dashboard again, and it said one, which was sort of puzzling, the math didn't seem right. He had picked her up at eight, and they had been talking pretty much the whole time. Did that really mean they had been talking for five hours? It felt like maybe three hours had gone by, at most.

He hoped he hadn't said anything suspicious, all that time. The risk of being recorded had faded fairly far into the back of his mind for most of the conversation. But maybe it was better like that. One way or another they could communicate with each other. He felt centered, everything was clear again now. He was a different person than he had been five hours ago.

Blake suddenly knew exactly what he had to do. He could just write her a note, hand it to her somewhere, under a table, maybe. 'Please delete any record you have of my San Diego number. If anyone asks I left San Diego on the 11th. Destroy this note and tell no one of this. B.' That sort of strategy had worked well enough with Joe and his business card. She would have his back, as of that moment he had no doubt of that.

Then he just sort of rode the wave, cruising down the highway. It was a nice sunny day, he was feeling good. He had a lot of energy. They were soon in LA, Laura looking at the map, figuring out the fastest route, giving him directions. She sent Jack a text from her phone, the battery on his was dead. They found the way without making a single wrong turn, and pulled into the hotel parking lot with time to spare.

22

The hotel was huge, and fairly flash actually, a big fountain and everything. Blake took a particularly visible parking space right out in front, and did grab the backpack with his computer. Maybe he had some diagrams he wanted to show them or something.

He saw stars when he stood up, but kneeling down to adjust his pant legs over his boots it quickly passed. As they crossed the parking lot Jack appeared out of the hotel's main doors, a wide grin on his face.

"Blake!" he said boisterously, shaking his hand, and giving a laugh. "We weren't sure if we were going to see you again!"

"Yes, sorry again about all that, it was crazy, you wouldn't believe."

Jack laughed again, giving a slight glance in the direction of Blake's boots. "We all just assumed you were off on some adventure." His tone was jovial, lighthearted, although he just quickly gave Blake a puzzled sort of look, it had meaning in it. Had he gotten the message then?

Jack said they wouldn't be ready for them for a few minutes, so they went into the hotel lobby, sat down on some plush chairs off to the side. Blake cracked another energy drink - Laura giving him a slightly disapproving look - and Jack started off about his trip.

It was actually the first time he had been anywhere in Asia, he had even managed to explore a little bit, it sounded like he really enjoyed himself. And maybe they *could* be selling more speciality products out there. It was a decent sale with the Thai company, and it sounded like it would be fairly steady. Laura looked impressed when Jack mentioned selling threads had been Blake's idea.

Blake tried to study Jack's mannerisms as he talked. There was always the chance that someone had talked to him, he could even be wearing a wire. But he again seemed pretty normal.

There was a pause in the conversation, then Jack looked over at Blake curiously. "And how have you been? You were saying you were on a ranch?"

Blake shrugged noncommittally. "Well, yes, for a little while, really I've been all over the place. Last few days I was just hanging out at the beach."

"Blake was herding!" said Laura with a laugh.

"Well, not really, just a little bit," said Blake, self-depreciatingly.

"Really, herding," said Jack, grinning and shaking his head. His tone went more serious, if still lighthearted. "We *were* getting a little worried about you though, you had been coming in almost every day. We were joking that armoured van robber guy got you."

Blake felt his stomach jump, that caught him off guard. He gave Jack just the quickest of looks, had he gotten nothing from their phone conversation back there?

"Ha, ha, no. Just got caught up in some business," Blake said, trying to sound as natural and nonchalant as possible. "I remember watching that on TV, it was a couple of days before I left town. I was going to drive out to Anza-Borrego to do some hiking, but I changed my mind after watching the news."

"They just caught him, did you hear?" said Laura, her tone mildly surprised, delivering an interesting factoid. Blake froze. They what?

"Really?" said Jack. "That's good to know, he seemed like a pretty tough character. I wouldn't want to run across that guy in a dark alleyway."

The room started spinning, Blake's vision again disappearing at the edges. He had a very distinct impression Laura just said they caught the armoured van robber. She had been keeping that from him all the way down?

"Did they say how they caught him?" he asked, hearing a small catch in his voice.

Laura gave a shrug. "I can't remember, it was on the news yesterday. I was making dinner, so I didn't really watch it."

What the bloody devil. Joe was supposed to be uncapturable in the woods. Had he done something stupid? Blake tried to think of a non-suspicious way of asking for more detail, but the conversation had moved on, Jack was talking about the meeting now.

Blake tried to nod along as Jack delved into the fabric needs of the hotel industry. He felt a rising panic. What was his situation, then, here and now? He didn't think Joe or Lee would sell him out, but him and Lee were known associates. Maybe he was the guy on the outside, an investigation could be starting right now. Teams fanning out, descending on the beach town, calling the car rental agency.

Jack was looking at him, he had been saying something about whether they would sell directly to the hotel chain, or to their manufacturer. Blake wasn't sure if some comment was expected of him, but then Jack's phone was beeping. They were ready for them upstairs.

Blake felt lightheaded again as he stood up to follow them towards the elevator. Was getting into an elevator his best course of action? He stepped in, and suddenly felt very claustrophobic, trapped in the little box. He wanted to flee, make up an excuse and bolt for the nearest newspaper. But he had come all this way, he had to stay for the meeting. He needed to maintain plausible deniability.

The elevator binged and the door opened to a hotel hallway. A couple of men in suits greeted them, an older scrawny fellow with glasses, and a youngish guy, chubby features with slick black hair, a fairly normal suit but a really loud colourful tie. This point in the afternoon it almost hurt Blake's eyes. He didn't catch the older guy's name, but he was vice-president of something, and the younger guy was Dan.

Blake dutifully shook their hands, then they were walking down the hall, getting some sort of tour. The rooms were pretty flash, Laura was clearly impressed, they checked out the view. They were all made to feel the sheets, Blake thought they were nice. But maybe they could chaff a bit, certainly.

The older guy was going off about fabric durability, Blake had trouble following him. It was very technical, corporatespeak, it was making his head hurt. Their marginal attrition rate for linens was limiting their potential to invest in other customer experience amenities. It was literally like that.

The young guy, Dan, cracked a joke, those duvet covers see a lot of action. Everyone laughed, Blake forced himself to laugh as well. Apparently they didn't actually get as many stains as you would think, being a hotel. Not that there wasn't a lot of undesirable stuff to clean up, but they had industrial strength washing machines. It was just the red wine, you had the smallest red wine stain, you had to throw the sheets out, people got freaked out.

Jack started talking about their new stain resistant fabrics as they went to look at one of the suites. As they continued down the hall they passed an open door, with a laundry cart outside. Blake could hear a TV on in the room, it sounded like the news.

He strained his ears, he could get a couple of words. They were saying something about a big merger in the energy sector. But then a vacuum started up, and they were walking again, back towards the elevator. They went up, near the top floor, into a medium sized meeting room. Apparently Jack had couriered them up some fabric samples, which were passed around.

Blake's mind kept racing. Had Laura actually said that, they had caught the armoured van robber? He had been preoccupied with that stuff, and he was sleep deprived. Maybe he was hearing things. He replayed the moment in his mind, he had asked how they caught him, and she had replied. Jack had said something about it as well.

The way Laura was talking, it sounded like it had happened yesterday. He felt like an idiot, he should have been checking the news. All he had been watching was that cheesy movie channel.

Dan was now telling a story about some guest who tried to escape his room naked out the window with a rope made of towels. Laura seemed skeptical, but he was insisting, no, it really happened. You couldn't make this stuff up, the guy tied like three of them together, he sprained his ankle, they had to take him to the clinic. Everyone seemed to think it was a funny story, Blake again made himself laugh along with the group.

He had a sensation that he was missing the meeting. He probably seemed distant, there in body only. He needed to be *there*, being at a meeting wasn't just being written into the appointment book. It was witty banter, important insights, new business connections.

"Towels!" Blake heard himself say. Everyone in the room suddenly went silent and turned towards him, it was slightly off-putting. "We could make you some amazing towels." He had been going somewhere with that, a second ago, his vision was beginning to fade at the edges again. "Then people could steal them, if you put your logo on them, and it would be advertising, word of mouth."

The older guy was nodding a bit, although he didn't look particularly convinced. Blake hoped he wasn't re-inventing the wheel for them. "You could make them out of space aged material, have them be quick-drying or something, so they would be a conversation piece, something that people would show off to their friends."

The guy was nodding a bit more, now looking perhaps slightly intrigued. Blake looked over at Jack, who was giving him sort of a look and making some funny little lateral head movements.

Laura then chimed in. "You could do it like a promotion, a free gift that every guest gets. You could even have a bin, down in the reception. That way it would be clean towels, so people aren't carrying around dirty laundry."

She paused a second. "It could say something like 'we throw in the towel'. You could have a little write up about how your guests love your towels so much they are stealing them, so you decided to just give them away. You could even attach a little survey, and get some free market research at the same time!"

"We do write off towel losses as an unavoidable cost, but we figure we get at least a third back through indirect advertising," said the older guy, rubbing his chin. "It's hard to quantify, but our research has found that our guests do associate tangibles from the hotel with their overall destination experience."

Blake's head was pounding, he was feeling nauseous. This had been easier when he didn't have to talk. Jack was almost shooting daggers at him with his eyes. Did Wildon Textiles make towel material? He couldn't actually remember seeing anything towel-like in the warehouse.

"Well, we're still working on perfecting our towel designs, so we might have to get back to you on that one," said Jack jovially, again giving Blake a look.

The conversation then jumped to shipping logistics, Jack went off about stain resistance gradients for a bit. Then Blake was made to show off his boots, everyone seemed to like them. He had been on a ranch, not so far from Austin. He had ridden horses a bit, and yes, even did a bit of herding. Just getting the animals in at night mostly, he wasn't sure if it even counted.

Dan asked him if there were tumbleweeds, Blake said yes, there were a few. He hoped there were tumbleweeds around Austin. What kind of a question was that?

Then Dan said he was transferring the hotel's New York branch, he'd be working at the big main hotel in Manhattan. Blake knew where that was, actually. There was a really nice pizzeria across the street? There was, Dan said he would probably be eating way too much pizza.

Then, a little out of the blue, Dan said he heard Blake had recorded the band Crass/Class? Dan thought they were totally ahead of their time. The New Direction Orchestra was doing pretty much the exact same thing, just without any substance, it was a total rip off. Blake felt a sudden flash of indignation. They could have at least been a little more political, the basic concept was punk.

Dream Embargo was on the same label, right? Yes, Blake recorded them as well. Then Dan asked him if he had a card, he didn't actually, but he took Dan's. They would go for drinks, Blake was going to be back in New York eventually.

Although for now he was thinking he might just go back to the ranch. The city was too much, after howevermany days in the country. He had culture shock, it was too much noise, the honking, the pollution. They all thought he should just go back.

Then goodbyes were being said – Dan had to run, he had some core competencies he had to leverage - and Blake found himself again in the elevator. From the sounds of it, a plan was being made amongst the three of them to get coffee in the hotel's restaurant below. Dan had recommended it, they had just remodelled it, apparently they just had to take in the ambiance. Blake said he could only stay a few minutes though.

They went to his car, Laura wanted to pick up her backpack now. She had some box ad designs for Wildon Textiles to show them. When they got to the car Jack's eyes went wide, he made a comment towards the end of never having seen that amount of mice.

Blake supressed his urge to flee, and they went into the café-restaurant. There was a big TV, with a game on. It didn't seem prudent to ask them to switch to the news. He couldn't see a newspaper in the entire place.

They had a big wall of donuts, with strange bizarre long names. Laura was laughing and reading off the flavours, 'avocado maple chocolate coconut', 'triple powder custard re-luxe'. None of it made any sense, it was just weird random arrangements of words. Joe was potentially captured, and Blake was trying to make sense of 15 syllable donut names.

In the end he just ordered a mango mint donut and a coffee, and they sat down at a table off to the side. Jack seemed to think the meeting had gone well. It was just groundwork at this point, but it was a good start. He was right in saying Wildon Textiles had higher quality material, wasn't he? The only issue was that it was a little more expensive, but they would make that back on increased durability alone.

Blake's mind was doing somersaults, he still couldn't process any of it. They had caught the armoured van robber? He tried to eat his donut, but it was pretty much pure sugar, and it was sort of a funny flavour combination. But maybe it would get back to the guys at the meeting if he didn't finish it. That was bad business, Dan had been raving about the café. Which in turn made it suspicious if he didn't finish it.

Blake had a sensation like he was skipping through a minefield. One false step, and it was all over. He tried to eat another bite, but it was burning his tongue. And it tasted like energy drink. What if he had drank too many of them, and now everything was going to taste like energy drink for the rest of his life?

Jack was looking at him. "What did you think of the meeting Blake? Do you think we'll make the sale?"

Blake gave some tentative little nods. "It seems like it went well enough, you never really know with these things, but I would be optimistic." He paused a moment. "Sorry about all that with the towels."

Jack grinned at him. "Well, we were talking about towel material back when you were in San Diego. I don't think we have any machines set up for it right now though." Blake nodded, although he had absolutely no memory of that. Jack was probably just being polite.

"I think you made quite an impression on Dan," said Laura, an ever so slight slyness in her smile.

Blake nodded, unsure of what to say. He needed to get out of there. "I have to go, I have to make a phone call to an investor on another.." as he was speaking, he could see a couple of cops walk up to the door of the restaurant and peer inside. He watched as they opened the door, then he quickly looked away. Jack and Laura were looking at him expectantly.

"On the other side of the planet," he finished, not knowing where on the other side of the world it was business hours.

Jack smiled at him. "Well, it was good to see you Blake. Can we expect you in San Diego any time soon? Maybe you can get started on towel prototypes, we've got a couple of machines that might actually work for that."

The cops crossed the restaurant, and were talking with the waitress. One of them looked over in his direction. Blake got his phone out of his pocket, went to turn it on, changed his mind, then put it down. He had been on a ranch, a couple of hours from Austin. He didn't have the address, but he could try and get it for them. He must have the guy's card somewhere in his bag.

"I might try and make it back to San Diego soon, my schedule's a little up in the air right now though," said Blake.

The cops were walking towards him. Maybe he should just run. That would be a give away, but given the circumstances it could be his best play. Was he better on foot, or in a car? The car might have tracking devices, and there were really a limited number of places you could drive, especially in LA traffic.

They were on him, right beside the table. Then they were walking past him towards the door, carrying a bag, one of them saying something about apple fritters. They opened the door, and were gone.

"Are you alright Blake? You look a little pale," asked Laura.

"Just a little tired," he managed.

Jack looked at him, concern now on his face. "If you ever need anything, or even just want to talk, just give me a call."

Blake nodded, if it didn't feel appropriate to come to Jack for advice on harbouring genetically engineered supersoldiers. He still needed to talk to them about the alibi stuff though, didn't he? Was that all out the window now, with Joe being arrested? Could well be it was all the more important.

He glanced around the bar, the sound from the TV was loud, there was no one else around. He had no reason to believe either of them were wearing a wire. He could talk to them. He spoke slowly, slightly exaggeratedly, deliberately.

"Mm, hey, I just remembered, I was trying to tell Laura that story you told me. She wanted to use it as an example in a presentation, but I didn't feel like I could do it justice." Laura looked at him, slightly confused. "The one about the shoe lining people. You told it to me the afternoon after that meeting I missed, with the furniture people."

Jack again got that weird look on his face, just for a second. "That's one of my favorite stories. I've probably told it to both of you a couple of times by now," he said with a quick laugh. "It's all about how you never know exactly how a customer is going to use a product, so you should never lie to them, even if you think it's for their own good."

"Yes, that's the one! You can tell her once I've gone," said Blake, looking at them intensely, trying to communicate the gravity of the situation with his eyes alone. Then he turned to Laura. "Oh, and I haven't given you my new number. Jack has it, he can just give it to you." Again he spoke very deliberately, and scratched his mouth in sort of a shh movement, now looking between the two of them. "I'm not using the old one anymore, make sure everybody deletes it."

"Ok, cool!" said Laura, still looking slightly confused. "Give me a call sometime!"

"Will do!" said Blake, and with that he was up and away, shaking Jack's hand and giving Laura a brief hug. He hurried towards his car, quickly started the ignition, and pulled out of the parking lot, panicking for a moment as the car lifted up and the wheel jerked to the side - he must have been up on the curb - then he sped off onto the open road.

23

Blake made a beeline for the nearest branch of the hotel that accepted Lee's anonymous corporate loyalty card. He wanted to put on the radio and look for the news, but even that seemed like too much. He hadn't been listening to the radio at all before.

He stopped at a little corner grocery store on the way. Unfortunately they didn't have newspapers, so he just bought a bottle of scotch and continued on his way.

After a couple of wrong turns he found the hotel. It looked like an anonymous enough place, with a big underground parking garage, so he drove in and parked. He figured it was still unlikely anyone could have bugged his stuff anywhere he had been parked so far, but it would be a real risk here, so he quickly threw it all into the duffle bag. Then he took it all out and carefully repacked it so everything fit. It was a logistical issue in and of itself, the amount of mice he had.

He hurriedly hauled his bags up the stairs, his pockets full and the DJ box in his hand. The receptionist looked distracted, all he had to do was swipe the platinum card and she was giving him a key. Once he got to the room he poured himself a scotch, which he downed in one go, then he poured himself another. Then he turned on the TV, jumping around between stations before settling on one that looked like Californian news.

He watched as they did the weather, a bit about municipal elections. Part of him wanted to just go ahead and get out his laptop to do a search, but that seemed like a bad idea.

It moved on to world news, failed peace talks, some kind of drought-flooding combination disaster somewhere. Massive casualties, refugees, a record heat wave was apparently responsible. He willed it to go faster, how much could really be going on in the world? He supposed that while Joe fleeing had been a big story, him being captured could well be the opposite.

Then suddenly there was footage of police lights on a dark

street, the announcer was talking about the armoured van robbery last February. The perpetrator had been shot and killed by police after a failed robbery of a convenience store.

Blake felt a blackness at his core, he couldn't process it, he was falling. The announcer was still talking, there was an ambulance, a guy in a t-shirt talking to a reporter. Blake couldn't understand any of it, it was all just noise. Everything they had been doing, all his maneuvers to look normal, it all suddenly felt like stupid little games.

Then a mug shot appeared on the screen, but it wasn't Joe, it was someone who looked vaguely like Joe. Whoever they were, it sounded like they were both the person who got shot and who robbed the armoured van.

His despair turned to relief, to confusion, was he hallucinating, what was going on? It really didn't make sense to have somebody else's mug shot. Were they going to say that was Joe, was it some kind of massive gaslighting conspiracy cover-up?

To confound matters further Joe's mug shot now appeared on the screen. Blake felt a baffled relief as the video switched to newsroom, the announcers were talking about how the original suspect was innocent.

"That's almost the bigger story here, isn't it Jane?"

Jane's eyes were wide. "Can you imagine?"

"It must be pretty hard to see your face up there on TV like that," said the other male announcer. "I probably would have gone into hiding as well."

Jane was nodding, her eyes still wide. "If you think about it, Jim, he'll be a hero now. It isn't easy to hide from the police like that."

"I wouldn't have lasted a day out there," laughed the chubbier announcer.

"The San Diego police have cleared Eugene Cudneck of all crimes, and are calling on him to come out of hiding," said the one male announcer, breaking from banter tone into statement tone. He then embarked on a PSA sort of speech about how in the rare event you were ever falsely accused of a crime, you should just talk to the police, or better yet get a lawyer.

Then the San Diego Chief of Police appeared on the screen. He was a maybe 50-something grey haired fellow, lean features, seemed a pretty respectable type. He was giving a press conference on the stairs of a courthouse, apologizing for their mistake. Cudneck had been cleared of all charges, and granted an official state pardon for any misdemeanors he might have committed as a result of their mistake.

Blake tried to get a read on the guy as he went into a boilerplate apology. There was something odd in his demeanor, an anger, a cynicism, maybe a bemusement, Blake didn't know exactly. Just little things, his enunciation, his facial expressions, points left to hang a little too long.

When he said 'the detectives working the case', it was like he was separating himself and the police department from them. Almost defiantly, he said there would be a review of officer conduct. Then he made an ambiguous reference to factors beyond their control, and mentioned a lack of information sharing in the early stages of the case.

And then it was over, the news going on to sports. Blake stared unseeing at the TV while his mind raced. All things considered it seemed a fortuitous turn of events, if he didn't know exactly what to make of it.

Given the whole thing was made up, he doubted they got the wrong man. Maybe they had taken it too far, it probably wasn't easy to fake an armoured van robbery like that. People started asking questions, when a fugitive was on the lamb that long. For all he knew they could have been about to transfer the investigation to another department where Joe's people didn't have any pull.

Could even be they had them on the run. They weren't necessarily going up against an all-powerful conspiratorial force. It was probably a small number of people who were up against constraints of their own.

Blake was about to pour another scotch, but he stopped himself. All things considered it didn't change much for him on the ground, here and now. Operation Groundhog. His mission was still going basically as planned, perhaps with a few hiccups. The only step left now was to disappear and make his way back to the cabin.

Lee had the motorcycle parked for him midway up the state. It would probably be best he try to shake a trail a couple times, he was new to all of this. He would have to assume there was a tracking device in the car he had now, so the first order of business would be to switch cars.

Although that in and of itself posed some logistical difficulties. He could switch cars where he rented it at the airport, but that would leave a trail. He'd have to assume they could get the plates.

It would just be weird switching cars, as well. What was wrong with the car he had now? Even if they weren't on him now, that would leave a trail for someone to find later. He supposed he could switch up to a sports car or something, maybe he felt like racing around in a slick roadster. Although his mice probably wouldn't even fit in a sports car.

His head throbbed a bit, he had been thinking about this kind of stuff too much already. What *was* he going to do with all his stuff? It would be a little strange to buy all that just to stow it away in a storage locker. Maybe he could store it with a friend for now, although then he'd probably have to hang out with them for a while. He didn't even know who he would call.

He could rent a motorhome. That would actually check a lot of boxes. It was a different enough type of vehicle that it justified returning his car. And it would be a place to stay, he wouldn't have to worry about getting another hotel. Likewise he could just park it somewhere and leave his stuff there, Lee could get someone to take care of it. It would even make sense to have his lawyer rent it for him, he generally used them for bigger rentals.

Blake set up his security system, then had a shower, thought it all over. Then he called his lawyer from the bathroom with the volume on the TV turned up. Could he get him a motorhome in LA? Special order, which was code for anonymously, which was generally how they did things like that anyways.

Blake said just a small one was fine, he wanted it tonight, optimally they could just leave it there for him to pick up. After about ten minutes on hold his lawyer came back on the line. He had found a place on the north side of town, they closed soon, but they could arrange to have someone stay late. Legally they had to have someone there to hand off the keys. That worked. Blake held, and five minutes later his lawyer was back on the line, it was all set up.

That just left the question of how to get to the motorhome place without being trailed. He could get a taxi, and leave the rental car here for the company to pick up. Although if there was someone staking out the hotel, they would probably be watching for any cabs that came and went. Did he think he could outwit them that easily?

There were those dial-a-drivers services. If you drove someplace then got too drunk to drive, they would come with two drivers, so they could drive you and your car home. He remembered them being regulated differently than taxis in LA, quite often they were just private cars without logos or yellow paint jobs.

And then they could take his rental car back to the airport. Which justified him getting the dial-a-driver in the first place. Otherwise he'd have to drive the car all the way to the airport then get a cab across town to the motorhome place.

Blake had a plan then. He turned on his computer, setting up the security system, then went to scout out the hotel. Wandering through the halls there were maybe three different ways he could get to the parking lot from his room. There was a camera in one of the main halls, another outside the parking lot. Although hopefully hotel cameras didn't matter.

From the parking lot, he did a loop around the hotel, just out to stretch his legs. It felt good to go for a walk, actually. A bit farther down the road there was a convenience store, he grabbed a sandwich, some chips, a drink. Then he walked back to the hotel, eating chips as he went. That seemed like something people who didn't think they were being watched did.

He went over his story again as he walked, it sort of worked, maybe it was a little weird. But any way of throwing a trail was going to look a little weird, and this seemed like it minimized any strange behaviour on his part.

It all seemed at least logically consistent. He was still used to ranch hours, getting up early. So he was in a hurry to get the motorhome tonight, as to take off unimpeded at 4 in the morning, long before the motorhome rental place opened.

It was probably best he didn't check out of the hotel though, the lobby was in a pretty visible spot. So maybe his plan would be to drive the motorhome back to the hotel tonight, and he would just change his mind once he got it. It would have a bed.

Back in his room he got out the hotel's phone book. The sun wouldn't set for another hour or so, but he felt like getting out there now. Given the choice people tended to flee under the cover of darkness, did they? Maybe it would catch them off guard, while looking less like a deliberate elusion.

He called a dial-a-driver place with a smaller, more amateur ad. After a couple of rings a youngish man's voice answered, bit of a Californian accent. Yes, they had a car available. Blake gave them the address, first left when they got in the parking lot, then left again at space 30, back into the little alcove just after the stairs.

Then Blake asked what kind of car it was. Did it have a logo or anything? Blake got ready to cancel, to say he just remembered something. But the guy said it was just a private vehicle, a blue sedan, in a sort of exasperated annoyed apologetic tone that suggested the lack of a logo had been an issue for them somewhere previously.

Blake waited a few minutes, then tried to carry his stuff back down to the parking lot as subtly as possible. After just a couple of minutes wait an oldish blue sedan turned down the lane. Blake waved at it, having a realization. The two cars would leave at basically the same time. If they saw his car leaving the parking lot with someone else driving it, any other car leaving at the same time would probably be pretty suspect as well.

The sedan pulled up next to him and they were getting out, introducing themselves. There was a brown haired guy and a blond guy, both maybe mid-late 20s, somewhat built. Both seemed to be in awe of his mice. Blake told them he was in a rush, so they quickly managed to fit his stuff in the car.

The brown haired guy went to start up the car, and Blake dug out his car keys to give to the other guy. There was one other thing, he had sort of a special request. Could the guy drive his car to the rental place at the airport?

At this the guy got a look on his face. That wasn't what they did, they were supposed to all drive to the same place. His friend would have to pick him up at the airport, it was the other side of town. He actually looked kind of pissed off, he was looking over across the way at Blake's car suspiciously. He wasn't going to pay for any damages.

Of course, of course, said Blake. He felt a little wave of panic, he supposed the guy could just say no, then where would he be? Blake said he understood it was a little unorthodox, but he was really in a hurry, he shoved a couple of big bills into the guy's hands.

All he had to do was drop the car off. He could put the keys through the mail slot and run if he wanted to. The guy looked pretty uncertain, looked over at his friend in the idling sedan, but he finally said OK.

Then just as Blake was opening the door to the sedan, he put his hand to his forehead. Reaching into his pocket, he pulled out the room key. He had forgotten it in the rush. Could the guy drop the key off at the reception, as well?

At this the guy really balked, but Blake said there were no damages or anything, he really was just in a hurry. He had only been there a couple of hours, actually. If the guy really pressed the receptionist she should give him a partial discount on the room, he could keep that as well. That was the official hotel policy, he might have to convince them though, they liked to keep it for themselves.

Blake threw the keys to the guy, who caught them, then just sort of stared at him slightly gape mouthed. But if he was going to complain they were off before he had a chance, Blake ducking down in the back seat and making fiddling with bag noises as they left the parking lot onto the road.

He reappeared with a couple of energy drinks, one of which he offered to the guy, who slightly nervously accepted it. Slouching down in the middle seat Blake gave him the address, and told him about the change of plans with the airport trip. Blake would pay extra, the guy guessed it was ok.

They talked a bit, the guy wasn't long out of college. Driving was a good job for now, he got to go to a lot of crazy LA parties, although only to pick people up. He was just glad Blake wasn't going to throw up in his car. Then Blake said he was going to lie down for a bit, that was cool, ya, he looked tired.

Maybe half an hour later they were there, the sky darkening during the drive. They parked around back, an annoyed looking guy in a suit and glasses appearing from the office. The motorhome was parked right there, it seemed nice. The three of them just unloaded Blake's stuff onto its floor. The guy then lectured him a bit about having to put it all away properly, everything had to be battened down in a motorhome, stuff flew around when you hit the brakes.

He was sure he knew how to drive a motorhome? Blake said he drove them all the time, which was a bit of an exaggeration. But he had driven one once before, a few years ago now, if it had been a lot smaller than this one.

Then the dial-a-driver guy was off, and the motorhome guy soon after, after giving Blake a further rundown on the vehicle. Both were given substantial tips. Blake quickly set in to putting his stuff away, although it took a bit of work to fit everything in. The motorhome was big, but there was only so much cupboard space. In the end his mice barely fit.

Finally he sat down in the drivers seat, put on a hat, and adjusted the mirrors. Pulling out of the rental place, the thing was a beast to drive. He would have to be really careful changing lanes, he wasn't 100% on how the rear-view mirrors worked. They stuck out on the sides, and had a mirror in the mirror.

Blake's mind started spinning again, did he think he had pulled that off, was there anything he was missing? He gave the dial-a-driver guy his key, but his story was supposed to be that he was originally planning on coming back to the hotel after renting the motorhome. He couldn't even remember why, this point in the evening, but every detail seemed important.

But he just sort of let it all go, let his mind slow down. He could go over it all later with Joe and Lee. For now it seemed prudent to dedicate all his mental energy to driving.

After about an hour he passed a mall complex with some motorhomes parked outside, so he circled around and parked there. He managed to get a few hours of sleep in the bed before heading out again, the bustle of people coming and going from the parking lot soothing him into sleep.

Early in the morning he reached the town where Lee had the motorbike stashed away. He parked the motorhome outside a mall, waited until it opened, then set up his computer security system and went in. He found a big clothing store, and bought a backpack, shoes, a couple new sets of clothes. Then he stopped in a grocery store, and made breakfast there in the parking lot.

From there he needed a place to stash the motorhome. He looked at the maps in the glove box, there were a couple of parks with campgrounds nearby. One wasn't far from the edge of town, so he drove out there to check it out.

It looked like a nice spot, bit of an oasis in the desert with some trees. The ranger's office wasn't open yet, but they had a self-check in system. That was perfect, he filled out the little form - putting his lawyer's information - and dropped it in the box with cash for a week's stay.

Then Blake just parked the motorhome, cracked one of the business books, and sat at the picnic table reading. He had to wait until dark to flee, so he just had to kill some more time, he felt like he was getting good at it.

Mid-morning he managed to fall asleep in the motorhome, which was a relief, it was well needed. Around noon someone knocked on his door, but he ignored it, he would assume it was the park ranger. Who knew if he would want to see some ID or something.

By late afternoon he was starting to feel reasonably rested, so he got up and went over a map of the town. There was a specific route he was to take to the motorbike, they had drilled it into his head in the cabin. He changed into his new clothes, putting a change of clothes in the backpack. Everything else would stay in the motorhome, nothing he had on him had ever been out of his sight.

Then he left for town, first taking a trail through the woods behind the campground, then a city bus. He walked a lap around town, got dinner at a little donair place, then made his way to the mall Lee had specified.

Studying the map at the entrance, he memorized where his exit was. Then he wandered around for a bit, browsed a comic book store, spent a bit of time looking at shoes. Then it was out the west exit, through a wooded area then across the street, down the second left. He could see it all on the map, he took the one side street past the three streets. Then he cut through the yard of a small apartment building, hurried down a narrow alley, and ducked into the parking garage of another apartment building.

In the corner was a motorbike, black with a sticker for a folk festival, as Lee had mentioned. He set the code into the key box and got the key. Opening the compartment under the seat he found some Kevlar pants, shoes, a puffy jacket, and a helmet with a big visor.

Blake put everything on, and stored the backpack under the seat. Then he stood there a minute, on the bike, took a couple deep breaths. It had been rather a while since he had been on a motorbike. Well, back in Italy, they had been on scooters. This one looked like it had some horsepower.

But time was a-wasting, he started it up and gingerly revved the engine. Then he was off, out onto the road, through another residential back alley into the night. He was soon out of the city and onto the same checkerboard of country roads he took on the way down. For the first time since Austin he truly felt like no one was watching him, not that he could really know. It was liberating, the cold night air rushing by, he went fast on the bike.

If he did ever start a co-operative in the automotive sector, it could just be motorcycles. That would be much more manageable than a whole car company. If he wasn't better off with something simpler still. Maybe appliances made entirely of replaceable parts, if that was a little boring, as a concept.

It wasn't until after midnight that he reached the cabin. Going up the driveway, it seemed impossible, he had actually made it back. Lee was out in the yard to meet him, a wide grin on his face and a scanner wand in his hand. Blake had triggered an alarm, well obviously. He had planned on giving Lee a full report, but he couldn't do it, he just stumbled to bed and collapsed.

24

Once Blake woke up he groggily gave Lee a detailed run-down of his time outside the cabin. Lee in turn said he had taken care of the car rentals without a hitch, and had put the stuff from Blake's apartment in secure storage.

Lee had sent Joe a message summarizing the news about the armoured van robbery, and now another telling him that Blake was back. All he had heard back was all-clear signals, as was to be expected.

Lee couldn't offer Blake much insight as to whether there had been anyone survielling him. Sometimes you just couldn't tell with these things. Lee didn't think Blake having to turn on his laptop was necessarily that uncommon - Lee did actually have an associate who followed airport security protocol fairly closely, and apparently that was happening more often these days. But it was evidence there was at least a flag on Blake's file.

Neither of them knew what exactly to make of the Police Chief's press conference. Lee thought he could be someone sympathetic to them, if they needed an ally in the corridors of power at some point in the future.

Lee was then quickly off to take care of some things, like getting the motorhome out of the campground. That meant Blake needed to watch the cameras, they needed to be on them like hawks 24/7 now that he was back.

Staring out at the black and white forests, it was worse than being alone in that hotel in the beach town. But there was nothing, no super agents, nor Joe. It was a good sixteen hours before Lee got back, Blake leaving his post once the whole time.

A day passed, then another. Joe was assumedly outside – he had said he would watch the cabin for a few days after Blake arrived. But if he was out there, they didn't see him. Someone drove right past Lee's driveway, sending them into a bit of a panic. But from the looks of it they were just lost, they went back the way they came.

The next day was opening day for baseball, so Blake had the games on during his shift. Brooklyn was playing Tampa Bay, it was a particularly epic game, lots of little one run innings. Then in the 8th it was 5-4, with the bases loaded. Blake was on the edge of his seat, when suddenly Joe was sitting there beside him, cheering when Brooklyn got a hit.

"Didn't see me coming, did you?" he asked, his grin wide. Joe then proceeded with stories from the woods, catching game, weathering storms, sleeping in the trees. He had been watching the cabin, and he was pretty sure nobody was watching them. Neither of them noticed the slice of pizza that was missing?

They watched all the news clips about the shooting. There wasn't much of anything new, coverage seemed to have dropped off fairly drastically after the first couple days.

Joe also thought the Police Chief said some weird things. He seemed a little nervous about it all, actually. From the sounds of it his people didn't do a lot of operations like that in America. If anything, it seemed like something they specifically tried to avoid.

Joe then made Blake go into excruciating detail on every single thing that happened on his trip. Blake wondered if he had been too obvious with the dial-a-drivers and all that leaving the hotel. Joe thought ya, he might have been, there were a couple of things like that. If anyone went to Wildon Textiles right now it wouldn't matter if Jack knew to lie, he was in Europe for the next couple of weeks. Or there could be a record of him specifically deleting his number in the chat with Laura. Hopefully none of that mattered.

In the end Joe agreed that some of the stuff that happened was a little weird, but his guess was that at most they might have been watching him for a day or two. Like maybe the guy in the mall with sunglasses - that kind of sounded like his people's style, and it had been the day of his flight. Joe had seen them do really small things to mess with people's heads, then wait for them to go crazy jumping at every coincidence.

Then they kicked back, put on another game - Oakland vs. Indianapolis – and had some pizza from the fridge. It was another epic game, but Joe was strangely silent, it seemed like something was bothering him. Finally, in a break between innings, he spoke up.

"I really got a chance to think about things out there, in the woods. Like about what we're planning on doing."

Blake snapped to attention, his pulse quickening. Joe paused a moment, seeming uncertain, then continued. "Like, this baseball thing, do you really think it's a good idea?" His tone was incredulous, like they weren't seriously thinking about doing that, were they? He looked over at the screen, then back at them, a sort of bewilderment on his face. "I mean, it would be really cool, if we could pull it off. But do you think it's even possible?"

They were all silent for a moment. Blake suddenly had a sensation that Joe must have really been giving it a lot of thought. "Well, I don't know. I've never been involved in a venture quite like this before," he said earnestly.

It was sort of a hard question, Blake still didn't feel like he could see it clearly. But he didn't want to lead them down the wrong path. Baseball had originally been his idea, hadn't it? Appraising ventures was his area of expertise, Joe didn't know these things, couldn't be expected to know these things. He felt like now was the time for him to call on all his investor savvy, and give them as realistic and objective an estimation of project feasibility as possible.

"It would certainly be difficult, a long shot at best, any number of things could make it impossible." Joe seemed to be hanging on his every word. "Although stranger things have happened." Blake tried to think of an example, but nothing came to mind. "One way or another, you'd have no trouble keeping up with the other players."

At this, however, Joe just looked glum. "Ya, I would be cheating, wouldn't I? Maybe I would make a ton of money, but I wouldn't deserve any of it."

Blake shrugged. "The way I see it, it's millions of dollars to hit a ball around a field. Someone's going to be making that money, it might as well be you."

Joe looked slightly offended. "Ya, but still, people take baseball really seriously. You know how pissed off people would be if they found out? Even if nobody found out, I'd feel like a fraud. What about the players on the other teams? It wouldn't be fair to them."

Lee grinned. "I wouldn't be too worried about them. Half the players out there right now must be using something. Have you seen the muscles on some of them?"

Joe was silent at this, looking a little wracked, so Blake continued. "Perhaps you would be an extreme example. But in the end, you would be no different from any other player who was on steroids. In fact, I would say you would be more ethical than they are. You didn't use steroids to get an edge playing ball, you just had that life thrust upon you. What if you would have played pro ball anyways, even if your lab had never gotten their hands on you? Is it fair they close that door on you just because you're a supersoldier?"

Neither of them looked particularly convinced by that. Blake felt like he had sort of ended on a weak argument, so he quickly continued. "And apparently baseball has always had a funny sort of relationship with cheating. I was just reading something about spitballs. They've been against the rules for most of the 20th century, but it's still seen as part of the game if someone throws one. Like it's just playing the game on another level."

They still didn't look convinced, he felt like he was losing them a bit. "And I don't think people would really see you as a cheater, if the truth were to actually get out. You'd be the romantic rogue, more akin to a bank robber than a steroid pumping juice-monkey." Joe nodded a bit at that, perhaps hopefully. "I think people would see it as a prank more than anything else."

Blake paused reflectively for a moment. "In many ways, that's what something like this would be, a prank. Maybe one of the greatest pranks in human history. Perhaps one that only a few people would know the true extent of, but they would be important people. Say it was declassified fifty years from now, I think people would see you as a hero."

Joe grinned at that. "I've always thought it would be cool to be in one of those declassified documents. Although fifty years would be pretty optimistic."

Lee spoke up, a mischievous grin on his face, it again seemed he was amused by all of this. "As a baseball player you would be a celebrity, a hero. You could talk about the real issues, the stuff the media ignores, and nobody could shut you up. As long as you kept hitting home runs, people would listen to what you had to say."

Blake nodded, that was a good point as well. If he wasn't sure which exact 'real issues' Lee was referring to. That was sort of a change of tact on his part, it almost sounded like he was behind baseball, then. Perhaps he had sat down and done the maths?

Joe however again looked glum. "Ya, I guess, that would be

good. But there are other people who can say those things, and probably talk better than me. But not a lot of other people are strong like me."

A shadow crossed his face. "I kind of feel like a deserter already. Maybe I just should have done my mission. Do you know how much it costs to make a supersoldier right now? Just under $24 million, that's what they told me, a bit before I escaped. That was an estimate, but it's something like that. And I'm gonna go play baseball?"

Blake shrugged at that. "Then drop 24 million dollars on the doorstep of wherever the lab is. What they're paying for sponsorships these days, you could make that much in an afternoon of getting your picture taken drinking soda."

He hoped he wasn't coming on too strong with all this. "And it's not like you'd have to play for the next twenty years. You could probably just do a couple of seasons, and you'd be set for life. From there you could even go on to do missions."

At this Joe's face did light up a bit. "Ya, well, what I was sort of thinking, was that the baseball season is only April to October. So I could do missions in the other half of the year. Although maybe that wouldn't be that different to how things would have been if I never escaped."

"The difference is independence!" said Blake forcefully. "Money is freedom. If you have your own money, you can fund your own missions. You're the one calling the shots."

It felt a little silly, talking about doing missions, like they were kids playing in the garden. Although he supposed Joe really did do missions. "You could still even work for them, the people who created you, if you wanted. It would just be on your own terms. If you didn't like a mission, you could turn it down. You could be freelance, work for whoever you thought was doing right."

Joe laughed, and shook his head. "Ok, so you are making a good case." Now he looked at them intensely. "But people get shot for less than this. We would be pissing off some really dangerous people."

Here Lee grinned wickedly. "It would be a PR nightmare if the truth ever did get out. Even if you don't want to go public, they don't have to know that. Whatever you do, we'll always have that on them."

Joe sort of nodded, and looked at them earnestly. "If we did something like that, there would always be a risk of the truth getting out. Even me being here now, it's a risk. And I don't even know what the implications of that would be."

"Well, the way I see it, there are a lot of reasons both for why the truth should get out, and why it should stay secret," said Blake philosophically. "And maybe no one can really know which is better for the world. But if that's the case, then from our perspective it's a moral coin toss - at worst it's just as likely our actions do good as they do harm. All we would be doing is throwing the coin in the air."

Joe got a funny look on his face, like a man possessed. "Maybe that's what we need, a coin toss, leave it to fate," he said. Then before Blake could stop him, he was reaching into his pocket, pulling out a penny, and throwing it in the air.

"Heads I play, tails I don't." The coin flew in a dancing arc through the air. Blake wanted to jump at it, grab it from the air, but it just landed on the table with a clink. Tails. A sombreness filled the room. Joe stared at the coin in dismay, almost disbelief.

"Screw it," said Joe. "Let's do it anyways."

25

It felt like something was resolved. If - talking about it again briefly over dinner - they did all agree that they weren't really locking into baseball, just continuing down that path. It would be tough enough just getting in, there would be plenty of opportunities to abort in the future.

The next order of business, then, was to get Joe a new face. Lee's plastic surgeon connection was still in hiding in South America, so he would have to get a recommendation from an associate. Lee would also talk to an associate - a different associate - about getting Joe a fake ID.

Lee set off to contact his people the next morning, which put Blake and Joe on the cameras for 12 hours a day each. It was again nerve-racking, even off shift neither of them really slept. Blake had to dig up some eye drops, his hands were getting sore from grabbing onto the arms of his chair. It was now that someone would make an attack.

But there was nothing, not even deer this time, just the swaying trees. Joe pointed out that implied they either hadn't been watching Blake's every move back there, or that he had successfully thrown a trail. There was something nice about narrowing it down to those two scenarios, if they did have very different implications.

Lee came back after a couple days, getting in late at night in a big SUV. He had gotten the names of a couple doctors that could be trusted - one in LA, another in Florida. The guy in LA sounded like the better doctor, and it was a lot closer, so that would be their destination.

They left a little after dark the next day, Lee driving with Blake and Joe hidden away in the back. The roads were empty as they cut through the middle of California, down the same checkerboard of country roads that Blake had used before.

They got to the safehouse Lee had set up for them well

before sunrise, the city suburb around still asleep. Joe immediately dressed in black and got out there to set up cameras. He was up on the roof, around the sides of the house, in maybe twenty minutes they had a security system set up.

Blake took the first shift on the cameras, while Joe set up the DVD player and video games. Once the sun began rising Joe was at the blinds, peeking out into the street. It was LA out there! He seemed quite amused just watching the people go by. A lady with a little dog, a kid on a skateboard, people jogging, the one guy was gay, right? If there were no movie stars, unfortunately.

Lee was soon awake, and they started their day by going over the doctor's website. Fanto was his name, and his before/after pictures seemed good. Blake supposed they always did, but it was a good sign. He had gone to a top school, had co-authored a book about major facial reconstruction. He also did a lot of different stuff, facelifts, noses, eyes, you name it. That was important, as Joe would need a few different things done.

Perhaps the bigger issue was that they didn't know him. Joe was pretty worried about that - people did just go to the police sometimes. And more importantly, he was going to see some next level stuff. Joe's face wasn't normal. He was only authorized to have facial work done by people with high level security clearance. They would be personally responsible if information about the technology got out, it was pretty top secret.

Joe thus suggested they put him under surveillance, then give him some sort of a test. Depending on how he reacted they could then use him, or try the doctor in Florida. It would be a bit of extra work, but Joe really did think they needed to do their due diligence on this one. It was sort of protocol, in fact.

Lee had fortunately brought along a rather extensive selection of bugs, hidden cameras, tracking devices, and the like. The first step was just scouting the doctor out, which fell on Lee's shoulders. So he headed out, while Blake and Joe settled in to taking turns between the cameras and a video game system.

Lee returned in the late afternoon, in a new car. He had staked out the guy's clinic, got some pictures of him when he went for lunch, then followed him home. As far as Lee could tell he lived by himself, a nice house not actually so far from where they were now.

They looked at the pictures of the guy, he was maybe mid-50s, white-grey hair. He seemed like a competent fellow, from what you could tell just by looking at photos of someone.

Probably had some facial work done, it didn't look bad, but maybe a little windblown, just slightly unnatural. Blake supposed you didn't give yourself plastic surgery, so it didn't really say much about his skill.

Lee had called the clinic - disguising his voice, with a burner phone across town - and had managed to make an appointment for a consultation tomorrow. Joe went over the pictures of the guy's house and the clinic, and said he would probably just bug the house. Best he do it while the guy was there, so he could bug his phone as well.

At this point Blake felt he had to raise some doubts. What exactly was he talking about, like breaking into the guy's house? Joe was strangely relaxed about it, Lee hadn't thought there was much of a security system, just the cheap kind any old house would have. He wouldn't get caught breaking in. And if he did, he would definitely be able to get away before the police arrived. Lee didn't see a dog, did he?

Blake was still skeptical, it sounded like a lot of risk. But Joe thought it was necessary, and it seemed like it was decided, they would do it tonight. Joe started making preparations, which wasn't much other than just going over some satellite images of the area around the house, then passing the rest of the day playing racing car games.

They set out around two AM, Lee and Joe in one car, Blake in the SUV. They parked in opposite directions from the house, Blake outside a waffle place about a kilometer away.

Blake was set up with a monitoring station on his laptop, he was to be HQ. He had a screen with little dots where each of them were, he could communicate with both of them on an encrypted signal, switch to a camera on the dashboard of Lee's car. It was really something, actually.

After a few minutes he got a message, Joe was going in. Blake watched the Joe-dot move towards the house, pause outside briefly, then enter through what would have been the side window. It was excruciating to watch, what the devil were they doing?

The dot bumped around the house for a little bit. Then maybe 10 minutes later it was leaving. Joe sent them a thumbs up message, and that was it. It was a little anti-climatic, actually.

Back at the safehouse Joe said it had been a breeze. Hacking the security system was nothing, the guy seemed like a heavy sleeper, the floorboards didn't even creak. Turning the system on, there were three video feeds of the house, a sound feed from the bug on Fanto's phone. They could hear the guy snoring. Joe said he had also put a keystroke logger on his laptop, and a tracking device under his car. And they had been giving Blake trouble for being paranoid back there on his trip.

The doctor was up early the next morning. They watched as he made a smoothy, did some stretches. Lee meanwhile had started working on his disguise before dawn - you wanted to fool a plastic surgeon, you had to go all out. He put on a variety of make-up, some powders, even injected something into his cheeks which made his face puff up. Blake wondered what the point of getting plastic surgery was, if they could just do stuff like that.

Before Lee left he put a wiretap device under his shirt. Blake also gave him some money and other valuables - if the doctor looked promising they would give him an initial good faith payment. Then Lee sprayed himself with a concoction that smelled of rotten sweat, cigarettes, and hard liquor, and they were off.

Blake and Joe parked in a green space a little ways from the clinic. They put on headphones, and Joe pressed record on the wiretap device. There were a few bumping around noises, then Lee was talking to the receptionist.

His voice was slightly slurred, with a dirty raspy quality. He had an appointment at 11. Yes, Mr. Richard Head she said, her tone falling as she said the name. She must have realized it was a fake, she gave a sort of forced unconvincing little laugh.

Lee then made some slightly flirtatious small talk. It was funny, it really didn't sound like his voice. The receptionists sounded nervous talking to him, told him to take a seat. The doctor would be ready for him in a few minutes.

There was a silence, then they could hear the receptionists talking to each other faintly in the distance, it was a sunny day yesterday. Their conversation sounded kind of strained. With any luck Lee was planting a bug right now. Then they said the doctor was ready to see him.

A minute later there was the voice of Fanto introducing himself, telling Lee to take a seat. Mr. Head, was it? Lee gave a sort of incoherent introduction, then there was a thud sound, as though something fell on the floor. Fanto said not to worry about it, his tone slightly annoyed.

Then Lee went off in a garbled voice, he wanted to be a new

man, make him beautiful, har har har. He really had a sick laugh, it was wheezy, gurgly. Fanto sounded uncertain, hesitant, was he sure he wanted extensive surgery? It didn't always meet patient expectations, he needed to understand the risks.

Lee babbled off a bit, well, he was getting fat, eating lots of chocolate bars. Fanto would be able to sculpt him. Lee started talking with his mouth full, offered the doctor some chocolate.

Fanto sounded flustered, he could remove fat, but he couldn't "sculpt" it. Maybe he should come back when he was feeling better, Fanto really didn't think he could do anything to help him, maybe he should try someone else. He had another consultation coming up in a few minutes, he needed to prepare for it.

Lee hollered no, he was sorry, he stopped talking with his mouth full. He didn't have a lot of time, they were after him. Fanto seemed like a good guy, he used to drink at a place called One Eyed Jacks?

At that an uncertainty entered the doctor's tone. That sounded vaguely familiar. Was it a bar on the East Coast somewhere?

Lee said it was. He started babbling again, it wasn't his fault, he had no one else to turn to. He was in the wrong place at the wrong time, he didn't know they were Mafia. He saw the boss take someone out, bang BANG and the guy was dead, lying on the floor. He didn't have anything to do with it, he was just drinking too long in the wrong bar, he saw too much. Now they were out to get him.

Fanto told him to calm down, lower his voice, he sounded really agitated. He wanted a facelift to get back together with his ex-girlfriend, was that what he was telling him? Who gave him his name?

Lee was almost bawling, he was his last hope. Take this money, there was more where that came from. He went incoherent for a bit, there was something about an international smuggling ring, some kind of business in Reno, they had the dogs after him.

Then Lee's tone changed. He could see right through him, couldn't he? It had nothing to do with the Mafia. He got even more incoherent, he considered the man a friend, it should have been a done deal. Things just went wrong sometimes, it didn't have to be that way.

Then his tone went clear, earnest. No fair jury would give

him anything worse than manslaughter. But those redneck fucks didn't even want to use the courts. Fucking inbred hicks, didn't know when to take the money and run. He would get them before they got him.

Fanto was silent, and Lee continued. He would owe him, for the rest of his life. He was a good guy to know. He was a human being, maybe a flawed one, but he wasn't a bad guy, he just made some mistakes. He was crying, blubbering like a baby. Brother, he needed help, he had no one else to turn to.

Then suddenly, Lee said he had a text, he had to go, right now. Urgent business. But the doctor had to help him, he would be back. There was a little park, just down the road, Lee gave the address. The doctor spoke quickly, neutrally, he knew where that was. Lee said he would be there next Monday, 10 pm sharp.

Then Fanto was again silent. Did he think he was wearing a wire? It would be a pretty expensive sting, for those cheap ass pigs. Here, have some more money, those were real diamonds, no, no, take it, take it, keep it, it was a gift. Did he want some meth? He had a line on top quality meth for almost nothing. Then Lee repeated himself, 10 pm sharp at the park, come alone, tell no one of this.

There was another thump of something being knocked over, and Lee was giving a slightly off-colour goodbye to the receptionist. Then his dot was leaving the clinic, speeding towards the side street where he was parked. Blake started the car, then drove in the other direction.

A couple of new lights had appeared on the wiretap console. As they drove back they switched from Lee's feed to the feed from the doctor's cell phone and the new bugs in the clinic. Fanto was silent for a while, he must just have been sitting at his desk.

Then they heard a little bumping around, the door opening. The receptionist was asking who that was, Fanto just said some drunk. Then he asked her if she could do his afternoon consultation. He might just go home now, he had a headache.

They got back to the safe house before the doctor got home, and watched as his dot moved towards his house, then as he appeared on their cameras. He looked pretty distraught, freaked out, he poured himself a drink, then another. He stood up and paced a couple of laps, sat down, then got up and paced again.

Then he got a look on his face, shook his head, laughed. And then again his face went serious. He took the diamonds out of his pocket, put them on the table, looked at them one by one.

It was a lot of money they had given him already. Blake wondered if they could get him to give it back if he didn't want the job. It worked like that sometimes, people didn't want your dirty money.

Lee got back, and went for a shower. The doctor opened up his laptop, and their eyes went to the key logger screen. He just did a couple of searches, 'reality TV', 'reality TV law'. It didn't look like he was reading much of the results, he just closed his laptop again quickly.

Fanto paced around a little bit more, then went to his bed, and lay down. Watching him lie there, with his chest heaving up and down, it really felt like an invasion of privacy. This was all really illegal, wasn't it? It seemed like a lot for due diligence, but it was Joe's call what they did to protect his secrets. Maybe it would help their case if they were ever up against a firing squad.

Around six Fanto got up, had a shower, then headed out in his car. Lee - who had already put on a new disguise - went to see where he was going, while Blake and Joe listened to the bug in his phone.

They watched as Fanto and Lee's dots moved across the map, ending up in a fancy restaurant a few miles away. Fanto met up with what sounded like a group of friends, maybe 5-8 people was their guess. The restaurant was loud, they could only get maybe half the conversation. People talking about their various jobs, TV shows, a little politics.

At one point in the night someone commented that Fanto seemed a little distracted. He had just had a long day. After that he talked a bit, told a funny story about the businesses beside his clinic fighting over parking spaces. He sounded pretty normal, if maybe his delivery was a little off.

Then they were all paying. Some of them were going to a comedy club, but Fanto said he would just turn in. Which he did, driving directly back to his house. Once he was back he paced a few more laps, poured himself a couple tall glasses of strong drink.

They then both passed a sleepless night, Blake watching the two sets of screens, the doctor tossing and turning in his bed. Fanto got up to stare out into the night for a while around 3 AM, and had another glass of whiskey, did some more pacing.

From the looks of it he bought Lee's story hook, line and sinker. Which was good, Blake had been a little worried Lee might have overdone it. He supposed that giving people that amount of money made things real. Sometimes people just needed to confess things.

Fanto was still at home when Blake woke up the next morning, watching movies with a blank sort of look on his face. Around one in the afternoon he got a call from a friend who was going to the bar tonight, it sounded like he was looking for a wingman.

Fanto said he would take a pass, but they talked for a while. From the sounds of it the guy was an old friend. Fanto waxed nostalgically about some time he spent working in Africa after getting his MD, wondered if he should have stayed on there longer. At one point he asked what happened with the 'car deal'. The guy went sort of defensive, he did it, and made some real money. That was that.

After the call Fanto put on yet another movie, so Lee took the opportunity to go meet with his associate who would be handling the fake ID. Blake, Joe, and Fanto then passed the afternoon watching movies, the doctor now in fact onto a comedy Blake had watched in the beach town. Which was a relief, they weren't sure who was going to trail him if he did leave the house.

Lee returned to the safehouse in the early evening. He had talked to his guy, and he could do it, but it wouldn't come cheap. He passed Blake a piece of paper with a number on it, and Blake balked. Lee hadn't given him the fellow's phone number by mistake? And it ended with $220, like it was that precise, they were sitting there counting everything down to the last twenty?

Lee got that it wasn't easy to get that much cash, did he? Lee just shrugged. Joe wasn't going to be using it to cross a border or get a job in a warehouse, it was spy grade fake ID. If they wanted something he could use to be a celebrity, it had to be in all the different databases, be legit on every level.

So Blake gave him the go ahead, then called his lawyer to get them started on very subtly setting up some transfers. His assets were already somewhat liquid with the defensive re-arrangement, but this on top was enough to get the IRS or some anti-money laundering task force investigating him.

The other issue was that Lee's associate would need a picture of Joe before starting on the ID. This was of course problematic, as Joe still had his old face. Lee had asked if there was any way they could do it without a picture, and his associate had said hypothetically yes. But he had been pretty hesitant, it might raise some red flags, get them all in trouble. Apparently it had been the first time anyone had made that particular request.

They could wait, but then who knew how long it would be before they could even get started. Joe's face would take a while to heal. After a brief discussion they decided the best approach would be to find a picture of a kid with a generic looking face - Joe had a rough idea of what he would look like after the surgery. And if it was an old picture he could say his face changed a lot as he grew up.

They spent the evening scouring the internet, as the doctor continued with the movies, a blank expression on his face. They ultimately settled on a picture from a photo of a grade 11 basketball team in Georgia.

Lee edited the picture, changing the facial features slightly, and taking out the background. He had some experience with fake IDs, having worked in the business on the side for a number of years. In the end it looked good enough - perhaps a bit blurrier than government ID was supposed to be, but that was probably for the best anyways.

As Lee was doing this, Joe spent a lot of time going over Fanto's before/after photos. He seemed to be getting a little freaked out - it was his face. Normally he would only be operated on by a top grade specialist.

Lee reminded him that he could still back out. Getting it done would mean that he could never go public with the story about being framed as an armoured van robber. It would be pretty hokey to say he used to look like Eugene Cudneck, but got plastic surgery.

That seemed to effect Joe a bit, he said it was a good point. Which surprised Blake, was he considering going public then? Blake thought that was off the table.

Fanto again had a sleepless night. After a couple of hours of tossing and turning he got up and poured himself a drink, paced around a bit. He knocked over his glass, which shattered on the floor, it looked like he cut his finger picking up the pieces. At one point he must have heard something outside - he was peeking out the windows, went and made sure the door was locked.

Blake was sort of glad he was freaked out. After a performance like Lee's you didn't necessarily want someone who was too eager to rush into the job. It was about finding someone who was the right level of unethical, he supposed, sort of a goldilocks thing.

Still, Blake felt bad, it was kind of a dark road they were sending him down. He wished the guy would just go to sleep. They were going to need him at his best, if and when it came time to operate.

Fanto seemed to have a frenetic energy the next morning, spending a couple of hours frantically cleaning the house. He washed the windows and everything. A little after noon he opened up his laptop, checked his email, looked up some tourist information for Brazil.

Then he typed 'Newspaper Reno', but didn't hit return. He just sat there staring at the screen, then deleted it. Good he was thinking like that. Then he was grabbing his keys, getting in his car. Lee was quickly out the door to follow him.

Blake and Joe watched as Fanto's dot pulled off down his street, onto a main road, went across town. He drove for about twenty minutes, then started driving around in circles in a commercial district. Was he trying to shake a trail?

Then the car stopped, parking by a bunch of stores. A couple minutes later they got a message from Lee. Fanto had gone into an internet café, and was on a computer. He was hidden away in the corner, but Lee would try and get on the machine when he was done.

They sat and waited almost half an hour. The only information they had was the clacking of keys from the bug on his phone. Then Fanto was leaving the café and going to his car, heading back the way he came.

A couple of minutes later Lee sent them a message, he was on the computer. Joe and Lee started messaging back and forth on an encrypted chat program. The computers there did a reset and clean after each session, but there were still ways you could undelete the search history.

They had to install a couple of programs, but after maybe fifteen minutes Lee had it. The doctor had done a number of searches, but hadn't accessed any email programs or anything like that. The first searches were for newspapers in Nevada, he had gone to a couple of sites. It didn't look like he had done much digging around though, he didn't really get much past the home pages.

From there he did a few searches on doctor-patient confidentiality. Then finally there were some searches about appraising diamonds. A lot of pages from 'appraising diamonds yourself', as well as the webpages for a couple of appraisers in the area.

About this time Fanto was getting back to his house, again appearing on their screens. Then he was getting the diamonds out, holding them up to a light by one of the cameras, he was right up there in their view. He put them down, and went digging around for something in a drawer, it looked like a DVD. Then he went and closed the blinds a bit further, and grabbed a little pump bottle from a nightstand.

"You, uh, might not want to watch this," said Joe. Blake felt his stomach do a flip. There was a metallic taste in his mouth, he wasn't going to be able to hold it back. He made a rush up the stairs for the bathroom, he almost didn't make it, warm acrid bile burning his throat as he retched into the sink.

It was all a little heavy, Blake just lay there on the bathroom floor for a while after that, staring up at the ceiling. This was sort of his life now, then, was it? In all of this he was suddenly very struck by the fact that he already knew everything Fanto would know, and more.

In the evening the doctor appeared to be getting ready for their meeting, so Lee and Joe both got into disguise. Blake then stayed in the house with the surveillance system while they went to secure the area around the park.

Fanto left the house a little before the meeting, taking neither the diamonds nor the money with him. Blake again watched his dot cross town, then bump around the park, which again seemed to be the sum of his role in all of this.

Fanto stayed out there for close to twenty minutes, before the dot began moving back towards his house. Joe and Lee soon returned to the safe house. It had been clear, just the doctor by himself. The operation was a go.

They went to work setting up one of the bedrooms as an operating room - blocking off the windows, covering the room floor to ceiling with plastic, moving the bed, that was Joe's job. Early the next morning Lee went out and got a wide variety of medical implements, drugs, and other paraphernalia.

The doctor had an operation that morning, a facelift. He sounded like he was in a bad mood, a man scorned, he snapped at his assistant a couple of times. After that he had a patient in for review, their eye lift recovery was going well. There was a consultation with a girl who was on the fence about a nose job, then he left to go home in the early afternoon.

Blake and Lee headed out in the two cars, Lee already

dressed up in another disguise, Blake putting on big sunglasses and a hat. The doctor was walking, so they just parked on a street he had taken on the way home before, Blake a ways behind Lee on the other side of the road.

After about five minutes Blake could see Fanto walking by. He stopped by Lee's car, and peered into the window, at what would be an open suitcase full of cash.

Fanto lingered outside a moment, then opened the door and got in. They stayed parked briefly, he must have been putting on the blindfold. Then the feed dropped for his phone - Lee would have taken the battery out - and they were off. Blake followed a distance behind as they took a roundabout route back to the safe house.

They left Fanto sitting patiently in the back seat as they changed into the outfits Lee had bought. They were big brown robes, sort of along the lines of what a monk would wear, with slightly creepy happy face/sad face theatre masks. Blake took the happy one, Lee the sad one.

Then they walked Fanto up the stairs to the operating room, and positioned themselves beside Joe, who was sitting in the operating chair.

"You may take off the blindfold," said Lee. Fanto did this, blinking confusedly and recoiling a bit, then doing sort of a double take.

"There was an armoured van robbery in San Diego a couple months ago..?" asked Fanto, slightly weakly.

Joe nodded, grinning. "I'm the actor who played Eugene Cudneck, and I'm going to need a new face."

"That drunk guy.."

"That was us," said Lee.

Then Fanto just sort of stood there gaping for a moment. Blake supposed he could just refuse to do it now, in light of this new information. In many ways they were asking him to do something significantly riskier. But then he nodded, and said OK.

Joe motioned the doctor to approach him, which he did. Joe then pulled a gun out from somewhere below the table beside him, and proceeded to reach forward and sort of tuck it into the front of Fanto's pants. Fanto stood there motionless.

"Ok, so I'm going to give it to you straight," said Joe, calmly, friendlily. "Not everybody in HQ knows about this operation, and we kind of need to keep it that way." The doctor gave a quick little nod, swallowing, he was going white. With his free hand, Joe reached into a bag beside him, and pulled out a CIA ID card, an FBI badge, then a NYPD badge, putting them on the table.

"I could get in a lot of trouble, if the truth did get out, and things didn't go exactly as planned. You aren't gonna tell anybody, right?" said Joe, his tone surprisingly friendly, relaxed. Just a precaution, buddy.

Fanto shook his head. "I won't tell anyone."

Joe pulled out an Interpol badge, put it on the table, then another one, with Arabic letters on it. "That's good. Because if you do tell anyone, I'm going to find out."

Joe removed the gun from his pants. A big friendly grin now came over his face. "And I want to look good too, ok?" Joe looked over at the briefcase, which was on a chair beside him. "You'll get your money, don't worry about that."

"I'm happy to help," said Fanto. He paused a moment, then leaned forward, studying Joe's face.

"I could reshape your eyes, suck in your cheeks. A bigger nose would really change the appearance of your face."

Joe shook his head, and passed him one of the sheets from his briefcase. "Just follow the directions. I've made some changes in pen, but I'll walk you through it."

At this Fanto's eyes went wide, an expression of awe passing over his face as he looked at the sheets.

"That doesn't exist," said Joe emphatically.

"We've already administered the anesthetic, so you can start working right away," said Lee.

And with that Fanto gave a little nod, then started his work. For hours he toiled away, nipping, tucking, using a wide variety of scalpels, forceps, and other strange tools. He asked for help holding things a couple of times, Blake was forced to watch as he cut deep around Joe's eyes, into his nose. Blake felt like he was going to be sick again.

They periodically made Fanto coffee, he had some pizza around dinner time. It was a long job, they worked late into the evening, then into the night. It was well past midnight when he finally said he was done.

They bandaged Joe's face up like a mummy, and Fanto gave him some instructions, recommended he take some things. Then Lee wheeled a TV into the room. He turned to Fanto, passing him a sheet of paper.

"This is a list of all the surveillance devices in your house and clinic. Please be sure to dispose of them properly. You shouldn't have even done those searches at an internet café."

Lee paused a moment, passing a card to Fanto. "If anyone does approach you about this, you may contact us at this number or email address. Make sure you have a secure connection. If you come looking for money, all you'll find is trouble."

Fanto looked aghast, gasped of course not. Then Lee pressed a button on the TV remote, and a video of Fanto holding a diamond up to the light came on. It was maybe a five second clip, playing in a loop, an eerily silent circle flowing into itself.

Fanto sat there stonefaced as a recording from the consultation began to play. There was Lee mentioning the Mafia, then Fanto asking if he wanted plastic surgery to get back together with his ex-girlfriend. Then the bit about no fair jury giving him worse than manslaughter, and Lee saying he would get them before they got him.

"What's your father's birthday?" asked Lee, holding up the briefcase. The doctor said the date, and Lee keyed it into a combination lock on the briefcase. "Do you have any allergies or adverse reactions to benzodiazepines?"

Fanto shook his head, looking confused. Lee nodded, then with a quick motion jabbed a needle into his arm. Fanto's eyes went wide for a moment, then they slipped into the back of his head, and he was sinking into the seat.

They carried the comatose doctor into the en suite bathroom, stripped him down, then gave him a thorough wash in the shower. It was vital that not even a strand of Joe's DNA leave with him. They all agreed they would have seen if he had tried to hide anything rectally.

Then they dressed him in a fresh set of clothes and carried him to the SUV. Hopefully he didn't have any particular attachment to his old clothes. They cleaned up quickly - Lee had already cleaned the rest of the house, and the operating room was mostly just a matter of gathering up all the plastic.

Then they were off, out into the warm LA night, Blake, Joe and the comatose Fanto in the SUV, Lee driving point about five minutes ahead in the car. This time of night in LA there was the risk of drinking and driving roadblocks.

They drove to a motel on the edge of town, where Lee had already booked a room. When no one was looking Blake and Lee drunk-walked Fanto into the motel, and laid him down on the bed, handcuffing the suitcase with the money to his arm. Blake took a brief sad last look at the money, that and the ID was getting to be quite a bit. Then they snuck out of the hotel and were back onto the highway, headed north towards the cabin.

26

Joe lay in the back of the SUV with his head elevated as they drove out of LA, Lee still ahead of them in the other car. Joe seemed talkative, his face felt funny, it was all tingly and numb. It was going to start hurting soon, that was going to be fun.

He thought it had gone really well though. The doctor seemed to know what he was doing. He would probably keep quiet, as well. Did Blake think the thing with the gun in his pants was too much? Blake thought it might have been, a couple of things, actually.

Ya, it probably was. He had done the thing with the gun before on a mission, it was really effective. All that was pretty tame, compared to some of the stuff his lab did. They could piss people off, then get them to flip out and do something illegal. Or get a liability claim against someone's assets then hold it over their head. He probably would have had to do something like that with the guy with the research lab, if he hadn't thrown the pool table.

Then Joe quieted down, talking was making his face bleed. After about an hour Lee parked the car in a residential neighbourhood off the highway, he would have someone pick it up later. They were soon back in the cabin, cleaning and disinfecting Joe's face, doing a proper bandage change. It was pretty unsettling, looking at him. His face was starting to swell up, the cuts and stitches were raw.

Joe followed an elaborate routine over the next few days. He would alternate ice packs and heat packs, take blood samples then pop pills to maintain his blood at a certain thickness or balance out his hormones. His face started swelling up like a balloon, to the extent that Lee had to re-stitch a couple of his cuts. They were getting worried about scarring – not only would it be evidence of plastic surgery, but of weird plastic surgery.

But other than that there wasn't much to do but set back into the movies, books, video games and the like. Lee had again stocked up, so they played old video game systems from ten years ago, some complex board games imported from Europe, were into the black and white movies.

Lee had found a box of old university textbooks, so Blake started pouring through those. Economics, social sciences, psychology, ecosystem biology. It felt productive, like this wasn't necessarily wasted time. It was probably the equivalent of a course or two. Really he was just taking all the time he would have spent reading books in the next five years, and condensing it into a couple of months.

Joe's face seemed to be healing well, and they were soon removing the stitches. If he was still pretty bruised and swollen. They began passing through May, the weather getting nicer with each passing day, birds singing outside, fresh breezes wafting in through the windows.

This was sort of ironic, as all it really meant was that Joe couldn't get out there to train now that his face was starting to heal up. They had some debates about whether they could go out on clear days, but Lee made some fairly persuasive arguments to the end that it was just a little bit too much risk. Just in general they had to be more careful now, it was the kind of backcountry people were known to occasionally wander through. Lee found the remains of a campfire and some discarded beer bottles just a couple of miles away from the cabin.

Likewise there was more traffic on the roads. It was now common to see several cars a day drive past the road that led to Lee's road. One week there were logging trucks driving back and forth every few hours. That was pretty unnerving, they were again on the cameras like hawks. It would be easy enough to hide an entire strike force in one of those trucks.

But aside from that there wasn't a lot of action. Eugene Cudneck's family was apparently now offering a substantial reward for information leading to him. The deadline for Joe's fake ID came and went, but Lee said everything was fine. There were just some delays, that was normal. Although now his guy wanted extra for backdated ID - apparently if you wanted ID with a picture from more than five years ago it complicated things. That sounded like BS to Blake, but they weren't in a position to negotiate.

As the days passed they did begin to worry that it had been too long since Blake's last public appearance. There was an argument he should just go live his old New York life for a while, although after a short debate they all agreed it wasn't worth the risk.

If nothing else he needed to send some emails though. So on the next supply run Lee downloaded his emails, and he started composing a batch of messages to be sent out to his friends. Blake only did the minimum, messages to a few key friends who would be wondering about him. It was crazy, he had been on a ranch, was thinking about coming back to New York, didn't know exactly when.

Jack had sent him a message, just hoping everything was alright. There was nothing from Laura. The Dark Ages historian had just sent a quick note asking if Blake had received his previous message.

There were a bunch of spam messages from some weird food safety organization, all about the various toxic chemicals that get added to food. They were a little morbid, riddly, otherwise health people getting sick out of the blue. The subject lines were a little creepy - they were health warnings, but they also read a little like threats.

Lee speculated there was at least the possibility it was a psychological operation. Emails were easy to send, and it wouldn't matter that Blake didn't know if it was something real, just that he worried about it. That sort of thing could wear away at someone who was paranoid, make them more likely to flip out and tell all, if they had an all to be told. But researching it - with a different secure internet connection – they seemed like a real organization, other people were complaining about the emails in some forums. Reading them again they weren't really *that* creepy.

They also decided to make a reservation in Blake's name for a three day whitewater rafting trip in Colorado, with a tour operator Lee had a connection with. This would be paid for with a credit card in Blake's name, with the confirmation going to his most easily accessed email address.

Blake would just never show up for it. The idea being that if Joe's people were in fact suspicious enough to be poking at him back at that beach town, they might send an agent to join him on the trip. This could then 'use up' that agent, as Joe's people might not want to use the same person twice - if they did, it would leave a trail that they or someone like that Police Chief could later find.

It still didn't feel like quite enough grid-marks though, so they finally decided Blake should at least join Lee on his next supply run. It was a full night and most of the morning driving - they chose Denver, as it was far away from the cabin, and near the rafting trip. Blake was dropped off at a holiday rental, where he picked up a minivan, then drove to a big outdoors chain he particularly liked.

Then it was an hour of quite enjoyable shopping. If it was a lot of stimulus all at once, between the flashy displays and bits of conversation all around him. One person had a seeing eye dog with them in the store. Blake bought tents, new boots, a couple of kayaks, a variety of nifty mountain climbing cookware and head flashlights and the like. Obviously they had mice, so Blake grabbed a couple of the one model. He would still be chipping away on the market research.

He had some longish conversations with the floor staff, they had to help him put the kayaks on the roof of the minivan. He paid with the same credit card he had been using in LA. Then once it went through he was on the clock, so he was right quick out of the parking lot then back to the holiday rental down the side roads. Then it was another huge long drive back to the cabin.

Lee had also picked up the makings for a small laboratory, and a wide variety of pills, serums, and tinctures - Joe wanted to start measuring and tweaking a variety of his biomarkers. They had managed to find some fairly detailed information on what testing the various baseball leagues did, so he had some exact targets to aim for.

Joe started testing himself multiple times per day, peeing in a cup, taking blood samples, even looking at his hair under a microscope. He seemed a little nervous about it all, but said he was making progress. It was kind of an art, getting all your levels right. Joe also said he didn't see any evidence of cancer or osteoporosis or anything like that, he seemed pretty relieved.

Whenever Joe was on shift he generally had a baseball game on in the background. It was a little frustrating watching the season pass by, and Blake was starting to find watching the games a little unnerving. But it was important research, the announcers alone were invaluable in explaining the finer details of the game.

Blake did begin thinking about how exactly they would get Joe into the sport. The most obvious place to start seemed to be scouting camps, which ran from mid-June into August. They basically seemed to be a place where amateurs could go and show off their stuff.

They definitely weren't the main way into pro-ball - for one thing they took place right after the draft, which was where the vast majority of new players were selected. Blake's impression was that it was when the scouts finally had time for less important stuff like that. But they would be a relatively safe and informal environment, where they could get Joe in front of real major league scouts.

Of course with someone like Joe they might be better off with a more unorthodox approach. Blake could just try networking with owners and managers, connecting them with Joe could even just be an afterthought. Maybe he could be a potential sponsor from an energy bar company. Or Lee could pretend to be a rich retiree who got it in his head he wanted to become an amateur scout.

After the original approach, however, it seemed like there was a fairly specific career path a player went through on their way to the big leagues. The first step into professional baseball itself was to be drafted by a major league team. After being drafted players generally didn't seem to go straight to the major leagues, however, but played in various divisions of the minor leagues for a few years. Only the best of the best would then graduate into the major leagues, and often only for a few games.

Just getting into the big leagues didn't turn out to be enough to make the big big money, however, no matter how good you were. The bidding wars that would naturally develop over the best players were supressed by the draft, as teams got exclusive rights to a player for their first six seasons.

But reading through the rules, Blake made an interesting discovery. Players who were passed over in the draft were free to sign with any team, and as long as they signed a contract that same year, they would be ineligible for future drafts. By his reading, at least, that meant a player like Joe could jump straight to being a free agent. He would have no limitations on what team he played for, aside from those in whatever original contract he signed.

Really it seemed like a bit of a loophole. The whole draft system was sort of based on the assumption that anyone worth drafting would be known by scouts before they even got to high school. It was also a huge draft, a three day affair with howevermany teams picking up to 50 players each. So anyone even halfway decent would usually get snatched up.

But if a player with major league skills could appear out of nowhere, they could dodge around the whole system, and get a full free market salary straight out of the gate. Joe wouldn't even have to be that good to start, just good enough to sign whatever short-term contract, get his foot in the door.

Maybe it would be a little unorthodox, but they could find some middling team who was missing something, some rare combination of skills that only Joe had. Like maybe they needed someone who could hit and pitch. Apparently that was really rare, and Joe could throw a decent fastball.

From there someone like Joe could become a star player pretty fast. Blake did some calculations on how many runs it took to win a game. The average was high enough, but some games were 10-0 blow outs. A player like Joe could just nudge a few 2-1 games over the line. If he made the difference in 5, 10 games, that could well be enough to get even a lower ranking team into the postseason. From there he could trigger a bidding war. They could even play it like he wanted to stay with his team, the money didn't matter to him. Joe could be into the multi-million dollar contracts in no time.

Blake might be getting ahead of himself, though. The more immediate issue was Joe's backstory, which was another thing they started working on. Obviously Joe would have to be the sort of guy who didn't talk about his past a lot. But giving some details would be unavoidable. Maybe he spent a lot of time working on farms, that didn't always leave a paper trail. He could have also gone from festival to festival selling stuff like jewelry and pipes from a blanket. Maybe he used to have dreads.

They spent a lot of time doing research, everything from job descriptions to tourist trip reports to festival playbills. Joe would try to dodge questions like where he grew up, although they decided on the balance it would be better to say he was from America. He could also say that he lived in Latin America for a while, maybe that was where he learned to play ball. He did actually speak a decent amount of Spanish.

They even studied a little cricket. Its history, star players, they made sure Joe had a good understanding of its rules. If he found it a little indecipherable at first. Joe being able to BS about cricket would open up a few different emergency fall-back stories.

Then finally one morning the skies blackened, and a cold rain began to pour down. They got up early in the morning, and were out in the meadow training the whole day. It had been a while since they had trained, but Joe did really well out there. He broke the speed record a couple of times at the start, but other than that nothing. And just in general he seemed a lot more natural. Sometimes it worked like that, you left something a while, you were much better when you came back to it.

His hitting control was getting pretty good, and there was a pretty big gap between just over the fence homeruns and epic record-breaking home runs. He was starting to master aiming it - pegging trees x meters away, hitting groundballs that bounced at certain points, pop flies that a catcher would run after before they landed in the seats.

What was beginning to bother Joe about hitting was the question of how much certain types of pitches lent themselves to certain specific types of hits. Could he just hit a bouncing groundball up left field off any pitch, or was it better off a curve ball, a slider, or a fastball? They went through the baseball books they had, searched online, but there just wasn't a lot of information.

Small details like that were starting to seem really important, it was putting them on edge. Joe was getting really good at catching, too good, they both agreed he needed to let more of them go. But which ones?

Watching games, they tried to classify different catches. A running leap catch, that was something a pro would only get maybe 50% of the time. A nearby dive was higher %, he could get most or all groundballs that came straight at him.

Then as quickly as the storms came they were gone, and the forecast said nothing but sunny skies. Blake had Joe practice pitching a bit at night, but there was a lot of stuff they couldn't do, Joe was getting pretty freaked out. He said his hitting was all off, the ball wasn't leaving his bat at the right angles, it was different than the players on TV. After a couple of days of sunny weather Joe was pacing around the cabin, going up the walls.

Finally he carried one of the pitching machines up into the big room on the second floor, and covered the walls and ceilings with mattresses, blankets, and other padding. Then he was up there for hours on end.

It was a little unnerving, hearing the steady stream of thwacks coming from above. Blake went in and tried it a couple times, and it was pretty intense. It wasn't a lot of space, and the balls left the machine pretty fast.

The days passed, and Joe's face began to properly heal up. It was all rather eerie, as the swelling went down he started looking like a normal person, just not Joe. Blake supposed that was the point, but it was still pretty strange, he had Joe's voice and mannerisms and everything. Joe's beard also seemed to be growing at epic proportions - apparently he had some sort of hormonal thing where his facial hair grew at close to twice the normal rate. Which was helpful, Joe figured he would have to keep the beard for at least a month or two, he would probably look pretty unnatural without it.

All in all it was getting to be a lot of time in a cabin. They did seem to be getting on each other's nerves a bit. Blake was banned from practicing bass, while Lee and Joe got into big arguments over Joe's conspiracy videos. Lee seemed to think they were designed just to distract you from the real conspiracies. Fortunately the cabin was spacious, and they were still all on different schedules – they were still basically doing eight hour shifts on the cameras, if they didn't spend every single minute with their eyes glued to the screen.

At this point Blake was developing a routine. He would get up at noon, starting his day with some short serial TV shows, then move up to a couple of movies, while playing video games at the same time. After a light lunch, he would play an empire building game, which didn't seem to get boring as long as he only played it for a couple of hours every day.

Then during his shift he would listen to a series of lectures on tape, or music, with Joe's movies on in the background. On the last supply run Lee had gotten him one of those ship in a bottle models, so he worked on that a little bit in his off time as well. It was a nice change of pace.

Finally, as they were passing through the third week of May, Lee returned from one of his supply trips with mischief in his eye and a big brown envelope. His guy had come through.

Joe's eyes lit up when he saw it, he looked a bit kid-at-Christmas. "Man, do you think he really did it? I mean, like a real ID that's gonna work?"

"I have utmost trust in my guy," said Lee, then with a dramatic flourish he opened the envelope. "Joe Soldao, you are now," he paused for dramatic effect, "Jamal Fulano Soto Chang."

"Jamal.." said Blake, reaching for the paper to see the name, a certain panic setting in, "Fulano Soto Chang? That's the name?"

Lee raised an eyebrow at Blake. "Is that too ethnic for you?"

"No, but I mean.." Blake stammered.

Lee shrugged. "Their technique is based on the old paper tripping system. We're using the name of someone who died, they only had so many options to choose from." He seemed rather nonplussed by the whole thing.

"Oh, so there was a real Jamal Fulano Soto Chang then?" Blake asked incredulously. He gave Lee a look. "How many other people with that name do you think there are out there? Is he just the other Jamal Fulano Soto Chang from," he looked at the paper again, "Baltimore, Maryland?"

"We needed someone with a diverse background, didn't we?" asked Lee, now looking distracted, flipping through the papers. "Without looking at the birth certificate, it looks like a Latin American naming pattern, two first names then two last names. If that's the case, then Soto would be his father's surname, and Chang would be his mother's."

Lee rubbed his chin, then continued. "Jamal suggests African American. There's a lot of Afro-descendant people from Latin America, but I don't think many of them are Muslims. So that could even suggest the original Arabic origins of the name. There are big Chinese and Middle Eastern diasporas down there, his family could just as easily come from any number of melting pots."

Blake gave Lee a look, feeling his frustration grow. What the devil were they going to do? "Well, yes, quite. But does Joe *look* Chinese to you?"

"I don't think someone's surname should define who they are, especially in this day and age. Are you saying that people who look like Joe shouldn't have Chang as a last name?" Lee's tone was exaggerated, a look of offense on his face.

"No, but I mean.." Blake stammered off.

Joe, who was looking at the papers, held up a picture of the original Jamal Fulano Soto Chang, a smiling African American kid in a suit. "I think I probably look more Chinese than he does." He held the picture next to his face, and made some fake-Chinese noises, then did some little martial arts moves.

"Relax," said Lee. "We need to change his name again anyways, this is just the first step in the process. The Jamal Chang name will be buried pretty deep. If someone does somehow manage to find it, we can tell them Jamal had some personal reasons why he needed to change the name before going into baseball. Or that he was involved with gangs, and it's a witness protection honeypot name. Something like that could stop a private investigation in its tracks."

Blake nodded. That would be another bloody thing to do then. Joe held the picture of the kid under the light, inspecting it closely.

"Does it say anything about who he was?" he asked.

"A teenager, from Baltimore, lived in the projects," said Lee, picking up a folder marked 'destroy' and flipping through it. "He died when he was 17, so that makes you," he thought for a second, "23."

"Good to be a little younger," said Blake.

"How did he die?" asked Joe, peering over Lee's shoulder at the documents. "I hope it was gang related, not an overdose or something lame like that."

Lee looked slightly offended at this. "Lots of good, strong people fall victim to drug addiction." He turned over the page. "Three bullet wounds, one to the head, from a passing car. He died instantly. The killer was never caught."

"Cool," said Joe. "Did he take anybody down with him?"

Lee looked over the papers, and shook his head. "There's no mention of anyone else."

Blake picked up the folder with the police report, it looked like the real thing. From the looks of it there had been some investigation into his death. A list of people they had talked to, some suspects. But it didn't seem like it had been particularly in-depth.

"That should be the only copy of that," said Lee, pointing to the report Blake was reading. "They took them from the police archives."

Then Joe gave a dismayed groan, looking at one of the folders. "Man, he only got to grade 10. Am I gonna have to go to High School?"

"There's a test you can take, the GED, once you have that you're eligible to play pro ball," said Blake.

They passed around some pictures, he looked happy, just a kid. He didn't seem like a gangster or anything. The police report had speculated he just got involved with the wrong people.

"Perhaps we should give a moment of silence, in honor of this poor boy whose untimely death we are profiting?" asked Lee. So they paused there a moment, standing solemnly over the yellow folders.

27

Now that they had the ID, their next move was to go to Portland, Oregon. Lee had requested a copy of Jamal Soto Chang's social security card be sent to an anonymous post box he had there, as a way of testing the ID. His people were good, but you never knew when the police would catch a whiff of something.

While they were sitting around dinner that night, Lee also brought up an idea, a bit of an insurance policy. He acknowledged Joe probably wouldn't be interested - he said he almost shouldn't even suggest it - but he would throw it out there anyways.

Basically, he was thinking about creating a sort of 'dead man's switch'. Something that would protect them in the unfortunate circumstances of, say, them being captured, or a variety of other scenarios like that.

It would be a recording showing Joe's super human powers, put onto a usb stick, then given to secure parties. Those parties would then be instructed to release it to a variety of governments, news agencies, private individuals, etc., if they went more than a prescribed period of time without receiving a message from any one of them.

Joe was immediately opposed, although Blake thought it could have some merit, if he found the name slightly off-putting. Lee added that they could use some fail-safes, there were secure ways of doing it. They could encrypt the files and split them up onto three different USB sticks, so you would need all three to view any of the information.

They could give them to banks, journalists they trusted, maybe one of Blake's rich friends. Collusion among two parties would be very unlikely, three even more so. It could also be set to automatically delete with any departure from protocol, such as repeatedly entering an incorrect password.

Strangely enough, Joe started to get behind the idea. It would be a pretty strong card to have up their sleeve. And he did know how to encrypt the shit out of something. If they did three different USB sticks that would be pretty secure, although maybe 4 or 5 would be better. After an extended debate about what could go wrong, to Blake's immense surprise Joe finally acquiesced.

They started by scanning a selection of the stuff Joe had brought with him when he fled San Diego. It was the first time he had opened his briefcase since getting out the plastic surgery diagrams, and Blake was quite curious to see what it contained.

Some of it was a little dry, chemical formulas for steroids, a little treatise on bone fortification technique, a list of people who were believed to be liaisons for secret agents around the world. Apparently some unspecified party had ten underground warehouses across America with about 5000 drones in each of them.

Some of it was really out there. It was a bit of everything, there was a lot of experimental stuff, but it had a grab bag quality to it. A couple pictures of a sniper in an elegant colonial building, Blake remembered an assassination a few years ago in Latin America.

There was genetic code for some kind of experimental drug-producing yeast. It built colonies on the walls of the stomach, then released the drug when it was exposed to certain sound frequencies outside the audible range of human hearing. Even a design for some kind of 50 foot tall bipedal war robot, a little space for a human pilot in the chest.

The more important task was making a video displaying Joe's strength. This was perhaps easier said than done - it was easy to fake those sorts of things, this day and age. All those magicians you see on TV, people could think it was just CGI smoke and mirrors. They figured the best approach would be for Joe to do a wide variety of superhuman feats, and record him from a bunch of different angles at once.

On a whim Blake suggested they trash the K-56. It was pretty expensive for a video you never wanted to get out, but they wanted it to have some flair. Be fun to trash as well.

The next day was really cloudy, so they drove it out onto a field and set up the cameras. Joe drove it in circles, did a little half jump, spun it around, showed it was a real car. Then he started picking it up, throwing it around. It was heavy for him, but he could lift it, throw it a few feet.

They did it up properly dramatic too, Blake reading from the car's sales literature as Joe threw it around in the background. 'Weighing in at a little over one and a half tons, the K-56's sleek lightweight chassis balances smooth handling with a surprising amount of pickup', that sort of thing.

Joe thought it was a terrible idea that Blake appear in the video. But Blake would take the risk, if it did get out he wanted to be there on it, was Joe crazy? Could be it might even protect him. They were using the K-56 already, there were only so many of those in America.

Blake also did a little speech about how Joe was a supersoldier, created by a secret lab, framed as an armoured van robber when he escaped. Joe having a big beard and a new face did put a bit of a damper on that, but Lee said he had some old footage from the security cameras.

From there Joe picked up some boulders, bent some metal, raced against balls shot by the pitching machine and grabbed them out of the air. Blake and Lee shot at him with the paintball guns, he didn't get hit once. All done with no cut scenes, twelve cameras recording at once. They watched the videos after, and it all looked really real.

Once they were done Joe dug a giant pit to hide the remains of the K-56. He was almost a blur, it was a big shovelful every couple seconds. It wasn't that Blake had forgotten he could do all that kind of stuff, but it was still a sight to see. It was less than an hour before Joe was dragging the K-56 into the pit and shovelling the dirt back on top.

Lee gave the cabin one last clean that night while they waited in the SUV, then they left for Portland a couple of hours before sunrise. They were all in a good mood as they drove north, watching the dawn from the forest highway.

As they were approaching a gas station to fill up, Joe leaned forward, a grin on his face. "Whaddya say I go pump the gas? Out of the three of us, I'm the least likely to trigger face rec or anything."

That was probably actually true. Joe's eyes were weirdly puffy, and he sort of had the face of a fat guy with a skinny guy's body. But he didn't look like Eugene Cudneck.

"Ok," said Lee. They pulled in and Joe was off, filling the tank, into the station. He came back with a goofy look on his face, and five bags full of stuff.

"Man, that was a trip. It's like a whole world in there," said Joe, his eyes wide. "There was this guy, and he just kept putting cheese on his nachos, it was overflowing the chip container. Are you allowed to do that? Then he bought a bag of chips, as well."

Joe held up the bags, looking slightly sheepish now. "And, um, I got some stuff. They had all sorts of cool stuff there."

Joe passed around the bags, which were full of a variety of chocolate bars, chips, and neon-packaged candies. They set in on the junk food buffet, then there was a cry of dismay from the back.

"Oh man," said Joe, "look at that." He was holding up a hamburger. Blake couldn't see anything out of the ordinary.

"That looks nothing like the picture. It was twice as big, and there was lettuce sticking out the sides. This is just crushed and damp." Joe stared at it morosely, holding up a thin film of rubbery lettuce, then flapping his hand in disgust to get it off him. "Do you think we should go back?"

"Get used to it," said Lee. Joe tried it, and conceded that it did actually taste pretty good.

Blake was setting in on a second bag of chips when Joe leaned forward again. "So, like, if I'm not going to be Jamal, then I sort of don't have a name right now. If anybody asked me my name in there, I wouldn't have had anything to give them."

"Seems like a fairly important detail, actually," said Blake.

Lee nodded. "We'll be doing the name change soon, so the sooner you figure it out, the better."

Joe got a perplexed look on his face. "Man, I dunno. I have no clue what my name should be."

It seemed like rather a momentous decision, all things considered. "You could really choose anything, I guess. Be nice to find something that has some meaning to it," said Blake.

"Ya, right," said Joe. "Who do I seem like to you, other than Joe?"

None of them knew, was he a Mike, an Alan, a Steve, a Sam? Hey Sam, pass me the chips. None of them really felt like him, he was Joe. Maybe he could keep Joe as a first name, although even that seemed like it could be too much. It was sort of hard, coming up with a name.

"We've got those baseball books, they might have something," said Lee. "Actually, there's a turn off for a mall up ahead. We could get one of those baby name books as well."

They all thought that was a good idea, so Lee left the

highway and they pulled into a sort of outdoor mall area. There was a big three story bookstore, so they parked beside it, and after a brief discussion it was decided Joe might as well go in again.

Joe spent maybe twenty minutes in the store, coming back with a bag full of baby name books, as well as a book on surnames, and a couple new baseball books. He said it had gone well, if he might have seemed weird at one point. The cashier had asked him 'are you expecting?', and he said no, the books were a gift for a friend. Expecting meant like his wife was going to have a baby? She had been talking about the baseball books right before that, her husband really liked baseball, and he got confused.

They started with the baby books. 'Angus' meant unique strength, or 'Ethan' meant strong, did he want to play off something like that? Joe thought 'Liam' was cool, but Lee noted that it had become more popular recently. Names that were popular today would be different from those that were popular twenty years ago.

Maybe they were going about it the wrong direction, they switched to the surname book. There was an argument they should figure out more of his backstory first, whatever name they chose was really relevant to that. They could give him a name that suggested a place of origin, something Spanish, Arabic, African, even South Asian. His family could be from another country - immigrants often lived in-between two worlds, that could explain why there wasn't much of a paper trail around him in either of them.

With Joe's linguistic background there were any number of countries they could choose from. Lee had connections in a few places, he could materialize some old friends. It would be committing to a backstory now, but it would let them set up lots of supporting details that would make that story more plausible. Like maybe he played a lot of cricket back in his home country.

Although there were complicating factors in that as well, for one there wouldn't be any record of him taking flights. All things considered he was probably better off with a commonly occurring American name that worked with a wide variety of back stories. Maybe he should just be Bob Jones or something. If nothing else they could pick names at random from the phonebook.

Then Blake had a thought. "There was an old Jazz player,

Robby Johnson, then another one a few years later, Franky Johnson. They did a shtick where they said they sold their soul to the devil to play wicked good horn. You could play off that, Stevie, Matty, maybe Tommy Johnson?"

Lee grinned. "Tommy Johnson? That sounds like a baseball player."

Joe's eyes went slightly wide for a moment, then he laughed. "Like I made a deal with the devil." He looked over at Blake. "Does that make you the devil?"

"Erm, yes, I suppose it would," said Blake.

Joe laughed again. "Man, I kinda feel like a Tommy. I mean, if I can't be Joe. And it is a good generic name." Joe stopped in reflection, a wide grin forming on his face. "Ya, that works, Tommy Johnson."

28

They arrived in Portland a little before noon, detouring briefly for Lee to pick up a second vehicle outside a warehouse. Lee went to drive a lap around the apartment building where the PO Box was, and they met up in the safe house, a vacation rental on the edge of the suburbs.

Then they were again killing time, as they weren't going to pick up the ID until about 3 in the morning. There would always be a small - but real - chance of a police chase. Likewise if anyone did come poking around at 4 am they would probably either be a cop or an undercover cop. The most important thing here was just knowing if anyone was watching the PO Box.

Joe started in on studying for the GED and practicing signatures. He would need a good copy of the Jamal Soto Chang signature soon for the name change, and hopefully a Tommy Johnson signature not so long after.

They had also been meaning to experiment with disguises for Blake. So they shaved off his beard, then injected his face with something, gave him a couple of pills, it would cause his face to puff up. It would pop right back, to exactly how it was before, would it? They said it would.

While they were waiting around, then, Blake raised an issue he had been thinking about. If they were going to do this baseball thing, then Joe - or well, Tommy – he would need to practice against a professional pitcher. Blake had gotten decent at pitching, and they had been using pretty top end pitching machines. But neither of those were anything close to a professional pitcher.

Tommy agreed, if Lee was immediately opposed. It was too much of a security risk, what if he did something beyond human capacity? Well, better he do it with one person on their payroll than in front of 30 aspiring amateurs, scouts, and soccer moms at a scouting camp.

Lee didn't like it one bit. There would be any number of little things a trainer could mention to whatever random person. He would assume they weren't going to pull anything like with the plastic surgeon on a trainer? But in the end he was forced to concur that if they were going to do baseball, getting a professional trainer would be a vital step.

The hiring of that trainer would also fall on Lee, Tommy and Blake both agreed that he should start looking for someone right away. So with an exasperated look Lee hooked up a secure phone connection.

They listened in as he called around, Blake now soaking his head in a chemical bath designed to change the consistency of his hair. There were some ads online, Lee tried a couple of college athletics departments looking for recommendations, even a batting cage place.

Lee spent a lot of time on hold, had to make a lot of call backs. He got through to a couple of trainers right away, but after brief interviews none of them thought they would do. Just something about their demeanor, the one didn't really have much experience.

Finally as it was getting towards the evening Lee got through to a guy who seemed good. His name was Mike Ciagorma, he had pitched relief for Los Angeles for most of a season a few years ago. Someone at a university had recommended him.

He was just doing freelance personal training right now, said it was good work, a little sporadic. He was kind of living between LA and San Jose, pretty much had a job lined up coaching at a University in San Jose in September.

From the phone conversation he seemed like a good guy. They dug up his stats, and there he was, playing for LA a little more than ten years ago. He had pitched about 20 innings, seemed like he had done alright, a decent ERA, if he got sent back down to triple A after the one season.

LA made it to the postseason the year he played, they had a lot of good players, pitchers especially. So he must have had a lot of competition just getting on the field. And he played more than ten years in the minors, which was a long career, he had experience.

One thing Blake noted was that his name started with 'CIA', but after a brief deliberation they decided that probably didn't mean anything. That was getting a little *too* paranoid, just because they're after you..

So Lee called him back, asked him if he was available in the next few days, made him an offer. Hearing Ciagorma's slightly confused response Blake got the impression he thought it quite fair. Lee told him to tell no one about the job, Blake would get his lawyer to deliver an NDA for him to sign. Then Lee hung up, they had a trainer booked.

At this point Blake's hair treatment was done, and his face was properly swollen up. Joe and Lee trimmed his beard, gave him some thick rimmed glasses to wear, and voilà, he was disguised.

It was almost eerie, looking in the mirror. Like it was this different person walking back and forth, waving his arms the same way he waved his. Blake tried changing his voice as well, but both Joe and Lee seemed fairly emphatic that it wasn't necessary. Nobody was going to recognize his voice, but sounding like he was doing a voice was something suspicious in and of itself.

Joe - Tommy - then got a grin on his face. Did they want to like, go out there, do something in Portland? If Lee put on a disguise none of them would be recognizable, what was really going to happen? They all concurred, Blake for one was getting a bit of cabin fever.

The rental place had a local newspaper, with a big section on events. Bands were playing, they could just go to a bar. There was a little write up about how there was a fair in town, apparently it was particularly good. They could pull off a fair.

Lee got into disguise, then they drove to the fairgrounds as the sun set. Once they were there they drove a quick lap around the grounds - there were lots of exits - then went in. Passing through the main gate it was an assault on the senses. Barkers yelled at them, the crowd was thick, a mixture of cotton candy and popcorn wafting through the air. Blake looked over at Tommy, and his eyes were wide.

The whole thing seemed to have a sort of bohemian, retro-carny atmosphere to it. Old style writing, red and white striped tents, apparently there was a bearded lady and a museum of oddities. They walked past some little stages, listened to a band playing on one. Sort of steampunk inspired outfits with accordions, violins and clarinets, a fellow in a vest singing nonsense lyrics.

A little further on there was one of those girls on a wheel, with a fellow throwing knives at her. Tommy gaped for a second, that couldn't be real, could it? Both Blake and Lee were pretty skeptical. It was hard to get a permit for that sort of thing.

Another circle of people were around a shirtless strongman with a handlebar mustache. They watched for a bit as he picked up rocks, spun people around on a bar, breathed fire into the air. It was a good act, if Tommy didn't seem particularly impressed.

Further along they passed some rides, just smaller ones. There was a food court filled with craft beers and locally grown, organic sorts of food stalls. Then they reached the games section, that was more their speed tonight.

It really sprawled out in every direction, it was a labyrinth. There was a lot of your standard stuff, basketball hoops, shuffleboard, darts, a whole stretch of like twenty of those claw games. A little further along there were some shooting galleries. Tommy gave them a grin, did they want to give it a go?

They paid the guy the money, and proceeded to fire BB pellets at pieces of paper with stars on them. It was good fun, boisterous, all of them yelling at each other over the racket. When it was over, the barker pulleyed the targets to the front. Blake's had the most shot out, and by quite a margin - he was the winner. If he hadn't shot out enough to get a prize.

The barker thought Tommy looked like he might want a rematch, but they continued on. After a bit Lee stopped them at another stand, a milk jug toss. It had rather a strange setup, big red velvet curtains flowing out on the walls, a bizarre assortment of art. There was a dead flower still life, a bag of chips statuette, a landscape painting with a UFO.

When Blake asked how much it was, the guy said it was free, and directed them to a big long write-up at the side of the stall. Apparently it was in fact an installation piece from a local art gallery, the write-up went off about challenging notions of commerciality and public space. As such there were no prizes - it was just a place you could go and throw balls at milk jugs, if you wanted to throw balls at milk jugs.

They threw a few, did pretty good actually. Blake for one had a lot of practice from pitching to Tommy. The guy was clearly impressed, said it was too bad they didn't give out prizes. There was a stall on the other side they could try, although he couldn't promise their luck would hold over there.

They continued on, now lost in the seemingly endless corridors of carnival games. As they got deeper in the crowd began to thin out, the carnies glancing boredly at them as they walked by.

Off over in a corner Blake saw something that caught his eye, a stall made out to look like a gypsy caravan. He motioned them towards it, it was something to do with Tarot cards.

"Want to know what the future has to hold?" asked Lee.

Tommy grinned. "We can use the cards as code names."

They sauntered up to it. Sitting at the stall was a proper gypsy fortune teller lady, bandanna, jewelry, a flowing white long-sleeved blouse. On the walls of the stand were Tarot cards, The Wheel of Fortune, the Magician, the Fool.

Blake looked at the cards up on the wall, it wasn't the complete deck. "Major Arcana?" he asked.

"Very good," she said, sounding unimpressed.

"Is it a game? How do you play?" asked Blake.

She exaggeratedly sized them up. "Game is simple," she said, in a passable Eastern European accent. "You get good card, is big prize. Bad card, is small prize."

Blake gave her a look. "I don't know if all the cards in the Tarot can be divided into good cards and bad cards."

She shrugged. "Is not all cards. Is just Major Arcana."

"Well, still.." said Blake, trailing off a bit. "Is the Fool a good card or a bad card?"

"Fool is good card," she said.

Blake flashed her a grin. "Well, ok then, those sound like good odds. How much is it to play?"

"$50 a card," she said, not missing a beat.

Blake gave a little laugh. "What?" He paused, not knowing what to say. These fairs could be overpriced, but that was ridiculous. The shooting gallery had been $15 for the three of them, and it had seemed steep. "How much is it really?"

She was stonefaced. "$50 a card, no discount." Now she looked kind of bored. "You don't have the money?" she asked skeptically.

Blake sort of wanted to walk, on principle alone. But something about her demeanor pulled at him, he suddenly very much wanted to get a fortune.

Giving her a grin, he passed her the bills for three. He looked over at Tommy and Lee. "Who wants to go first?"

Lee stepped forward. "How about new ventures?" he asked, and she held out the deck for him to touch, which he did. Then she raised one hand in the air in a flourish, there was a flash and a bang. Tommy jumped back a bit, and smoke floated up

through the air. Then she pulled the top card from the deck. It
was the red and blue of a man hanging upside down.

"The Hanged Man!" she said dramatically. Lee gave a laugh.
"Well, that's not a good sign, is it?"

"No, no," she quickly said. "Look at man in card, he is calm,
serene! Is card of surrender, giving up control and just flowing
with whatever the universe gives you," she said, her accent
disappearing slightly for a moment. "Hanged Man means giving
up on false hopes, breaking old patterns, winning by losing, it is
liberation. If you are on wrong path, the faster you walk the
further you go in wrong direction."

At that Lee sort of gave them a look, and nodded
philosophically, a grin returning to his face. "Maybe that's not so
bad then."

Tommy nervously stepped forward. She gave him the deck
to touch, and again there was a bang and a flash, smoke rising up
from her hands. With a flourish she flipped the card face
upwards. It was a skeletal figure on a pale horse.

There was momentarily a noticeable shock and fear on
Tommy's face. "Death," he said hoarsely. "What does that mean?"
He asked, his tone sort of relaxed, joking, but shrill at the end as
well.

"Do not worry! Death does not always mean death! It also
means transformation, an ending and a beginning. Like moving
to another town, or changing jobs," she paused a moment. "Often
it means deeper changes, to something at the very root of your
being. Perhaps you are moving from one stage of your life to
another?"

At this Tommy seemed noticeably relieved, there was even
a bit of awe in his face. "I am sort of going through some
transformations right now."

"The Tarot is wise in its mysteries." She now turned to Blake,
her pupils wide and a mischievous sort of look on her face,
holding up the deck for him to touch. He did so, then she again
made with the pyrotechnics, and flipped over his card. There was
a large horned figure, with a naked man and woman chained at
his feet.

"The Devil!" she said, gasping dramatically. They were all
silent a moment, Blake staring at the card. By some measures
those were the worst three cards in the deck. He didn't know what
the odds were for that, must be one in a thousand, probably less.

"Devil is self-explanatory, actually," she said, grinning at him smugly. There was another silence, then she reached under her table and pulled up a box of trinkets. "Three small prizes!"

They dutifully dug through the box, Blake taking some kind of old looking foreign coin with weird writing on it, Lee a miniature horseshoe, Tommy a rabbit's foot. Apparently it wasn't real rabbit, ethically sourced! Then they turned and sort of shuffled away from the stand.

"Let's not use those as code names," said Tommy, looking kind of freaked out. Lee seemed to find it all amusing.

Blake gave them a look. "That wasn't real, right? I mean, what are the odds? She had long sleeves and was doing those firework things. She just made us touch the deck, not pick a card. I mean, fortune tellers are supposed to fan out the cards and have you pick one, right? I've worked with a couple magicians in the past, that's all classic sleight of hand." Blake felt his temperature rise a bit. He patted at his pockets. "Check your wallets."

"Ya, I guess," said Tommy, looking relieved.

Blake still felt slightly unnerved, nonetheless. Was it even legal to do that, was she drawing 'The Lovers' for couples every time? He actually knew a bit about festival law, in New York State, at least. You could have a rigged game there, as long as there was a prize in the end. Then it wasn't a game, but an 'attraction'. But who did that, she didn't know anything about them, how they would interpret it.

They continued through the games section, now trying to find their way out. It really was a maze, they passed the shooting gallery a couple of times. They were finally reaching the edge when Tommy stopped them.

"Man, look at that," he said. There was one of those hammer games, a red target to hit and a tall tower with a bell on top. "Whaddya think?" he asked, mischief on his face. Blake and Lee looked at each other, uncertain, then nodded. Tommy separated from them and approached the game.

There was a big crowd around it, a barker in a pinstripe suit and top hat calling on them all to step right up. A group of mostly guys - frat boy types, from the looks of it - were taking turns on it. Blake and Lee joined the crowd on the opposite side from Tommy, and watched as a hefty looking fellow grabbed the oversized hammer and swung at the target.

The puck jumped up the meter, making it maybe three quarters of the way up. There was cheering from the crowd, the guy showed off a bicep. He went over to the prize tent on the side, picked out a teddy bear for his girlfriend. It was a really big tent, with some pretty nice prizes. There was even one of the video game systems they had at the cabin.

Then another guy went up, seemed to be part of the same crowd. They all stared intently as he swung the hammer. He didn't do as well, his friends were cracking jokes. So he took another go at it, did better. Then one of the girls with them went up, hit it up pretty high, gave her friends a defiant look.

Then the group was done, and the game left open. The barker danced around the stage, show your strength, win a prize. The stage was empty for a moment, then Tommy stepped up, passing the barker a couple of crumpled up notes.

Tommy positioned himself, got loose, then took a small swing. The puck went up about halfway, to a couple of sedate boos from the frat boys, who still seemed to be hanging around. Tommy just gave the crowd a grin, then lined up for another swing.

Blake suddenly felt nervous, he wasn't sure if it was a good idea to attract attention to themselves. Looking over at the prize tent again, there really was some nice stuff. The video game system would have to be worth a few hundred dollars, for one. It was a pretty linear game, if that wasn't a prize for ringing the bell, why was it there?

Tommy wound up, then again swung the hammer, cutting through the air in a smooth forceful arc. With a smack it connected, and the puck zoomed upwards. Blake felt panicked as it raced towards the top, slowing a little as it approached the bell. He looked over at the barker, whose face wore an expression of fear and disbelief.

The puck continued up, ever more slowly as it neared the top, until it finally slowed to a halt, just maybe half an inch under the bell. Then with a groan of disappointment from the crowd it slid back down.

"Man, that was awesome! You almost hit it!" said one of the clearly impressed frat boys. "You should try again!"

Tommy shook his head. "Nah, man, maybe later, I think I hurt my shoulder," he said, rubbing his shoulder and moving his arm. The relieved-looking barker quickly motioned Tommy over to the prize tent, a few people from the crowd following with him.

"You can take any prize except the ones on the top left," said the barker, the top left being where the video game system was.

Tommy stared at the prize wall a moment, then pointed. The barker passed him a professional looking wooden baseball bat.

The frat boys were now surrounding Tommy. "Man, that's a sweet bat, do you play ball?" asked one of them.

"A little," said Tommy, slightly nervously. "Just hitting them for the diligence!" he continued, which didn't make a lot of sense to Blake. There was a silence after this, the frat boys still in awe, one of the girls sort of smiling at Tommy. Blake felt distinctly on the spot, just watching him there.

Tommy swallowed, then glanced nervously around the crowd. "Anyways, gotta go," he said. Then he just wasn't there anymore.

Lee looked at his phone, then motioned Blake away from the games. "Do you want to loop back and head for the car?" he asked.

Blake was confused for a second, what, shouldn't they find Tommy first? But no, that was code, they had agreed on it earlier. What did that even mean, there was potentially someone on them, he was to follow Lee's lead, that was it.

Blake tried to remain calm as they made their way back through the crowd. Adrenaline pumped through his system, the carnival around them now seemed to take a sinister hue. It felt like the jugglers and fire-breathers were looking at him, the music wafting in from the Ferris wheel was dissonant, almost warped.

Lee however was now going off about a BBQ he was thinking about buying. It was expensive, but sometimes it was worth it, for a good BBQ. He bought a cheap one last time, and it broke after two years. Blake agreed, if it lasted longer that alone made it worthwhile. If you were going to cut corners in life, well it should be something other than your grill.

29

Once they were back in the car, Lee just said he was a little peckish, and they agreed to get something to eat. The pre-agreed upon protocol was now to drive to a diner nearby and wait for further instructions. Blake wanted to ask what was going on, but he supposed the car wasn't guaranteed to be secure. Lee probably wouldn't have much information anyways.

The diner was just five minutes down the road, it was a classic Americana sort of place. They went in and sat down, Lee having a little chat with the waitress about their 24-hour breakfast special. They all agreed it was a particularly good deal, and two breakfast specials were ordered.

Blake didn't particularly have an appetite, but he forced it down, made some more small talk with Lee. A free games stand, that's what good art was about. Blake felt all his worries from the beach town come back, he wondered if he was sort of traumatized now. He had to hide his hands under the table, they were shaking. Just a bit, but that would be all they would need to see. It felt like a mistake to be in a public place like a diner. Glancing around there was only one exit, the way they came in.

He was downing his coffees a little too fast, the waitress kept coming back and refilling his cup. Lee checked his phone after a bit, and said he was going to do the meeting next week. That was the all clear.

After another couple of coffees Tommy appeared at the window, giving them a quick wave. Meeting up with him in the car, he was really apologetic. He was almost certain it was a false alarm. He was just a little jumpy, people were looking at him, one guy in the crowd had a camera.

They were still on to pick up the social security card though, right? He was actually kind of pumped now. They went back to the rental place, and got Tommy into a new disguise. This one was more full-on, big platform shoes, a layer of makeup, a slight gut. When it was done he did look like an older version of the kid in the ID, but not like he looked now after the surgery.

They took off around two in the morning, Lee and Tommy again in one car, Blake in the other. Blake's job was again to be HQ, he parked in a residential neighbourhood a couple of kilometers from the apartment building.

It was the same as with the plastic surgeon, he watched as the Tommy and Lee dots moved around the screen. Lee had already tapped into the building's security cameras - which Blake thought was really going the extra mile on his part – so they had a video feed of the mail room, another in the hallway.

Blake listened as Lee and Tommy scouted it out. There was one main road the cops would probably take if they investigated, Lee would park a car with a camera along there. Apparently there was no evidence of a stake out or anything.

Blake did sort of feel useless, sitting there, Lee and Tommy doing all the real work. Headquarters, it was almost patronizing. You had the most important job of all! Tommy had said that were something to happen he might turn off all communications. It was safer that way, there would be no risk of them tracing where the signal was coming from.

It wouldn't make a particularly good story, for one. Oh yes, I sat outside in the car while they did everything. Not that Blake should be planning on telling stories about all this. Nor complaining, did he really want to be out there running from the police if things went sour?

He got a message, Tommy was going in. Blake watched Tommy's dot approach the apartment, pause at the door. Then there he was on the camera, walking down the hallway, appearing in the mail room. Tommy looked around exaggeratedly as he opened the PO Box, he looked as guilty as they came. Blake supposed he was doing that on purpose, they might not be the only ones watching this.

Then he was quickly out the door, his dot cutting diagonally away from the apartment building. It was zipping down side streets, lots of right angles, through the park, and a grinning Tommy was opening the door and holding up the card.

They decided to head south immediately – Blake for one was still flying off the caffeine from the diner. Lee would stay there to observe the area for the next few hours, then meet up with them in a couple of days, after meeting with his associate about the name change.

They again watched the sunrise from the road, stopping to get breakfast at a drive through fast food place. Tommy thought the fair was pretty awesome, if he seemed slightly preoccupied about something as well. It was pretty lucky the hammer game had a baseball bat for him to win, wasn't it? Blake didn't think it was too superstitious to take that as a good sign.

As they were getting towards Oakland they stopped for groceries. They both went in, and Tommy seemed pretty blown away. They really had a lot of stuff. He never really thought much about where people got supplies from, but he wouldn't have expected something like this. Like, you couldn't actually see to the other side, and it was straight all the way across.

They stocked up on enough food to probably last them a month - as well as every movie and celebrity magazine at the checkout counter - then went to the safehouse. It was a little row house in a commuter suburb, it seemed pretty anonymous, the keys in a combination lock box under the stairs.

Tommy had a nervous energy the next morning, he was pacing around the house. It was a big thing, to train with a real trainer. He had been reading about the season Ciagorma played with LA, it had been pretty epic.

Getting ready there was some question as to whether Blake should participate. It might be good to have a third person for some of the exercises, and Tommy was a little nervous about hanging out with the trainer by himself. What if he said something weird?

In the end it didn't seem like it would be much of a risk, as long as Blake only gave his first name. Likewise Joe would give the name Tommy, but not Johnson. There was no need to give the guy that much information, but Blake thought that if things went well they might want his help networking with teams. Best he had his 'real' first name.

They got to the field about 7:30 in the morning, and did a couple of passes around the neighbourhood. It was a biggish field, a little run down, out of the way on the edge of another commuter neighbourhood and an industrial zone. Tommy deemed it a secure place - really it was in fact perfect. Blake wondered to what extent Lee had researched it, and to what extent they just got lucky.

Ciagorma showed up about ten minutes early, with a couple of big bags full of baseball paraphernalia. He seemed like an agreeable fellow, friendly if slightly nervous. Maybe mid-40s, brown hair, about 6 foot, a bit of paunch on him. He was wearing a Bakersfield jersey, which was apparently the minor league team he had spent the most time pitching for.

Introductions were made as planned, and they did a bit of small talk. The three home run game San Francisco had yesterday, Oakland's management strategy. There was something refreshing about having a conversation with someone who wasn't Tommy or Lee.

But they quickly got into the training, the day was a-wasting. Hitting was what Tommy needed to work on the most, so Blake suited up and took the catcher's mound, and Ciagorma started pitching to them.

Tommy started slow, swinging and missing most pitches, knocking a few into the end of the field. They had agreed beforehand that he would stay under a 0.200 batting average - they didn't know if Ciagorma was pitching his best stuff, but one way or another there was no need to show off.

Ciagorma alternated types of pitches, throwing him sliders, then curve balls, then fastballs, then mixing them up. Some of them were really hard to catch, Blake had to scramble. He caught a couple in the mask, the shoulder, marks were left.

Eventually Blake had to stop catching, they could just throw against the fence. Ciagorma was a professional pitcher. Blake went out to the field, and started gathering up balls, made a few epic running catches.

As the morning progressed they started working on Tommy's stance and swing mechanics, so Blake went to sit on the bleachers. It was a nice sunny day, the air was fresh. This wouldn't be such a bad way to make money, would it? And Tommy seemed to be enjoying himself, passing the morning zinging balls into the fence. He would be the one to benefit the most from all this.

Blake felt a little pang. All that was assuming Tommy had at least a snowball's chance in hell of playing baseball in the first place. It felt like bringing on a trainer was crossing an invisible line. Any point before now, maybe it was just a lark, nothing they were seriously considering. But hiring a professional trainer really said something. Maybe this was the exact point where he had officially made an ass of himself.

Hopefully it would all become clearer with time. Who ever even knew with these things? If there was one thing he had learned in life, it was that there was only so far you could ever go trying to second-guess business ventures. Sometimes you just had to see how they played out, and hope you didn't get taken to the cleaners. The normal economic physics didn't apply here, it was potentially a billion dollar venture.

Ciagorma looked to be taking a break, sending Tommy on the rather pointless exercise of doing sprints around the bases. Blake came down from the bleachers and joined him.

"Man, that guy can hit," said Ciagorma. He had a far away, unbelieving expression on his face. "That felt like I was back in the majors for a little while. I wouldn't want to pitch against that guy." He gave his head a little shake, looking over at Tommy running the bases.

"Yes, well, I'm not really a baseball expert, but I thought he did seem quite the gifted player," said Blake, slightly depreciatingly. He made a brief turn-down-the-knob motion at Tommy as he ran by on one of his laps.

"He's got some stuff to work on, his stance and swing is all wrong. But the way he's hitting them, maybe he shouldn't change anything." Ciagorma shook his head again. "Where did you say he went to high school?"

"Dropped out," said Blake, slightly tersely. He didn't know exactly how to respond to that, he felt a little on the spot. "GED."

They were both silent for a moment. "You got the NDA my lawyer sent you?" asked Blake, knowing that he had signed it and sent it back to them - quite quickly in fact - but wanting him to confirm nonetheless. There were people in this world who would sign an NDA, then tell your investment idea to all their friends at the bar the next evening. It wasn't some meaningless technicality like the terms of use for an online alarm clock.

"Ya, I signed it and sent it off."

"Great! Tommy's a newcomer and we don't want anyone talking about him just yet. It would probably be best if you didn't even mention that you were training someone up here at all, or talk about anything related to this whatsoever."

"Ya, of course." Ciagorma gave Blake an earnest look. "A couple of summers ago, I was training a guy from Mexico. There was a lot of paperwork.." Blake gave the smallest of non-committal head movements, well enough if he believed something like that.

Tommy finished his laps, then sort of collapsed onto the field, panting heavily. After a little rest they got back to training, and Tommy mostly struck out for the rest of the afternoon.

Ciagorma thought he probably overdid it.

They were just getting ready to go when Blake got a message from Lee. They needed to take care of the errand today. They said goodbye to Ciagorma, then sped to the safe house. Lee was there with six months of night janitorial pay stubs for Jamal Soto Chang, as well as lease documents for an apartment.

He had talked to his guy, and the planets were aligned. Apparently someone was out of town at the courthouse, but they were expected back any day now. And it was much better if they did the name change while they were away. The courthouse stopped accepting new applications at five, so as long as they hurried they were good.

Tommy looked freaked out, they were really going to do it already? He didn't even have a middle name picked out yet. Maybe the middle name was the one you didn't use, but it was still a big thing. Likewise Blake felt distinctly unready, he was exhausted. And it was at a courthouse now? Lee had never said anything about courthouses.

They got ready really quickly, Tommy having a shower and Blake just sponging off in the sink. Then they were out the door, Lee and Tommy in one car, Blake in the other.

Blake felt an intense nervousness as he drove towards the courthouse. It was something a step up, they were off to do dirty business in a house of law. It all felt sketchy, Tommy with his big beard, who the devil went to change their name with a big beard like that? He supposed if you had a beard, you wouldn't shave it off just to get your name changed. But still.

Blake was again headquarters, setting up in a café just down from the courthouse. He ordered a coffee, took a seat in the far corner, then put on earphones and turned his laptop on. He had a visual feed from a camera in Lee's car in the courthouse parking lot, and an audio feed from Lee's phone. There was some ambient room noise, he couldn't hear too much. Then there was Lee's voice, cracking a joke about how maybe it would go faster because it was the end of the day.

After a bit Blake heard someone say 'Jamal', there was some bumping around. Then a woman was introducing herself, asking how they were. Blake didn't get her name, but he would guess African American, middle aged, she had a friendly voice.

"My friend Jamal would like to change his name," said Lee, his tone friendly yet professional.

"Ok," said the woman, then there were some little hmm

noises for a bit, the shuffling of papers. "Ok, all the paperwork looks good."

"He helped me fill it out," said Tommy, Jamal.

"Why do you want to change your name?" There was a moment of silence. "You don't have to tell me if you don't want to," she said, and there was another silence.

"Ok, I'll file these," she continued, her tone routine, professional. "You also have to make a court appearance after all the forms are processed. You can do that here at this courthouse, and you can check online if your application is processed yet here." Blake could almost see her circling a webpage on a sheet of paper. "You'll also have to publish the name change in a California newspaper for two weeks, there's a list of acceptable newspapers here.."

At this juncture Lee made a small, almost imperceptible noise. They were all silent a moment, then Lee spoke. "There was," he said, pausing, his tone now strained, "abuse."

"Now, we can connect you with some programs.." she said, her voice conveying it all, a little heartbroken, a little concerned, perhaps impressed in some way as well. Blake supposed there might be some sort of paradoxical effect, if you were talking about abuse with a big guy like Tommy it made it all the more believable.

"No need to dig up old wounds," said Lee. "Just a precaution."

"You'll have to talk to the magistrate then. Do you mind if I.." Lee told her to go ahead, and she made a phone call, Blake couldn't catch all of it.

Blake was feeling distinctly nervous, it felt like this whole thing could go really wrong really fast. He doubted this lady they were talking to was Lee's 'guy'. How many people were going to be involved in this? Maybe they should have stayed with the Jamal Soto Chang name. There were people who had the same name as other people, even if they had big long names.

"The magistrate can see you now, actually," said the woman, a slight note of surprise in her voice. "He's on the fourth floor, room 403."

They thanked her, and a moment later there was the tromping of two pairs of feet echoing in a stairwell. Then a knocking, and someone telling them to come in, come in.

"Jones!" said a man's voice, in a friendly, boisterous tone. "And you must be Jamal, or I guess it's Tommy, is it?" he continued, and Blake could almost hear a wink. Should he even be saying that? Blake hadn't heard the whole phone conversation, but he didn't think the lady had mentioned the name Tommy, or even Jamal, for that matter.

"Not quite yet," said Lee, his voice slightly sharp, annoyed, even. The two of them talked about the weather a bit, the traffic around the courthouse, apparently the guy commuted in everyday from deep in the 'burbs. Then the magistrate asked to see the documents, there was the sound of paper shuffling, him mmm-hhmming a bit.

"Well, this all looks good." The magistrate paused, reflectively. "I understand what you've been through, Jamal. I'll make sure there's no risk of anyone dangerous to you finding out about the name change. With abuse cases like this we can really bury things, the FBI would have trouble finding your old name." Blake could almost hear another wink. "Technically you're supposed to make a court appearance, but there's no reason we can't just do it all here."

There were more sounds of papers shuffling, a couple of little bumps. "I just have to go downstairs and get it stamped, I'll be back in a minute," said the magistrate, a bit of nervousness here entering his tone, perhaps even a note of wish-me-luck.

Again there was silence, Tommy making some brief comment to the end that it was going well. Blake willed the guy to speed up, to pull it off. He hoped Lee knew what he was doing with all this.

Something caught his eye over at the other side of the courthouse parking lot. There was a cop car pulling in. He watched as it parked near the entrance, another cop car close behind it. Three cops got out of the first one, then another couple got out of the second.

Blake stared at the screen. You expected cops at a courthouse, didn't you? But five was a lot, those were the sort of numbers you went after someone with. If he wasn't watching for that, what was he watching for? He squinted at the screen. The chest of one of them stuck out, were they wearing bullet proof vests? They were all turning, going into the courthouse, so he couldn't see.

He sent a message to Lee. Still looking for investments, this was the fifth company he had looked at, he wasn't sure what to do. A message appeared on his phone, keep looking into it, but don't buy anything yet, keep me posted.

Blake switched on the mike on his phone, Lee would be able

to hear it if he put on headphones. Then he was quickly out of the café and crossing the street towards the courthouse. He had really been hoping to sit this one out, of all their little operations. For one he was exhausted, and he just didn't like courthouses. There had generally been something unpleasant going on any time he had ever been in one.

The courthouse was a tall, imposing sort of building. Maybe slightly run down, with none of your classical columns or anything, more just a utilitarian greyness. Blake felt a dizziness as he went in, and a strange sensation of déjà vu.

Up the steps the doors opened into a large reception hall, with a high domed roof, a couple of different teller windows, wide hallways at the side. It was somewhat busy, people milling about, sitting on the chairs along one wall. The police were standing in a group, over to the far side of the room.

Blake wasn't sure what his strategy was, or what he was even trying to achieve. He supposed all he could really do was try and listen to what they were saying. He walked a little ways into the room, trying not to look like he was looking at the police. They were sort of off in their own space, not really close to anything. There weren't a lot of reasons to go up to them.

The closest thing was a teller window, and there was a little line. He walked over towards it, and stood in line, angling himself as close to the police as he could without looking suspicious.

They were standing in a semi-circle, talking to themselves. He couldn't make out a lot of words, just the buzz of conversation. Was it an aggressive buzz, a relaxed buzz, a getting ready to go take out a supersoldier/identity forger buzz? Blake couldn't tell. Did he hear the word hallway? He thought he did, and that was something spatial. Hallways were the sort of thing people who were planning an attack talked about.

The line moved forward, so there was just one person between him and the teller. What was he there for? Blake's mind spun, he had no idea what he was doing with any of this. He just wanted to go and find a hole to sleep in.

The person in front of him just dropped some papers off, then it was his turn. "Do you have the paperwork for small businesses here?" he asked.

The teller looked at him, slightly annoyed. "To register a small business?"

"Yes, that's the one," said Blake, and the teller passed him a couple of forms. Blake stepped away from the window in the general direction of the police, and stood there, looking over the forms.

There was a pause in their conversation, then one of them said 'are we going to do this?' The others made noises in the affirmative, and they headed towards the elevator.

Blake felt his stomach drop. The elevator, Tommy and Lee were upstairs. What did he do? He felt like he had been standing by the teller's window for too long. It was a transient thing, you just stood there with your body angled towards it briefly while you made sure you had everything you needed.

He needed to see where they were going. Moving against his instincts, he walked up to the elevator, taking a space beside the police. One of them had pushed the up button, the elevator was going down, 6th floor, 5th floor, 4th floor, where it stopped. That was where Tommy and Lee were. He wondered if he should maybe take the stairs, run up to the fourth floor and see if they got out there.

The light stayed on four, it was really getting to be an abnormally long amount of time. Did that mean anything in and of itself? It made Blake nervous, he glanced around the courthouse.

"Does it usually take this long?" asked one of the cops. It felt like he had sort of said it in Blake's direction. And none of the other cops were saying anything, the question was just sort of hanging there.

"No, I don't think so," said Blake. His mind raced, what did that mean, was that abnormal behaviour, the police asking him that? Maybe it was a little test, maybe people like him came out of the woodwork when you did raids against escaped supersoldiers or identity forgers. Maybe that was even a *mistake people made*, they appeared out of nowhere to follow the police up elevators.

He hoped that wasn't what was happening right now. The guy had sounded pretty relaxed, casual. But maybe that was just how they operated. One way or another Blake had just committed to having some familiarity towards average wait times for elevators in this particular courthouse.

The light was still on four. "I wonder what's going on up there," Blake said, immediately regretting his words. That was going to sound like he was fishing for information.

The cop gave a dry laugh. "Probably some kind of scam."

Blake forced himself to breathe, his lungs were crushing

down on him. He felt a little like he was going to be sick. Why was it a scam, why would he say that? He gave a mirthless laugh himself, the mirthlessness being fairly easy to pull off at that point. "Most likely," he managed, which seemed like an acceptable enough response. Then the elevator was moving again, the light went to the 3rd floor, the 2nd floor.

There was a ding, and the elevator doors opened, a greasy looking guy in a suit stepping out. He was followed by a blond guy in a cast with crutches, a look of mortal agony etched on his face as he painedly dragged himself out of the elevator. Then the cops went in, the one giving Blake a weird sort of knowing look. Blake hesitantly followed them, seeing that the lights were on for the fourth and fifth floors.

He didn't press any buttons, and stood in the corner of the elevator. As the doors closed he reached into his pocket, and fingered the volume button on his phone. If he held that down it would send the emergency code to both Tommy and Lee.

The elevator started going up. He was probably sweating, he probably still smelled of sweat after his sponge bath. What were the interpretations, there were the two floors selected, were they splitting up, could they come at them from above, what exactly? They were uniformed police, that might suggest an operation against an ID forger more than a rogue supersoldier. Should he try to distract them? He might be made already.

The elevator reached the fourth floor, then stopped. Blake felt himself tense up, ready to move, his hand clasping his phone. There was a bing, then it felt like the doors were opening in slow motion.

Behind them were a couple of African American teenagers, standing in a hallway. They just sort of stared in at the elevator, staying where they were, as did the current occupants of the elevator. Then the doors slowly closed again, and the elevator was going up.

The doors opened on the fifth floor. With a gracious motion Blake let the police leave before him, then he hurried out in the opposite direction. It was nothing but offices, closed doors with name tags on them. He went around a corner, then down the empty hallway, there were stairs down so he took them.

There was another long hall with more closed office doors, so he continued down it. He passed room 403, and nothing seemed to be going on. So he sent Lee an all clear message, then continued a few doors further down the hall.

One of the offices had a plastic box filled with flyers beside the door. It was something to do with a bill on campaign finance reform, so he stopped there and grabbed one. That could be his excuse, if anyone ended up asking him why he was up there today. Maybe Lee's alibi guy had been complaining about it.

The flyer itself was sort of strange, it was all about changing how much could be donated to political campaigns. But it was badly written, wouldn't get to the point, reading it was making his head hurt. He wasn't even 100% sure if it was pro or against the bill.

Five minutes passed and no one appeared in the hallway. Blake sent Lee another all clear, and got an all clear in response. So he hurried down the stairs, and sauntered boredly out the main entrance.

30

There was some dipsy-doodling involved in Blake returning to the safehouse - after the events in the courthouse they needed to make absolutely sure he didn't have a trail. He ended up driving for more than an hour, and took a walk in a park. Then finally he had a long dinner at a French restaurant before getting the all clear.

Once they were all back in the safehouse they did a debriefing on the name change. Blake should avoid talking to cops, he knew. Lee thought it had gone well, it was all out of their hands now. His associate would finish the final details and they could expect it to go through within the next week or two.

At the last minute Tommy chose 'Leon' as a middle name, purely on the grounds that he thought it sounded cool and it meant lion. He seemed to have a bit of buyer's regret though, like Tommy Leon, it sounded like some kind of lizard. Blake and Lee both thought it was fine, ya, he guessed it was.

Lee said there was no evidence of any investigation of the mailbox in Portland. Then he wanted to know how things had gone with the trainer. He seemed a little nervous about it, Blake got the distinct impression that he still thought the trainer was an unnecessary risk. But both Blake and Tommy gave Ciagorma a shining review, he seemed like a trustworthy guy.

And he knew his stuff. Tommy said he learned more in the one day of training than in a week at the cabin. And he hadn't had too much trouble hitting anything that Ciagorma threw at him, as long as he sped up his perception. With a little more practice, he would probably be able to hold his own at any level of baseball.

Lee concurred, but wondered if he might not have learned most of what he was going to learn from the one session? But Tommy thought it was pretty important. Optimally he would train with the guy for a few months before even thinking about stepping onto a field. In the end they all agreed that - at least for now - continuing with the trainer was a necessary risk.

On that note, Lee raised another thing, seeing they were so gung-ho on baseball. All the Bay Area teams were out on away games right now, but they would be back in a few days. Lee could get them tickets anonymously, that was easy enough. If this baseball thing was what they were doing, it would make sense to go check out a game, wouldn't it?

Here it was Tommy who was opposed. It would be a lot of risk. There was security, thousands of people, once he was in the stadium seating there wouldn't be a lot of places to run. He looked a little freaked out just at the idea of it, as was Blake. The whole thing was decidedly unsettling.

Lee insisted though. If it was too insecure to go watch a game, how was he ever going to play in one? In the end Tommy conceded that it might be a good idea. They could get some perspective on the whole thing.

The next morning they resumed training with Ciagorma. They did a wide variety of exercises, batting left handed, catching balls with the sun in his eyes, even some slides. After a few hours they stopped practicing fastballs - which Tommy had no problem with - and focused on a variety of sliders, curveballs, changeups and the like.

Ciagorma seemed a little puzzled by this. In general he seemed to think they were choosing weird exercises - fastballs were one of the most important pitches in the game. But Blake said they had a system, Ciagorma was happy to go along with it, if Blake got the feeling he didn't think much of it.

This time they stayed out there until the sun set, all three of them exhausted by the end of it. Ciagorma said he was happy keeping at it though, so they booked him for the next week and a half. Tommy would train with him until it was time to leave for the scouting camps.

They were out there bright and early the next morning, and the day after that. They did quickly stumble across some problematic areas, however, in terms of Tommy's overall realism. It soon became clear that there was a rather large incongruity between his ability to hit and his ability to throw.

Turned out that if someone could hit at a near-major league level, it would look weird if they weren't throwing at anything near a major league level as well. Even if they were really good at throwing. Throwing a ball all the way across a field, right into somebody's glove, that was really hard.

They might not have even realized, but Ciagorma seemed to be puzzling over it, he asked if Tommy had an arm injury. So Tommy made something up on the spot about an accident on a farm where he had been working. Ciagorma looked a little concerned, but he thought it would be alright. It was getting better by the day.

Likewise there seemed to be a similar incongruity with Tommy's knowledge of baseball. He did know quite a bit about the sport, and had been following it fairly religiously for the past few years. But that was still nothing compared to anyone else who would be playing at his level.

This was remedied easily enough, however, just by having Blake step in to ask questions. In general Ciagorma was a wealth of knowledge. He would talk at length about the unwritten rules of the game, the intricacies of what went into a coach's decision to play one pitcher over another, the various approaches towards signalling technique.

They hung on his every word, and he regaled them with stories about crowded buses and stinky dorms in the minor leagues, 14th inning pitching battles in the rain, chasing skirt after the games. Apparently it was pretty nice when you were in the bigs. Food from caterers everywhere, five star hotels, just being up there, he got kind of wistful. Once you got in, you sort of got hooked, but it was a tough game.

Ciagorma also offered them some fairly detailed insights towards the treatment of foreign players of questionable legal status. This he did completely spontaneously, with no prompting from them whatsoever. Which lead Blake to think he had filled in the gaps in their story by assuming Tommy did in fact have visa issues.

Some of it was quite useful information. Apparently in one of the A-ball minor leagues, they just didn't care, they hardly checked IDs at all. Ciagorma was sure there were guys who didn't have work visas, there were a lot of guys from south of the border playing there. He thought they even got better players than they should, at least until they got legal and went to AAA. If you wanted to watch some good minor league baseball, that was the place to go.

Blake did also get the impression that he got there was something else a little weird going on, beyond Tommy's potential visa issues. But if he did, he kept it to himself. If anything he was more accommodating, going out of his way to explain things that Tommy should probably have known already. All things considered Blake was impressed with how he was handling himself. He could be a valuable asset in terms of getting Tommy into the sport, from the sounds of it he knew a few people in the business.

They settled into a good rhythm. Starting bright and early, Blake getting them lunch from an Indian place down the road, training late into the afternoon or the evening. There was a group of neighbourhood kids who watched them a couple times, Tommy hit one out of the park for them once and they all cheered. They made Blake nervous, but they never hung out for too long. It would probably be more suspicious to try and chase them away.

It felt like everything was coming together, the preparations were almost behind them. The first scouting camp was now just under two weeks away, in Des Moines, Iowa. Which was going to be quite a road trip, maybe 24 hours of solid driving, they weren't going to fly there.

Blake still however felt unprepared. He had been doing a lot of research, but they were doing something pretty unorthodox, and baseball's rules were complex. He had a hovering feeling like they were going to get blindsided by something. With any other investment he would generally have had his legal team look over it months ago.

So he raised the idea of going over it all with his lawyer. Lee was again skeptical, how many people did he want to bring on? Blake didn't think he was 'bringing anyone on', he would just be asking for general information about how the rules worked. After a medium-lengthed deliberation over what could go wrong, they agreed it should be safe enough. Blake's lawyers were discreet.

Blake took the day off from training, and they set him up with a secure line before leaving. His lawyer was glad to hear from him, said that everything was progressing well with the European real estate. Blake briefly considered asking him about Oregon state fair law, but decided against it.

Was he available personally to do some research? He was. Blake would rather they didn't use paralegals on this one, it was rather a sensitive project. He would pay the special rate.

Blake laid it out for him, hypothetical situation, say it was for a bet. Incredibly talented baseball player, complete unknown, wanted to get into the sport as quickly as possible. What would be the legal issues, what would they have to do, what would the weaknesses be if people got in their way?

Blake also went into detail about the Free Agency loophole. His lawyer thought that was a funny thing. The hypothetical player could potentially make a multi-million dollar salary right off the bat, if Blake would forgive his phrasing.

His lawyer said he would start right away, and call Blake back later in the day. Blake then passed the morning flipping through baseball's official rule book. It was sort of dry reading though, and it felt like he was having trouble focusing on anything involving baseball right now.

Blake made a couple of teas, had another breakfast, some lunch, then his lawyer called him back. In general it seemed that Blake's research had been pretty accurate. His lawyer still couldn't say 100%, but it did seem like the free agency loophole would work. He didn't think it would really happen in the real world though. A top level player would pretty much have to appear out of nowhere, the amount of scouting there was these days. Did Blake win the bet?

Going over it all, however, his lawyer had found one thing Blake had missed – a central database that all players across the sport needed to be registered in. As far as he could tell it was mostly just a technicality. His impression was that coaches generally did all the registering and updating as a part of their normal start of season housekeeping.

Blake went to the website where you registered. It had a few fields, name, date of birth, height and weight, emergency contact, that sort of thing. He almost wanted to fill out the form now. They had a secure connection, and it would probably be another whole big thing with Lee.

Clicking on the education option, Blake saw that it had GED. But when he selected that, another field appeared, 'accrediting institution'. They both figured that was the school that awarded the GED. It had a star beside it though, it was a required field - he couldn't submit the form without it.

What happened if they didn't fill out the form? The hypothetical player might not have the GED yet. His lawyer said a player would need to have the GED before the start of the draft to be eligible to play that year. You couldn't be passed over in the draft unless you were registered for it in the first place.

Blake felt a panic wash over him. He had thought you just needed the GED before starting to play. His lawyer said there was some contradictory information in the rules, but if you read both sections it was fairly unequivocal. Blake told him to keep researching it, then hung up, feeling dizzy. It was Friday today, and Tuesday was the first day of the draft. He sent Lee and Tommy a message to come back to the safe house. Then he did a search for GED testing on his laptop, found a number, and called it immediately.

After a brief wait he spoke to a confused sounding girl, who said it usually took at least a couple of weeks to a month to process. Blake inquired as to the possibility of a rush fee. There was no way to do same day marking? She didn't think so, she put him on hold while she went to ask her supervisor.

After a bit she came back on. She was sorry, but there was no rush option. But it was usually marked within 10-15 working days. Could he talk to her manager? Price wasn't an issue. She didn't think he was available. It was important, Blake could hold.

After a long wait he was put through to a manager, who seemed even more clueless. He finally got him to put him through to *his* manager, who sounded suspiciously like the first girl doing a voice.

She insisted there was no option to rush the test. It was official policy and they had to treat everyone fairly. Blake pleaded a little bit more, but she said it was the absolute minimum. How bloody long did it take to mark a bloody test? Someone was sitting there for ten days straight, were they, up at dawn working into the night?

When Blake hung up he saw his lawyer had called, so he called him back. His lawyer said having the diploma awarded before the draft would be best. But they could probably build a legally defensible position around using the date the test was taken. There was some precedent.

Blake thanked him, and went back to the GED pages. That would leave them Monday, maybe Tuesday, to take the test. He searched through the testing centre's pages, they didn't seem to offer the test that often. There was one on the 20th in Palo Alto, another on Wednesday in Sausalito.

Just as panic was beginning to set in, he finally found one. There was a test on Monday, in Fresno. Looking up at the cameras he saw that Tommy and Lee were pulling into the safe house. They appeared in the living room, looking concerned.

"You've got to take your GED on Monday," said Blake.

"Monday, what? There's no way, I'm not ready yet, I haven't

studied half the stuff," said Tommy, panic appearing on his face, while Lee looked on with mild curiosity.

"It's our only option, my lawyer's stumbled across a speed bump." Blake proceeded to explain the exact nature of the situation, highlighting the importance of no one being able to kick them out on a technicality. Especially in the context of using a loophole to achieve free agency, or a top secret lab wanting them out of the sport.

"Well, we can't do much about that," said Lee. "He still doesn't have Tommy Johnson ID, you realize? I highly doubt the name change is going to go through by Monday. And even if it did, he still has to get a new picture ID, that's another week. Do you want him to write it with the Jamal Soto Chang ID?"

Blake steadied himself on a chair. There was that, wasn't there? "You can't just get him a temporary fake ID in Tommy Johnson's name?" He looked at Lee hopefully, he was the master of getting that kind of stuff at the drop of a hat.

Lee shook his head. "They'll need ID that connects to whatever databases they are using. They've all got their own unique number, which you can't get until the ID arrives. There's no way around it, they'll need to scan the magnetic stripe, which might have unique identifier codes of its own. They're pretty strict with the GED, people have been known to pay other people to write the test for them."

Tommy was now giving Blake sort of a weird look. "Do you really think I'm going to be able to play this year? We're already a couple of months into the season."

"From the sounds of it you can't even play in the minor leagues unless you get the GED now," Blake said, a little unsure if that was exactly what his lawyer had been saying.

An idea occurred to him. "What if you did take the test with the Jamal Soto Chang ID? Then you would have legally written the test. If we need to produce it, we can. I'm sure once the name change has gone through we could just talk to the GED people and get them to change the name on the certificate. People change their names, don't they?"

Lee looked at him like he was crazy. "Then that's a record of the name change, in the public school system. Do you know how much work it's taking my guy to keep it off the books?"

Blake shrugged. "We don't have to change the name on the diploma, Tommy could just write the GED again after the name change goes through. It would just give us the option of producing a GED dated before the draft if we need it. What were you saying, we need to do things to test the ID?"

Lee looked exasperated. "You want to write the test here, he'll probably need California ID. The Jamal Soto Chang ID is Maryland."

Lee went over to the computer, and Blake felt the ground drop away a bit again. They probably couldn't risk him getting on a flight with the Jamal Soto Chang ID. Maryland would be a pretty long drive. Although then they would be a lot closer to the first training camp in Iowa, they had to go out that way anyways.

"Aha!" said Lee, looking a little bit too proud of himself for Blake's liking. "All students must take the GED in their state of residency."

Blake stared at it. "Residency isn't determined by what state your ID card is from, is it? You can have a Maryland ID and still be a resident of California. We already have those pay stubs, that's what they were for, right?" He picked up the phone, and started dialing the GED office again.

"Who are you calling?" asked Tommy.

"The GED office. There's a girl there who seems to have some limited understanding of how their testing system works."

Tommy sort of gave him a look. "I just set up that phone to call your lawyer. I thought we said we were all going to talk to each other before making phone calls."

"Right," said Blake. He had said that, hadn't he? "Should I call from this phone then? I've already called them once."

Tommy thought about it a moment, Lee with a sort of grimace on his face. "I guess it's ok."

Blake nodded, and made the call. The same girl answered again, she seemed to remember him. He just had one more quick question, did she know exactly how the residency requirements worked? If he had an out of state ID, could he still take the test?

Tommy and Lee stared at him as he listened. She said it was possible, but they might ask him for proof of residency. Pay stubs, rent receipts, that sort of thing was usually good. That was perfect.

Lee threw his hands up into the air, and mumbled something about never having gotten behind baseball. They called Ciagorma and told him he could take the weekend off. Then Lee immediately took off to buy every book he could find on GED preparation, while Blake and Tommy started in on the study materials they already had. That was the whole other aspect of the plan, he had to pass.

Tommy seemed to have received a good education during his training. Certainly it was at least the equivalent of a high school diploma. But as they progressed through the study guides it became clear that it was rather uneven, from the perspective of the American curriculum. A knowledge of American history or particle physics had only limited use in infiltrating a terrorist cell or getting past a foxhole on a motorbike. If he did actually know a surprising amount about American history, given that he had originally been measuring his time there in hours.

With the maths questions, for example, he would really ace some of them, but then be completely lost in terms of solving for x. Likewise he knew nothing about ecosystem interdependence or mollusk physiology, but found human biology a breeze. He got all the sample questions right on the first try, if he thought one of their questions about the testosterone system technically had the wrong answer.

Fortunately there were some areas where he was solid across the board. His grammar was amazing, for one. He actually knew the difference between adverbs, nouns, verbs, all those things. After maybe 20 minutes they just stopped studying it. Blake supposed you picked all that up, learning however many languages it was he spoke. He would be the one guy wishing there was more grammar on the test.

Working against them, however, was the fact that the test was designed so you needed to get a minimum score on each section. He couldn't just ace a few sections and let the average work out.

Tommy studied late into the night, got straight back to it over breakfast. Blake and Lee tried to contribute in any way they could, taking note of things he had trouble with, making up mnemonics for him. They kept going until about 2 AM Sunday night, Tommy only stopping because they forced him to at least get a couple hours of sleep.

First thing in the morning they filled out the form registering Thomas Leon Johnson in the baseball database. On Blake's suggestion they just put Blake's lawyer's information for emergency contact and address, people did that often enough. A fake residential address would look like a fake residential address, should a league detective or journalist or some such investigate him at a later date. While an upscale Manhattan law firm could discourage any potential perturbances. Then they clicked submit, legally the baseball people had 24 hours to contact them if there were any problems.

They did Tommy up to look more like the kid in his Jamal Soto Chang ID, then drove down to Fresno in two cars. Blake by himself, Lee driving Tommy. The test was in a medium sized community college, which didn't seem too busy, it was summer session now.

Blake was again HQ, with their locations on a map and the central communication system. Tommy obviously wouldn't be able to communicate with them once he was in the test, but they set his phone up with five different ring tones for emergencies.

Lee went to scout out the test center to start. After about half an hour he sent them the all clear, then Tommy went in. Blake put on his headphones and turned on the live feed.

There was some ambient noise, a door opening, footsteps echoing down a corridor. Then another door creaking open, and Tommy was speaking.

"Is this where I go for the GED?" he asked.

"Yep, this is the place," said a youngish woman's voice.

There was some rustling. "Here's my ID and the payment," said Tommy. There was another silence, and Blake could faintly hear some typing noises.

"Jamal Fulano Soto Chang," murmured the girl. There was another pause. "That's funny."

"What's that?"

"It says here you're dead." Blake's heart jumped, and he instinctively reached for his car keys, and put them in the ignition.

"Dead?" asked Tommy, his tone humorous, a little incredulous, although Blake could hear a note of nervousness slip in as well. "Um, that's weird."

"1351 Rumbo Sur Boulevard?" she asked, her tone perhaps more perplexed than suspicious.

"Ya, like years and years ago," said Tommy, fairly lightheartedly. "It really says I'm dead?"

"Must be a bug in the system. The database is kind of wonky sometimes. I've never seen anything like that before, though." There was another pause, more faint typing in the background.

"Ok, there, I've fixed it for you. You're alive again."

"Great, I feel much better!" said Tommy jovially. The girl laughed, and then gave him some information about the test. Four sections, fill in the answers with a led pencil, no cell phones or anything once the test started. Then there was ambient room noise for a moment, a phone ringing, and she was talking to someone about wheelchair accessibility.

Blake sat back in the car seat, breathing in and out. He sort of felt like he wanted to throw up. Bloody school records, with what they were paying he would have expected Lee's guy to fix those.

Were they going to ruin his whole identity right here and now? He could imagine some great government computer scanning through data, finding multiple suspicious connections with Jamal Fulano Soto Chang. Agents could be leaving for the test centre right now.

Blake switched to Lee's feed to see what he made of it. And, presumably, get his ear chewed off. But Lee seemed to be on the phone. He was having some sort of conversation about ramp width and angulation, there was a strange buzzing sound in his feed that hadn't been there before. It didn't make any sense, he was just droning off about all these different numbers, different slopes, lengths and widths, it was a hard conversation to follow.

Lee was asking, did she think they could put in a reinforced wooden ramp? Yes, she thought they could put in a reinforced wooden ramp, said a female voice. That was the girl from just there checking into the test, was it? Blake turned off the feed. Lee could probably hear him breathing on his end, he didn't want to distract him. How did he even get her number?

Then it was again just a matter of killing time. They gave you up to ten hours to write the test, and he imagined Tommy would need all the time he could get. On Lee's advice Blake set up in a hidden away study carrel in the library. He played around on his computer, flipped through some history journals that had stuff on the Dark Ages.

He kept compulsively looking up sample GED questions though, it was a lot riding on one test. Some of them were pretty difficult - he didn't know if he could pass, if it was him taking it today. If you thought about it, it was equivalent to the whole 12 years people spent in school, in one test. They couldn't make it too easy.

What if Tommy did fail? Would they be cruising around high schools trying to find some dirty official? Blake couldn't stop thinking about all the things that could go wrong, this and everything else. It was too many little things, too many singular do or die moments where one false step could bring down the whole house of cards. In the end he just had to force it out of his mind, there wasn't much he could do about it here and now, and it was giving him indigestion.

31

It was getting dark by the time Tommy finally finished the test. After a reassuringly uneventful drive back they did a debriefing at the safe house. Tommy didn't really know how he did - there was some stuff he didn't know, but the stuff he did was spread out. He didn't feel like he did badly on any one part.

Overall he was optimistic. One thing he was a little worried about was an essay he had to write, on a job experience that taught him something about life. He made up something about hurting his shoulder while working on a farm, he hoped it was realistic. He didn't really know much about how things worked on farms.

The next day was their last with Ciagorma, so they got out there early to get a solid day in. They started in on fielding practice, Blake pitching to Ciagorma and Tommy diving for the balls. He was feeling exhausted though, and even Tommy seemed pretty out of it – Blake wasn't actually sure if he was missing some of them on purpose.

There was a game about to start, Los Angeles at San Antonio, so they decided it was in their collective best interest to go watch that instead. They walked to a big sports bar a little down the way - Tommy fortunately not being asked for ID - and got the bartender to put on the game.

Ciagorma and Tommy were immediately off talking about the players, analyzing each team's season, making predictions as to how the game would go. Los Angeles got up 2-0, and the conversation moved on to the finer details of the game. Overall statistical fielding trends, the matchup between the pitcher and the batters. All his time researching the sport, and Blake understood maybe half of it.

It was sort of strange, watching a game, he hadn't actually been watching a lot lately. There was a guy who looked a little like Tommy going up to bat, it was just unsettling. Then the camera panned over the stands, the cheering crowd. It made him dizzy, looking at them all, he felt a little sick.

The conversation got on to how the market was for new players these days. Apparently there was a lot of demand right now, it was the best time to be a player in years. Guys were getting snatched up like crazy. Although Ciagorma seemed to think the main reason was all the steroids scandals - they were doing way more testing these days. There were a lot of guys on suspension, from the minors up. So it was good news and bad news, from their perspective.

It seemed like a good opportunity to ask what he thought would be the best way for Tommy to get into the sport. Ciagorma sat back and thought about it. That was actually kind of a funny question, he wasn't sure. So he really never played high school ball? There weren't a lot of guys at Tommy's level who weren't already playing somewhere. The way scouting was these days, they had files on kids before they started shaving.

He thought Tommy could try college ball. How was he academically? Once he got in, he would probably get a scholarship pretty fast. There were leagues at all levels with baseball, as well. He could just start in a little bush league somewhere and work his way up.

The more immediate plan was the scouting camps, so Blake asked him about those. Ciagorma had never been to one, so he didn't know what they would be like. Maybe teenagers and amateurs, guys who had never gone pro and wanted to see if they could cut it. He didn't think anybody really got into the game through them. But there would be real scouts there, definitely.

There was a pause in the conversation, then Tommy looked over at Ciagorma earnestly. "So, like, you've seen me play. What do you think my chances really are.." he swallowed, "like, out there?"

Ciagorma looked slightly put on the spot by the question. "You showed some good stuff." He looked at Tommy with respect. "You've got a good shot. Probably one of the best shots, out of everyone I've worked with."

Blake felt a relief at that, it was about the level of ability they had wanted to send out. Ciagorma rubbed his chin, then continued. "Don't let it go to your head though. Like I said, you're good, really good. But out there in the big leagues, it's another world. You never want to get overconfident." A warble entered his tone, a certain sadness. "Just because you're getting hits off me doesn't mean you're going to get hits in pro ball, even in the minors. Those guys can throw."

Ciagorma paused a moment. "I mean, don't let it get to you either. You don't want to be too confident, but you don't want to doubt yourself too much as well." He shook his head. "The game messes with your head, especially once you get up to the higher levels. Guys have trouble with the pressure, or they get hit by a pitch, and they lose their game."

He stopped a moment, thinking, maybe unsure if he should say anything, then continued. "I noticed something, a couple of times we were out there, and those kids came by? I don't think you were hitting as well when they were watching you. You gotta watch out for that. If a bunch of neighbourhood kids effect your game, wait until you get in front of hundreds of people in the minor leagues."

"Ya, I do kind of get self-conscious," Tommy said nervously.

"You gotta be Zen up there. Like I said, you're good. Maybe really good. If you keep at it, keep training like you've been training with me, I could see you in the bigs in as little as four or five years."

"Four or five years is pretty fast, then, is it?" Blake asked, trying to sound curious and nonchalant, although he heard a catch in his voice. He had been noticing that, reading player biographies. Even the big names seemed to have spent a lot of time in the minors. It had sort of been nagging at him, actually.

Ciagorma shrugged. "Ya, you gotta put in your time in the minors, pay your dues. A lotta guys take even longer. Although if you don't make it after maybe seven or eight years your odds really start going down." He paused, watching an LA batter ground out. "Like that pitcher that got picked first. A guy like that I could see in the bigs two or three years from now, although some of his stuff still needs work."

That wasn't exactly what Blake was hoping to hear. "There aren't a lot of players who go straight to the major leagues then?"

"I think it used to happen more often, maybe back when the President was still selling used cars?" Ciagorma shook his head. "I remember there were a couple of guys, but they fizzled out pretty fast." He paused, like he was trying to remember, but didn't name anyone. "But in double or triple A you start getting good money. I was eating at restaurants every night, and they comped my hotel any road game. Some of them were pretty nice hotels."

Ciagorma looked over at Tommy. "I dunno, the way you were hitting them, you might be able to get into the minors by next season. Although no offense, but a big guy like you is gonna be guilty until proven innocent. They might want to do a couple rounds of tests before they even let you step on the field."

He paused a moment, then continued, sort of philosophically. "The more I see, the more I think they kind of just want to get to know people first. It isn't always 100% about being the best. Ballplayers are heroes to a lot of people, they want to know if someone is going to get drunk all the time, or beat up their girlfriend or something."

He gave a shrug. "Sometimes a lot of it seems like BS. Guys get frustrated, nobody ever gets to the bigs as fast as they want. But you've always gotta play by their rules. They've got their way they like doing things, and it's kind of their way or the highway, even if it doesn't always make a lotta sense."

Blake tried to grin philosophically. "A couple years in the minors doesn't sound so bad."

He felt like he should just see it as another obstacle to overcome, but it was all starting to feel like too much. Baseball executives would probably be shot-calling ballers who wouldn't take any nonsense from the likes of them. It was just how those things worked, anywhere where you had so many people who wanted in.

Blake was getting the impression that baseball was a particularly long road, even just compared to other sports. He had been reading some articles about cricket, and for a top player the salaries were actually fairly comparable.

There would be advantages and disadvantages to an international sport. But he had a feeling it could be a lot easier to get onto a team somewhere in the developing world. In many ways they had chosen the worst place possible – America was a bureaucratic nightmare where things were done by the book, and you could go to jail just for paying a bribe.

But if they had their pick of countries, they could choose the one with the most favourable conditions for things like drug testing or fake IDs. It would be slightly distasteful, but really a little dictatorship somewhere might work best – they could just give the head guy a cut, and the doors would open up. He wondered how much the central sport body managed things, and how much of it was up to the individual countries.

Ciagorma was now going off about the minor leagues, they were pretty awesome, actually. In many ways he had enjoyed his time there more than the majors. Well, the majors had been pretty awesome as well, but it was different, a lot more pressure, for one.

From the sounds of it he had quite a wild time pitching for LA. And after, he had gone back there once his major league career was over. Apparently you could sort of milk it, even just as a relief pitcher you were still a minor celebrity once you left the game.

It turned out he and Blake both knew some of the same bars. The 4 AM dive place, the crazy one with way too many disco balls, the 24-hour diner everybody went to.

Then Ciagorma got sort of a funny look in his eye, and swivelled on his stool a bit towards Blake. "Hey, did you used to have," he stopped, looking lost for a moment. "Like, I don't remember, a boat with a fire on it?"

Blake quickly gave him a quizzical look, his heart jumping. "A boat with a fire on it? Can you have fires on boats?"

Ciagorma looked a little confused, and slightly sheepish. "Like a fireplace maybe? I don't remember, it was something like that." He rubbed his head. "Ya, maybe not, it was a few years ago now, at some party at a beach house. They had this really huge pool with a fake beach, but it was right on the beach, it was crazy."

"It wasn't me," said Blake. He remembered the place well, if most of the time he spent there was a blur. It was a movie producer's mansion, he threw some epic parties.

Ciagorma continued, scratching his head. "I remember there was this guy, you really remind me of him. Somebody was making him tell a story about some kind of a boat with a fire on it or something."

"What, like a bonfire on the deck?" asked Tommy. "I don't know if I'd want to sail on that boat."

"Ya, it sounds like a crappy boat," said Ciagorma, laughing, they all laughed.

Ciagorma got a far away look in his eye. "Man, those were good times." His voice was slightly choked up, and he gave Tommy an earnest look. "I wouldn't trade it for anything. What I wouldn't give to be up there again, one last season, even just a game. If you've got any chance of making it in the bigs, I'd go for it. Even if you don't make it past the minors, it's still a good life."

His eyes were kind of misty now. Then he looked over at

Blake. "You guys seem pretty up to date. You don't know about anything that could sort of.." he paused, now uncertain, nervous, with lowered voice, "put the spring back in somebody's step?"

There was an uncomfortable silence, Blake didn't know what to say. "I'm not sure exactly what you mean. Tommy has some special exercise regimes, meal plans and nutritional supplements that he finds useful."

Ciagorma mumbled something that sounded like an apology, he looked aghast a moment just at having said it. It then felt sort of awkward, they returned their attention to the game. It was getting pretty intense, 3-4 for LA, top of the 8th. San Antonio tied it up, but then in the 9th LA blasted one out of the park and won it 5-4.

Ciagorma said he had to run. But he was going to go watch a game tonight, actually, down in San Jose. If they weren't doing anything they were welcome to come check it out. It wasn't anything big, just bush league. But they played a good game, and he knew some of the guys on the team. They might all go out afterwards, it was always a good time.

Blake looked over at Tommy, who looked like he was considering it. But then he said they couldn't make it. They thanked Ciagorma for all his help, and Blake again reminded him of the need for discretion with all of this.

Blake also passed him an envelope full of cash and a bunch of random gift cards. Blake found gift cards to be a good way of paying extra when you wanted to downplay the size of a tip. Sort of like he didn't even know how much was on them, maybe they were going to expire soon.

Back at the safehouse, Lee seemed pretty freaked out that Ciagorma had recognized Blake. Tommy and Blake both thought Ciagorma believed him when Blake said it hadn't been him with the boat. But the fact that he asked about steroids immediately after was a bit worrying. That would have been around the time Blake was dealing.

Either way it just underscored the risk of having Blake go out in public. Today might have been a near miss, but they might not be so lucky in the future. What was worrying Tommy more, however, was Wildon Textiles. The more he thought about it, the more it seemed like there were some dangerous loose ends there.

For one, he didn't think his people would necessarily talk to Jack Wildon in person, and their strategy had kind of been orientated around that. Investigating Blake would probably be a low priority for them, and any noise they made doing so could lead him to connect the pool table incident with Eugene Cudneck. Blake had some clout in the world, Tommy's people would tread lightly around him.

That meant they would probably focus any investigation purely on whatever clues were left on the grid. Blake was basically done if they found his San Diego number, and people were backing up their contact lists on the cloud these days. There was always going to be the risk his people could access those databases.

Bill, Steve, the receptionist, anybody at Wildon Textiles could have Blake's name and phone number saved away on a server somewhere. Blake had sort of told Jack to get people to delete that number, but there was no way they could assume that he had systematically gone through everybody's phones.

There was that, and emails. Someone could have easily sent an email that mentioned the details of Blake's disappearance. Blake had been saying there was maybe enough to figure some stuff out, just in the emails he had access to?

Tommy went to the computer, and pulled up an article from a tech magazine. Apparently the company Wildon Textiles used to manage their IT stuff was getting bought out by a bigger tech company. Tommy knew them, and they were pretty loose, from a data security perspective. Or at least his people had no problem getting access to their data.

He was keeping track of stuff like that? He was. There was only so much they could do about people's emails. But Blake's impression had been that the Wildon Textiles people generally used their @WildonTextiles.com addresses to communicate with each other, right? Most or all of the messages dangerous to them would probably be on Wildon Textiles' email server, and it would be the place Tommy's people would be most likely to look.

What did Blake think about hacking into their server? He would have to go down there for that, but Tommy thought it would probably actually be pretty easy. He could ask to use Jack's computer, and put a keystroke logger on it. From there he would just have to get Jack to log in to the administrator account, maybe Blake could ask for a new @WildonTextiles.com email address.

Blake supposed that could work. As a concept it made sense, but in terms of actually doing it he would be a little nervous. Although compared to breaking into houses to set up surveillance systems and the like it seemed pretty straightforward.

They would think it over, then. Tommy still wasn't sure if it was a good idea. Sometimes trying to cover your tracks just drew attention to them. Just even having Blake spend time in San Diego entailed some degree of risk.

Either way, it would be good for Blake to call Jack now, if nothing else just to check in. While he was at it he could call Laura, as well. Actually, maybe he could even try and do lunch or a coffee with her before they left. She might still have his old number in her phone.

So Tommy rigged him up a phone, and they headed out into the country, driving for more than an hour before finding an out of the way rest area where the signal was right. Lee and Tommy put on headphones to listen to the calls, then Blake dialed Jack's number.

Jack answered after a couple of rings, and sounded happy to hear from him, it had been a while. Had Blake been back on the ranch? Apparently everything was going well in San Diego, the weather was great, they were in the midst of manufacturing a huge order of tablecloth material.

Jack just had a call with the hotel people. They hadn't made the sale yet, but it looked promising. That's how these big deals were, lots of groundwork, he almost didn't know if it was worth it. Although ya, it probably was, ha ha.

Then they just chatted a bit, his son was trying to choose which universities to apply to, there was a corruption scandal that had been in the news. Blake had sort of liked some of the politicians, who knew.

After a bit Blake said he'd let him go. But he was thinking about coming down to San Diego, finally, at least for a week or two. Jack said they could take the sailboat out, the weather had been amazing.

Then just as they were hanging up, Jack said there was one other thing, paused a moment like he was really considering his words. Blake steeled himself, that could be a few different things. He had to act under the assumption the phone was tapped.

But then Jack just said something about how they had never paid him anything for all his help with the management consultancy stuff. That sort of caught Blake off guard. He said what, no, no, they could figure it out later. Actually, they didn't even have to worry about it. Blake brushed him off when he protested, no, really, they were even, they had given him such a good deal on the little share he bought.

Blake hung up, and they all thought the call had gone well. So Blake took a deep breath, then called Laura's number. It rang a few times, but finally she picked up.

She sort of sounded happy to hear from him, but also a little distant, maybe hurried. Things had been crazy busy with her work, she was actually trying to get a really big project finished up right now.

Blake tried to be witty, suave, put on his A-game. It sort of felt like at any given point in the conversation she was going to say she had to go. He felt kind of awkward though, having the guys listen in. And he didn't know what to say. His A-game usually involved tales of epic luxurious exotic adventure, but any stories he might have generated in the past weeks he couldn't tell.

So he talked about how he had been out in the woods, had done a lot of kayaking, it felt like a white lie. Lee held up a note, 'sea kayaking off Big Sur if she asks'. She did seem to warm up a bit there, a bunch of them had been planning to go kayaking, but it fell apart at the last minute.

It turned out she had been down in San Diego a couple of weeks ago. Wildon Textiles had some really neat new machines. Blake said he would have to check them out, he was planning on going down to San Diego for a little bit in the near future. Apparently she would be there as well, things with the satellite office were really picking up.

Blake said they should hang out, if they were there at the same time. Although actually, he wasn't far from San Francisco right now, that was why he was calling. He wouldn't have a lot of time, but did she want to get lunch or a coffee or something in the next couple of days?

She had a couple deadlines, and then she was going camping for the weekend. But after a brief hesitation, she said a whole bunch of them were going to the bar tomorrow night. He should come! Blake said he wasn't sure if he could make it, he looked at the guys. Maybe he would get back to her.

Then she said she really had to run. As soon as the call was finished Lee started up the car, and they pulled out onto the road. All of them thought the calls had gone well. Laura had sounded a little cold towards him at first, Lee thought that could even be a red flag. But maybe she just thought he was weird, after all that the day of the meeting. Blake admitted that could well be the case. He felt like they had basically ended on a good note in LA, but sometimes people looked back and got creeped out, certainly.

Either way she had warmed up, and sounded natural. They all agreed it was unlikely someone had talked to either of them. The big question, then, was whether he should go to the bar tomorrow.

What Tommy was thinking was that it could be a good way of testing the waters. He had been thinking about what had happened to Blake, while he was in LA and that beach town. Some of it was kind of weird. Was it normal to get your hotel room cleaned late in the afternoon?

At this point in the game, it was pretty vital they know if there were people on Blake. It had a lot of implications for what they did next. Like having him go to Wildon Textiles to wipe the email server, for example.

Blake concurred, a lot of his financial rearranging he would really only want to do if he was sure he wasn't being watched. Moving his gold, adornment, and precious stone holdings involved a lot of paperwork, for one, and they would spend a couple days in transit before they were in international waters.

And it would just be fun to go to the bar, Blake needed to make another appearance on the grid anyways. They turned on the music and drove, up through forested hills, taking turns at random. Passing through a thickly wooded area they saw a sign for a park. Grinning at them, Tommy suggested they go for a hike.

They parked and set out, the trail map said there was a five mile loop. There was something exhilarating about being out in the woods again. Even in the cabin they had hardly been outside, or when they had they were distracted with the training. The air was fresh, birds chirping around them, lone sunbeams cutting through the thick canopy.

They all seemed to share his good mood. If Tommy admitted there was a good case that going for a hike was an unnecessary risk. They were only so far from where they made the calls, someone could be putting a tracking device on the car at this very moment.

Or maybe they were being too careful. They all sort of agreed, at some point you just had to accept that stuff was out of your control. Had they really needed cameras two kilometers from the cabin? Maybe they should just leave Wildon Textile's email server alone, for one.

Although if they were going out into the world doing things, Tommy thought there was a good argument they should be even more careful. They should never underestimate his people. But nonetheless they continued on through an open meadow, the sky blue above them, sauntering along for any satellites to see.

On that note, Lee mentioned they had the game in a couple days. He had the tickets already, if they wanted to go. Tommy thought it would actually be kind of cool to go to a game. It probably wouldn't be much of a risk at all.

Although here Tommy went silent for a moment, and looked back at Blake, an apologetic uncertainty now in his eyes. "Man, some of that stuff Ciagorma was saying. I think it might actually be really hard to get into professional baseball."

Blake made a little noise in the affirmative, and Tommy continued. "Like, it sounds like it takes years and years, and they're doing all that testing? I dunno if I'm gonna be able to pass those tests. I was never designed to look like I wasn't on steroids, just not to look like a supersoldier. And there's the GED, or the fake ID. I was watching some player biographies and it sounds like they really researched people."

"Yes, well, there certainly are a lot of hurdles, perhaps some of which would be rather difficult to get around. It was always a long shot," said Blake, hearing himself use the past tense.

For a moment he wanted to raise the idea of cricket. But suddenly, finally, there in the woods, he could see it all clearly. Tommy, Joe, he was never going to play professional sports, was he? There were just too many things wrong with it, the fundamentals weren't there. He had been involved in ventures like this too many times before. It was the undersea apartment project all over again. Or refined catnip, for that matter.

He felt a certain disappointment, but it was bittersweet. There was something strangely liberating about it, it felt like a great burden had been lifted from his back. In truth he felt more relieved than anything else. The plan was to drive across the country in a couple of days for the scouting camps, he wondered if he should just save them all the time.

Joe had moved on though, and was now talking about how cool it would be to start some sort of a detective agency. It even sounded a little bit like a pitch. They could do jobs for people, or just go around looking for wrongs to right. Find some random bad-guys who were doing evil shit, then thwart them. With a detective agency they wouldn't have to worry about half the stuff they had been working on, they probably could have even done a mission or two already.

Did they think the three of them would be enough of a team? Joe *maybe* might be able to get some of the other supersoldiers to turn. It would be hard just getting in touch with them, he didn't know. Lee knew some people as well, a bounty hunter, his fake ID guy was pretty badass. Not the magistrate, the guy who got it in the first place.

Blake thought he might know a couple people, he had met some characters in his day. Or maybe he could help more with the advertising. He had a lot of connections with well-heeled people who might need that kind of service.

Sometimes finding jobs was the hardest part. How did you even find super-villains in the first place? They generally just sulked around in the shadows hatching elaborate plots. Joe had been wondering about that, actually. He had always just gotten missions assigned to him. Lee seemed to think there were plenty of super-villains operating out in the open.

It all made Blake a little nervous – super-villain types could be the vengeful sorts who didn't like having their plans thwarted. But there was a good case they would be less likely to end up getting shot with a detective agency then trying to play pro-ball. And they could get some high paying gigs, with someone like Joe. Really it suddenly seemed like the much more obvious thing to do.

Blake started going over some numbers as they walked. Just rough estimates, who knew how many jobs you would be expected to have per year, what the expenses would be. From the sounds of it Joe would want to do a certain amount of pro-bono work.

Well, it really didn't feel like the time to do a cost:earnings estimate. Who really knew what the future would hold for them? On some fundamental level it had always just sort of felt like baseball was what they were going to do, he wasn't exactly sure why. But maybe the story didn't have to go that way, they were all free to write their own destinies, weren't they?

Blake didn't know, but for now it was enough just to walk through the trees. For once he felt relaxed, at peace. He half listened as Joe went off about stealing some kind of stealth submarine. Apparently otherwise travelling internationally would be a recurring issue, having a sub would solve a lot of problems at once. Blake didn't think about any of it, he just basked in the day's last rays of light, shining in like a mosaic through the layers of leaves and branches thick around them.

32

It seemed all too quickly the hike came to an end, the sun now setting over the trees. They made it back to the parking lot without incident, Joe sliding under the car to give it a once-over for bugs.

Once they were back in the safe house, Lee got changed into a disguise, then went to scout out the bar for tomorrow night. He returned a few hours later with a rough schematic map of the bar, some photos from his hat-cam, and satellite print-outs of the surrounding area.

Turned out it was a huge place, a complex of like five interconnecting bars. It was also located in a fairly busy area, with plenty of escape routes. All things considered they couldn't ask for a better place for the operation - with lots of space to move around it would apparently be easier to see if someone was watching Blake.

So Blake sent Laura a message - from an email address Joe thought his people would be able to access if they wanted to - just saying he would be there tomorrow night and confirming the address. Over his breakfast the next afternoon they put him to work studying the maps. There would be an extra car and a motorbike stashed in strategic locations around the bar, should he in fact need to make a hasty exit.

Blake's mission would be fairly basic. Beyond being his normal suave relaxed self, he would have to wander around some specific routes, and do a fake exit at some point during the night. Lee in turn would surveil him in disguise, while Joe would just be HQ for this one - they didn't want him anywhere remotely near the action if anything did happen.

They waited until fairly late in the evening to leave, Lee getting into disguise with a big beard and looking about thirty years younger. Lee then dropped Blake off about half an hour's walk from the bar, and went to scout it out.

Blake tried to relax as he walked, shake off all his anxieties and paranoia. A nice jaunt through the warm night was a good way of doing that. Nonetheless worries kept running through his head. For one he couldn't stop thinking about their operation against the plastic surgeon. It had been rather heavy, that.

Joe's behaviour there would be a direct reflection of how his people operated, wouldn't it? Who all was staring at security cameras and maps with little dots right now? Just in general he didn't know how he felt about all that business with the doctor, going forward he would rather avoid that sort of thing.

As Blake was arriving at the bar he got a message from Lee. Laura and company were in the pub, he was to use the long pub-nightclub-lounge maneuver upon entrance. A bouncer patted him down then motioned him through, and he went down a little hall, into a long sprawling bar. Blake stood up tall and glanced around the bar, looking for Laura, who didn't seem to be there. Seemed like a good crowd though.

He made his way across the bar, then into a sort of hallway space, with wide stairs going up and down. That hallway past the stairs was the best exit to flee from, if it did come down to fleeing. It lead to the smokepit, he would have to jump a fence, but then there were lots of places to run. If it had a disadvantage it was that it was too obvious, apparently.

Blake went down the stairs into a big sprawling underground nightclub, with really loud music, boom boom boom. Down here was a bit worse for exits, just the stairs up, although there was an emergency exit beside the bar.

Blake did a lap around, it was fairly big actually, but still no Laura. So he went back up the stairs, then up the other stairs, which lead to a fairly fancy looking lounge. It was quite nice actually, a lot of plants, a patio, some decent scotches behind the bar.

There was no Laura there either though, so he headed back through the first bar and into a nice pubby sort of place. There they were! Laura stood up and waved when she saw him, then gave him a quick hug.

They made eye contact for a brief moment, and there was something there. A puzzlement, uncertainty, a bit of nervousness, maybe a touch of cynicism. He wondered what exactly Jack told her, after he left that day.

Blake was quickly introduced to her friends, it was a big

group of people, spread across a couple of tables. Laura told the group around them about how Blake was working with Wildon Textiles, they talked about the meeting with the hotel. She had seen his pillowcase designs, they were awesome.

It felt a little weird, unnatural, talking to normal people again. Blake couldn't help but feel like he was coming across as slightly gauche. Just the way he was speaking, his timing was off.

One of Laura's friends - a brunette girl who worked for some non-profit - thought he sure must know a lot about textiles, managing a company like Wildon Textiles. It felt like she was giving him the third degree, she wanted to know all about their polyester to cotton ratios, he didn't really even know what she was talking about.

Then she went off with a bunch of questions about the factory in Mexico. He sort of had to dodge around the fact that he hadn't been there yet. And when he said girl did he mean woman? At least she wasn't asking him about the ranch.

The conversation moved on to the guy sitting beside Laura, a dark haired fellow in a particularly nice suit. He seemed to have a sort of smug perma-grin which Blake found mildly annoying. Apparently he had just made partner at the law firm where he worked. It was a pretty big deal, he was the youngest person ever to make partner at that firm.

Blake thought the trend was towards that these days. He did seem really young actually, closer to Laura's age than Blake's. The guy went off about a totally bogus patent case he had been working on. A phone company had been trying to keep anyone else from using the best encryption. It had been a real fight, but they won in the end. Anybody could use triple symmetric inverse cypher encryption now.

Blake actually remembered something about that, Joe and Lee had been talking about it. It had seemed like a reasonably big case, actually. He knew a bit about patent law, he wondered if they had played up the fair use angle at all? No, they had focused more on precedent, and what were the acceptable boundaries to a patent. Fair use wasn't actually that relevant, the guy said, that was more for copyright.

A group from the other side of the table now seemed to want them all to go downstairs to the nightclub. So they all sort of gradually finished their drinks, got up, then headed down that way. The nightclub was a little busier now than it had been, the music a little louder.

A bunch of them went onto the dance floor and sort of bounced up and down, while Blake got a drink and hung out with his back to the wall. It seemed like there were a lot of opportunities for people to bump into him out on the dance floor, and Joe really didn't want anyone bumping into him. Depending on the exact nature of the bump, Blake might have to go check for bugs, it could compromise the whole operation.

A couple of Laura's other friends were nearby, so he struck up a conversation with them. They seemed like interesting people, he felt like he was finding his rhythm again. The ranch came up, and he told a story about chasing chickens, they all laughed when he did some pantomime.

He got a text from Lee - just a so far so good, and a reminder to pace himself. After a bit Laura, the lawyer guy, and a few people joined their little group. Blake couldn't hear exactly what was being said, but it seemed like people were thinking about heading up to one of the other bars. The lawyer guy made sort of a boom boom boom motion following the bass, and it was decided, they would head upstairs.

They went to the first bar after the main entrance. It had gotten busier, and the bar was long and thin, there wasn't really a lot of space for everyone. Blake was starting to feel awkward trying to position himself, but then he got another text from Lee. He was to go back down to the nightclub and make himself available.

Blake detached from the group and headed back downstairs. He got another drink, briefly joined a few of Laura's friends who had stayed down there. That was a cowbell in the drum track, wasn't it?

Then he went and sort of half-danced on the edge of the dance floor for a bit. Nobody came and talked to him, although one kid was really flailing around, even howled a couple times. He was getting in Blake's space, it was a little annoying, it put him on edge. The guy must have been on something.

Blake now had another message, long bar again. He went back up the stairs, to find the bar even more crowded than it had been. Laura's table was full. So he got another drink, and just leaned against the bar.

He saw Laura was still talking to the lawyer guy, they seemed to be getting along pretty well. Were they an item then maybe? He had never asked her if she had a boyfriend. It did seem like something that would have come up already, but you never knew with those things.

One way or another the two of them had been together most of the night so far. That could even pose some logistical issues, just in terms of getting a chance to talk to her. In his experience, a situation like this he would be better off waiting for her to come to him, even finding another girl to talk up, make her jealous, perhaps. But he didn't know if he would have time to play it like that, and he would need some fairly specific conditions to talk to her. It would be a narrow window, he wasn't even cleared by Lee to have that conversation yet.

She was looking over at him now though, and she gave him a little wave. There was a space free beside her. He made his way through the crowd - dodging around a couple of people who could have easily bumped into him - and sat down beside her.

He was having a good time, ya, it was quite the bar, huge. They started off on Wildon Textiles, it sounded like everyone was doing well. Bill and Steve had been hard at work setting up some new machines, they had moved everything around in the break room, there were a couple of new factory staff. Blake made a mental note of that, it was another complicating factor.

From the sounds of it she had actually been spending a decent amount of time with Wildon Textiles. She was doing some more work on the box ads, and was going to help them redo their website.

Then - slightly shyly, now - she told him about an event she was helping to organize, a promotional show for a clothing company. They were going to have bands, and a skateboarding contest, a big clothing giveaway. Apparently her boss had sort of thrust it on her at the last minute, it was one of the things keeping her crazy busy.

She had been running around trying to get everything organized with the venue, there was a lot of red tape with the permits. They still had to book a couple of the opening bands. Blake said he knew bands, and knew people who knew bands. He could probably help her find someone. That could actually really help her out, she admitted to feeling in a little over her head.

Then her lawyer friend appeared at the table with a tray full of shots for everybody, Tequila! Blake took the shot, it was good tequila. One of Laura's friends then wedged in between him and Laura, starting in on a story about some crazy guy downstairs in the nightclub.

Blake sort of found himself in a conversational island,

everyone nearby talking to someone else. He got out his phone and flipped through it, just to look busy. It was a special security phone, so there wasn't really much to do on it, he just sort of browsed through the settings page.

As he was doing this, a message popped up, are you still around? That was code for him to make his fake exit. Blake continued flipping through his phone nonchalantly, and went to the route mnemonic, went over it a few times. Every turn had to be correct. Apparently Lee had in fact parked multiple vehicles with hidden cameras at strategic locations along the way.

Then Blake just sort of slipped away from the group. He gave a sort of final, uncertain look at Laura, who was now deep in conversation with the lawyer guy again. Sort of huffily he went to the other bar, trying to look a little lost. Just seeing what was going on, maybe.

Then after a pause he went down to the nightclub, just peeked his head in. The music wasn't that good, and it was too loud, the place was really crowded, lights beaming into his eyes.

He gave his head a little shake, then headed decisively up the stairs towards the exit. Maybe he wasn't feeling it tonight, maybe he was playing some kind of petty little game with Laura, maybe he had just had a long day. And leaving an event without saying goodbye was a thing, wasn't it? 'Ghosting' or something.

Blake was out the main doors of the bar and onto the street. From there it was left down the main road the way he had originally came, one, two, three streets, then left again onto a darker side street. He walked a little ways down it, looked around slightly confusedly, then turned right onto an even narrower street.

After one more turn he was walking beside a largish park in a semi-residential neighbourhood. With a furtive glance around he went in, hurrying down the little stairs from the satellite map, then quickly into the trees. The park was particularly well placed from the perspective of someone who wanted to flee the area, there were four narrow side streets around it that would be perfect to disappear into.

He hurried into a particularly dark section under a tree. Digging around in his pocket he found the joint that Lee had given him, and with another furtive glance lit it up. Lee's logic had been that the steps one took to find a place to smoke weed in a crowded downtown core were in fact amazingly similar to the steps taken in shaking a trail and disappearing into the night.

He stood there, puffing away, hiding himself a bit when some people walked past on the street. The weed made him cough, but he didn't feel particularly high. It was a low-THC strain that would at most give him a light buzz.

His untimely departure explained, he headed back towards the bar. As he was arriving he got a message with a thumbs up from Lee. That was the all clear - there had been no evidence of anyone trailing him.

It seemed to have gotten a lot busier in his brief absence. Laura and company weren't there in the one bar, so he got another drink before going to find them. As he did so a 30-something Latino guy cheers'd him with a bottle of water, struck up a conversation, the place was packed, huh?

Apparently he alternated, two drinks, one water, no hangover. Blake thought that was a good system, maybe he would get a water after this. They talked about the bar, it was huge. The guy had actually been there last night as well, and it was a lot busier today. It wasn't even the weekend.

The guy said he was an entrepreneur, it was kind of technical, but he worked in turnstile system engineering. Something to do with the counting mechanisms, Blake didn't exactly get it. But Blake remembered, he had seen something. Denver's baseball stadium was going to do a complete overhaul of their turnstile systems. The announcers had been talking about it, there had been a little puff piece about how they were selling the old ones as collector's items.

The guy thanked him, that was a good tip, wow. Blake couldn't help feeling a little paranoid, could he be an agent? Although if they had given him the all clear he could probably relax a little. The guy didn't ask any probing questions, and was soon off to find his friend. Blake almost wished he had gotten his card. Turnstiles, that sounded like a decent industry to be in.

Blake then went to find Laura, although as he was crossing the bar he sort of got caught in a big crowd of people. He tried to step aside to get out of their way, but bumped into a big South Asian guy with a beard.

"Man, it's crowded in here!" said the guy to Blake. It was Joe's voice.

"Ya, I can hardly move," said Blake, trying to sound normal. They both sort of backed into an alcove in the bar.

"I totally shouldn't be here, but I thought it would be fun. Everybody's gotta live a little, right?"

"I guess." Blake glanced around, they were pretty hidden away from the rest of the bar. But still. "Are you sure we should be talking here?"

Joe shrugged. "I think we're ok, as long as we stay in this exact spot. Now that I'm here talking to you, it isn't going to matter if they slipped a bug in your pocket."

"We're all clear then?" asked Blake, still feeling a little freaked out. Looking at the guy, he really didn't look like Joe, his face, his build, it was all different.

"I think so, we're pretty sure no one was following you on your walk, and we haven't seen anyone here." Joe gave Blake an intense look. "I'm going to leave in a bit, I guess we'll find out for sure then."

Joe then grinned at Blake. "I was talking to a girl from Philadelphia, she seemed really cool. She's just down here for the summer, but she's going to try and move here if she can find a job." He held up a little piece of paper. "I got her digits."

"Nice work," said Blake, still feeling a little dizzy.

"Anyways, we shouldn't talk for too long." Joe cast a glance around the bar. "Laura is in the nightclub downstairs right now. Lee said the guy in the suit was hitting on her, but she looked kind of bored. If you take her to the fancy lounge upstairs Lee will be saving you a table where it's safe to talk. Look for the guy in the ball cap."

"Ok, cool, I think I can do that." Blake felt a little rush of victory. That was valuable information.

And then just like that Joe was gone, Blake didn't even see which way he went. Blake made his way through the crowd and down the stairs into the nightclub, which was even busier now. He saw Laura across the way, just sort of hanging out, she wasn't dancing. She looked over at him, and he motioned for her with his head towards the stairs. She gave him a little smile and made her way over.

"You want to go check out the lounge upstairs?" he yelled, and she nodded. They made their way through the crowd and up the stairs into the bar. It was fairly crowded as well, they spent a moment on arrival looking for a place, but then a little table off to the side opened up. They quickly snatched it up, Blake ignoring completely the kid with the ball cap that vacated it.

They picked up the menus from the table. "Oh wow, this is really expensive!" said Laura.

Blake waved her off, if the prices were actually fairly

ridiculous. "One drink it's not so bad." He looked around. "And it is a nice atmosphere, isn't it?" She nodded to this, looked like she was about to say something, and then she gave him the weird curious sort of look again.

He waved to the waitress and they ordered, him getting a Manhattan variant and her trying some gin concoction which was the cheapest thing on the menu. Then they were silent a moment. Blake didn't know what to say, he wondered if he should just jump straight into it. Who knew how long he had her for, one of her friends could arrive, someone could just stand next to them.

But then she said something about how the bar must be doing well - it was pretty full given the prices - and that got them off on a conversation about the economics of running a bar. The overhead, how much advertising there was, the implications of dealing with drunk people. Blake thought it was a harder industry to make a profit on, it was generally over-supplied because people just wanted to own bars. If you wanted to make money, you were better off manufacturing staplers or something.

Then from there they got into talking about business books again, she had read another one, Blake had read a few, in fact. She had been meaning to read one of the ones he mentioned, so he gave her his take on it, it was probably worth reading, certainly.

Then she sort of gave a laugh, and threw her hands up in the air in an exaggerated way. "You know what? I think the song playing right now is based on a business book, or something like that."

Blake gave her a quizzical grin, and she continued. "I mean, do you feel like all our lives revolve around business sometimes? Everything I do is all work, work, work. I'm always obsessing over the next promotion, or checking my investments, it's always something like that. It's like I can't escape it. There's more to life, right?"

Blake felt he was somewhat forced to concede her the point on that one. "I suppose I do tend to get focused in on the business side of things sometimes."

She gave him a sort of I-know-right look, then they were silent again. It wasn't particularly awkward, the silence, but he felt panicked. Now was the time to talk to her, but how was he even going to do it? Just giving her his new number wasn't enough. He needed to see what contact information she had for him, and make sure she deleted it. Everything else aside, raising a new number was something you did at the end of the night, not when you were having a moment in a fancy bar.

But then she spoke, again giving him the weird look. "So, like, was there something going on back there, with Wildon Textiles?" She looked nervous now, like she wasn't even sure if she should be talking about it. "Jack was talking about some stuff, around the time you left San Diego..."

The message had gotten through then, in some form or another, had it? Blake looked into her eyes, he could see confusion, a little bit of fear, but also a strength, even a camaraderie. He suddenly felt very sure that he could trust her. He was best off just laying his cards on the table.

"There is something going on." He flashed her a grimace. "I need to have left San Diego on February 11th, and I need my San Diego number not to exist." A distance crossed her face for a moment, an uncertainty, but then she nodded, biting her lip.

He fixed her in his gaze. "Do you have my San Diego number anywhere? I deleted it from the chat history where I first gave it to you."

"I had it on my phone, but I deleted it after I talked to Jack." She paused a moment. "I think I might still have it on my computer somewhere."

"Delete it, anywhere you have it. Do you think you said anything that would give away the day I left in any emails?"

Again she thought about it, then nodded slightly, looking kind of nervous. "Me and Jack talked about it a bit. I don't think we mentioned any dates, but there might be something, I don't really remember." She looked him in the eyes. "You left on the 7th, right?"

Blake gave a quarter nod. "You said you were going to do some web design stuff for Wildon Textiles?"

She looked uncertain, but she again nodded. "Ya, just prettying it up, making it look more professional." She swallowed. "Um, why?"

"Do you have the administrator passwords to access Wildon Textile's email server?"

"No, just the website, I think. But maybe I could get them."

"If you could get that for me.." he said, and she nodded, her lips disappearing.

"I can try."

"And there hasn't been anyone asking about me or anything?"

She shook her head. "Not that I know of."

"That's good." He paused, then gave her a serious look. "Don't tell anybody about this, don't even talk to me about it unless I bring it up first. Assume your phone is bugged, and people are reading your emails, all of that. Because they might be." He paused a moment, now feeling unsure what exactly to say. "Sorry to involve you in all of this.."

She grinned at him, a wide-eyed mind blown expression now on her face. "That's cool. I hope you're not in trouble. I've got a friend who sells weed..."

Blake shook his head. "Nothing like that." He gave her a look, and a grin. "You wouldn't believe the half of it."

She gave a nervous laugh. "Ok. Wow. Ha ha. Crazy." Then her face sort of went straight, a little perplexed, uncertain. "I've got something.." she looked at a loss for words, "to sort of, confess? As well."

She took a deep breath. "Full disclosure." She looked like she was going to say something, then stopped, now looking kind of vulnerable. "I'm kind of, um, like, rich."

Blake gave a little laugh, trying to process the implications of that. "Well, ok then. It was a secret?"

She went noticeably red. "No, it's just.. I dunno, people treat you differently.. like, rich guys..." She threw her hands a little ways up in the air. "How do you even tell people? It doesn't just come up in conversation." She looked at him shyly. "My dad kind of does a lot of construction on the east coast."

Then she laughed again. "It feels good to say it!"

"I'll say, I say it to myself several times a day," said Blake with a grin, and she sort of gave him a look. Then she looked up across the room, and gave him a little kick under the table. The lawyer fellow was coming towards them, a slightly nervous look disappearing from his face, a blond girl Blake had never seen before hanging off his arm.

"Hey, did you guy see Jim? I wanted to talk to him about that Yosemite trip, I dunno if he's left yet," he asked in a slightly strained tone, coming up to the table.

"I think he left already, he has to work early tomorrow," said Laura.

"Ok, well, we're going back downstairs to the club," said the lawyer guy, slightly awkwardly, like he hadn't meant to interrupt.

Blake had a small sense of victory, that was a party-foul.

"We'll join you, we were just going down there," said Laura, smiling. She waved to the waitress for the bill, holding up a credit card.

Blake's head was spinning as they headed down to the nightclub. She was rich! And he had sort of recruited her. Good thing his microphone hadn't been on, he wasn't sure what he was going to tell Joe and Lee.

There was a big group of them sort of bouncing around on the dance floor, so they joined them. Blake didn't know if the music was any better, but suddenly he was feeling really good, he tore it up a little. There were a couple of rounds of shots, tequila again one time, some kind of over the top sour thing. Laura danced with him, they all sort of danced together. The lawyer guy seemed to have disappeared.

From there the night began to blur together, they were all up in the one bar, then back in the nightclub again. Blake had a big long conversation in the first bar with the designated driver guy and one of the girls about some tech company, the guy thought their shares were going to go through the roof, there was some big regulatory change in the works. He was upstairs for a while somewhere playing pull tabs from a vending machine with Laura's friend from the non-profit and a bunch of people, it was pretty raucous, but they didn't win anything.

Then they were all back in the nightclub, one of Laura's friends was dancing on a table, the DJ was really rocking now. There was a black guy with a beard and an afro tearing it up on the dance floor. He looked like he was roughly Joe's build, give or take, but Blake didn't even try to figure it out.

Suddenly a new song came on, and everyone was booing. Laura told him they always played that one at the end of the night. Then he was sort of grabbed up, he didn't know what was going on. A congo line had spontaneously formed, Laura with her hands on his hips, they snaked through the bar.

Then the lights were on, they were all moving with the crowd towards the stairwell. His phone buzzed again, with the all clear. He wasn't even sure what that meant, that point in the night.

He went with Laura and her friends to the coat check, she had a jacket there. Then they were standing outside the bar, in the warm night, a light breeze in the air. People milled about around them on the street, flagging down cabs, buying hot dogs from a stand across the road.

Laura looked at him shyly, and smiled. "I had a good time tonight."

"Me too," said Blake, quite genuinely.

"Let me know if you're going to be around," she said, looking him in the eyes. "Anyways, I've got to go, our DD has a lot of driving ahead of him." She paused a moment. "Do you need a lift anywhere? I think there's an extra seat."

Blake shook his head. "No, I'm good, I feel like a walk, then my driver's parked not so far down the way."

At this she gave him a little look. Then there was a honking from across the street, Blake could see the DD guy waving at them from a minivan. With a quick 'Ciao' Laura was off, and Blake was left standing alone on the street.

He started off on the pre-agreed upon route, it was pretty much just a couple of turns then straight down the way. It was a decent walk, but he didn't mind in the slightest, he could walk for the rest of the night and be happy. The air was fresh around him, the sounds of revellers in the streets, he felt good. If there wasn't anyone on him, he could go find an afterparty, could he?

A little ways further down the road he passed the tattoo parlor Lee had mentioned, and turned onto the side street as instructed. Further down that street a blue station wagon pulled up next to him, Joe sitting in the front seat.

Blake got in and sat down in the back. He expected them to start up and drive, but they both just sort of looked at him. Then Joe held up his phone, pressed a button, and a recording started.

"Hello, this is a call from Professional Baseball's office of recruitment. This message is for Thomas Leon Johnson. Congratulations, you've been drafted by the San Jose Knights in the 48th round!

Sign up to my mailing list!

mail@dylankyle.com

www.dylankyle.com

Made in the USA
Monee, IL
15 May 2021